Beach Cute

BETH REEKLES

BeachCute

Delacorte
Romance

Text copyright © 2024 by Beth Reekles
Cover art copyright © 2024 by Art of Nora

Visit us on the Web! GetUnderlined.com

Educators and librarians, for a variety of teaching tools,
visit us at RHTeachersLibrarians.com

Library of Congress Cataloging-in-Publication Data is available upon request.
ISBN 978-0-593-80906-8 (trade pbk.) — ISBN 978-0-593-80907-5 (ebook)

The text of this book is set in 11-point Adobe Garamond Pro.

Editor: Kelsey Horton
Cover Designer: Trisha Previte
Interior Designer: Megan Shortt
Copy Editor: Colleen Fellingham
Managing Editor: Tamar Schwartz
Production Manager: Shameiza Ally

Printed in the United States of America
10 9 8 7 6 5 4 3 2 1
First Edition

For the Physics gang: Amy, Katie, Harrison, Jack and Emily. You dorks changed my life for the better. Stay stellar.

BOOK NOW!

The all-inclusive luxury resort that lets you reconnect with reality!

Switch off from the hassle and stress of the outside world and engage fully with the here and now at the coveted Spanish getaway, Casa Dorada. Relax and reset from the very first moment you set foot in this luxe, lavish resort on the Majorcan coast. Upon arrival at the recently refurbished hotel, you will exchange your phone—and all your worries—for a glass of bubbly and a room key.

Each suite is decorated with touches of natural fabrics and local artwork bursting with color. Take in the views of our award-winning gardens or the ever-inviting ocean from your window. And, rest assured, our staff will be on hand to cater to your every whim.

Ideal for the solo traveler or groups looking to reconnect with the world around them, Casa Dorada is the perfect choice this summer to help you detox and disconnect from the hustle and bustle of your everyday life. For couples looking for a more intimate getaway, we are now taking advance bookings for next year in the new and improved luxury villas on our private beach.

With a wide range of activities, there's something for everyone: early-morning coastal walks, open mic nights over sangria, games of water polo, and day trips to local attractions guided by friendly staff members who will be only too happy to answer your questions . . . or mix you another cocktail!

Book now to avoid disappointment! >

1　𝓛𝓾𝓷𝓪

"No," I say, pushing my printed confirmation across the counter. "See? I booked hold luggage. It's right there."

"I'm sorry, miss, it's not in our system."

I gulp. What kind of useless, cheapo airline is this? Well, not *that* cheapo, since they're currently trying to charge me again for my supposedly unbooked hold luggage.

My palms are sweating. I hate stuff like this. I hate *arguing* over stuff like this. If there's one thing I normally avoid like the plague, it's confrontation. But I am *not* paying that money. Liam would've dealt with it so well; he was great at stuff like this—especially because he knew I wasn't.

I get a pang in my chest just thinking about him, and push that feeling deep, deep down. I've got the entire week ahead to get my head around that. Right now, I need to deal with the fact that this woman wants to charge me fifty-eight pounds for luggage I've already paid twenty-three pounds to put on the plane.

She's smiling at me as if she'd like to load me onto the conveyor belt just to get rid of me, clearly waiting for me to cave and pay the money.

Come on, Luna. You can do this. You're almost twenty years old. You're an adult now, and adults know how to handle these things.

I inhale a deep breath through my nose and tap the paper on the counter. I'm so glad now that Mum insisted I print everything out "just in case."

"But I paid for it. Look, it's—it's right here. Confirmation of payment, see? That's what it says."

The woman suppresses a sigh, but gives me a too-wide toothy smile and says, "Let me go find my manager and we'll get this sorted for you."

"Thank you," I say, but I don't let myself feel relieved yet—I'm already mentally drafting an email of complaint demanding a refund, just in case this all goes south.

(Confrontation is a lot easier on the other side of a screen, after all.)

I remain on tenterhooks, feeling pissed off and more than a little bit tearful until I've had the same argument with the woman's manager, who looks my booking up on the system just to tell me I need to pay the fee, and I try not to lose it as I push my printed email toward her, too. I can hear people in the queue behind me grumbling because I'm causing trouble and taking so long.

Don't worry, I want to snap at them. *The plane won't leave without you.*

Even though I know I'd be doing exactly the same in their position.

And even though I am worried the plane might leave without *me* at this rate.

Eventually, the manager concedes that I have in fact paid the fee due and lets my baggage through. My boarding pass is handed back to me with a smile. "So sorry about that. It must be because you booked through a third party. Have a safe flight, miss."

"Thanks," I mumble, praying I don't have the same trouble at the hotel. Maybe booking this whole thing when I'd had a few drinks wasn't my smartest move . . .

Then again, there are a *lot* of things that make the "Luna's Completely Lost It" list lately—and a solo trip to Spain isn't even the most drastic of them.

I turn away, examining my boarding pass and checking my seat number for the billionth time. I'm so focused on it that I walk right into someone trying to get to the counter to check in.

"Oof!"

"Sorry, sorry! I'm so sorry," I say as the girl starts apologizing too. "Totally my fault," I tell her.

She fixes the sunglasses perched artfully on top of her head, where her blond hair is piled into a messy bun. "No worries, hon."

She looks so zen, a pale-blue travel wallet clutched between fingers with lilac nail varnish on long nails, a small and lazy smile on her face. She's wearing a white camisole tucked into gray linen shorts and a long, almost see-through white cardigan with a fringe that brushes her knees. The look is tied together by a chunky turquoise necklace and giant cork wedges with brown suede straps that match the brown leather bag hanging from her elbow.

For a moment, all I can think is: *She's so Instagrammable.* In spite of the fact that she only looks about my age, I wonder for half a second if she's some popular influencer because my next thought is: *Who dresses like that to travel? She'll have to take those shoes off*

3

when she gets to security, and I bet that necklace buzzes when she walks through. And how can she fit her hand luggage in that handbag? It looks mostly empty.

As I get out of the way so she can wheel her small suitcase to the check-in desk, I take another look at how glamorous she is. She's joined the back of the queue and is holding her travel wallet between her teeth, bags on the floor, as she takes a video of herself wiggling her passport in the air for the camera.

I feel like such a slob in my most comfortable leggings and T-shirt, with my big rucksack, Vans and thin hoodie. We always dress comfortably to go on family trips, and it's a habit I'm apparently not breaking anytime soon. Traveling alone is nerve-racking enough without suddenly throwing new habits into the mix.

Well, the joke's on Instagram Girl, I think, hiking my rucksack higher onto my shoulders and heading toward the escalator to make my way through security. *Her legs will be cold on those airplane seats.*

It takes me forever to get through security. I remember being tempted in my moment of madness (or rather, drunkenness) by the security fast-track option, for however much extra money. I'd talked myself out of it then, but standing in the queue in front of a man in a suit talking loudly on his phone and behind a family with a screaming toddler and a little boy who keeps running under the ropes, I regret it.

The line crawls along. I get my phone out, clicking out of my boarding pass now that I no longer need it and instead tapping aimlessly across social media. Not much on Threads catches my attention, and my headphones are in the bottom of my bag somewhere, so mindlessly scrolling TikTok isn't much of an option. I have one rubbish email promoting a makeup brand, which I delete, and just as I'm about to check Instagram, my phone buzzes.

Liam.

For a second, my heart stops. Then it launches into a somersault, leaving me feeling queasy in the pit of my stomach.

> Saw on Insta you're off on vacay.
> Hope you have a good time x

I stare at the message for a while—long enough that Mr. Noisy Talker behind me taps me on the shoulder and says, "Excuse me, could you move forward?"

I do, and before I can even decide whether I should reply or not another text comes through.

> Roger brought my stuff over. I'd have
> come to get it if I'd realized you were
> moving out early. Thanks though

The dots reappear while he types another text.
They disappear.
They come back again.

> I miss you

The guy behind me clears his throat, pointedly enough that I look around. He nods irritably in front of me, and I shuffle along into the space between me and the family.

What am I meant to do about that? What am I meant to do with an "I miss you"?

Especially when I've spent the last couple of weeks wallowing in regret because I've realized I miss him, too?

I knew Liam was The One from the second I met him. We were introduced by friends a few years ago, when we were fifteen. He went to a different school, but we've spent practically all our time together since then. I was thrilled when we both got into Newcastle University, so I didn't have to worry about what the stresses of long distance might do to our rock-solid relationship. I thought things would only get better for us.

Usually, I'm more sensible than to believe in things like love at first sight, but Liam ticked every one of my boxes. He was smart, funny, popular among our friends and even his tutors—and he was close with his family. I liked that most about him.

His laid-back attitude was at complete odds with my compulsion to control everything, but we worked; we balanced each other out. He's tall where I'm short, lean where I'm curvy, outspoken while I'm reserved and thoughtful. He pushed me outside my comfort zone and helped me have a busy, vibrant social life when I might otherwise have wanted to stay in.

And he loved me.

It was always so easy to picture my future with Liam: we'd graduate at the same time, find jobs near each other, rent a place together while we saved for a house deposit. We'd be on each other's car insurance, share a Netflix account, argue over what to call the cat we both wanted. He used to laugh when I'd say things like, "I want to be married by the time I'm twenty-five, and have kids by the time I'm thirty," but then he'd kiss me and say that was good to know—he'd keep it in mind, block out his calendar so he'd remember to go ring shopping in plenty of time.

We were going to be in the same houseshare next year at uni; it would be good practice for when we lived together, just the two of us.

He was supposed to be my forever.

I haven't heard from Liam since I broke up with him a few weeks ago.

I guess I don't have much right to wish he'd get in touch when I was the one who ended things, but it still hurts to go from having my whole world wrapped up in him to . . . nothing.

Well, not *exactly* nothing, because any time I open an Insta-gram Story from one of our friends, bam, there he is. Out with everyone. Having fun with everyone. Not wallowing at home, heartbroken, his entire future in tatters, like I was—if only because nobody had invited me along to give me another option.

I was the one who asked our mutual friend Roger to come grab the things Liam had left in my room. I was too much of a coward to face him myself because I knew if I saw him, I'd end up breaking down in tears and begging him to take me back. Which

I would've done already if he hadn't been out with all our friends, carrying on as if everything were the same. As if the last four years just meant . . . nothing.

Until that text, I hadn't even known he missed me.

I shove my phone in my pocket; I can guarantee that given half a chance I'll get drawn back in and try to win him back when I already tried so hard all of last year just to *keep* him. I think about the vision board I threw in the bin, the pages I tore out of my journal in a flood of drunken tears the night I booked this trip. I think about all the time I wasted being with him, and the time I'm about to waste trying to get over him.

A lump forms in the back of my throat, and I choke it down.

The *last* thing I need right now is to dissolve into floods of tears at the airport, for God's sake. I can even hear my brother in the back of my mind, teasing me for being so sensitive.

(Although he was pretty devastated when I told him about the breakup. He really liked Liam.)

I draw a shaky breath and square my shoulders.

Get it together, Luna.

I slip my phone out of my pocket. Liam's text is still up on the screen.

Going from seeing him every day to not even sending him a video I think he'd like has been torture. I don't think I've ever felt so lonely.

There's no reason we can't be friends, I think, once we've both moved on. I'd like to be. Isn't that what grown-ups do? And we *are* grown-ups now. And if we can be friends, then everyone else will stay friends with me, too.

"Miss?"

I look up, fingers hovering over the on-screen keyboard, ready to tell Liam I miss him, too. But instead I'm being beckoned forward, toward the empty trays behind the security belt.

"Please place all electronic items in the tray separately. Any liquids . . ."

I tune out but follow the instructions, placing my phone in the tray next to my iPad and Kindle.

By the time I've gone through the metal detectors and picked up my tray to begin putting everything back into my rucksack, my phone screen is lighting up with an incoming call from Liam. My heart stops.

Is it because he thinks I've moved on if I'm going away without him, and wants to patch things up before I leave? Or did he just find one of my textbooks while packing up his room and wants to know what to do with it? No—no, he misses me, he still loves me, this is all just a horrible mistake, a big mess and . . .

I stare at the screen for a second, hardly even able to breathe for hoping, but then I'm being jostled along by other people coming through the security scanner, and when I snatch my things out of the tray I accidentally cut off his call.

I wince, but . . . maybe it's for the best. I broke up with him for a reason, didn't I? And this vacation was supposed to be a chance to have some space and get over him. Or at least stop me from running back to him.

Standing out of the way, I cradle my phone in my hands and put it on mute.

Sorry, Liam. But this week is all about me.

2 Rory

My big sisters are way too good to me, I think, breezing past the people in the hideously long security queue with the fast-track pass my eldest sister, Hannah, bought me without a second thought.

"I don't need that," I'd told her, watching her click the box as she booked my trip. If I were a nail-biter, my nails would've been in shreds at that point. *I should stop them,* I kept thinking. *I shouldn't let them do this. I should just grow the fuck up and take some goddamn responsibility for my shitty life.*

But I was letting them do it. I was even recommending the resort and pulling up a promo code from an Instagram ad I'd seen about it. I was far too excited about the idea of running away from all my problems for seven days in paradise.

(A little *less* excited about having to give up social media for a week, but . . .)

"Oh please," my other sister Nic had scoffed. "It'll give you more time to nose around in duty-free or grab a coffee."

"You know I can't afford flavored syrup in my coffee, right, let alone anything in duty-free?" I'd pointed out to them, but now my travel wallet is thick with euros that our parents gifted me. It's a total pity gift, but I think they prefer the idea of me jetting off to get some sun rather than moping around my childhood bedroom, withdrawing even more than I already have.

All this makes me feel spoiled and bratty, and I know I should be feeling guilty as hell, but I'm just *not*.

I'm about to spend a week in the Spanish sun, in a luxury beachside resort, sipping on mojitos and nibbling at tapas, with no responsibilities other than "having a break," and I feel pretty damn great about it. Who wouldn't?

Not to mention it's the perfect opportunity to run away from the impending doom of A-level results and university once summer ends. I can bury my head in the sand (maybe literally; that is very much to be determined) rather than deal with reality.

A few weekends ago, I'd gone out for lunch with my sisters, letting them pick up the bill because I couldn't afford it on my zero-hours contract, and knowing full well it was our parents' idea of a gentle intervention.

"You've just seemed so down in the dumps lately," Nic cooed, pouting at me.

"Me?" I scoffed. "I'm fine. You're the one with a new baby and getting, like, no sleep. And, Hannah, you've got your fancy promotion and have to work twelve-hour days—"

"Aurora," Hannah snapped, and I'd felt the blood drain from

my face. I couldn't remember the last time either of my sisters had used my full name like that. "We're serious. We're worried about you."

"Maybe you should go back to the doctor," Nic suggested gently.

And because I couldn't face going down *that* road and having *that* conversation again I'd declared, "I'm not depressed. I'm just . . . I'm nervous about starting uni! That's all. Moving out, making new friends, having to try not to burn pasta! Did Mum tell you? I ruined the pan. How does a person even manage to burn *pasta,* I ask you! So much for a fail-safe, student-friendly meal."

Either I did a good enough job of convincing them or they felt straight-up sorry for me, but they decided that what would *really* do me some good was a vacation. And a digital detox one at that—because apparently I spend too much time on my phone. Which is ridiculous, if also absolutely true. And it's a vacation generously paid for by them because my savings account has less than fifty quid in it.

I may not have touched a single book from the suggested reading list for my new course, but I definitely have a head start on the whole "broke student" vibe.

I breeze through the fast-track security like I do this all the time, and wander around duty-free, sniffing perfume samples like I'm actually considering buying something. I take a free chocolate and chat to the lady on the stand, telling her I'll have a think and maybe come back later, even though we both know I have no intention of doing such a thing.

I've got half an hour to kill before they announce the boarding gate, so I work my way through to the Costa café and splurge (using my own money this time) on a venti chai latte with whipped cream. A dusting of cinnamon on top and it looks—and smells—like heaven. Drink in hand, I have to stand for a few minutes, peering through the heaving crowds, before I spy a couple leaving a table. I make a beeline for it.

As I slam my cup onto the table, someone nearby huffs.

Ha, I think, seeing a guy roll his eyes and turn away with his tray, *I win.*

I rummage through my bag, tipping out my notebook and a couple of pens. Blue and green felt-tips and my favorite Biro. I can work with that.

I have one week on an all-inclusive digital detox vacation to stop thinking my life is tragic (because it isn't *really*) and instead consider what to do after the summer—and map out a plan.

I've never been much good at planning, but maybe this will be the week that it finally happens.

Maybe inspiration will *strike*!

Maybe, when I come back, I'll find my TikTok account has totally blown up and I'm being slammed with offers to work with brands. Maybe I'll have sold something off my Etsy store, after a monthslong dry spell. Maybe my parents will see it and think, *Wow, look how good Rory is at this thing!* And maybe I'll finally find the guts to turn down the uni offer I never actually wanted in the first place.

I scoff at myself as I press my notebook out flat to a clean set of pages. Not likely. But hey, I can hope.

Before I get started, I take a video of my coffee and the airport to add to my "Come away with me!" TikTok video, then I stand up and lean over the table to snap a flat lay for Instagram. I fix the filters, tag my location and Costa Coffee, Tiffany & Co. and the independent online shop where the notebook is from.

> Unwinding at the airport with some organization and a latte . . . Going to be off the grid for the next week. Try not to miss me too much! xxx

> PS Has anyone checked out the new @tiffanyandco perfume? Talk about YUMMY

I polish it off with some hashtags and put my phone face down on the table in an attempt not to pay too much attention to the notifications. Hannah and Nic kept telling me to make the most of this trip, so I guess I should probably start practicing being without my phone a bit.

This week is supposed to be all about being "restful" and "rejuvenated," and I don't want to waste it. I do not intend to come home with just a tan to show for it. Plus, I know my family wants me to get something out of this break. Mum told Nic she hopes I come back "a bit less depressed," which Nic wasn't supposed to tell me, but obviously she did, because that's what sisters do.

This week is my chance to turn it all around.

To feel like I know what I'm doing with my life. To stop moping and start succeeding. I don't usually go in for all that manifestation stuff, but I'm tempted to give it a shot for a change. Send some positive vibes and a can-do attitude out into the world.

What I need is a bucket list.

I sip my latte, then smack my lips and click my Biro. Time to get to work.

The Vacation Bucket List

1. Write pros and cons list of actually doing the law degree you got an UNCONDITIONAL OFFER FOR
2. Write pros and cons list of doing literally anything but that
3. Consider other degrees to apply to through clearing?
4. Write pros and cons list of a gap year, just in case
5. HAVE FUN! BE RESTFUL! PRACTICE MINDFULNESS!
6. Talk to strangers (make friends??)
7. Try something new!
8. Figure out how to tell Mum and Dad and Nic and Hannah I don't want to do the law degree, never wanted to do the law degree, never will want to do the law degree, and might cry if someone mentions the law degree one more time
9.
10.

I stare at the blank spots for nine and ten for a while, tapping my pen absently against the page and then chewing the end of it, then tapping again while I drink some more coffee. It bugs me there's only eight things on the list instead of a nice round ten (ten would make for better content, I can't help but think), but hell—I've got the whole flight to come up with two more things to do this week.

I embellish the page with a couple of tiny doodles with my felt-tips, then drop the lot back into my handbag and reach for my phone. It's been maybe ten minutes, which I think is a pretty good start to the digital detox. That's about the longest I've left my phone alone in years.

I have a few notifications, mostly consisting of overenthusiastic messages from my parents or my sisters telling me to have fun. There are some from my friends about how jealous they are, which I reply to with a selfie of me grinning in the airport. I do feel a bit superior about it, but in my defense, they're all off on a group getaway to Ibiza this year and I have to miss out because it clashes with the family trip to Tenby, and Dad wouldn't let me bail on that. Which royally sucks, but I do love the family trip to Tenby. And Mum and Dad *are* kind of footing the bill for whatever trips I go on, so I can't argue too much.

Not that it's that big a deal anyway, because there's plenty of time this summer to hang out with my friends. The girls from netball, some of the gang from art club, a few people from my classes . . . I do feel a bit proud when I see all their different faces popping up as they read my update in Messenger. All these different people I've brought together. It's a nice feeling.

But before the group chat can start sharing their Ibiza plans and make me the jealous one, I swipe over to the comments section of my #GRWM #getreadywithme TikTok from this morning—and my stomach plummets when I see it only has a few hundred views, making it a total flop in comparison to most of my other videos. My views have been going steadily down for weeks now, and my number of followers has hit a plateau—none of which is helping my recent grand total of zero sales from my Etsy store.

Why? What am I doing so wrong? Did I upset the algorithm by switching to a different filter on my videos? It doesn't make sense. Plenty of my videos have tens of thousands of views. And a GRWM is always popular!

What gives? I want to yell.

Is this it? The beginning of a downward slope into nothingness?

Not to be dramatic or anything, but it sure feels like a pretty firm sign to pack in any ideas of pursuing a creative career and do the boring, sensible, stupid law degree that, for some unfathomable reason, my parents suggested might be a good fit after the careers teacher said I had "tremendous potential" and that, for some even more unfathomable reason, *I said sounded like fun*. It's the universe telling me I'm a joke.

Furiously biting back tears (because I'll be damned if I'm going to *cry* in the *airport* over one measly, pathetic video), I throw my phone back into my bag and down the last dregs of my latte, which has gone almost cold by now.

My nails sound loud and sharp as they tap on the tabletop. A woman at the next table clears her throat, jerking me back to reality. It's only then that I realize I've been huffing through my nose and my lips are twitching like they're making argumentative replies to my parents, to the algorithm, to that awful letter of doom congratulating me on a place at Bristol Uni.

I take my phone back out—but only to check the time.

The gate should have been up four minutes ago. Dad joked about how I'd probably get so distracted, traveling alone, that I'd miss the flight, and I cannot prove him right. Not after everything my family has done to try to cheer me up with this vacation. Quickly gathering my things, I take a deep breath and stand up, bag slung over my shoulder. A quick scan of the table to check I haven't left anything behind, and I pick my way between the tables that are packed way too close to each other to the nearest board.

I stand under it for a few minutes, not quite seeing it.

Then I say, "Shit. You've got to be kidding."

And a voice says, "Are you delayed too?"

I look at the girl next to me, with mousy brown hair pulled taut in a tiny, high ponytail and wearing the most outrageously bright pink trousers I've ever seen in my life. She's got to be about my age, and her mouth is twisted in sympathy.

"Yeah. To Majorca."

"Same. Ugh, the perfect start to a vacation, right? Apparently there's a fault with the plane, but I don't think we're supposed to know that."

"Where'd you hear it?"

"One of the airline staff. I kind of badgered it out of him."

She shoots me a quick grin, giving me the impression she did a bit more than "kind of badger" the guy. She starts tapping her phone rapidly against the palm of her hand.

I take a guess. "Nervous flier?"

"Kinda."

So I say, "I reckon there's something wrong with the left phalange."

As soon as I say it, I regret it. Because if she doesn't get the reference, I've probably made this poor nervy girl even more anxious, and I'll have to explain the whole thing, and it won't even have been worth it.

But to my relief, she laughs. "Here's hoping, huh? I mean, it's only delayed twenty minutes. It can't be that bad if it's just twenty minutes, right?"

"Right," I say, unconvinced, but what else does she want me to say? I know I said I wanted to "talk to strangers" and "make friends," but I didn't necessarily mean with the first person I bump into . . . Honestly, I'm enough of a shit show on my own—I don't need to tag along with a nervous flier.

Already backing away, I offer a polite smile and say, "I'd better go buy a drink for the flight, actually, before we board. I bet it won't even be that long a delay. Ten more minutes, max."

3 *Jodie*

By the time we're boarding, eighty minutes later than scheduled, I'm frazzled.

I'm seriously considering downloading Twitter just to message the airline and complain, but I figure I've done enough of that with the staff here in the airport.

I like to think of myself as a go-getter. I am the *dictionary definition* of "strong, independent woman," thank you very much . . . but I am *terrified* of flying, and haven't traveled abroad for the past few years. Whatever tolerance I built up in my early teenage years seems to have vanished without a trace.

I'm glad there's nobody I know here to see me falling apart now.

I smile through gritted teeth at the perky flight attendant and show her the boarding pass on my phone. She points me in the direction of my seat, and I think about how that's a practice I'll never understand.

I mean, there's literally only one way to go, other than the cockpit. You don't have to be a genius to figure out where row eleven is.

But I say, "Thanks," and make my way down the aisle on wobbly legs, stopping every so often as people in front of me get to their row and take forever to stow things in the overhead locker, or they have the window seat and need the rest of the row to get out, all of which stretches out the torturous process of settling in for my flight. Like this wasn't already bad enough without me seeing who'd be too slow to move out of the way in the event of an emergency . . .

When I get to my row, there's a girl in my seat.

"Excuse me," I say to her.

She must be about my age. She's bundled up in a hoodie and wearing leggings so worn I can see the bobbles on the fabric. Her short, curly black hair is held back by a headband, showing off a simple pair of sparkling studs in her ears, and she glances up with wide green eyes from a book she's only three or four pages into.

"Sorry, but I believe you're in my seat."

"Oh God, I'm sorry," she blurts, smiling awkwardly and half standing. "I just—I really like the window seat. I've got the aisle seat. Would you mind?"

I have never minded anything less in my whole life.

I relax a little, saying, "Actually, that's perfect. I hate the window seat."

"Match made in heaven!" she declares, sinking back down. She smiles at me again and then returns to her book. Some cheesy romance with loopy writing on the cover, like Gran would buy.

I clutch my bag on my lap, waiting for the plane to fill up and for someone to stop next to me and ask me to move so they can get to the middle seat. But then the attendants start shutting the doors on the plane and everyone's in their seats, buckling themselves in or setting up iPads with movies, and I realize nobody is sitting beside me.

At least something's gone right today.

First, I'd been delayed getting to the airport—Mum had insisted she'd left enough time, but had to stop to fill up with petrol, then she took a wrong turn at the airport and we spent another fifteen minutes driving around trying to get back to a drop-off point. *Then* the airline said I couldn't take two bags on the flight, so I had to pay a ridiculous fee to check my suitcase, after I'd worked so hard to squash everything in so I could get away with just hand luggage. But it didn't end there as *of course* I got stopped going through security, which is never fun . . .

And to top it off, the flight was delayed. By *eighty minutes*.

It doesn't help that I've never flown alone before. I wasn't even totally sure about this trip, but Gran and Mum convinced me in the end, and two years of frugal student living and a part-time job where I consistently take on extra shifts meant I had the savings to cover it.

Plus, they'd made such a compelling case.

"You've just wrapped up your second year of uni, you're home for the summer, you're at a bit of a loose end with no plans before you start your summer job at the café . . . and you work so hard!" Mum had grinned at me, Gran nodding along fiercely behind her. "Nothing wrong with a little break! You deserve it, Jodie. When was the last time you treated yourself?"

"I bought that coat from Zara a couple of weeks ago. And I have a millionaire's shortbread from Starbucks every Wednesday after my computational methods lecture."

"It's not all about material goods, missy," Gran barked, before

Mum could wheedle me into it. "When was the last time you went out and *did* something?"

It had shocked me that I couldn't actually answer her, even after spending several nights lying wide awake, considering it. So . . . here I am. On a flight to Majorca. To take a weeklong vacation in the sun all by myself.

Which, admittedly, I *am* excited about.

But this has *got* to be the worst preflight in history.

All I can think is that it doesn't bode well for the rest of the trip.

I fumble through the pockets of my bag for my headphones and then quickly stuff my bag under the seat in front of me once I've got them. The cabin crew take us through the emergency procedures and point out exits and things, as though they're not already clearly signposted. The captain apologizes for the delay—a delay arriving, due to adverse weather conditions on the flight out.

I let out a small sigh of relief. Not entirely convinced it wasn't a problem with the plane, but . . .

Maybe it *was* a problem with the left phalange.

I smile a little as I remember that. That was funny.

When the plane finally starts taxiing down the runway, I remember my travel sickness tablets. I bend down and try to get them out as discreetly as possible, without moving my bag from under the seat in front of me.

I stuff two in my mouth and swallow them dry. They don't go down easily, and I cough, pulling a face.

"Are you okay?"

The girl in my assigned seat has set down her book to look at me with a mixture of sympathy and *Oh God, please don't puke on me.* The plane picks up speed, and I can't reply except to grind my teeth, squeeze my eyes shut, wrap my fingers tightly around the armrests and nod stiffly.

Fake it till you make it, Jodie. Come on, get a hold of yourself.

Oh right, a voice in the back of my mind bites back. *Because that mantra has served you well so far, hasn't it? It's not like you wake up sick with dread over lectures or expect to be told you've failed every piece of coursework and every exam . . .*

"Do you want me to talk to you? Will that help? My brother used to be a nervous flier and it always helped him." I don't manage to answer, but she barrels on regardless. "Are you heading to Majorca for a vacation? I am. A week away, all-inclusive. I can't wait. Well, I'm a bit scared, to be honest, because it's my first time going away by myself, but I'm sure it'll be all right once I'm lying next to a swimming pool with a book. My boyfriend—ex-boyfriend—was always much more keen on adventures than just chilling out, so that'll be a bit of a nice change, I think."

This is where I'd say something about being a fellow solo traveler and how I'm hoping to relax this week, too—but I can't even relax my *jaw* right now to get the words out.

The girl carries on. "The last vacation I had, we went to visit my dad's family in Jamaica, which should have been *way* more exciting than it sounds—it was only for some cousin's wedding, and I ended up with food poisoning for half the trip. Do you want some water?"

We're in the air.

Thank God.

"No," I churn out. My voice sounds dry and cracked. I clear my throat. "Thanks."

She grabs the water bottle out of her seat pocket, uncaps it and hands it over anyway.

I take a sip, kind of worried that if I don't I might throw up. "Thank you."

"No problem. You're not as bad as my brother—he used to cry. He's older than me, so he'd always act all butch and macho and important, but then we'd get on a plane and he'd turn into a total wreck. I used to love it. I'd tease him about it relentlessly in front of his friends."

"Bet he loved you for that."

"Well, he deserved it. He'd tease me for crying over Pixar movies."

"I thought everyone cried over those."

She laughs. "Not my brother. Those first ten minutes of *Up*? Not so much as a sniffle. If he didn't use to cry when we got on a plane, I'd have thought he had a heart of stone. Do you fly much?" She glances around as if trying to work out whether I'm traveling with anybody.

I shake my head. The plane is noisy and a little rattly, and they haven't turned the seat belt sign off yet. The perky flight attendant who pointed me to my seat is getting something from an overhead locker. She staggers ever so slightly going back down the aisle. My right hand hasn't unfurled itself from the armrest yet.

Dictionary definition of "strong, independent woman," huh? *Yeah, right.*

"Not really," I tell the girl. "I think last time I went away was with some friends from school?"

"Ooh, those trips are always a riot, aren't they? We all went to Amsterdam during reading week, end of last year. Stayed in this god-awful hostel because nobody would listen to my suggestion about sharing rooms in a nice hotel. One of my flatmates got high and accidentally hired a sex worker. We ended up playing Uno with her."

I peel my eyes open a little wider, my neck stiff as I turn to give her a baffled look. She's smiling at me, a gap between her front teeth, chattering away as if we're old friends. I can't quite decide if it's weird or comforting, but the alternative is thinking about all the ways this plane might crash (I should *not* have let Gran convince me to watch that Tom Hanks film about Captain Sully last week), so I decide to roll with it.

"How does that happen? I mean, how do you *accidentally* hire a sex worker?"

"Honestly, I have no idea. We were all too busy trying not to pee from laughing so hard, we never figured it out. Great story, though, isn't it?"

"Most definitely."

There's an electronic *ding* throughout the cabin.

"Ladies and gents, the captain has now turned off the seat belt signs. The cabin crew will be providing a trolley service shortly where you will be able to purchase food and drinks. If you are removing any hand luggage from the overhead lockers, please be careful as items may have moved during takeoff."

The girl next to me goes quiet, and I've relaxed into my seat.

"I'm Jodie, by the way," I tell her.

There are hundreds of hotels in Majorca, but we still have to spend the next couple of hours on this flight together; I can't redo the first impression I made, but I can try to make up for it a little bit.

I stick my hand out toward her, which she looks at in amusement before I realize that this is probably a really weird thing to do. It's an airplane, not some networking event. What, do I expect a keynote speaker from Glossier along with the trolley service?

She grins, though, and shakes my hand firmly. "Luna."

When the trolley comes around, I let her go first. She asks for a cup of tea and a Twix. I jump in straight after with my order, telling the guy I'll pay for it all.

Luna blushes furiously and says, "Oh gosh, no, please. You don't have to do that."

"You didn't have to be nice to me during takeoff," I tell her, and hand over the cash for our drinks and snacks before she can protest again.

When I pass hers along to her, she purses her lips and quirks an eyebrow at me as if to chastise me, but then she grins again and says, "Thank you."

We chat a little more, but I can feel the conversation fading—I notice her fidgeting with the book in her lap, and I have a few podcasts downloaded I was hoping to listen to. We both let the conversation drop off, turning to our own in-flight entertainment for the rest of the way.

I find myself breathing a sigh of relief I didn't know I was holding. Maybe I can do this after all—*relax*. Have a *vacation*.

Despite all the hard work I've put in, I'm not very *good* at the whole university thing. But this isn't molecular biology—or even rocket science. This is a break, and a well-earned one. And I can *definitely* spend a week not worrying about what's next and just enjoy some sunshine and a trashy podcast to take my mind off everything.

4 Luna

The baggage carousel is broken.

It takes forever for the bags to appear, and even then they only show up three or four at a time. Then the carousel stops for another couple of minutes, churns out another few and stops again. It's torture.

I tell myself the bus won't leave without me, but I still find myself chewing on my thumbnail while the seemingly endless wait for my suitcase drags on. *It won't leave without you. It's a resort shuttle bus. They have a list. They'll wait.*

I can't help but remind myself about the whole prepaid checked baggage debacle back at the other airport, though, and I can feel my heart jump into my throat every time the carousel groans to life again and starts moving.

While I'm waiting, I fire off a couple of texts. I had one from Dad almost as soon as I landed saying, *I see you've landed. Let us know when you're at the hotel.* I text my brother, bemoaning the baggage carousel and grinning at the string of GIFs of Captain Holt from *Brooklyn Nine-Nine* that he sends back.

As I'm replying to let him know what a dork he is, a new message pings through.

It's from Liam.

> Tried calling but guess I caught you
> when you were already on the plane.
> Just wanted to say I hope you have a
> nice time. Would be good to talk if you
> get chance x

Does he want to talk because he wants to fix things? Does he even realize that there were parts of our relationship that *needed* fixing? As much as I miss him, as badly as the space in my heart where he used to be aches, I immediately recall the sorts of things that pushed me to break up with him.

Messages that went unanswered, hardly speaking to him for days on end, even with him only living across campus. How I was always the one putting in the effort to make plans for us because if I didn't, he sure as hell wouldn't. The fact that he prioritized his new friends over me again and again, and made me feel like *I* was the one not spending time with him if I didn't go along on a night out—just for him to practically ignore me if I did.

I miss Liam, but I *really* don't miss all that.

It's those memories I focus on as I fight the urge to text him back—not the ones where I was wrapped up in his arms like that was exactly where I belonged, or all the fun day trips or times out with friends I would have missed if he hadn't coaxed me along, and the way my heart sang when he sat there with his arm around me and smiled like I hung the moon.

We probably should talk. The breakup—my break*down*—was so out of the blue I probably at least owe him more of an explanation.

But not right now—and not this week. This trip is supposed to be completely self-indulgent and an attempt to get over him. If I'm still hung up on Liam by the time I get back home, maybe I can tell him that I miss him—and *only* then.

I mute the notifications from him until the end of the week.

A text comes through from my service provider saying WELCOME TO SPAIN and reminding me about all the tariff details. I open up the WhatsApp chat with my friends from uni to message everyone and see how they're doing. It's been quiet lately, which is weird, because with seven people in it, there's usually some conversation going on.

In my group chat of friends from home, which has also been quiet for a few weeks, I send a longer message saying that I'm off on vacation, ask how everybody's exams were and say it'd be nice to catch up properly when I get back next week.

I get one bland, brief reply from the uni crowd a few minutes later, and something heavy settles on my chest. It's the same feeling I get when I see the photos they've recently posted, which include Liam but not me.

He would have told them about the breakup. That's always been the way with us: Liam's the extrovert, forever on his phone, messaging people, and we were together constantly, so he'd read out whatever was going on and I'd pitch in to the conversation via him. Of course he would have told them what happened, they're our friends, but . . . Hardly anyone from *either* group has reached out to me about it, and the way my messages go unanswered now feels like a line in the sand.

The luminous orange suitcase strap I borrowed from my parents catches my eye, and I'm saved from having to speculate about the fact that my and Liam's friends might *not* be mine anymore.

I shove my phone into my hoodie pocket while I lunge for the suitcase strap, puffing slightly as I heave the suitcase off the belt and turn it upright onto its wheels.

Nineteen kilograms of luggage is barely enough to get me through the week, but now that I have to carry it I'm kind of regretting it. I hope this resort isn't full of little winding staircases I have to lug it up.

I follow the SALIDA signs, glad of my Spanish GCSE I can just about remember, and make my way toward the brightly colored stands where vacation reps in polo shirts wait.

I don't see the one I'm looking for, though.

Someone in wedge heels brushes past me with a four-wheel suitcase and stops in front of a TUI rep. It's Instagram Girl, from the check-in desk. Her messy bun still looks just as stylish as it did earlier. How it hasn't fallen out must be some kind of miracle. I wonder if it's locked in place by a hundred hairpins I can't see or by sheer willpower.

"Excuse me, hi, sorry—I'm looking for the Casa Dorada resort?"

My ears practically twitch toward the conversation, but I try to look like I'm not eavesdropping.

"Er, what, sorry?"

I'm so glad the rep is English. Much less glad he doesn't seem to know what we're talking about. (*She*—what *she's* talking about.)

"Casa Dorada?" she presses, and I can hear the nervousness seeping into her voice. "There's—there's meant to be a shuttle bus for it, but I haven't seen one. Do you know about it?"

"I'm, er . . ." He trails off as Instagram Girl taps on her phone and holds it out to the rep, presumably showing him the resort confirmation email. I know I could step in and back her up to try to help out, but all I can do is hang back nervously and listen to her handle this. "Hang on. Hillary—Hillary, come here. Casa Dorada?"

Another rep excuses herself from a family of five and steps over briskly, clipboard at the ready. With a distinctly French accent, she asks, "What is this?"

Instagram Girl tries again, showing her phone to Hillary.

"Oh! Yes, yes, I think . . ." Rep Hillary looks around. "I don't think they have a stand like us, yes? They will be waiting by the taxis."

"Really? Oh, thank you so much!"

By the taxis?

I can't help but pull a face, unconvinced. Shouldn't they be with the other reps? Isn't it . . . more *official* that way?

I have a sinking feeling in the pit of my stomach, but march off after Instagram Girl anyway.

Outside, I spy Jodie, the nervous flier from the plane, standing in a small crowd near someone with a sign. Well, first I spot her luminous pink trousers, which stand out a mile away. She spies me, too, and gives me an awkward wave.

Didn't she mumble something during landing about Casa

Dorada? She'd been fairly incoherent, talking so quickly and quietly I'd missed a lot of it. Mostly, actually, I'd talked *at* her in an attempt to distract her while the plane raced toward the tarmac.

(And to try to keep myself from thinking too much about Liam and whether I should reply to his texts once we landed. As good as my book promised to be, it hadn't been enough of a distraction on its own.)

Instagram Girl has stopped to peer around, squinting against the sunshine pouring in from every window to pick out the sign for our resort among all the names held up by prebooked taxi drivers or for the business class travelers.

I suck in a deep breath before I pluck up the courage to tap her on the shoulder. "Casa Dorada, right?"

"Oh! Yeah. Are you looking for it too?"

I point in Jodie's direction. "I think it's that way."

She flashes me a quick smile and then strides off on her long legs, leaving me to hurry after, hindered even more by my suitcase.

Sure enough, there's a man in beige cargo shorts and a white button-down with bright-blue swirly writing on the breast pocket declaring he's from Casa Dorada. The uniform is some comfort, I suppose.

Although he doesn't have a clipboard.

"Names?" he asks us.

"Luna Guinness," I tell him, and Instagram Girl says, "Rory Belmont."

"Then we are all here! Bueno. Please, please, with me."

There are seven of us altogether waiting for the bus: a couple around my parents' age who are busy bickering in very quiet voices, an old man who looks weathered and broad and makes me think of the oak tree in the neighbors' garden, and a woman with a wrinkled face wearing a long peasant skirt. I end up walking behind her and catch a faint whiff of something I'm pretty sure is weed.

Outside, it's hot. The kind of still, stifling heat that presses up against you, and I can feel myself sweating already, despite still being in the shade of the airport.

I need a lemonade in my hand and a pool lounger, stat.

Instagram Girl had the right idea traveling in those clothes, I think. My leggings are clinging to me in all the wrong places, my hoodie is weighing me down, and I think my rucksack might crush me face-first into the tarmac if I bend forward even a little bit.

Our hodgepodge group shuffles single file out of the airport. The man guiding us eventually stops at a smallish shuttle bus that's probably white under the thick layers of dust. He gets in the driver's seat, puts the key in the ignition and starts up the air con. The whole van chugs and churns with the effort. He gets back out and comes around the back to take our luggage.

When it's my turn, I say, "Excuse me, but—well, shouldn't you . . . Don't you have a list or something? What if you left someone behind?"

He gives me an indulgent smile. "No, Miss Lola, not to worry. I have a wonderful memory, ¿sí? I know who I am collecting."

I don't point out the irony that he's misremembered my name.

He heaves up my suitcase, cheeks puffing out. "Ay, Miss Lola, it seems you have brought all the lists on my behalf!"

He's so busy laughing that I don't try to mumble some kind of explanation or defense, just flush and walk away to get on the bus.

Instagram Girl—Rory Belmont—is already onboard, tapping away at her phone from a back seat. She tilts her head and pulls a neutral, not-quite-pouting face to take a selfie, then clicks at her phone and does the same thing but moving slightly as if it's for a video, and goes back to typing. Jodie, sitting near the middle and in front of the now-deathly-silent couple, has earphones in and is mumbling into her phone—talking to someone, I guess. She's got her eyes closed and her forehead in her hands. I wonder if she's still feeling rough from the plane, but don't want to interrupt her to check whether she's all right.

I pick an empty seat near the front of the bus. A quick call-up of Google Maps says it's a fifty-minute drive in current traffic to our destination.

I wish I'd saved some of my water from the flight or bought another bottle at the airport. I'm so hot and so thirsty, and now all I can think about is having to be hot and thirsty for the next fifty minutes, and about the cool lemonade I'm suddenly *desperately* craving.

Liam would be huffing and puffing and grumbling by now. We went to Lisbon last summer before uni, and he was so irritable in the heat. I got snappy at him for not loosening up and enjoying the vacation, even though I was kind of struggling too. I guess at least this time it's just me I have to worry about.

Just me.

Four years of always having someone to share *everything* with, always having plans scheduled with friends and people to join in with, and now it's *me*. Alone for the first time—ever.

Oh my God, what was I thinking?

What do I think I'm *doing*, taking myself off to Spain for an entire week all alone? And on a trip I booked on a drunken impulse! It's bad enough that I broke up with the guy I thought I'd spend the rest of my life with out of *nowhere*. I'm not this person. I don't just drop everything and jet off somewhere, I'm not outgoing or spontaneous or anything remotely like . . . *this*. Just because Liam's out with our not-so-mutual-after-all friends all the time, and drunk me wanted to prove that *I'd* moved on, too . . .

The problem is, I don't know how to *be* alone.

We haven't even left the airport yet, but I'm already starting to think this trip cannot be over soon enough.

5 Rory

My top lip is sweating. The backs of my knees are sweating. There's a trickle of sweat running down my leg, hovering around my ankle in all its grossness.

It takes way too long for us to get to the hotel. The air con begins to sputter out halfway through the trip, and even though it makes a valiant effort to carry on, I don't feel cooled down. I feel sweaty and gross. My (disgustingly warm and not-too-refreshing) Diet Coke is running precariously low, and I wish I'd thought to buy more water at the airport.

Note to self: you can *never* buy too much bottled water.

I grab a quick snap, trying to look as cute and polished as possible, and put that advice on my Instagram Story. *#TopTip.*

There seem to be roadworks on all the routes we take, resulting in heavy traffic. According to the incredibly detailed itinerary Nic made for me, we should've been at the hotel well over an hour ago.

My phone battery is almost as low as my Diet Coke supply, and I've already drained my portable charger. I turn off the music to conserve the battery and keep myself entertained by looking around at the other people on the bus from my vantage point at the back.

The short, dark-skinned girl at the front—what did she say her name was? Lola? Luna? Something cute like that—looks chilled out and half-asleep. She must be getting the best air-con supply from her seat. Second best, after the driver. Although I seriously do not know how she isn't melting in those leggings and that thick cotton T-shirt.

There's the old man built like a mountain, wearing Beats headphones and watching a Studio Ghibli movie on his iPad. He keeps grumbling to himself and twisting in his seat to move the screen out of the glare of the sun. What he's doing on a digital detox retreat, I have no idea.

The lady just in front of me, however, I can totally see on this kind of trip. With her hemp tote bag, long wavy hair and beaded bracelets, she reminds me a bit of Mum that time she went to a '70s party dressed as a hippie. I wouldn't be surprised if she doesn't even own a phone.

The couple on the left must be in their forties, maybe fifties, and they've been sniping at each other for a good twenty minutes now. He thinks he forgot to pack the sun cream, but *she's* the one who screwed up the online check-in and ended up getting them seats at the back of the plane near the toilets and made them the last ones off. And *now* he's checking his email, *again*. ("Really, Andrew?" she hisses, and I think, *Yeah, Andrew, really?* and do a quick check of my own emails, but there's nothing to see.)

The other person on the bus is the nervous flier from the airport. Left phalange reference-getter. I think she's a little older than me. She's been tapping furiously at her phone with such a deep frown I think she might need twelve rounds of Botox to get rid of it. She looks even more desperately in need of a break from reality than I do, which is *really* saying something.

Outside is less interesting. We rattle down main roads with high, sandstone-colored walls of rock, and sparse brown-green shrubbery poking out from the cracks in them. Then we're traveling down narrow streets, somehow squeezing between two rows of parked cars and blockish white buildings.

I feel like I should appreciate it all. I *want* to appreciate the sights, but it looks so . . . bland to me that I can't find any awe-inspiring beauty in it. Just a street with houses, or the side of a road.

Frankly, I don't see anything worth getting my camera out for, but I grab a couple of shots anyway.

My stomach twists. Why do I get the feeling this doesn't bode well for our end destination?

I turn away from the window, fidgeting.

Is it so bad that I want to check my social media, see how my content is doing after all the effort I've put into it? Refresh my emails in case the handful of brands I pitched content to have responded—whether good or bad? What if my group chat is going off and I'm missing some drama?

I *hate* the not knowing. I hate that limbo. I hate feeling like Schrödinger's damn cat—except sometimes I think a nice quiet death by poison while trapped in a box might be preferable to the crippling anxiety of not knowing things.

I ping Hannah and Nic a text in our WhatsApp chat.

Rory

Still on the way to the hotel. Don't know how much longer. Slowly dying of heat and exhaustion and lack of phone battery

Nicola

Just as well you won't need your phone the rest of the week then!!

Hannah

Get off your phone. But also send pics when you get there, I want to see what I've paid through the nose for in all its pixilated glory

Nicola

What WE paid for!

Hannah

That's what I said

Rory

I'm on 18%. Later losers xo

I close WhatsApp and turn my phone face down. I switched vibrate off over the last couple of days in an attempt to ease myself into the whole digital detox thing, but I don't think it's worked very well so far—within about thirty seconds the FOMO hits and I turn my phone back over to see if anything new has happened.

Of course, when the bus stops, I feel like this has all been worth it.

The resort stretched out in front of me looks exactly like the photos online, and every bit as picturesque as the advert made it out to be. The way it was going this morning—the busted baggage carousel, the delay—I was almost (read: totally) expecting some ramshackle hut.

But it's not, and I could almost cry with relief.

There's a breeze stirring the shrubbery and palm trees. I can *see the sea*. It's even close enough that I can hear waves crashing softly. The sky is an unnaturally bright shade of blue and there's barely a cloud in sight. The air smells like salt water and sand and—

And I'm pretty sure I can smell my own sweat.

Gross.

I pull out my phone, snap some pictures and take one snippet of video to use as the grand finale of my vacation TikTok. I can probably get one last quick upload before I have to turn my phone in . . .

The hotel is another white block, three stories with lots of windows and wide black wrought iron balconies. It doesn't take up much space, but the rest of the resort, at least according to the pictures online, is a collection of luxurious villas made of logs and with straw roofs, sprawling across the sand. I can only assume they're on the other side of the hotel. On this side, the one away from the beach, there's a big grassy area full of shrubbery with vibrant yellow, pink, red and white blossoms that brighten up the scene.

The driver sets our suitcases down, and we all collect our own.

"I can't believe you lost the luggage strap," Mrs. Andrew mutters at Andrew.

"If you'd bought the cheap ones like I said, maybe it wouldn't matter so much," he snaps back. "Sixteen quid on a luggage strap. Honestly, Linda."

Honestly, Linda, I think, watching the whole exchange shamelessly. I spy Nervous Flier hiding a giggle behind her hand.

"This way, por favor," our driver says with a sweep of his arm, and leads us to the hotel. He leaves the bus key in the ignition and the doors wide open, and Lola/Luna eyes the key nervously, as do I. Shouldn't he take it with him, even if he doesn't lock up the bus?

Not that there's anybody about, I guess. We seem to be miles from anybody and everything. The road to the resort was little more than a dirt track through grass and along the coast.

But *still.*

Driver Guy leads us down a path I didn't notice through the flowering bushes, and we lose sight of most of the beach but end up with a better view of the hotel. I steal a few more pictures, trying to be subtle in case I'm told to put my phone away before I've even checked in. The whole bottom floor of the hotel is open, like some grand pavilion with columns. It's white everything everywhere, except for the blue cushions that adorn the white wicker furniture at reception. It's a *much* better clip to end my video on; I'm so glad I hadn't posted it yet.

I hope my room looks this inviting.

And then I realize we're all coming to a stop.

"Gracias, Rafael," says a man with the most immaculately groomed twirly mustache I've ever seen in my life. The driver nods his head slightly. To us, the man gives a broad smile and opens his arms, palms up.

"Bienvenido a todos," he declares. "Welcome, all, to Casa Dorada. I am honored to have you here with us today. My name is Esteban Alejandro Álvarez, and I am manager of this resort. Alma?"

There's a lady at his side who I didn't see before because she was hidden by the huge old guy. She steps forward, holding a tray of champagne flutes filled with sparkling golden liquid.

Oh God.

This is *so* perfect.

Like, beyond perfect.

Hannah and Nic have never been so right, and I've never been so glad to let them take charge of my life like this. I try not to do the greedy grabby-hand thing when Alma and the champagne come my way, but I think I do anyway.

Mm.

Delicious.

I think it's only prosecco or cava rather than proper champagne, but I honestly wouldn't know the difference. After years of parties with whatever alcohol my friends and I could scrounge from older siblings—or sneak from our parents' kitchen cupboards—until we were old enough to purchase our own liquor, I can't say I have a particularly refined palate. But it's chilled and bubbly and everything I need right now.

Even Linda and Andrew seem to mellow a little.

Esteban announces, "Anything you need this week, my team and I are at your disposal. We are here to ensure your stay is . . . one to remember, ¿sí? Now, if you will all follow me, we will check you into your rooms, collect your phones and begin the trip!"

6 *Jodie*

A few people start following Esteban Alejandro Álvarez, but all I can do for a minute is stare at his retreating back.

He *cannot* be serious.

"Excuse me," I blurt, jogging forward (carefully, so I don't spill the bubbly in my glass), suitcase abandoned. Esteban stops and turns to look at me. "Sorry, but—did you just say *collect our phones?*"

"Did you mean passports?" Luna pipes up, her face pulled into a fearful grimace. She's clutching her phone tightly, which is exactly what I feel like doing.

Esteban laughs, not unkindly. "No, señorita, I meant phones. My English is quite good, I can assure you."

"Why do you need our phones?" I demand, because I'm still not convinced I heard him right.

My brain rattles through what other words sound like "phones," but I can't come up with anything. Maybe he just means they need our mobile numbers? So they can contact us during the week? Maybe it's in case of emergencies? Yes, that must be it. There's a totally reasonable explanation for this. Everything is fine.

Esteban turns to the other guests with a confused smile on his tanned, weathered face. "You are aware this is a gadget-free resort, ¿sí?"

There are nods throughout the group, except from me and Luna, who looks every bit as stricken as I imagine I do right now.

This is *not* happening.

"I'm sorry," I say as patiently as I can, "but you mean we can't use our phones? The whole week?"

Esteban laughs again. It's one of those nice full laughs, but right now it's grating on me. That laugh and that silly mustache with the twirly ends and the sheer *audacity* that he's wearing an Apple Watch and— "Yes, señorita, the whole week. Now, if we are all clear on that, maybe we can proceed with check-in."

Luna hangs back to walk next to me, eyes wide and still clutching her phone desperately. The tall blond girl at the back of the group who made the joke about the left phalange catches us up.

"So I'm guessing you guys didn't get the digital detox memo?" she asks, looking at us with sympathy.

"Definitely not," I mutter. "I mean, I know it said stuff about 'switching off' and 'detoxing' when I booked it, but I just thought it meant, like, you know, *relaxing*. Drinking some green tea and having a mud bath or something. I didn't think it meant *literally*."

Looking down at my phone, my stomach twists into knots. I know it's not exactly like I'll be missing out on that much when it's only a few days, but . . . This is a lot to get my head around. I don't remember the last time I spent more than a few hours without my phone or any kind of internet connection.

And damn it, I was planning to use this time productively.

Get ahead on the job search. Grad schemes open in September and I need to start applying. I was going to brush up my CV, perfect a cover letter . . . Now I'm just supposed to spend the whole week doing *none* of that, leaving those tasks to eat into my part-time job this summer and the studying I was going to do to get a head start on next year?

And what about Mum and Gran? I chat with them *every day*.

How am I supposed to go *the entire week* without talking to either of them?

"I definitely didn't read anything about a digital detox," Luna all but snarls, glowering at Esteban and the rest of the group. Then, all of a sudden, her face relaxes and she lets out a brief giggle. For a second I wonder if the sun's got to her already and she's delirious, but then she says with a self-deprecating sigh, "Then again, I was absolutely smashed when I booked this."

"You booked a vacation *drunk*?" Blondie asks, aghast—no, I realize, not aghast: excited. Like it's the most scandalous thing she can imagine, in the greatest way possible. Getting a better look at her, she barely looks old enough to drink. She stumbles slightly on an uneven paving stone in her wedges. "Really?"

"Oh, I was in full-on crisis mode," Luna admits, a bit sheepish. She looks at me instead of explaining further. "What about you?"

"My gran found it in a magazine. To be honest, I was more focused on checking how many stars it had on Tripadvisor than examining the fine print. I mean, come on, a digital detox! Are they kidding? Who even *does* that? What kind of crazy social media addict do you have to be to need to *detox* from it?"

I realize as soon as I say it that Blondie from the back of the bus is here voluntarily and is probably one of said crazy social media addicts, and I cringe. Luna and I both look at her, and all I can think is: *Well done, Jodie. Another stellar first impression, you're really nailing it today.*

She shrugs in response, thankfully not looking too offended.

She also doesn't point out that dreading the idea of giving up my phone for a week makes *me* sound like a crazy social media addict.

We're in reception now, waiting while everyone else gets checked in. The bickering couple are in front of us, arguing about who had the passports last.

"I bet it was Andrew," Blondie whispers to us. "The muggy bastard."

"Are you kidding?" Luna scoffs. "It's *definitely* in her bag. You think she'd trust him with the passports?"

I can't help the sudden giggle that bursts out of my mouth. I fake a coughing fit to cover it, smothering my mouth with my hands, and concentrate on not so much as glancing at either of them until I've recovered.

When was the last time I giggled like that?

I know they're total strangers, but this is the most girl talk I've had in . . . months. And that's a conservative estimate.

After the old man and the other lady have checked in, Rafael scurries into reception, wielding passports. "Tortolitos," he calls out. "Tortolitos, you left your passports on the bus!"

Andrew and Linda glare at each other.

"What's tortolitos?" Luna asks, butchering the pronunciation.

"Um," I say, already on my Google Translate app. I smirk and show them the screen. I'm worried if I try to say it aloud I'll dissolve into giggles again.

"Lovebirds?" Blondie says, scoffing, then snorting. "Our man Rafael has a great sense of humor." Then she gasps. "Oh my God. What if they use words we don't know? What if the menu's all in Spanish and we can't translate it without our phones? *Oh my God.* I did *not* even think about that."

I don't know her very well, but I think she might be about to hyperventilate.

"The staff seem pretty fluent. I'm sure they'll help."

Lips pursed together so tightly they turn pale, she swallows loudly and nods. "Yeah. Yeah, you're totally right. I'm sure."

"I have a GCSE in Spanish, if that helps," Luna offers up.

"I did A level," I say, not that it's a competition. Except A level is really quite a lot harder than GCSE, so.

Blondie looks mollified, and swallows again, still nodding. In the least Spanish-sounding accent I've ever heard, she says, "Fantástico. Gracias, ladies."

I let Luna and Blondie go ahead of me after the tortolitos have checked in, but Luna steps aside too. I get the feeling she does it just so she can have those few extra seconds with her phone. She's furiously typing out some texts by the looks of it.

Which makes me think, *I should do that, too.*

I fire off one to Mum to let her know I'm not MIA, I'm just at some stupid no-phone-zone—no-*fun*-zone more like—resort. I ask her to let Gran know and apologize that I won't be able to talk to them for a few days. I copy and paste the text into the group chat with the girls from school, before reconsidering and deleting it, instead typing out:

> At the hotel and WOW, it's every bit as gorgeous as it looked online! So excited to get stuck into a cocktail (it's five o'clock somewhere, hey!) and do some sunbathing. Is it raining back with you guys? PS Can't remember if I said, but this is a phone-free resort, so will be offline for a few days! Fill you in on all the deets next week. Missing you all already! xx

I bite my tongue as I hit Send, wondering if they'll see through my positive spin, and knowing that it's not them I'll miss. It's the knowing what's going on, which is the way it's been since we left school.

"Rory Belmont." Blondie introduces herself at the counter, pushing across her phone and passport.

"Welcome to Casa Dorada, señorita. Are these all your devices?"

"Sorry?"

"All your devices," Esteban repeats patiently, picking up her phone. "Do you have an iPad? A computer? An e-reader?"

Rory stammers, and Luna shoots me a look of alarm.

"Well, I—I have my tablet, but—but that's for art. It's not for the internet. It's not really *digital* per se . . ."

"E-readers don't count, do they?" Luna asks nervously.

"E-readers definitely don't count," I declare, fixing Esteban with my sternest look. This is a drastic situation, after all: I didn't bring any physical books. Mum had made the case that they'd take up extra space in my luggage, so I borrowed her Kindle and downloaded a bunch of e-books. I don't even know what most of the books that I bought in my little Amazon spree yesterday are about—just that they're of the rom-com variety and each cost no more than £1.99.

The only books I've read in the past few years are whatever everyone was talking about, either in group chats or at university. Usually some Booker Prize winner, but occasionally a book that got turned into a Netflix series or some crime thriller that had gone viral because of its epic plot twists. I was kind of looking forward to reading something just for fun.

"Any unauthorized devices will be confiscated," Esteban tells us flatly, mustache twitching, eyes narrowed slightly as he looks at each one of us. "*No* electronic devices. No phones, no computers, no tablets, no e-readers. If you are found with any prohibited devices, certain privileges will be revoked during your stay, and you may be asked to leave the resort."

"Privileges?" Rory echoes, looking mildly faint.

"Leave the resort?" Luna squeaks.

"Sí, privileges." He sighs, the furrow in his forehead deepening. "Did you read the information pack?"

"What information pack?" I ask.

"You should have been sent an information pack via email

after your booking was confirmed," he tells us, the words slow and clipped. "Did you receive this?"

The three of us look at each other. I'm not sure why I think these relative strangers will be able to tell me if I got the email, but the blank looks on their faces is some comfort—even if I can feel a headache coming on.

"I got the booking confirmation," Luna says meekly, lifting her phone almost nervously, like Esteban is about to snatch it right out of her hand before she can even pull up the email.

I do a quick check of my junk mail and feel like a prize fool because, lo and behold, buried under lures of compensation I could be owed and nameless threats that my webcam has been hacked while using adult websites, there it is.

I look at the girls in defeat. "Junk mail."

Esteban sighs once more, and says, "There is a copy of the information pack in each room where you will find everything you need to know for the week. Now, please, Señorita Belmont, your devices."

Grudgingly, Rory dumps her bag on the counter, removing a Microsoft tablet and an e-reader. A handful of styluses spill out, and she shoves them back into her bag.

"Is this everything?"

Rory's lips twitch, but then she sighs and hands over an iPod Nano, the kind I haven't seen in years.

"Muchas gracias. You are in room two-oh-five, señorita. Enjoy your stay."

Rory watches Esteban load her things into a tray marked 205

and take them into a back room. She snatches the key up from the counter and gives us both the quickest of smiles before stomping toward the lifts.

"Ah no, you must take the stairs. The lift is out of order," Esteban calls to her.

"Oh, *wonderful*," Luna mutters next to me, with a glare at her suitcase.

I know how she feels. Mine clocked in at fourteen kilos (and a bit) when I checked in—well over the weight allowance for hand luggage, as I found out at the airport. I'm really starting to regret bringing heels. Why couldn't I have just packed one spare pair of flip-flops and be done with it? Why couldn't I be a light packer, like Rory so evidently is?

Luna gets room 206, and makes her way toward the staircase. Then it's my turn, and I'm loath to give up my laptop.

So much for getting a head start on next year.

Handing over my Kindle is the worst, though. Farewell, entertainment for the week.

Esteban gives me room 207 and a bright smile I'm so not in the mood for. I grimace back, taking my key and following the sound of Luna grunting and her suitcase knocking against the stairs somewhere ahead of me.

At least I know two other people will be suffering right alongside me this week.

7 *Luna*

I'm itching to be on my phone complaining to my family and friends about this, but I can't because *they took my phone.* And I'm not sure my friends would even bother to reply anyway. Instead, I'm stuck with the next best thing, which is venting to Rory, whose room is across the corridor from mine.

I knock on her door a bit more aggressively than is really necessary, and she looks a little startled when she answers and sees me huffing and wielding the information pack.

"Have you read this?" I ask.

"I'm putting it off," she announces breezily.

There are tiny travel-sized bottles of shampoo and conditioner in her hand. It looks like her suitcase exploded all over her room, and I think, How did she fit all that into her bag? The bed is a patchwork of clothes in whites, grays and light pastels. Chunky, brightly colored jewelry spills out over the desk. There's another pair of wedges near the foot of the bed.

I'm staring, and we both know it.

"How did you fit all that in your case?" I ask.

"My sister used to travel a lot for work. She's a pro packer. Don't you roll your clothes?"

"I thought that made them crease."

Rory shrugs. "Sometimes, I guess." She jerks her chin at the information pack, then disappears into the bathroom with her toiletries while calling to me over her shoulder, "So? What's the damage?"

I stand in the doorway. Maybe it was rude to barge over here and pound down her door, but it still feels like a step too far to just let myself into her room. (And, besides, there's nowhere to sit. Everything's covered in clothes.)

"Did you know there are scheduled activities for us to participate in? Yoga at six a.m. Aqua aerobics at ten-thirty and again at two-thirty. A HIIT class at five. And that's just the tip of the iceberg."

The door of the next room opens. I look over my shoulder and it's Jodie, dithering slightly. "Sorry. I thought it was you guys I heard. Are you talking about the introduction pack, or whatever it's called?"

I nod.

"It's outrageous," she erupts, striding over. "Three activities recommended each day? Are they kidding? This week was supposed to be relaxing, not boot camp."

"Tell me about it!" Rory calls from the bathroom. There's clattering as she rearranges plastic bottles. "I knew they had some stuff planned to help keep us entertained, but come *on*. Do they seriously expect us to sign up for *three* activities a day?"

"Well," I say with a snort, flicking back to the page, "it's 'highly recommended.' If you want to get the most from this retreat."

"I do not," Jodie deadpans. "I mean, if it's only recommended, what can they do?"

"Yeah," says Rory, emerging from the bathroom and rooting inside a floral pink toilet bag for more bottles. "Like, what were these privileges Esteban was banging on about?"

"It sounds like the activities *are* the privileges, from what I could tell . . ." Jodie shrugs, not looking too sure of herself.

"That's what I thought," I say. "But privileges also include— wait for it—*alcohol.*"

Rory groans loudly. "In that case, I'm playing by the book. *They may take my phone, but they can never take my schnapps.*" She says it with a growly Scottish accent, then, in her normal voice, asks, "So what's the sitch with the booze and stuff, Smarty-Pants?"

They both look at me, so I guess I'm Smarty-Pants.

Well, it could be a worse nickname, I suppose.

"Um, where was it . . . ? Oh right," I say, pointing at the paragraph. "Privileges include alcoholic beverages, access to the private beach, the day trip to the Hidropark, the morning excursion along the coast, the afternoon trip to Palma with the visit to the Basílica de Sant Francesc and the military museum . . . the day at Katmandu Park . . ."

"Christ," Rory says, staring at me with wide eyes. "So much for seven days of relaxation!"

"I think the trips are optional," Jodie says, standing closer to me and leaning over the page. She blinks. "Ugh, I shouldn't have taken my contacts out. Can't see anything. Um . . . yeah, there— look." She points. "'These outings are encouraged, but not mandatory as part of your stay.'"

"What, and they're all just . . . included in the cost?"

Jodie squints again, taking the booklet from me. "They all have a small additional fee. Ten euros for the trip into Palma, twenty-five for the theme park . . . It's pretty cheap actually. Probably just contributes to travel or ticket cost."

Rory starts to pull a face, but then Jodie says, "Hey, don't look like that. You might be so bored without your phone, music and books that you're living for these trips out."

"True. God, I cannot believe that jackass took my Kindle!"

"Same."

"I saw a bookshelf in reception," I say. "I didn't get a good look, but it seemed pretty well stocked."

"Bet it's all Lee Child and Agatha Christie," Jodie says. "Beach resorts always have crime novels."

"And I brought loads of books. I mean, they're mostly all romancey things . . ." The best kind of beach reading, I always think. Well, the best kind of any reading. Even though I'd brought my Kindle, I'd made sure to pack a small stack of my TBR pile, too.

"I'm keeping you onside," Rory says, grabbing me by the shoulders. "Library of Luna, open for business. In return, I can offer you one melted Twix and my everlasting gratitude."

I laugh. "You can keep the Twix. But if you drop one of my books in the pool I'll come for it."

"Deal."

"You're welcome to borrow them, too," I tell Jodie. "If you want."

"You're my hero."

I blush, mumbling, "It's nothing. Just don't hurt my books."

Jodie claps her hands. "Thank you so much. Well, I'm gonna get changed and hit the pool for a couple of hours before dinner."

"What time are you guys going to head down to eat later?" I ask.

I suddenly realize I'm probably press-ganging them into dinner, but . . . without my phone or anything, this is going to be one long, lonely week. I don't know what it is about them, but I feel like we've already forged some kind of bond—and I *do* know that I want them to like me.

Rory looks startled for a moment, but Jodie says, "About seven, I guess? Seven-thirty? What do you think?"

"Seven-thirty sounds good. Rory?"

"Uh—um, yeah. Yeah. Sounds great." The shocked look finally vanishes, and she beams at us. "See you guys then. But I think I'm gonna skip the pool and take a nap. I'll see you down there for dinner later, though!"

Phew. Well, that totally paid off.

If I have to spend the week struggling through this enforced digital detox and "strongly recommended" structured activities, at least I'm not going to have to do it alone. These girls might be relative strangers, but for the next week they're all I've got.

8 Rory

I plonk myself down on a sun lounger next to Luna (not Lola—I need to remember) and Jodie (who's lying on her stomach and who I wouldn't have recognized if not for the fact she was next to Luna). Luna's wearing a white bikini, and I can't help but look at her thighs and her belly, wishing I had that kind of confidence in my body. Jodie's wearing a black one-piece with a low back that shows off the edge of a tattoo on her shoulder.

Luna drags her head around to look at me. "What happened to your nap?"

"I got bored."

I am really, *really* missing TikTok right now.

I don't remember the last time I fell asleep without my phone in my hand, the red tint of night mode lulling me to sleep. God, I hope I can sleep tonight without my phone.

The pool is big and square and the bright turquoise of chlorinated water. The sun loungers are all white with a thick foam seat cover, not that hard, unforgiving woven stuff that leaves a grid pattern all over the backs of your legs and makes your bum numb.

There are umbrellas galore, but the ones near us are all lowered and tied up.

If I moved a meter or so to the left and crouched down to get the sun in just the right place in the top right, it would make a beautiful Instagram shot.

This is just what the doctor ordered . . . Switching off for some self-care—as soon as I grab a margarita! #totalbliss #sunshineandfuntimes

I wonder how many likes it would have got. It would have been pretty enough that if I'd shared it on TikTok with the right sound it might have gone viral.

No use thinking about that now, I remind myself, fingers twitching for a phone I don't have.

The hotel's busier than I expected. There are maybe forty people around the pool. I don't see the lovebirds, Andrew and Linda, but I do spot the big old guy, and the woman from the bus smoking what I can only assume is a dubious white roll-up.

I psych myself up for a second before peeling off my white crochet cover-up dress that doesn't really cover much up now that I think about it and drape it over the back of the lounger before lying down to sunbathe.

All I need now are my podcasts, I think, lamenting all the unlistened-to episodes of *The Morning Toast* I had downloaded on my iPod.

I know this is a digital detox retreat, but . . . I didn't think it'd be this *extreme.*

My tablet doesn't even have its own data connection, for God's sake. It's, like, barely even *digital* without the Wi-Fi. I thought the detox was only about disconnecting from the outside world or whatever. I cannot believe they took what is essentially a glorified drawing pad and set of paints from me.

Albeit one with two seasons of *Stranger Things* downloaded onto it, but you know. Still.

How am I supposed to "disconnect" and leave the stresses of the real world behind when I'm stuck with nothing to do but listen to my own thoughts circling and spiraling? I'll go home more frazzled than when I left.

That said, I've been lying down barely five minutes when someone in a white polo shirt and khaki shorts comes over and offers me a towel and a bottle of water, just the over-the-top quality service I was promised in the ad. I can't help the way my eyebrows shoot up, but I say, "Thanks—uh, gracias," and take them.

Once he's gone, I turn to the girls. "Do you think it'll be like this all week?"

"Almost makes up for the fact they stole my phone," Jodie mumbles, lifting her head from her arms to reply.

"I can see why people pay a grand for this," Luna says. "Glad I got it on a good last-minute deal."

"Oh, tell me about it," I say as though this isn't a pity vacation *#gifted* by my sisters.

At least there's one thing I can tick off the Vacation Bucket List: talking to strangers and making friends. When they'd discussed dinner plans earlier, I hadn't especially thought I'd be included, but it's a relief to know I won't be alone in the whole technology-free week. (Especially now that I don't have my e-books and podcasts.)

I don't know them too well, but they might provide some good entertainment and be a decent distraction.

With the sun beating down on my bare skin, the sound of people swimming, the Latin music playing softly from the cabana, I tell myself that, despite all the issues with the flight, this week is off to a great start. And, in the end, I do take my nap.

I plonk down my plate from the buffet. Pasta, two slices of pizza and some chips. I reach for a bread roll from the basket in the middle of our table. It's hardly a picture-perfect plate, but when in Rome . . . (Or, in this case, a Spanish hotel, with nobody to Instagram this food for . . .) It feels like some sort of sneaky indulgence, like ordering takeaway in the middle of the week. I have this nagging little voice in the back of my head reminding me that if it's not the sort of thing I can share, it's *wrong*.

But the carbs, the carbs are calling. Jodie and Luna show no restraint, either, both with plates piled high.

"Okay," I say, raising my eyebrows at Luna. "So, tell me more about this drunken crisis that led to you booking yourself on a surprise digital detox. That is a story I *have* to hear."

Luna slurps down her noodles and chews for a while before answering. Jodie's watching her expectantly, too.

Maybe I shouldn't have asked, but *come on*. She can't just throw out a comment like that and *not* expect anybody to follow up on it.

Luna frowns for a moment, as if bracing herself for something, and takes a long gulp of wine before sucking in a loud, deep breath and launching into what I *really* hope is an epic (and, okay, messy) tale.

So sue me. I'd like to not be the only one here who feels as if their life has spiraled out of control.

"So I had it all planned, right? I thought I'd end up marrying my boyfriend—*ex*-boyfriend. I was with him for years. We even picked out our future kids' names! We go to the same uni, and I thought everything was going to be so perfect. We'd arranged to be in the same houseshare next year and everything, it was all in the five-year plan, but . . . I had a bit of a meltdown, I think. I broke up with him, right in the middle of exams. A couple of days later, I got drunk, got an email advertising this place and the rest is history."

"Why'd you break up with him?" Jodie asks, mouth full of lobster, eyes bulging. I feel way less guilty knowing she's enjoying this as much as I am.

Luna scrunches up her face. "It's hard to explain. I'm not even sure I did the right thing . . . It was just—lots of things piling up, you know? He's always been really sociable and liked going out to parties and stuff. He always encouraged me to come along and join in so we could spend more time together, but at uni . . . I know it's a big part of the culture, but sometimes it just got a bit *much*, you know? It started to feel like it was getting out of hand, and we didn't get to spend any quality time together. He'd be really grumpy and miserable when he was hungover, and he was *always* hungover. So I'd make the effort to go and hang out with all our friends or organize something as a group because that was what I knew he wanted to do . . . But then I'd look like a sourpuss the times I wasn't drinking or went home early. Or I'd feel like I was being a nag if I wanted him to walk me home, but he wanted to stay out . . ."

She sucks in a deep breath, then her green eyes open wide as she exclaims, "But, you know, these friends we hung out with were *my* friends, too, and it's what everyone was doing . . . and things used to be so great between us! It's almost like as soon as we got to uni he just decided, screw it, he didn't need to bother with *us*. Like I was just—there. Secondary to all his fun plans with friends and new carefree lifestyle. He was never like this before, I don't think."

She gets a faraway look on her face, like she's playing out a montage of Luna and (Ex-)Boyfriend's Best and Worst Moments, trying to pinpoint when this guy changed. He sounds like he's having the uni experience of my dreams. But I'm also jarringly aware that he sounds like a total *dick,* at least when it comes to being someone's significant other.

"Anyway," Luna says, that distant expression not budging one bit, "it got to a point where I came back from this really rough exam and I was super stressed out about it, and he didn't seem to *care.* He said it was our first year so it didn't matter anyway, and I just . . . snapped, I guess. I didn't want to waste my time nursing hangovers or making so much effort to make *him* happy when he didn't return the favor ever, and honestly, the whole thing was like some out-of-body experience. I just remember screaming at him to get out. I told him that I was sick of not mattering to him, and that we were done. It was all a bit of a blur."

Oh wow.

Okay, that took A Turn. I hadn't expected her to spill *everything* like that.

I let out a long, low whistle.

Luna pauses, blinking as she takes in our shell-shocked expressions before blurting hastily, "But he could be so great. *So* great. The best. He could be really sweet. And he *got* me. We just gelled right from the start, you know? It had always been easy with him, *before*. Like, I wanted to marry him. And I was having such a rubbish day when I broke up with him. I think we were going through a rough patch? I mean—that happens, right? So all this was probably a mistake, and I'm not sure I was even thinking straight. It was just . . . yeah. I don't know."

Jodie says, "That sounds horrible. I'm sorry, Luna."

As I start mm-hmming in sympathy, Jodie suddenly backtracks, sitting up straighter and placing her hands flat on the table. "Whoa, whoa, wait, hang on. You have a five-year plan?"

Luna blinks. "Don't you two?"

"I barely have a one-week plan, babes," I say with a snort.

She shudders.

Then Jodie reaches for a bread roll and declares, "I think I want to drop out of uni. That's why I'm here."

Now we stare at her and wait.

While Jodie stalls, buttering the roll and mulling over her words, I grab a roll from the bread basket myself and reach across for her half-used butter. It's only when she gives me a startled look that I think to ask, "Do you mind?" and she shakes her head, letting me take it.

I dig into my food, and Jodie finally continues talking.

"I don't have a five-year plan or anything, but I was doing it all *right*. Or, you know, I thought I was. I got good grades at school, and I was supposed to be the first in my family to go to uni. It's just me, my mum and my gran, and they were always so *proud* of me," she says, spitting the word and scowling like she can't imagine anything worse than her family being so supportive.

"They really encouraged me, and I knew it was what I was supposed to do. But I got to uni and it was *not* the one. I thought it was what I wanted, but I can barely keep up. I'm completely out of my depth. I don't even *like* being a student, but I don't want to let everyone down, you know? I don't. So I just threw *everything* into uni. And now I'm on track for a 2:1 if I can keep it up next year, and before long I'll have to start applying for grad schemes and jobs and . . . It all just got very real, very fast. It feels like I've been on autopilot for the last two years."

Jodie's breath shudders out of her, and she seems to fold in on herself. She tears off a bite of bread roll, focusing on chewing it before she can carry on.

If she's just finished her second year, Jodie must be about two years older than me. Right here, in this moment, she seems to age a decade or more, though, shrinking under the weight of her problems. It's only now that I notice the sallow look to her skin, the bags under her eyes, too deep to be travel-related.

Will that be me in two years? Will I be run-down and miserable, doing a degree I hate?

There's a sick feeling twisting through my stomach, and I wriggle in my seat as Luna reaches a sympathetic hand out to pat Jodie's shoulder.

"So have you quit?" I ask. *Tell me, tell me how.*

Jodie shifts upright, face screwing up. "No. Not—not yet. Maybe I won't. I don't *know.*"

"Because of your mum? Your nan?" I ask, ignoring the almost reproachful look Luna gives me, as if I should be allowing Jodie some space—like she didn't *volunteer* to tell us all this stuff.

Like I don't desperately need to know how she's going to deal with it, so I can find out how I'm supposed to tell my parents I don't want to do the law degree I'm meant to start in September. Jodie feels like my Ghost of Uni Experiences Yet to Come.

"Sort of," Jodie admits. She's still tearing chunks off the bread roll, but leaves them on her plate rather than eating them. "Not just because of them. I don't feel like they'd disown me or anything if I quit. I mean, they've always encouraged me to work hard for what I want. And this is what you're *supposed* to want, isn't it—the university degree, the good grades, the impressive job afterward? So that's why I've worked so hard to get through it. I swear, every time I talk to my friends, everyone's just bragging about how great everything is, how amazing our lives are. Or, I don't know, maybe that's just me, and it only feels like that's what they're doing. Plus, if I pack it all in now, waste the last two years for *nothing* when I'm so close . . . what's everyone going to say? What if this is all just some silly crisis moment like when dads buy a sports car, and I'll leave uni only to regret it later?"

She looks at us, so defeated it's obviously a rhetorical question, and it's like a vise tightens around my lungs. *What's everyone going to say?* That's my biggest fear, too.

"Anyway," she declares in a significantly more blasé tone,

"exam season just finished, and my mum and gran said after all the hard work I'd put in I deserved a break, and suggested this resort. Seemed as good a place as any to run away from everything."

"Up until they stole our phones and threatened us with an organized good time," Luna mutters, and Jodie and I both crack up, our laughter washing away the tension that had gathered around the table.

Jodie takes a glug of her wine and I top up everyone's glasses, not too surprised that the bottle we shared is already empty. The wine's going down faster than the food—which is saying something because we were all *starving*. I'm startled to realize my plate is already empty, and debate going up for more when Jodie speaks again.

She sets her wine down with a flourish and crosses her arms, leaning over the table. "And what about you, Little Miss Impossibly Long Legs?"

I blush. "They're not that long."

"They look it to me and my five feet, five inches," she says with a snort. "What're you? Five eleven?"

"Five ten. Plus the heels." I poke my leg out from under the table to waggle my shoe at them.

"Well, in my book that's tall and leggy."

"What are you doing here?" Luna asks curiously, and drinks some more wine. "I mean, you *knew* this was a digital detox. You were all ready to hand over your phone. Bad breakup? Stalker ex?"

I scoff. "Hardly. I'm not much of a relationship person. Well, not the *serious* relationship type anyway."

"Then why'd you book this week away?"

I think about what I could tell them. I could flick my hair over my shoulders and say breezily, *Oh, me? I read about this place online and wanted to check it out, and you know, it's supposed to be* such *an uplifting, centering experience to give up your phone for a while . . . Me? I'm not here to fix or run away from anything. I'm just here for the ride.*

But they've been brutally honest, and I've had enough wine by now that I blurt out with a sardonic smile, "I got an unconditional offer for a law degree that I only applied for because my family are all boring, sensible people who think art is a waste of time, and maybe they're right? I do a lot of social media stuff and . . . I'm actually pretty good at it? Like, middling levels of popular. But they just think I'm obsessed with my phone, and they're kind of not wrong. I don't want to tell them it's because I've been trying to build a brand to flog my artwork on Etsy, because I've flopped and have made a grand total of seventeen sales in the two years since I set it up."

That's the first time I've said any of that out loud. I have the girls hanging off my every word, which gives me the same kind of adrenaline rush as seeing comments on one of my videos pour in.

"Anyway, I've backed myself into a corner with the law degree because everyone seemed so happy about it and I was like, 'Yeah, why not! Sounds a great idea!' Which it was when I applied because it seemed *ages* away and like I had time to turn it all around. I thought if my Etsy store did well enough, it might overshadow the whole 'unconditional offer' thing. But obviously that hasn't happened. So now they're worried I'm in one of my *moods* and I'll end up back on antidepressants, which is why my sisters booked me this trip. They said I needed a digital detox to have a proper break. They thought it would be *mindful* and *restful* and help me 'gain some perspective'—and it sounded like a better option than going back to a therapist. And a *way* better option than just telling them the truth."

I wait for their responses with bated breath, doing my best to appear casual and unconcerned. My heart is hammering furiously in my chest, and my hand starts to sweat around my wineglass. I wait for them to ask what I've got to be so depressed about or why I'm wasting my time on social media, or to use their great Wisdom and Experience as Older Girls to tell me my family are right: I should just suck it up and do the law degree and stop being such a brat about it.

But what Luna says is, "Your sisters just . . . packed you off on vacation?"

"Yeah, pretty much."

"Oh my *God*. My brother would never."

"Now I wish I wasn't an only child," Jodie says. "If only I had big sisters who'd do that for me."

"If only I had my shit together," I deadpan back at her.

Jodie laughs. "I'll drink to that."

Luna raises her glass high over the center of the table. "Hallelujah!"

9 *Jodie*

When I drag myself to breakfast at about nine-thirty, sinking into a seat with a plate of toast, fried eggs and a heavy hangover I definitely deserve, I groan quietly. I'm such a lightweight. I don't remember the last time I had more than a single glass of wine—none of my usual crowd at uni are heavy drinkers—but I must've had near on a bottle last night. Rory had a generous pour; it was easy to lose track.

I set my elbows firmly either side of my plate for a moment, lay my head in my hands and groan again.

"Ah, Miss Jodie," says a voice that's already irritatingly familiar. I drag my head up to give Esteban a smile that feels more like I'm just baring my teeth at him. Go away. Leave me and my throbbing head in peace, por favor, Esteban.

He says my name like "Ho-dee," despite his otherwise flawless English.

"Are you not feeling well?" he asks with a sympathy that I'm, like, ninety-six percent sure is fake.

Yesterday, my first impression of him was good. Competent, capable, charismatic.

Now the charm has turned to chiding, and the whole thing seems like a carefully constructed facade.

(Or maybe, I concede, I am just very grumpy when hungover.)

"I'm fine, thanks. Just—bit tired."

He keeps smiling, and I want to dunk his face in my plate of eggs. I'm not in the mood for cheerful and overly friendly service this morning.

"I see, I see. You missed your morning yoga."

"Huh?"

"You and your friends last night, you all signed up for morning yoga for the duration of your stay. Sofia, my colleague, said that you did not turn up."

"Oh. Right. That."

I have zero recollection of signing up for yoga.

How much wine *did* I have?

They shouldn't ask people to sign up for classes when they're drunk, I almost tell Esteban, but my head can't handle an argument right now. So instead I just say, "Sorry."

"Mm." He knows I'm not sorry. "We hope you will make it tomorrow, then, Miss *Ho-dee*."

After he's gone, Rory scurries into sight, head ducked and one hand raised to hide half her face. She sets down a cup of coffee on the table, claiming the seat opposite me. She peers out from between her fingers, bloodshot eyes the only visible sign of a hangover. I can't help but feel a little jealous, thinking of my lank hair shoved back in a ponytail and the bags beneath my eyes. Nobody should be allowed to look cute in this state.

"Please tell me he's gone. I cannot deal with another telling-off from Señor High-and-Mighty. Cute glasses, by the way."

"Thanks. You missed yoga, too, then?"

"Honey, I don't even remember signing up for it," she says, running her hand over her face.

"Me either. Do you think he's just making it up so we feel bad and actually show up?"

"Wouldn't put it past him, the Kindle thief."

I smirk and dig into my food. Rory eyes my plate for a while before hauling herself out of her seat and going up to the breakfast buffet. I wander back over to make myself more tea and get more juice; when I come back, she's got a full English breakfast *and* an omelet.

"How does someone as skinny as you eat that much food?" I ask, half in awe and half plain envious. I'm not plump and curvy the way Luna is, or skinny and willowy like Rory; my body is soft and untoned, something I'd rather keep covered up and definitely have never felt confident about.

Mouth full, she tells me, "It doesn't count when you're this hungover. Ugh, how much did we drink last night?"

"I don't know, but I get the feeling that also doesn't count when you're on vacation."

Rory laughs a little, then winces like even that is too much effort. *I feel you, girl.* "It does when you end up signing up for six a.m. yoga classes. God. Do you think we signed up for anything else?"

"I hope not. Are you going to go tomorrow?"

She pulls a face, then looks over her shoulder and spies Esteban laughing cheerily with a group of five who must be pushing seventy. "I feel like if we don't, he's not gonna let us hear the end of it. Have you seen Luna this morning?"

I shake my head, but minutely, because I don't want to aggravate my raging headache any further. "Nope. She probably slept in, too."

Luna, it turns out, didn't sleep in. She's one of those horrible high-functioners who doesn't suffer from a terrible hangover after drinking too much. "Unless I mix, then I'm a goner," she explains when we're sitting around the pool later that morning, divvying up her collection of books. (I'm starting to see why she had such a hard time lugging her suitcase up all those stairs: she's brought enough to stock a Waterstones.)

When Luna says the alarm on the clock in her room had gone off at twenty to six that morning, I gasp. "Oh God, no, I do remember! You said you'd set an alarm. Promised to get us all up."

"I did knock," she says, looking guilty. "But only a little. After Rory was sick last night and you almost fell asleep at the table"—I do *not* remember that, but Rory shrugs and looks unabashed—"I wasn't so sure you guys would want to go."

Rory and I shake our heads. "Definitely not."

"Sofia, the lady running the class, asked me where you both were. I said I thought you weren't feeling well, but I don't think she bought it."

"Esteban definitely didn't," I tell her with an eye roll. "How was the class?"

"All right." Luna shrugs one shoulder. "Lots of tree pose and concentrated breathing. It wasn't so bad, actually."

"How is anything at that time of the morning not so bad?" I mumble. I pulled my fair share of all-nighters at the library, no problem, but getting up to make it in time for a nine a.m. lecture was always a trial.

"Watch out. Incoming," Rory says, putting down the two books she's choosing between and nodding behind us.

Luna and I turn around to see a hotel rep making his way from a group a few sun loungers down from us. Light-colored khaki shorts, neat haircut, white polo shirt . . . and a clipboard in hand. Wonderful.

"Buenos días, ladies. How are we today?" the man says, smiling broadly.

And then he waits for an answer instead of just telling us whatever he's come over for.

So I say, "Er, yes, great, thanks."

He helps himself to a seat on the sun lounger next to Rory. "My name is Oscar. I am one of the activities reps here at Casa Dorada. I am assuming you have all read the information pack, so you will be familiar with all the activities we have on offer here. Are there any you would like to sign up for?"

My eyes dart to the girls. Rory is looking at us with wide eyes, forehead crinkled slightly in helpless confusion, waiting for one of us to take the lead. Luna peers wistfully down at the book on her lap and strokes its cover. It's clear from both their reactions that they feel the same way as me about the organized activities: completely and utterly unenthused.

When neither of them volunteers an answer, I tell Oscar, "I think we were actually hoping for a bit of a quiet week. Lounge around with some books by the pool, have a couple of drinks, go down to the beach . . ."

"But you read the information pack, yes?" Oscar keeps smiling broadly, showing a set of perfectly straight pearly whites, but his tone is a bit less perky now.

"Well—yes . . ."

"Then you will be aware that the purpose of Casa Dorada is to reconnect with the world and yourself. Our activities have been designed specifically to center around this mission and are a chance to embrace some local culture. For instance, our trip to the Basílica in Palma is a wonderful opportunity to take photos to share with your friends back home."

Rory perks up at that—she literally sits up straighter, frown disappearing. "Photos? Does that mean we'll get our phones back?"

Ooh. Now we're talking. *Gran would love to see the Basílica,* I think. Maybe I could FaceTime her and Mum to show it off and squeeze in a chat at the same time?

Oscar laughs. "No, you will get your phones back at the end of the week, of course. You can purchase disposable cameras in our gift shop, but we *do* ask that you do not use them around the resort."

"Vintage," Rory mutters, her frown reappearing.

"Perhaps our coastal walk? The views are magnificent."

Luna gives a small appreciative hum, like she's considering it. Maybe she's only being polite, but Oscar latches onto it.

"Rafael will drive the group down to a point on the coast and we will set off on a three-hour walk. The bus will collect us at the end of the route. We recommend that you wear sturdy shoes, for safety reasons. Refreshments will be provided. The bus leaves at seven."

"What a shame," Rory says, really laying it on thick. "We've signed up for morning yoga. And I didn't bring sturdy shoes."

She waggles one flip-flopped foot at Oscar.

"The yoga class will be finished in plenty of time; it is only forty-five minutes."

"I think we were planning to go to the beach," I say, desperate for any excuse now. Because this guy is *persistent*.

"The beach is private access for our guests," Oscar says. His smile is tighter now, his words more clipped. "A *privilege* for the guests who are *participating*. You will remember that to get the most out of your stay we encourage you to sign up for three activities a day? We find this is particularly helpful for those who are struggling to be parted from their phones."

He punctuates this with raised eyebrows and a pointed look at each of us in turn.

I *am* feeling kind of lost without my phone, but in all honesty, it's mostly because I want my Spotify playlists and podcasts, and less because I'm missing social media or the internet.

I mean, I am missing Wordle, but I'll live.

It's . . . actually pretty nice not seeing messages from my friends and constantly feeling like they're doing anything and everything better than me, making me feel guilty and annoyed at all the things *I* should be doing to push myself, to one-up them, to prove I'm doing something worthwhile, too . . .

Yeah, I'm definitely not missing that.

Rory asks, "So we can't use the beach if we don't sign up for things?"

Instead of answering, Oscar says, "Have you signed up for any of our other activities yet?"

"Not yet," Luna mumbles. "Just yoga."

"Perhaps our aqua aerobics class, then? You have already missed this morning's, but we run the class again this afternoon."

"Um . . ."

"And this evening we are holding an improv night. Many of the guests have signed up already. That would be your three activities for the day."

No. *No.* Morning yoga I might be able to stomach, but improv night is where I draw the line.

"If we sign up, do we have to perform or can we just watch?" Rory asks.

"Yes. Everyone participates." Oscar grins again like improv is so appealing, because what more could we *possibly* want from a vacation than getting up to make prats of ourselves in front of a roomful of strangers?

Kill me now.

Okay, I think, taking a second to be rational. *This guy is clearly not going to let up, so we'll have to compromise somewhere . . . And better to do that on* our *terms than* his.

"There's a visit to a water park, right?" I look at the girls. "That could be fun. What do you think?"

Luna nods, face brightening. "Sure, a water park sounds good."

"I haven't been to one in forever," Rory says, and smiles back at us. "Screw it, let's do it. Go on then, Oscar. Sign us up for the water park."

"Wonderful! There will be a small additional fee, but we will add this to your bill at the end of your stay. The Hidropark visit is tomorrow. The bus will leave at eight o'clock, and we will be returning for dinner."

"Sounds great!" Luna says. "What about the theme park?"

"That will be on Friday. Would you like me to sign you up for that?"

"Can we think about it and get back to you?" Luna says, with an apologetic smile. "Chat between ourselves and decide?"

"Of course, of course. I will leave you with this . . ." Oscar pulls a sheet out from his clipboard and hands it to us. I take it. "This is a copy of the itinerary for the week. I will be around throughout the day, or you can find me in reception. I will leave you ladies to decide, and you can tell me later today what you are signing up for."

"Great," Rory mumbles, as Luna politely says with a far more enthusiastic tone, *"Great!"*

"And we will see you all later at the aqua aerobics class. Please be careful not to eat too soon beforehand."

Before any of us can object and point out we never agreed to sign up for aqua aerobics, Oscar is already gone, moving on to the elderly couple a few sun loungers away. I swear under my breath and Rory snatches the itinerary from me.

"Jeez, please say we don't actually have to do all this crap? Look. *Look* how much stuff they've got going on! A table tennis tournament, boules at three p.m. every day . . ." Rory tosses the sheet aside with a huff.

"I don't mind doing the theme park," Luna says. "If you guys are up for it."

"Can do," I say.

"I think we'd better," Rory agrees. "I'll be crawling the walls by then. That's *four days away*. I'm already going nuts without my phone."

"Tell me about it," says Luna.

"You're the only one of us who knew what you were getting into with this digital detox lark!" I laugh, flapping a hand at Rory accusingly, rather than admitting I'm not missing my phone so much. "It's only the first proper day."

"It's been nearly twenty-four hours," she laments, tipping her face up to the sky. "I miss Pinterest. And Instagram. And, like . . . being able to check the *time*. Not all of us wear watches."

"I like to be prepared," Luna says haughtily, hugging her wrist-watched hand to her chest. But neither of them can stay serious, and we start giggling. Luna pulls a face at us and says, "Oi, carry on and I'll revoke your privileges and take my books back."

I scoff. "All right, calm down, Esteban."

She pushes me, pulling another face, but then turns serious. "Do you think they'll really stop us using the beach if we don't sign up for enough activities?"

"They can try," Rory grumbles, and then stands up, dropping the itinerary in my lap. "I'm going for drinks. Lemonade okay?"

"Yeah, cheers."

"Orange juice, if they've got it," Luna says. "Please and thank you."

"Roger that. You guys can look at the list of living hell and decide if there's anything else worthwhile."

10 Luna

An hour after he's given us the itinerary, Oscar loops back around to ask what else we'd like to sign up for. Grudgingly, we stay signed up for afternoon aqua aerobics and put our names down for a couple of evening salsa dance classes later in the week and the theme park.

Oscar looks disappointed that we're not signing up for more. I can't work out why it makes me feel like I'm in trouble at school—maybe it's just because he's around my parents' age—but signing up for anything else seems like such a chore. I'm glad the other girls resist letting him push us around. I think if I'd been on my own, there's every chance I would've caved and signed up for whatever he told me to, just to end the conversation.

Jodie finally gets him to leave by saying we'll consider what else we'd like to do on the days we haven't committed to three activities. I'm relieved that he buys it, and when she hisses at us as soon as his back is turned, "We are *not* signing up for anything else."

This week is supposed to be *fun*. It's meant to be relaxing and a break from the heartache I've been nursing; the thought of being dragged to a military museum or on a coastal hike makes me want to shrivel up. I'm sure someone would like it, but it's definitely not my idea of a fun vacation.

And, thank God, not Rory's or Jodie's, either. I bet if they'd signed up, I would have ended up tagging along just so I didn't feel left out.

The aqua aerobics class after lunch doesn't turn out to be so bad, and when it's closer to dinnertime, the pool starts emptying, people disappearing back to their rooms or to other predinner activities like the HIIT class.

"I think I'm going to head up to my room," I say, piling my sun hat and book into my straw tote. "Wash my hair before dinner."

"Mm, good shout," Rory mumbles, the words muffled by her crossed arms, which are pillowing her head. "I'll go up in a sec."

"Once I finish this chapter," Jodie says, gesturing with the book she borrowed from me. She's hardly put it down all afternoon, and I'm glad I brought so many. (I'd had trouble deciding which ones to bring, and then I bought another two at the airport, even though I'd known there was no chance I'd be able to read them all in a week. It's nice to have some choice, that's all.)

"See you guys at seven-thirty, then, yeah?"

On my way back to my room, I think maybe I should call my parents and let them know how it's going. I want to tell them about Rory and Jodie and how it feels like I've known them forever already, and how we've been press-ganged into signing up for structured activities, and how, even though some of them sound okay, it's so awful. Why didn't I see it written anywhere that this was some bizarre resort where they've banned phones and fun?

But obviously I can't do that because they *took my phone*, and I feel my face scrunch up angrily. Stupid Esteban and his stupid rules. Stupid Oscar and his clipboard. Stupid Sofia with her nasty, judgy look when she asked where my friends were this morning and went, *"Hmm,"* like it was all my fault.

I'm muttering under my breath by the time I'm in my room, upending my tote bag and putting my things away before I shower.

This week was supposed to be bliss. It was supposed to be relaxing.

I can't even book a vacation right! This is not who I am. I'm usually so organized! This is the sort of silly, rash, careless thing Liam would do.

Even just thinking his name reminds me of the tight, red-hot pain in my chest, which I'd done such a good job of ignoring all day. Until now. I put my hands over my face, not sure if I want to scream or sob.

Things only get better when I lean into the shower and turn it on. The water sputters, then stops entirely. I remember something in the small print of the information pack about the ongoing renovations and that the water may "occasionally" be "a bit temperamental" and "thank you for your understanding and patience at this time."

My patience is *extremely* tenuous right now.

So much for a week of sun, sea and sand to try to self-soothe after my post-exam meltdown and the horrible fallout from it. Is this what it's come to—that I burst into tears for not being able to take a shower?

"Oh, come on . . . ," I mutter. I twist the knob off and on again a few times, and eventually the water starts working. It's barely warm, but I'm too riled up to care. A broken shower really would've been the cherry on the cake.

Even as I'm mentally drafting the scathing texts I'd send my family about this luxury resort fast turning into a hellhole, I should probably be counting my blessings that I actually *don't* have my phone this week. At least I can't be swayed by Liam's "I miss you" text and the plea for us to talk, and even if I do get a little tipsy at dinner, there's *no* chance now that I'll leave him a drunken voice mail begging him to forgive me and take me back.

Despite knowing I'm six days away from being able to message any of my friends, my mind goes over what I'll say to them and how the conversation will go. The uni gang might not be very responsive if they think I've been a bitch and broken Liam's heart, but there's still my friends from back home, from school.

I wouldn't have minded a girls' trip with them. That would've been fun.

But the more I think about that, the more I doubt it *would* have been fun, and the more relieved I am that I'm here by myself and didn't beg any of them to come with me. If I'm being brutally honest with myself, that group chat is stilted at best, and the last time we all hung out, during the Easter break, it wasn't the same. It hadn't been *awkward* exactly, I guess, but it hadn't been as easy as it used to be when we were at school together. It was more like we were playing the part of besties, while counting down the minutes until we could go home and relax properly again.

I know part of that is probably my fault, though. Maybe I would've made more of an effort to keep in touch with them if I hadn't been with Liam, or busy trying to make new friends on my course or keep up with Liam's mates.

I'm not really close enough to any of my uni friends to have made plans to meet up with them this summer. Actually, things had been looking pretty desperate and lonely without Liam, which was another reason I'd felt so compelled to book this trip.

At least stuck with Rory and Jodie for the week, I won't be lonely.

A bit desperate maybe, but definitely not lonely.

I knock on Jodie's door to go down to dinner.

She's ready to go, almost like she's been waiting at the door for me. I say hello, then go knock on Rory's door.

She throws open the door, looking less than impressed and less than ready for dinner.

"Ughhh."

"Run out of time to dry your hair?" Jodie asks her.

Damp blond strands are plastered to Rory's face. Her half-finished makeup and floaty pink dress with its off-the-shoulder ruffled sleeves make me feel horribly underdressed, even though I'm in a dress, too. Her shoulders are bright red—sunburnt.

"My air con is broken. The shower was really hot, and I couldn't get it to go cold, and the room was full of steam—it's so hot and oh. My. God." She huffs and barges back into her bathroom, grabbing a wad of toilet paper and dabbing it under her arms and around her face and neck in full view of us, with zero sense of shame. She tosses it down the loo, then twirls in front of the mirror, trying to see her back.

"Do I have a sweat patch on my back? I'm so sweaty, it's actually disgusting."

"You're good," Jodie says.

"I've got one of those little handheld fans, if you want," I tell Rory.

"Of course you do," she says, laughing. "But thank you. That'd be a godsend. I'd hug you, but I'm so gross and sweaty right now, I wouldn't want to inflict that on you. Hey, can one of you take my room key? This outfit doesn't have any pockets."

She finishes her eye makeup, dabs her sweaty neck and armpits once more, and then we head down to dinner. This time, we get soft drinks instead of wine.

"I do not want to be signing up for any more activities," Jodie says firmly, splaying her hands with their bright-blue, apparently freshly painted nails out on the table. "I'm not touching a drop of booze until the reps are all out of sight."

It's Italian night tonight, based on the green, white and red bunting draped around the buffet area and the sheer amount of pasta and pizza on offer. We're all stuffed by the time we decide to head to the lounge. Unlike last night, the staff are trying to usher people out of the dining hall when they're done—presumably to encourage us to watch the improv show even if we've not signed up for it.

It's astonishing just how militant they are when it comes to organized fun—and how almost everybody else is happy to go along with it.

The three of us find a table at the back near the bar, give up on the soft drinks and grab a bottle of white wine that we split between three glasses as the show starts. The rep who introduces it talks enthusiastically about how so many guests have signed up. A lot of people look genuinely excited.

"Are we really miserable for thinking this sounds terrible?" Jodie asks.

"Damned entitled kids ruining the improv industry, that's what we are," Rory deadpans, and I laugh so suddenly I choke on my wine.

The first few minutes aren't so bad. It's a group of people in their fifties. I overheard them talking earlier before aqua aerobics; they're all parents who know each other and who have kids off on their own group vacations. They do some skit about being lost, arguing about maps and directions and making jokes about getting old.

The three of us clearly don't find it as enjoyable as most of the audience because we don't laugh anywhere near as much as them.

The next person up starts monologuing about her ex-husband's erectile dysfunction, and Rory stands up, grabbing her wineglass.

She doesn't say anything, just leaves.

Jodie and I look at each other before snatching up our own

glasses and ducking out after her. I feel like we're going to be stopped by a big, burly hotel rep acting as a bouncer—or jailer—but I also don't have the guts to tell them to sit back down or to stay here by myself.

"Where are we going?" Jodie asks in a loud whisper.

Rory whispers back, "I saw something in the info pack about a beach bar. The pool one closes at seven, but I think the beach one might still be open."

"We don't even know where the beach is. And why are we whispering?" I ask.

"*Shh!* I bet if they see us leaving they'll drag us back. *Come on.*"

Rory skirts around the pool, following a path into a bunch of trees and tall plants with huge leaves. I'm not convinced she knows where she's going, but I keep my mouth shut. There are a few low-lit orange lamps along the path, but no signs to suggest which is the way to the beach or the bar.

Jodie yelps, jumping back and knocking into me when a lizard dashes in front of her and she almost steps on it. Some of her wine spills onto my feet as she murmurs to the lizard, "Aw, sorry, little guy."

My apprehension gets the better of me. "Are you *sure* about this, Rory?"

"No, but the path's gotta go somewhere, right? I think I saw people coming up from here earlier."

"Okay, but I'm just not sure—"

"I think I can hear music." Jodie interrupts, flapping a hand to shush me. I strain to listen, and hear the refrain of some pop song a little way off. We carry on and eventually the plants and trees give way to sand and a clear view of the night sky and the inky sea.

Rory turns to beam at us. "Ta-da!"

Jodie peers in the direction of the music, which is louder now. Without all the foliage in the way we can see a large hut-like building with a flat roof and little warm-white lanterns strung up around it artfully. There's a large decking area dotted with wicker tables and chairs, and the square bar has stools lined up along it.

Nobody's there, save for the bartender.

11 Rory

Um, whoa.

Those two words play on loop for a solid minute before I get a grip—because *um, whoa.*

The bartender is, like, the epitome of what you'd think a fit Spanish bartender should look like. Olive skin, shiny black hair with a soft curl to it that swoops to one side and is just long enough to run your fingers through. He's wearing a white shirt with the loopy blue font on the breast pocket declaring him an employee of Casa Dorada. The sleeves are rolled up, and I'm such a sucker for guys with their sleeves rolled up.

And he can't be *that* much older than me.

He sees us just before we step up onto the decking and straightens up from his slump over the bar with a wide smile on his face. His bottom front teeth are kind of crooked, but he has dimples and, oh my God, this guy . . .

Um, whoa.

Even without the hot bartender, this place is pretty *whoa.* The dark wood of the hut contrasts with the white-gold sand, and the rows of bottles behind the bar glitter like jewels. The string lights, twinkling like stars, give it a cutesy quality, and even though it's open to the elements, the collection of tables and chairs scattered over the polished decking makes the place feel cozy. Intimate, even. There's a little sand on the floor, but rather than looking messy, the place looks welcoming—not like it's so perfect that our mere presence will mess it all up. The pictures online didn't do it justice at all. In this light, I think what a good shot it would make. I can already see Jodie and Luna perched on barstools, drinks raised, smiling at the camera as I upload it with some caption like Here's to new friends!

A little way off, I notice the silhouettes of a string of small buildings. Those must be the luxury private villas, I realize. It's too dark to see if they're even better than their photos on the website, too.

The bartender is still looking at us with that broad, charming smile, and all I can do is stare back, gawping, thinking about how I've never actually seen someone this beautiful in real life.

He makes the guys I've dated the last few years through school seem like messy, gross, immature *boys*. This guy—he's all man.

I'm pretty sure the other two girls are as stunned by him as I am. Jodie squeaks. I swear to God, she *squeaks*.

"Are you open?" Luna asks, and I'm glad she does because the bartender turns his attention to her then, and I get it together enough to shut my mouth and tell myself not to be such an idiot.

I'm pretty sure Luna blushes when he looks at her, her dark cheeks turning distinctly pink. Even if she's nursing heartbreak, she's not immune to this man and his drop-dead gorgeous smile.

(Besides, he's probably got a girlfriend. And he probably smiles at *everyone* like that. He definitely smiles at everyone like that. It's probably in his job description. It's probably why they hired him.)

But he's so *beautiful.*

While Luna steps forward, the only one of us whose brain hasn't turned to *complete* goo, I grab Jodie's wrist and mouth, *Oh sweet Jesus.*

"We are," the world's most beautiful bartender replies. "I'd ask if I can get you ladies anything, but I see you already have some drinks. Please, take a seat."

Luna and I set our glasses on the bar and pull out stools. I notice that Jodie has to shake herself before she follows suit. Putting the bottle with its little bit of wine left in front of Luna, she clambers ungracefully onto the stool, battling with the slim cut of her maxi dress and the fact that its hem has no stretch.

I try not to laugh. She's already blushing furiously and casting furtive glances at the bartender in case he's noticed.

"Escaping the improv night?" he asks, acting oblivious to Jodie's sudden clumsiness.

"How'd you know?" Luna says.

"There's always a few." He laughs, and oh my God, that laugh. Taylor Swift could write entire albums about that laugh.

Jodie, now planted firmly on the stool, looks as if she's trying to say something, but her mouth just sort of . . . gawps. Wide open. Her eyes glaze over for a second like she's mentally rebooting.

"Guess you got lucky and pulled a shift out here, then," I say, to cover up the silence.

"I try to stay away from as much of the . . . structured entertainment as possible," he says, and laughs again. He says "structured entertainment" in the same skeptical tone and with the same exasperated look as we've been using.

A kindred spirit.

I may have a new best friend.

Jodie giggles. Actually *giggles,* all high-pitched and girlie. It sounds so weird coming out of her mouth when she comes across as so no-nonsense.

Someone has clearly got a major crush. And it only took, what, a minute and a half?

She's blushing again, and I can see the horror dawning on her face that she thinks she's making a fool of herself, so I start talking loudly to draw attention away from her.

(Not that I'm not also crushing on him, *but . . .*)

"We've done it," I declare, turning toward Jodie and Luna and gesturing at the bartender with my glass. "We've found the only other person in this place who hasn't bought into the crap they're peddling about self-fulfillment and being centered and all the rest of it. It's a goddamn miracle."

"Cheers to that!" Luna cries out, laughing, and Jodie raises her glass to the sky and says, "Preach!" before guzzling half of her wine down.

"If you're open, how come nobody's out here?" Luna asks our new buddy.

"Improv night is always very popular. People losing their inhibitions, ¿sabes? Much like you Brits in Magaluf. Tan loco."

"I never did the Maga vacation," Jodie says.

Apparently, she's got control of her brain again. She swirls the wine around in her glass and takes a large, fortifying gulp.

"We went camping after sixth form," Jodie says. "It was the worst. Rained the whole time. The food got soggy. The showers were grim. Nobody got *any* sleep. And one of my friends, you know, *did it* with her boyfriend against a tree and ended up covered in rashes from stingy nettles. Like—all over her back. Everywhere."

"As I said," the bartender pitches in, eyes sparkling as he glances at Jodie, "loco."

He's looking at Jodie with the kind of eyes that make it very obvious she's completely his type, his gaze long and lingering, and I feel like I'm intruding just noticing it. Okay, I decide, scrap my crush on him. I mean, *anybody* would have a crush on this man. He is beautiful. Hell, Tom Holland would blush for this bartender. Now I need to find out if this guy has a girlfriend. Like, right now. Because if he doesn't, I'm *so* going to try and set him and Jodie up.

They would be so cute together. I can imagine the adorable, loved-up Insta photos. No soft launch needed—not for a guy who looks this good.

"Somehow I don't think the people enjoying improv night are going to start dry humping in front of the stage and doing suicide shots of tequila," Luna says, not quite catching on to their vibe—and kind of ruining the moment. But the bartender just smiles and shrugs.

"Sí, probably not."

The bartender leans away from us, leaving us to chat and drink our wine. I can't help the way my eyes follow him, which is why I see him reach into his pocket and take out— "*A phone!* Bar Guy, you have a *phone!*" I exclaim, completely talking over whatever

Jodie's just started to say. I lurch over the bar, pointing at him, only to realize how desperate and pathetic I must look.

I wish I could blame that on alcohol, but I know I'm not even anywhere near tipsy yet.

I just really am that desperate and pathetic.

"Quizás," he says, flashing a grin.

I don't even know what that means—he could be telling me I'm a loser for all I know—but it sounds really sexy, so he can say it all he likes.

"And my name is Gabriel."

"Are you guys allowed to have phones?" Luna cries out. I'm relieved to see she's just as agog as I am.

"The staff are not permitted to use their phones on shift," Gabriel tells us. "Our phones are locked behind reception."

"Then what's that?"

"Qué, you think I don't have a decoy phone?"

"What if the guests see? They could tell Esteban." I gasp. "*We* could tell Esteban."

"I don't get caught using my phone around guests. I would be out of a job if that happened. I have had enough warnings by now," he adds with a laugh. "But I think you chicas will keep my secret."

"Please, can I look on Instagram? *Please?*"

I'm so desperate and pathetic I'm actually *begging,* but I don't even care.

I want to see if my follower count has gone up. Or, like, at least not gone *down.*

Which is vain and sad and the only thing I can think about now I've seen that phone.

Gabriel laughs and comes back over. Instagram is open on his phone. It's sad how excited I am to see such a familiar little screen, even if the text is all in Spanish.

"How about I make you ladies some sangria? And while I'm doing that, you can use Instagram. But I'm sure your boyfriend is missing you too much to post," he tells me. He winks, too. He's teasing, I realize, after a moment. Flirting? I wish. No, he doesn't have that twinkle in his eye like he did when he looked at Jodie, the lucky bitch.

Oh well. I guess I *did* come here for rest and relaxation, not to get railed.

Luna snatches the phone up with a strangled noise before I get the chance to find my own profile. Jodie and I both lean in to watch her search for "ldhaynes0" and scroll through the account of one Liam Haynes. A picture of a toastie. A picture of him and the lads at a pub table. A picture of him and some of those same lads with girls in a club, their arms all around each other.

He hasn't even used any *filters*. And the caption on the toastie picture isn't even funny. What a bore. Plus, he's tagged the town he's in instead of the restaurant in the second post, which screams absolute amateur. I don't know what's so interesting about his account that Luna was dying to check it.

She puts the phone down quickly. "What if he's moved on?"

"What?"

"Liam. What if he's already moved on? He said he missed me and I didn't even *reply*. He'll think I've ghosted him—after all this time! What if he's started dating other girls?" She picks the phone back up and goes to the picture from the club. "Look. That was only on Friday night! Do you think he kissed her?" She points at the girl on his left, at the end of the group, the one he has his arm around. "They look cozy, don't you think? Oh God. What if they went home together?"

Jodie and I exchange a look. Now it makes more sense: Liam Haynes is the ex.

"I thought *you* broke up with *him*?" Jodie says gently.

Luna reaches for her wine and chugs it—a drastic change from the refined sips she was taking earlier.

"I did. But—it wasn't *that* long ago. Just yesterday, he was telling me he *missed me*. And I'm not saying he should be at home crying over me or anything, but we were together for so long. And he didn't see it coming. I mean, I didn't either, but . . . Don't you think that's a bit quick? To move on from a long-term relationship like that?"

"Maybe he didn't even kiss her," Jodie says, not too helpfully.

I say, "And, if he did, it wouldn't have meant anything. He's on the rebound. So what?"

Luna looks at me. There are tears in her eyes.

Jodie started it, I almost snap.

"He did it before, though. When we were still together," Luna says, the words rushing out of her.

"Hold on, this guy *cheated* on you?" I shriek, both outraged for her and secretly willing her to go on and spill the whole story.

She shuffles awkwardly on her stool, something defensive in her features when she says, "Not really. It was . . . just a *kiss*. And he was drunk. It was on a night out a few months ago, so it . . . it wasn't anything major."

"Oh, hon," Jodie says with a sigh, reaching over to pat her arm. Whatever other sympathy she might have offered, or what other weak defenses Luna might've parroted for her ex's shitty behavior, we're interrupted by our friendly, contraband-smuggling bartender.

Gabriel, who has paused the sangria-making to come over, swivels his phone around. "He's not worth it. You are clearly better off without him. Look at his sneakers." He shakes his head, then goes back to cutting fruit.

Luna lets out a wobbly laugh. "He wore those to my grand-parents' fiftieth wedding anniversary. Everyone was dressed up smart, and he wore those sneakers."

"They're awful," I say, trying not to make things worse again. Although as far as I can tell, they're just sneakers. "I mean, is he serious?"

"And that *hair*." Now Jodie's scrolling to a pouting selfie of him. "Ugh. Duck face. Really, Liam, really? This isn't 2012, and you're not a fourteen-year-old girl. Even if it's meant to be funny and ironic—just no. Stop."

It's my turn to snatch the phone. "Oh, Luna, no. Tell me you didn't go out with a guy with a puka shell necklace?"

"It's a Throwback Thursday post," she mumbles, but even she's laughing now, looking less on the verge of tears by the second.

I read the caption. "Yeah. From *last year*."

She bites her lip.

"It's okay," Jodie says, all serious, and puts a hand on Luna's shoulder. "I once kissed a guy who wore tweed jackets with the weird little elbow patches, and bow ties."

"God," I blurt, repulsed by the mental image. "What was he, fifty?"

"He was twenty-four!" She pulls a sheepish face. "He was kind of a PhD student who was tutoring me, but . . . Anyway, the point is, Luna, we've all been there."

I pitch in, "I dated this boy for three months before I found out he was cheating. On his girlfriend. With me. *I* was the other woman."

"No!" Luna gasps, grasping my forearm. "That's horrible! How did you find out?"

"His girlfriend confronted me. One of her friends had seen me with him in town and recognized me. The girlfriend was just screaming at me in the middle of this pub like it was all my fault."

"Didn't you say anything?"

"I was too busy thinking how I was going to kill him and feeling like some awful home-wrecker. They'd been together for, like, a year or something."

"It was hardly your fault, though!" Jodie exclaims.

"Oh yeah, I know. She realized that, too, once she got over it."

"Men are trash," Luna says, still glued miserably to her ex's Insta.

"Cheers to that."

"On behalf of men—" Gabriel starts to say, but Jodie holds up a hand, cutting him off.

"I swear to Dios, if you say not all men . . ."

"I can only apologize," he says, laughing. "And hope this sangria is good enough to take your minds off terrible ex-boyfriends and PhD students with elbow patches."

With a smooth, swift motion that doesn't seem like something people should be capable of except in cartoons, he swings three glasses up from under the counter and onto the bar and pours us each a sangria. Luna's wineglass is empty and so is Jodie's. I push mine away, and we let him take the bottle, too.

Well, *Jodie* does. She hands it to him, and Gabriel catches her gaze with a slow, close-lipped smile, his fingers brushing hers as he takes the bottle. She blushes, and the whole thing looks so wildly intimate that I have to look away.

There are voices behind us, on the beach—it's the tortolitos, both whining about improv night. Gabriel slides his phone back into his pocket and moves across to get their order from Andrew while Linda takes a seat, arms crossed. I mourn what may have been my one chance at checking up on my social media, but not for long.

"I feel like we should make a toast," Jodie says.

"To being well rid of terrible ex-boyfriends," adds Luna.

And to fit Spanish bartenders with contraband phones, I think, and we clink our glasses.

12 Jodie

"Come on!" I whisper, and stumble over my own feet. I giggle, then clamp a hand to my mouth as Luna shushes me frantically. Rory runs ahead and stands flat against a pillar, singing the *Mission: Impossible* theme tune under her breath, then looks side to side before dropping and doing a forward roll across the foyer. She ends up splayed out on the floor, and Luna starts giggling, meaning it's my turn to shush her. We hurry over to help Rory up and dash the rest of the way to the desk, dropping down onto the floor in crouches once we're behind it.

"Should they really leave this unmanned?" Luna says. "What if someone's checking in late? Or what if someone needs help? I'm sure I read that there's someone on reception twenty-four hours a day."

"Yeah, well, not right now," Rory says. "Lucky for us."

I paw across the desk—there's a computer, which must have an internet connection, but we have bigger plans right now than trying to crack the password to it—and find a set of keys.

I turn back to the girls, spreading the keys out on the palm of my hand. "Which one do we think?"

Rory looks me dead in the eye and says, "Gotta try 'em all."

And Luna starts singing the Pokémon theme song.

"Guys!"

"I dunno! Try all of them."

Huffing, I do. I crawl to the door behind the desk. I jiggle the handle first, but it's locked, so I pick a key at random and wedge it into the lock. It doesn't work, but the fifth key I try does. The door swings open, and Rory whoops—loudly, but not as loudly as me—and Luna shouts, "Shh!"

I clamber back to my feet and snap the light on, then go into the room. There's a shelf unit with boxes lined up on it, each one with a number painted on the front. I find our boxes and take them all off the shelf. I knock another box with my elbow and it clanks noisily against the one next to it. I cringe, then dash back out of the room with our boxes.

It's not easy to get our room keys into the locks, just like it's not easy to walk, or be quiet, when you've had enough sangria, but it was so tasty, and Gabriel was pretty yummy-looking, too . . .

I blush, although the memory of him has turned fuzzy around the edges from drink. Am I imagining how attractive he was? It's possible; I was *definitely* imagining how it seemed like he was being a bit flirty with me . . . There's no way. No chance. I could barely string a sentence together! And next to curvaceous, pretty Luna and chic, confident Rory . . . I shake my head at myself for how delusional a sexy smile and a little wine has made me.

Eventually we get the boxes open, and then we're scrambling for our phones, turning them on as soon as we grab hold of them.

They buzz frantically with notifications we've missed, and I watch Rory cradle her phone to her chest.

She sighs softly. "How I've missed you, 4G."

I have a few messages, mostly from my mum about this whole surprise digital detox thing. I'm just replying to tell her I'm having a good time and found some fun people to hang out with for the week when a LinkedIn notification comes through: *Congratulate Mia on her new job!*

I abandon my messages to click the notification.

Mia and I have known each other since primary school. We're friends, but not really. She always seemed like a better version of me. She has a boyfriend and a joint savings account with him. She's a soloist in her uni's choir. She's doing an internship this summer at some bank.

Why do I want to be Mia?

I don't even like choir.

I actively opted to *avoid* doing any kind of internship or corporate job this summer just to enjoy the peace and escapism I find working in the local coffee shop, so I could push away the glaring reminders that I might be ballsing up my future if I quit uni now.

Apparently, Mia just got an offer for a place on a graduate scheme for next year.

There's a long-winded message in the group chat all about it, too. Appropriately humblebragging, all *#blessed* while letting us know just what a coup it is to get the job. I grit my teeth, bile rising in the back of my throat.

Rory slaps her hand against her leg, grunting in frustration and distracting me from the group chat. "Damn it! Screw you. I didn't want to work with your stupid company anyway. *Shit*. A hundred and eighty-one? Are you kidding me? *Almost two hundred unfollows?* What the hell?"

"I think he's seeing someone. Look," Luna says. "He's been liking all her photos. How does he even know—shit, *shit,* I just liked one of her photos. Oh my God. Oh God. It's from three months ago."

"Ahem."

"Guys? Guys, how do I undo this? She'll get the notification. Oh my God. Should I unlike it? Is that worse? Guys, tell me. Is it worse if I unlike it?" Her fingers snatch absently at my arm.

Rory doesn't even glance up from her phone to ask us, "What do you think Gabriel's surname is? Did you catch his Instagram handle? He's got to have a girlfriend, right? Guys like that always have a girlfriend. But then, like, if he works here, when does he see her? Oh man, I bet she works here. Goddammit. I was really rooting for you and him to become a thing, Jode. Would've been such a cute vacation romance."

"Huh?" Me and who? Whose girlfriend? I'm too busy looking through Mia's feed, reading up on her fancy-schmancy new job to pay any attention if Rory bothers to answer me.

"Ahem."

"The information pack went to my junk mail, too, Jodie. Look . . ."

I mumble like I'm going to look at the offending email any second now, but my eyes are fixed on my screen, on Mia's post. My brain is going a hundred miles an hour, my fingers already scrolling to trawl the chat for updates from my other friends, in case they're sharing similar news. I wonder out loud, "I thought all these grad schemes didn't open for applications until September at the *earliest*. D'you think I've missed the boat already?"

Would that be such a bad thing? Maybe that'd be my "get out of jail free" card . . .

"¡Señoritas!" a voice shouts.

We all look up, and I feel a sense of dread creeping down my spine. Or maybe it's just the alcohol sweats.

More likely the creeping dread.

Esteban looks *pissed*.

Luna's whole face is shiny; Rory bites her lip, eyes darting around. I gulp, and it sounds so loud.

"¿Qué haces?" he asks us, even though he can see very clearly what we're doing. He sighs and shakes his head. "I am very disappointed."

"We were, uh . . . we were just . . ."

Stealing our phones back, but that sounds so pathetic and is so obvious that I trail off instead of finishing my sentence.

Instead, I bark at him, trying to ignore my slurred speech, "You know, Esteban, you really shouldn't leave the desk unmanned. It's very unprofessional. What if people were checking in late? Or needed help?"

Mustache twitching, Esteban comes around the desk. "Por favor," he says, and gestures with his arm for us to leave. We put our phones back in our boxes in sheepish silence before shuffling out from behind the desk. I stumble over my own feet, and Luna bumps into Rory.

"Buenas noches," Esteban tells us with a stern sort of finality that makes me feel like I'm ten years old and have just been grounded.

The three of us trudge up the stairs in silence, and it's clear that Luna and Rory feel as embarrassed as I do.

We stop outside our doors, hesitating.

"Do you think we're in trouble?" Luna whispers.

"Maybe he'll let us off because we were drunk? Give us a warning or something?" Rory shrugs. "I feel like if he was going to give us a bollocking for breaking the rules he'd have done it."

I snort, wondering what kind of rosy sunshine world she's living in. *Spoken like someone who's never gotten in trouble for anything,* I think. But I keep my mouth shut, if only because I'd like to hang on to the sliver of hope that she's right and our escapade somehow won't be held against us.

"I suppose so," Luna mumbles, and I wonder if she's thinking the same thing as me. "Well, night, then."

I nod and put my key in my door. "Yeah, night."

Luna knocks on our doors to get us up for breakfast, and we head down together, bags in hand and ready to go to the water park.

"You would not *believe* the morning I had!" Rory exclaims. "So, the shower cut out while I still had shampoo in my hair, and when I finally managed to get the bath tap working, I barely managed to rinse the suds out before *that* gave up the ghost, too! Can you even believe? And my air con's still broken." She wipes her sweaty forehead. "I mentioned it at the desk yesterday, but I bet Esteban won't fix it now. As punishment."

"They can't do that, surely," Luna says.

"If they do, we'll definitely leave them some really bad reviews on Tripadvisor," I tell her.

"Believe me, I'm already working on it." She taps her temple.

We're all quiet at breakfast.

I know they're thinking the same as me: That we're in Trouble, capital *T.* That we screwed up, and we broke the rules, and we got off lightly. And that we're more hungover than we expected—the sangria was stronger than we realized.

It had all been Luna's idea. She was obviously hung up on wanting to snoop on her ex—but honestly, from what she's said of him so far, I can't for the life of me imagine why. He sounds like a total prat. Rory hadn't taken much convincing to take part in our little jailbreak, but they'd had to wheedle me into it. It was less that I was scared of getting caught and more that there hadn't been anything on my phone I was *that* eager to get back to. My regret stems mostly from the fear induced by seeing Mia's post, rather than the fact we got caught.

"We missed yoga again this morning," Rory mumbles, halfway through her eggs on toast.

Luna tsks. "I forgot all about yoga. Sorry, girls."

"It's not your fault," I tell her. "You seem like a mother hen type, but you know you're not actually our mum, right? It's not your job to get us out of bed."

Maybe I say it a bit too harshly because she slumps in her seat a bit and sounds a little dejected when she says, "But I said I'd set the alarm."

"She did say she'd set the alarm," Rory adds, but teasingly, and she knocks her shoulder into Luna's. "I feel like they didn't miss us anyway."

When we head through reception to get the bus, there's a group of people on their way out the door, bags in hand and sunglasses in place. We join them and make our way over to where Rafael is ushering people onto the bus and Oscar is checking them off on a clipboard. The tortolitos are there, bickering about towels, but disappear onto the bus before I catch any more of the conversation.

"Miss Lola!" Esteban calls out. It's annoying how familiar his voice is now. "Miss Rory, Miss Ho-dee."

We stop in our tracks and exchange looks. I get the same sense of dread as last night. It's definitely not alcohol sweats this time, though.

Esteban gives us a "sorry" sort of smile. It doesn't reach his eyes. "I am afraid you will all need to return to the hotel."

"What? Why?" I demand.

"As you will be aware from our information pack, and as I mentioned when you all arrived, if you do not abide by our rules at Casa Dorada, privileges will be revoked. I am afraid I cannot allow you to go to the Hidropark."

"What?" Luna bursts out, clutching her bag.

"You can't stop us going," I argue. "What are you going to do—drag us off the bus?"

"I am afraid I cannot let you on the bus. Por favor, if you will all return to the hotel . . ."

If he says, "I am afraid . . ." with that smug so-not-sorry tone again, I'm going to scream. Luna cowers behind me and Rory looks like she's been slapped. I grit my teeth and square my shoulders. Mum and Gran would *not* stand for this. Absolutely no way, no how.

"But we paid for our tickets," I say.

"You will not be charged."

"We're getting on that bus."

Esteban's expression is stony and unimpressed. "Of course, you are right, Miss Ho-dee. I cannot stop you. But here at Casa Dorada we reserve the right to evict you from the premises if you do not follow our rules."

"Evict?" Luna squeaks, horrified.

Is he serious?

"Are you serious?" I bark.

"It was in the information pack."

Yeah, in two-point font, I bet.

"Maybe we should just go back inside," Luna mumbles.

"Look, we're really sorry," Rory says, stepping forward. She plasters on the kind of pitiful smile that says, *Please forgive me.* I bet she always got her way when she was a kid. Especially being the youngest of three. I bet she still does. "We'd had a bit too much to drink, and we just . . . We thought it was a bit of fun. We realize now what a mistake it was, and we're really sorry. Er, siento."

Luna corrects her. "Lo siento."

"Lo sentimos," I mutter, but it's more of a question because I'm not sure that's actually right. My Spanish is so rusty.

"Right," Rory says, even though she probably didn't get any of what we just said.

Esteban shakes his head again. "Sí, Miss Rory, entiendo, but I still cannot allow you to go on the trip to the Hidropark today. And I am afraid I cannot let you on the visit later this week to the theme park, either. We have certain standards to abide by here at Casa Dorada, you understand, and even if you had not used your devices, you still broke into a room containing guests' valuables and private property . . ."

Oh *please*, I almost snap at him. It's not like we were there to steal anything—and if they were *that* worried, maybe they shouldn't have left the desk unmanned or the keys out in plain view.

Rory's smile turns into a frown, but then she composes herself. Her smile is sickly sweet and she bats her eyelashes at Esteban. "Of course. We understand. But we're still *very* sorry, Esteban, really. It won't happen again."

He follows us back into the hotel, and Rory heads straight out to the pool, Luna and I trailing behind her just like we did last night when she left the lounge. Rory throws herself down on a sun lounger.

"Is it too early for a drink? I feel a restorative G&T coming on. And I swear to God, if that man so much as looks my way again today, I'm going to swing for him," she snarls, her sweet-as-apple-pie expression gone and her face twisted into something furious and ugly. "*Cannot allow us to go to the Hidropark,* my arse."

"Can he really kick us out of the hotel?" Luna says, sitting down, too, teeth worrying at her lower lip.

"Well, if it *is* in the information pack . . ." I say, grinding my teeth.

"I'm so sorry, guys." Luna looks between us, fingers fidgeting with the bottom of her T-shirt. "This was entirely my fault. It was my idea to go all *Mission: Impossible* and break our phones out, and all because I'm freaking out at the idea that my ex might be getting over the fact I broke up with him. Now you're missing out on the water park, and I know how much you were both looking forward to it. I was, too."

"It's not your fault." Rory shrugs. "We went along with it."

"Exactly," I say. "And besides, it probably didn't help that I told Esteban off for not having someone manning the desk in reception. Your *Mission: Impossible* bit wasn't the problem. We should've just taken our phones and run. But we sat there out in the open like idiots."

"Idiots!" Rory concurs with a grin. "Seriously, Miss Lola. Listen to me and *Ho-dee,* and stop looking so stressy. It's not your fault."

"But—"

"But nothing," I tell her firmly. "Come on, sit down. I'll get the drinks in."

"Do they do tea?" Luna asks, still fidgeting. "I don't think I can stomach booze at this time of day."

"I wasn't serious about the restorative G&T," Rory says, laughing, although I'm not sure I'm entirely convinced. "Get us some waters, Jode, and see if they've got tea for Miss Lola, even though it's *wrong*, and basically criminal. Drinking tea next to the pool in sunny Spain. You'll find her wearing a fleece and sneakers by the time you come back, having officially turned into my mum."

"Oh God, no." Luna scrunches up her face, visibly relaxing now that she's sure we're not mad at her. "I'll be wearing my mac and wellies. Proper British summer gear, that."

"That's more like it. Seriously, though, Luna, don't blame yourself," I tell her, squeezing her shoulder on my way past to get our drinks. "We all effed up. It's not the end of the world. So what if we're missing out on the water park? We can still have our own fun."

13 *Luna*

"Up until we got caught red-handed, last night was fun."

Maybe not my first choice of fun, but . . . well, it *was*.

Stalking Liam's Instagram and seeing what a good time he and our friends are having without me, convincing myself he's already moved on—that was a bit of a gut punch to say the least. But sneaking around with Jodie and Rory, the solidarity of a shared little adventure, definitely put a smile on my face.

I've finally stopped beating myself up about the phone jailbreak and getting us into trouble; the girls couldn't be *less* annoyed with me about it, so I've cheered up considerably as the day has gone on—even if we *did* get roped into the morning aqua aerobics class.

"Definitely," Rory agrees, and turns a smirk on Jodie. "And we saw you making goo-goo eyes at the bartender, missy, don't think we didn't. Your jaw was practically on the floor. I'm pretty sure I even saw some drool. Although I totally don't blame you. He is *gorgeous*."

"Oh, shut up," Jodie says, shoving her and blushing. Then she bites her lower lip, face scrunching up. "He didn't notice, did he, d'you think?"

"No," Rory and I say at the same time. Although, personally, I'm pretty sure he did. Jodie stared longingly at him half the night. But then again— "He was flirting with you, though, wasn't he?"

"Was he?" Her tone is dismissive, but there's also something hopeful in it. Like she doesn't believe us, but wants to. She sits up straighter, twisting toward us. "Did you think so?"

"I thought he was. He seemed to be paying you a lot of attention."

"Isn't that his job, though? Flirt with everyone so they buy more drinks?"

"It's an all-inclusive resort," Rory points out. "And even if it was his job, he definitely flirted with you way more than he did with me or Luna. Like, *way* more. Didn't he touch your hand at one point?"

Jodie mumbles incoherently, but judging by her blush, that moment is all too clearly embedded in her brain. I remember being like that with Liam at first. The giddiness of those early days of *Oh my gosh, he likes me back!* All the effort that went into those initial dates, the overwhelming warmth in my chest of falling in love for the first time . . .

The nostalgia hits me hard, and I bite back a smile, not wanting Jodie to think I'm laughing at her. She doesn't strike me as the kind of girl who blushes when a boy shows interest in her, or like she's the naturally flirty type, so I'm not surprised to see her looking quite so awkward over it.

It's been so long since I properly flirted with someone and wasn't in a relationship, I bet I'd be exactly the same if I fancied a guy.

I wonder when I stopped flirting with Liam.

Was it before or after he stopped flirting with me?

The thought is sobering, and my stomach knots.

Maybe I was too hasty in placing the blame on him for our strained relationship and my own feelings? Maybe *I* should have tried harder. Or at least not placed so much pressure on him when I felt a bit lonely or annoyed about things. I bet I came across as a total nag and a real bore sometimes. Had I grown too comfortable with Liam, been too neglectful of his feelings all this time?

Liam, who despite the pre-vacation text that he missed me, hasn't sent me any more messages since. Is it really awful of me to have hoped he would message again? Is it weird that he hasn't?

Is it weird for me to be dwelling so much on Liam when *I* was the one to break up with *him*? It's selfish, I think, and it's not fair of me—but . . .

But I loved him. I think I still do, maybe, a bit.

My thoughts circle back to the girl on his Instagram, the one whose profile I'd started to look through, the one I think might actually . . .

It's all too easy to picture. Liam, with his big rugby-playing arms and close-cropped hair, dancing in some club with the lights flashing bright and blinding, and that girl, short and curvy like me, writhing against him to the music. His hands would be on her waist and he would be grinding against her, the same way he used to dance with *me*. How she'd turn to him and he'd bend down to kiss her the way I'd grown so used to—soft at first, teasing, and then firmer, coaxing his tongue into her mouth while her arms wrapped around his shoulders.

It's a vivid mental picture that's plagued me for months, ever since he came into my room abashed and upset at three in the morning, stinking of sweat, vodka jelly and another girl's perfume.

"Luna, baby, I'm so sorry," he'd said, and I'd *known*, known deep in my bones. My heart sank even before he told me, "It didn't mean anything, I swear, but—I needed to tell you. I'm so sorry, so sorry."

And he had been. He'd been clear-eyed, steady, and he'd cried, and then I'd cried, too. He'd held me, reassured me that he loved me. I let him in and fell asleep beside him, though my imagination's warped, nightmarish conjuring of the image of him kissing another girl has followed me ever since.

Suddenly I wonder what I'd been thinking to let him into my bed while he still had another girl's scent clinging to his clothes.

I feel sick, repulsed, just remembering, and push the memory away quickly. That's a whole new panic I don't even want to try to unpack just yet—and shouldn't, I tell myself sternly, not when we're talking about Jodie right now.

But Liam *had* tried so hard to make up for it. He invited me out with him and his friends, so I didn't need to feel insecure if he was out without me; bought me flowers; made dinner even though he was a *rubbish* cook . . .

"And you were kind of flirting back," Rory carries on, successfully pulling me out of my thought spiral over Liam—at least for now. She gets up from her sun lounger and sits on mine. I bring my legs up and cross them under me. "When you weren't too busy drooling over him."

"Shut up, I was *not* drooling. And I don't think I even remember *how* to flirt. It's been forever since I met a guy I wanted to date, or . . . whatever."

"By 'whatever,' you mean bone, of course."

"Of course," Jodie says a bit awkwardly, then sighs and sits up. "It's just impossible to meet guys, I swear."

"Do you try?" Rory asks. Her tone is brash, but I don't think she means to sound unkind. "Bumble, Hinge, going to bars, asking your friends to set you up . . . ?"

"Not . . . exactly," Jodie confesses. "I—I barely even take a break to go home and see my mum and gran. I've been spending weekends catching up on sleep or on coursework for what feels like forever." She huffs, fidgeting. "Fine, I guess I haven't *tried* to meet any. But that's beside the point. It's been a while since I put myself out there, okay? Knowing my luck, if I actually try to flirt with Gabriel, I'll just end up asking him if he likes chicken nuggets."

"That is a vital question," Rory says gravely.

I groan, unable to shake the nervous, nagging thoughts circling in my brain. I know I should be *listening* to the conversation, but it's so difficult when all it's doing is reminding me that (a) I'm also going to have to "put myself out there" at some point, and (b) maybe I should've tried harder to fix my relationship with Liam, rather than facing all that.

"I don't even want to think about dating anyone else," I say quietly.

"Are you *that* hung up on Liam?" Rory asks.

I can't work out if she's judging me or just asking a question.

Yes. Completely and utterly. Maybe. Kind of. I think?

Except I don't want to sound as pathetic as that makes me feel, so I say, "Not that—I just mean, when you put it like that, it seems so daunting. I've only ever had one proper relationship, and that was Liam, and we've been together since we were fifteen. It's been four years. That's—it's not *nothing*, but I feel like I threw it away as if it were. Maybe I shouldn't have broken up with him. He *told* me that he missed me. Maybe . . ."

"Nope, don't even. You did the right thing. Remember those sneakers? Not to mention the *cheating*? Um, hello?" Rory pulls a face. I flinch; I forgot I told them about him kissing another girl, though I feel a rush of gratitude at the way they're both sticking by me.

With my group chats still bleakly silent, it's clear that none of my friends back home have thought it's worth sticking by me.

Although I don't really know if I actually *want* them to back me up. Right now, I want them to tell me I was a fool and should beg Liam to take me back the second I get my hands on my phone again.

"Those sneakers *were* pretty shocking," Jodie agrees gently, and all I can do is roll my eyes. Liam's idea of getting dressed up was wearing matching socks and clean underwear. Which I don't say out loud because I know how shallow it would sound, but it was about *respect*, about making an effort.

Did he stop making an effort because I did? Or was it the other way around?

Still, even thinking about it irritates me. And when I do think like that, it's a little easier to remember all the things in our relationship that grated on me and tell myself I should work on getting over him. The way he prioritized everyone else over me.

Dismissed my feelings about my exam. And a string of other tiny, inconsequential annoyances and upsets before that. Texts that went unanswered, the nagging worry that if he wasn't with me maybe he'd stray again, maybe I wasn't worth sticking around for, that I wasn't fun or exciting enough, or . . .

"I bet he's not even single," Jodie mutters, lying back down.

"Who? Liam?" I ask.

"Gabriel," she says.

"Oh!" Rory exclaims, waggling her fingers at Jodie. "I started looking up this place on LinkedIn to see if I could find him in the employees and get his last name. I was going to try to find him on Insta to see if he had a girlfriend."

"That's some serious sleuthing." Jodie almost looks impressed, though, and I am, too. I never would've thought of that.

"What if he's some weirdo who only posts obscure photos of trees with really long, annoying captions telling you all about their day?" I say, all too glad of the excuse to shove Liam out of my mind.

Rory scoffs. "Tell me about it. I mean, what if he's a Pisces?"

"You're into horoscopes?"

"Oh please, like you don't love reading yours and tying it into your day." She rolls her eyes at me. "Let me guess. *You're* a Pisces."

"Did you look my birthday up on Facebook last night?"

"And you . . ." She squints thoughtfully at Jodie, head tilted to one side. "I'm betting . . . Capricorn or Leo."

"All right, that's just spooky. I'm a Capricorn."

"I do palm reading, too, if you want."

"Seriously?" Jodie scoffs.

"What? I think it's fun. It's a good party trick. Even the people who get on their high horse about it love it after a drink or two. Hey! Maybe I should teach you. You could read Gabriel's palm," she teases, kicking a foot out at Jodie's knee.

"What, and"—Jodie reaches over and grabs my hand, pulling it toward her palm up, and I let her—"ooh yes, Gabriel, this line means you'll find the love of your life, and this line here means she's sitting right in front of you. And this line means you'll have really, *really* great sex with her."

I burst out laughing. "Oh man, please say that to him. I'll die."

"*I'd* die if I said that. Can you imagine? And anyway, maybe he does have a girlfriend. I'd end up completely humiliating myself."

"You could just ask him," I say.

"No way! That just makes it super obvious I have a ridiculous little crush on him, and if he does have a girlfriend, makes it really awkward. And if he doesn't, but doesn't like me back, which is *just as likely*, it's even more awkward. It's lose-lose. This is why I don't do the whole dating thing. Life is stressful enough without all *that*."

"Unless he doesn't have a girlfriend *and* he likes you back," Rory points out. "Then it's win-win."

"And pretty much impossible. Ugh, I should've had a nose on his Instagram when we had his phone. Besides, it's not like it *matters*. We're only here a few more days."

"Doesn't need to stop you having some fun," Rory says, grinning.

Jodie pokes her tongue out. "Shut up."

But, judging by the grin on her face as she dips her head to hide it, she'd love just that.

I can see Rory falling asleep on her sun lounger, despite her insisting every time I ask that she's not. Those sunglasses aren't hiding the way her head lolls forward and she snorts, waking herself back up abruptly. I probably wouldn't hate a nap, either, and frankly, I'm worried about Jodie getting sunburn. In spite of all the sun cream she's applied, her shoulders are looking rather pink. No matter how many times she moves our umbrella, we don't seem to get any shade. And Rory seems to be laboring under the delusion that one spritz of sun cream this morning was plenty, even with her shoulders already bright red from yesterday.

They don't take much persuading to get out of the sun for an hour or so. The three of us slouch back toward our rooms in easy silence.

At reception, something drips from the ceiling, landing just in front of me. I wrinkle my nose, not wanting to know what it is. A little further away, there's a bucket and more steady drips plopping down from a wet patch on the ceiling.

I exchange a glance with the girls, who look about as unimpressed and unsurprised as I am. It's as if the hotel wants to prove how far from "luxury getaway" it is at every turn.

Upstairs, Rory slumps against her door and opens it, still half-asleep by the looks of her. Jodie roots around in her tote bag for her key, and I turn to say I'll see them in a bit.

Except Rory screams, and Jodie looks up, eyes wide, shouting, "What the—"

I hurry over and the three of us press into Rory's doorway.

There's a gaping hole in the ceiling, debris from it fallen on her bed, and water is pouring down in an unrelenting stream. There's a small flood on the floor, which Rory sloshes through, making horrified squeaks and flapping her hands uselessly.

"Oh my God," she says. "Oh my God."

She rummages through the bits of ceiling on her bed and clutches clothes, a shoe, a bottle of hair spray to her chest.

I think about the dripping reception ceiling and look at the gaping hole above Rory's bed. Glancing back out into the corridor, I notice a damp patch on its ceiling, too.

The same thought must cross Jodie's mind because she and I exchange panicked looks and hurry to our own rooms.

Jodie lets out a string of curses, and I can only stand in my doorway in shocked silence.

The ceiling's intact, but there's water dripping from it. It's less aggressive than the river cascading onto Rory's bed, but it's right over the dressing table, drenching the things I put there. A couple of soggy books, my toilet bag and useless headphones sit in puddles of water. Nothing that can't be saved, I tell myself. Still, I feel a prickle at the back of my eyes and in my throat. It'll be fine. It's just some books, a tub of moisturizer . . .

"It's in my shoes!" Jodie wails from across the corridor.

My stomach drops the longer I look at the water trickling from my ceiling, the sound of it hitting the dressing table and floor like thunder. I think maybe Rory's crying. Jodie's still swearing at everything, none too quietly.

Do something, Luna. You need to fix this.

I throw the wet things from the dressing table onto the relative safety of the bed and then run over to my open suitcase and close it for good measure, just in case.

"I'm going to get Esteban," I announce to the girls.

It's a pitiful sight, Jodie kneeling in a pool of water and clutching a pair of suede sandals, and Rory standing holding a pile of wet clothes and staring at the wall, looking helpless and hollowed out.

To Jodie, I say, "Help Rory get her stuff together. They'll have to put us in new rooms."

Jodie doesn't look up, but as I run toward the stairs, I hear her getting up and the splash of water as she goes into Rory's room and says, "It's okay, sweetie."

And then, a beat later— "Oh shit, no wonder it's flooded in here—you left the bath running!"

Downstairs, I'm relieved to see Esteban talking to a lady behind the desk at reception. I didn't think I'd ever be quite so happy to see his toothy smile and twirly mustache, but right now I could throw my arms around him.

"Miss Lola," he says brightly, "is there something I can help you with?"

I don't even care that he gets my name wrong. I grab the counter, hands shaking. I can feel my heart somewhere in my throat.

This is *not* the luxurious, relaxing week I was supposed to have.

"There's a problem with our rooms," I say, my voice coming out ragged and desperate and not at all calm and collected like I was trying for. I shake myself and try again, fingers gripping the desk even tighter.

You can do this, Luna, come on.

"There's a leak. Flood. Um, water. Agua. In our rooms."

Esteban's smile slips and he frowns, lips pursing. He says something to the lady at the desk in such rapid Spanish I don't have a hope of guessing what it is, then steps from behind the desk briskly and walks with purpose, leaving me to hurry after him. He takes the stairs two at a time, which makes me hate him a little less than I did this morning. He'll fix this. Despite our little phone jailbreak attempt last night, he'll sort this out for us. He has to.

"Dios mío," he mutters when he sees the ceiling and the mess in Rory's room, where she and Jodie are bundling things into her suitcase and a carrier bag depending on whether they're wet or dry. The two of them are chattering quietly.

"Ay, señoritas, qué lástima. What a disaster this is! On behalf of the Casa Dorada resort, I am so sorry for this inconvenience."

"Inconvenience?" Jodie all but shrieks, making me wince. "Are you kidding me? This is a bit more than an *inconvenience,* Esteban. Our rooms are flooded. Our things could've been *ruined.*"

"Then it is a good thing you have only some clothes, and no electronic devices in here, ¿sí?"

For a second, I think Jodie's going to punch him in the face.

In all honesty, I wouldn't blame her.

And then Esteban laughs, all jovial, like this is part of the experience, and says, "It seems you got your day at a water park after all!"

Jodie gives him a glare that makes *me* feel like I should back away quickly.

"My notebook!" Rory wails when she finds it under a piece of plaster on the bed. "It's okay," she mutters as if trying to convince herself. "It's okay. I can fix this. It's not ruined. It's not."

She lays the dripping notebook down on one of the few dry surfaces, then yanks open a drawer and grabs the hotel hair dryer.

"Rory—" Jodie starts, and Esteban says, "Ah, Miss Rory, please, if you could not—"

"It'll be fine—I just need to dry it out," she says, and jams the plug into the outlet.

There's a spark, a shriek, and all the lights go out.

"Oh dear," says Esteban with a sigh.

Rory starts to cry, and Jodie shakes her head before stepping over to comfort her and check that she's okay.

Esteban just stands there, looking into the room with a judgmental smile that grates on me, and my temper flares. He's the *manager.* He should be *doing* something.

I wish I weren't such a goody-two-shoes. I wish I had it in me to yell at him, like Jodie did, instead of just—just drafting a scathing review in my head that I'll never actually post online.

I give it a shot, clearing my throat to say in the steadiest voice I can manage: "Obviously, this flooding is a big problem. We can't stay in these rooms."

I sound like I'm about to demand a refund and speak to his manager. I dial it back down quickly, feeling too awkward to insist on anything.

"We'd, um, we'd really appreciate it if you could sort us out some alternative rooms for the rest of the week. Please. Por favor."

Esteban smiles what I think might actually be the most

irritating smile in the world at me and nods. "Of course, Miss Lola. Of course you ladies cannot stay here. Please, if you would pack up your things and bring them to reception with you, I will see what I can do. And please, I ask you: do not attempt to plug anything else in at this time."

The three of us stand there, waiting until we can't hear his footsteps on the stairs anymore, and then Jodie says, "Let's hope some new rooms aren't too much of an *inconvenience* for him."

14 Rory

Talk about #vacationsfromhell . . . LOOK at the state of my room! When they say you can roll right out of bed and into the pool, this is not what I was hoping for. Give me ten ccs of vodka, stat, and get me on a plane home

No, maybe that's a bit strong . . . I wouldn't share a photograph of the carnage in my room—it would ruin the whole aesthetic of my feed. And I'm not stupid enough to bad-mouth this place, not when I occasionally reach out to small brands, hoping to work with them on my modest platform; that would be social media suicide. Maybe a picture of one of my pairs of dry shoes balanced on top of my suitcase, with that potted tree in the background on the right-hand side of the frame and the doors out to the pool on the left—yeah, that would be cute, as long as I didn't get the bucket in the frame.

Embrace the unexpected. When life gives you lemons, make lemonade. When life floods your hotel room, go swimming. #goodvibesonly

Yeah. That would be much better. Cuter. TikTok would be a different story, though: I'd have taken a shot of the room in all its horror-movie glory, ready to compare it to whatever pristine, plush room we're going to be relocated to. I'm sure there'd be some catchy, silly viral song going around this week that would work perfectly for it. Sort of "Chrissy, Wake Up," except in the end I do, in fact, like this.

God, I wish I had my phone.

We've been sitting around in reception with our bags for almost an hour after we packed up our rooms, carrier bags at our feet filled with whatever was caught in the water. Jodie and Luna got off lightly compared to me.

I don't bring it up, though, because I get the idea that Luna might tell me that's what I get for leaving my room in such a state. It's the sort of thing my sisters would say to me.

Not to mention I left the bath running. But how was *I* supposed to know that when the water cut out this morning? That's not my fault.

(It is totally my fault.)

And it *does* look like it's very much my fault that the power went out across the entire hotel. It didn't take them *that* long to get it all back up and running, and nobody seems that bothered about it, but even so—I know I effed up.

Honestly. What was I thinking? Plugging that stupid hair dryer in when the room was flooded? I'm lucky it just tripped the power and I didn't get electrocuted. (So Jodie tells me anyway, in what I think is meant to be a reassuring tone but that sounds kind of pissed off. Not that I can blame her.)

Actually . . . no, I *don't* wish I had my phone, because then I'd feel basically obligated to tell Hannah and Nic and our parents what was going on, whining and probably crying about it again, and I *know* I wouldn't tell them about the bath, which is very clearly down to my own carelessness, or about the hair dryer incident, because they'd only tell me how stupid I was, but at the same time *not* telling them would just make me feel even worse about the whole thing . . .

While I sit there coming up with Instagram captions and imagining the videos I'd take to follow this shit show in real time, Esteban and a few others—plumbers included—go back and forth between the reception desk and our rooms. Some guests are brought in from activities or the pool and return to reception with their suitcases and bags, ready to be reroomed. A couple of staff have packed up some rooms themselves—I guess for the people at the Hidropark.

Jodie goes to talk to one of the women at reception, then comes back to inform us that it's taking so long because the hotel is still undergoing renovations and most of the rooms are incomplete, so they're having to play a weird game of Tetris rehoming everyone.

"I did ask if the flooding was because of the renovations," she adds, "and she got kind of shifty, so I think it probably was, but they're not about to admit it. As soon as they admit something, they're probably open to all sorts of insurance claims. I bet that's what it is. Either way, they're leaning on the fact that you left the bath running, Rory, and it caused issues with the pipes, so . . ."

Someone comes over a little while later with a pinched face, but he only says, "Ladies, I apologize for the strange request, but would you be open to sharing a room?"

The three of us exchange a look.

I shrug, not caring either way. They can't be worse roommates than my sisters when we used to have to share on vacation, or when a bunch of us from school booked a cottage in Cornwall last summer and the girl in the bunk bed below me snuck one of the guys in and shagged him *right there with me in the room.* I mean, she thought I was fast asleep, and it took all my willpower not to laugh and embarrass the pair of them, but still.

No chance of Luna or Jodie doing that kind of thing, at least.

But Jodie turns a stark shade of white, spine jolting stiff, and bolts upright. I almost laugh, wondering if being an only child has made her territorial of her space. Luna frowns and says hesitantly, "Is that really necessary?"

"Due to the damage from room two-oh-five"—he cuts a look at me, and I smile sheepishly in response—"many of the rooms on the first floor are also unavailable, and we are having some difficulty finding space for our guests."

Whoops. Okay, that one is *very* much on me—it just sucks that Luna and Jodie have been lumped in.

"Would you be open to sharing?" he asks again.

I don't get included in the silent exchange this time: Luna gives Jodie a withering look, and Jodie rolls her eyes before saying, "That's fine."

The man sighs in relief, thanking us profusely before scuttling back to Esteban.

Eventually, a few people are escorted back upstairs and some bags are taken up, presumably to new rooms.

Until we're the last ones left waiting.

"He's doing this on purpose, isn't he?" I mutter, glaring at Esteban, who chuckles at something a guy with a mop says to him. "He's punishing us for the whole phone-stealing thing, isn't he? And for not going to all those activities and participating in the structured entertainment."

"Or maybe he's getting us the best rooms," Luna says, but I think we can all tell she doesn't believe it. Her lips twitch in an attempt at an optimistic smile before she looks back down at her lap, where she's wringing her hands.

Jodie keeps moving in her seat. Crossing and uncrossing her legs. Tapping the arm of the chair. Standing up to pace for a minute, then sitting back down. Huffing and puffing like she's going to blow the whole hotel down.

I'm so glad they're here, even if we only just met two days ago. I could *not* cope with all this on my own. At home, when things go wrong, Mum and Dad are always there—or, if it's something I don't want them to know about (like that time I got locked in the park on some drunken dare and had to call Nic to help me climb over the fence and get me home), my sisters are always there to help fix everything.

Not that Jodie and Luna are anything like Nic or Hannah, but still. They seem to know what they're doing a little more than I do.

Eventually, Esteban makes his way over to us, and immediately I know something's wrong. His stupid smile isn't as jolly as usual, and he clasps his hands in front of him.

It's an apologetic sort of look.

Yet somehow still smarmy as hell.

My stomach drops.

No. No, no, *no,* this isn't happening.

Before I can start to argue (because whatever it is he's about to say, I know it'll be something worth arguing over), he takes a breath and starts talking.

"Señoritas, I am so sorry for the delay. We have had to inspect the cause of the damage and many of the other rooms, you understand. A burst pipe. These things happen, no? And, of course, some damage to the mains caused by Miss Rory *and* the bath in her room left running all morning . . . We have had to clear out a section of the hotel near the damage and relocate many other guests. Unfortunately, however, this is a very busy week for us, and with the rooms we have had to close off and the rooms undergoing renovation, we are, sadly, full."

He leaves us with this for a minute, and it takes me a second to get it.

"Full," I repeat. "Like . . ."

"Like no room at the inn," Jodie says, equally disbelieving.

"Like you don't have anywhere for us to stay?" Luna cries out, standing up and clutching her hands together even tighter.

Esteban gives a light chuckle. "Of course we have somewhere for you to stay, Miss Lola, no te preocupes. We have a series of private villas under development near the beach. Unfortunately, you ladies will have to share, but I am sensing this is not a problem for you all. And, of course, as a gesture of goodwill, we will only be charging you for two nights, instead of the entire week. A *significant* discount, you understand. Please, if you will follow me. I will have someone bring your bags along shortly."

Okay, I think. A private villa. That doesn't sound so bad. I'm pretty sure I remember some fancy-looking villas in the ad . . .

Luna walks a little ahead of us, putting on a brave face. I nudge Jodie in the side, trying to lighten the mood. "Villa on the beach. Bit closer to lover boy and his bar."

"Oh, shut up," she tells me.

But she smiles like she knows I make an *excellent* point.

Esteban leads us to a stretch of path set just off the beach, not far from Gabriel's bar, and flourishes a hand proudly at a row of half a dozen villas. They look . . . compact, I guess is the word for them, but they don't look *bad*. Not as good as the photos I remember. In need of some TLC, is all. Each villa has a porch with metal furniture in the same style as the hotel's balconies.

Esteban brings us to the nearest one—number seven, according to the bronze plaque on the door—and takes out a key.

Instead of unlocking the door, though, he turns to the three of us, and my stomach immediately starts to knot.

"Now, señoritas, as I mentioned, our villas are under development. This is a situation we have not found ourselves in before, but I have had this villa cleared out for your use for the rest of the week. And I would like to remind you that you will not be charged for the remainder of your stay."

Why does he make that sound like such a bad thing?

My palms begin to sweat with trepidation.

I don't look at the others, worried I'll see they're as uneasy as I am right now.

Esteban unlocks the door and steps inside with a sweep of his arm. Gingerly, I follow Jodie inside, with Luna trailing me. The floorboards creak and I feel grains of sand crunching under my flip-flops.

Luna lets out something between a gasp and a whimper and presses a hand over her mouth. Jodie's face contorts in disgust. I'm a bit busy looking at the flaking, yellowing paint on the walls to even try to compose myself.

The knots in my stomach get worse.

I might actually be sick.

I thought it looked compact from the outside, but this is . . . *tiny*.

There's a rickety little table with two chairs, the wood so faded and cracked I think it might spontaneously collapse any second. It'd definitely give you splinters if you got too close, I decide.

There's a bookcase against one wall, but there's nothing on it except a couple of cobwebs that catch the light.

Gross.

A mismatched sofa and armchair positioned around a small square table take up the rest of the space. The ocher armchair is stained with brown patches that I really don't want to wonder about for too long. The sofa is a sad-looking dark red. It's probably in a similar sort of state to the armchair, but it's hard to tell because it's covered by a couple of blankets and a pillow.

They, at least, look clean. Soft and fresh, like the ones in the rooms we were just forced to vacate.

I don't really register *what* that pile of blankets means, though, not until Luna says, "Wait, is one of us sleeping on the sofa?"

Esteban gives one of his sighs that grate on me like nails down a blackboard. "As I mentioned, you will have to share. These villas are intended for our couples retreat package, though that is currently unavailable while the villas are under development."

"So . . ." Jodie looks up at the ceiling and then back at him. "There's only one bedroom?"

"Sí, that is correct. Well, I shall leave you to it. Your bags will be along shortly. If there is anything else you need, please ask. Hasta luego, Miss Lola, Miss Rory, Miss Ho-dee."

I follow him to the door—if only so I can slam it shut behind him.

The door is loose on its hinges. Of course it is.

I spin back around to face the girls. "If we need anything else. Yeah, right. The way this is going, the only thing we'll get is the plague."

If I had my phone, I'd pan around the room with my camera, put a black-and-white filter on the video and maybe some music from a horror film or something. Screw social media suicide. At least this would be authentic. And this is *exactly* the kind of thing that should be shared—#vacationsfromhell #howaboutnope #imnotacelebritybutgetmeoutofhere.

"Maybe it's not that bad," Luna says, starting upstairs.

Jodie shrugs at me, and we follow her. The staircase leads straight into the bedroom, which at least looks clean. Ish. The walls are pretty grim, like the ones downstairs. They're about ten years overdue being fixed up. The door to the bathroom is open, and I go in to look while Luna inspects the wardrobe.

She screams, then runs and leaps onto the bed.

"Spider!"

"I've got it," Jodie says, sighing.

I peer around the bathroom a little more carefully. Ew. *Ew.* I can feel my skin crawling already. "One in here as well, Steve Irwin."

"Wasn't he the crocodile guy?" Luna says.

"As far as I'm concerned, he's the scary-creature guy. Including spiders."

I back out, cringing next to Luna until Jodie's done a sweep of the bathroom, too. She finds more spiders than just the one I saw in the bath.

Then she says, "Ooh, a lizard!"

And I think I might actually faint.

"Aw, he's cute," she says, coming back into the bedroom with her hands cupped. "You guys wanna see?"

"Please, no," I say.

"You're right," Luna tells me while Jodie coaxes the lizard out of the bathroom window. "She is basically Steve Irwin."

"All clear," Jodie tells us, and I go back in to inspect the bathroom.

It could be worse. It could definitely be worse. There's a shower over a bath and plenty of counter space near the two washbasins. It does actually look relatively clean—like they sent someone to give it a quick once-over before shipping us in. There's a pile of nice fresh, fluffy white towels. Jodie reaches into the shower. The pipes churn and chug for a few minutes before water spurts out. It looks pretty weak, but there is steam rising from it. At least we can have a warm shower.

And even though the tiles could use a proper scrub and there are cracks in the bath and sinks, it could be a lot worse.

"This is not what I think they mean when they talk about luxury private villas," Luna says with a sigh. "I saw the pictures in the brochure at reception, and it is *not* supposed to look like . . . like a glorified shack."

"Shack is generous," Jodie mutters.

"At least the sheets and the towels are clean," Luna points out, and I grunt in agreement, because God only knows what the old ones would have looked like. And if this is the villa all cleared out for us . . . I dread to think what it looked like a couple of hours ago.

"And hey, look on the bright side!" she continues, grinning at us. "There's *no way* Esteban will kick us out of the hotel if we don't do all those silly organized activities every day, hmm? No more early-morning yoga, no more improv nights . . . And I've gotta be honest, girls: I really wasn't looking forward to the salsa class we had on tonight. I've got two left feet, and being paired up with some rando to be spun around a hall . . . Really not my idea of fun."

I manage a faint smile; that is a silver lining, I guess.

(Especially when the shoes I'd been thinking of wearing for salsa night are soaking wet.)

There's a knock at the door signaling our bags have arrived, and we thank the two guys in their khaki shorts and white polo shirts who carry them in for us.

"So . . . who's taking the sofa?" Jodie asks.

In the end, we play eight rounds of Rock, Paper, Scissors. I lose five times.

I'm taking the sofa.

15 *Jodie*

We unpack our stuff and try to clean things up a little with soap and water and wads of loo roll, if only to convince ourselves the villa is properly clean. It turns out the manky coloring of the whole place is more down to age than any kind of dirt, though, which is reassuring even if it means our efforts at cleaning are pretty useless. Rory takes a spare sheet and covers the dining table downstairs, saying it's so she can put some of her things on it and not have to worry too much about getting splinters. It looks as crappy as we expect.

The whole mood is pretty sour, actually.

"This wouldn't have happened if I hadn't convinced you guys to steal our phones back," Luna mumbles. "It got us into trouble with Esteban, and clearly the man can hold a grudge."

"No, it's *my* fault," Rory says. "You saw how pissed off he was about me tripping the power. Not to mention I left the bath running and caused the whole flood . . . Not on purpose, obviously, but still. God, I was so stupid."

"It's neither of your faults," I tell them firmly. I mean, it's kind of Rory's, but she's not really to blame for the busted plumbing in this place. Of all the things to compete over, this isn't it. "These things happen. That burst pipe was a freak accident. The bath—that was just unlucky. Someone would've ended up in this villa, and let's face it, they probably would've stuck us here anyway. I mean, three girls like us? Traveling alone? We're the youngest people here by like, twenty years—at *least*. Rory's barely old enough to drink! We don't exactly look as if we're about to sue them. Not like Linda and Andrew would."

"No one would mess with Linda," I agree.

Ignoring us, Rory throws herself onto the bed, hunching forward and burying her face in her hands. A sob tears out of her mouth, startling me.

"I can't do anything right! I'm so sorry, you guys. I'm such a colossal fuckup! How was I supposed to know I turned the tap the wrong way when the water cut out? Then I trip the power and get us banished here, and I'm going to be stuck doing that shitty law degree and end up in a job I don't even want *forever,* and everybody always saying, no, Rory, you did the right thing, you'd never have made it as an artist, you're *just not good enough,* that's why your Etsy store is a total failure, just like *you.* Sorry, Rory, that brand you pitched to rejected you! This one didn't even bother to reply! Nobody is buying from your store! You're bleeding followers, and that brand you started to build for yourself is crumbling already for no apparent reason! Nobody cares about your stupid art or your boring social media—you're wasting your time with it all. Because you can't do *anything right.* I'm so fucking *stupid*!"

I look over at Luna, not sure where Rory's outburst came from. Luna shrugs at me and finishes hanging a dress in the wardrobe before walking over to put an arm around Rory. "Hey, come on, it's not forever."

"See, this is why my sisters signed me up to this. So I would have to get out of my head about everything. They don't even know about all my social media stuff or my Etsy store. I have decoy accounts for them to follow! I have a Finsta just for them! They already think I won't get anywhere with art and should just be sensible and keep it as a *hobby,* but if they knew . . . God, if they *knew,* it'd just drive the knife in. Like—like, as long as they don't know I'm trying and failing, it's Schrödinger's career. But it's not, because the cat's already *dead.*"

Luna and I wait, but Rory doesn't carry on. Her breathing is noisy, ragged, and she's shaking. Luna rubs her back with a sympathetic expression. She catches my eye for a moment, but I can only shrug helplessly. I know Rory said before that she didn't want to do the degree she's due to start in a couple of months, but . . .

I didn't expect *this.*

She comes off as so blasé, so cool and self-assured. But now she just looks young and scared, and I feel for her. I can definitely sympathize with feeling stuck about uni, anyway.

Rory seems to be done venting for the moment, so Luna takes it upon herself to try and comfort her.

"I know it's not the same thing, but I kind of get where you're coming from—at least about feeling like a failure. Ever since I broke up with Liam, I've been so in my head about whether it was the right thing to do or not, thinking that I've ruined things, let myself down. Mostly it's that I feel like I wasn't enough for him somehow? Or for our mutual friends? Like it's all a failing on *my* part and that's why I had to call it off, rather than anything he did. And I keep trying not to think about him, but it's not that easy. After I saw those pictures on Instagram, and that girl . . . And, you know, I was sure in one of them that she had one of those polo shirts on like they wear here? I didn't get a chance to check properly, though. That was when Esteban showed up. So now I'm driving myself crazy thinking what if she *does* work here?"

Rory sniffles a little. "I'm sorry, Miss Lola, but what the *fuck*? You know how paranoid that sounds, right?"

"No, I'm serious. I—I know how it sounds. That's why I didn't bring it up earlier. The girl in that photo on his Instagram. Remember when I looked on Gabriel's phone and I was panicking Liam had moved on? Well, he'd tagged her, so obviously I snooped on her profile—remember when I accidentally liked one of her old pictures? I was trying to zoom in. I can't remember now because, you know, sangria, but I'm *sure* she'd posted another picture more recently where she was wearing a polo shirt that looks *just like* the kind they wear here."

I stare at Luna, not exactly sure if she's exaggerating in an attempt to distract Rory. She looks so stricken, though, that I quickly realize she's not.

"We should never have checked our phones," Rory laments, clutching Luna's hand.

I look between them both for a minute, knowing it's my turn to pitch in. It's my turn to say how much I wish I had my phone or how much I wish I hadn't seen something.

Except—

Well, except, I don't. I don't have anything to say like that.

I'm glad I didn't have time to see all those other notifications on LinkedIn and that I didn't have time to read everything in the group chat, that I didn't have to reply to it.

It's kind of nice not feeling like I have to prove myself all the time to everyone.

But Rory and Luna look so *morose* over this entire thing that I end up saying, "Yeah. I know. I mean, I'm so mad about all my friends doing better than me. At everything."

It sounds like a lie even as I say it, and I think they notice my heart isn't really in it. I surprise myself at how much I suddenly want to distance myself from that feeling of competition that only drags me down, rather than driving me.

So I say, "Look, it's nearly dinnertime. Why don't we get changed, head to dinner and then hang out at the beach bar again tonight? Get away from Esteban and the whole crowd of people and whatever rubbish they're putting on tonight."

"I guess being your wingwoman for the night might make today a little less crap," Rory sniffles, managing a smile.

"Yeah, that and a few tequilas," Luna mutters. "Count me in."

The hot water is more like lukewarm by the time I get my shower, so I make it quick and try not to be mad about it. With the three of us clustered in the bedroom trying to get dressed, do hair and makeup or find something that isn't still damp from the pipe disaster, it gets to feel a little claustrophobic.

Rory doesn't appear to be at all shy about sharing the space, and Luna seems considerate of both of us whenever she's moving around. I might be comfortable hanging out with them, opening up to them about some stuff, but it feels *weird* to be taking a shower with them just on the other side of the door, hearing them chattering away. Even though I put my underwear on in the bathroom, I wrap my towel back around me to go into the bedroom to pick out some clothes, which makes them both laugh.

"No need to be shy," Rory tells me. "We've seen you in your swimming costume, hon—that's basically the same thing."

I *know* she's got a point, and it's not like I have any specific hang-ups about my body, just . . . you know, general ones. All-encompassing hang-ups. Plus, it's plain *weird* to not have my own space to get ready in. I don't have siblings and never shared a space with a boyfriend.

I get a sudden surge of panic about how I'm going to even do a number two, knowing they'll be just outside the bathroom. I'll have to sneak back by myself when they're out at the pool or something.

As relieved as I am to be sharing this shack with the girls rather than enduring it alone, I mourn for my privacy.

Maybe it *is* actually all Rory's fault, I think before I can help it. She deserves to be on the sofa. She caused that flood from her bath. She tripped the power. Maybe we'd have been fine if that little mishap hadn't happened.

But then again, they did *ask* us if we were okay to share a room, so we basically volunteered to be here. And Rory's not the only one who annoyed Esteban and broke his precious rules; I got a bit nasty with him, and Luna started the whole *Mission: Impossible* stunt . . .

It's not like we can do anything about it now anyway, so I don't say anything, and smile at Rory when she asks me to straighten the back of her hair for her.

We don't stick around long at dinner. Both Luna and Rory seem a little preoccupied, and besides that, it's like there's a dark cloud hanging over our table. It's all too clear that everyone knows we had something to do with the whole rerooming thing, judging by the frowns we're getting and the way people whisper to each other and look over at us.

"I heard they broke into the office and took their phones back," one lady mutters to her friend behind me at the buffet, where I'm piling lasagna on my plate. "Absolutely outrageous. Why bother coming here if you can't hack it?"

Her friend bursts into giggles. "*Hack* it! Oh dear!"

We shovel our food down and get the hell out of there.

"Did you hear the guy at the next table? He said he'd heard we caused the power outage. He was complaining that it was the reason behind the ice machine on his floor being out of order," Rory rants. "Half my stuff was ruined. I wanted to shove his *head* in a bucket of ice."

She keeps ranting all the way to the beach bar, and Luna and I let her. Keeping quiet seems easiest.

Rory strides ahead of us, throwing herself onto a stool at the bar and collapsing over it like a Disney princess who's lost all hope after having been told she absolutely cannot marry that man she met just once in the woods. Luna snickers next to me, like she can read my mind.

"She's such a drama queen—I love it."

Gabriel leans on the edge of the bar next to her and clears his throat as Luna and I take our seats. "Am I to assume a stiff gin is needed?"

Rory groans. "Not tonight, buddy. Give me a mocktail, stat. I've got enough of a headache without adding a hangover to it."

Luna pats Rory's shoulder, and then Gabriel turns his dashing smile on us. "And for you ladies?"

"Uh," is all I can manage because, oh, I forgot how good-looking he is.

He's *so* good-looking.

With his perfect hair and perfect smile and perfect arms . . .

His sleeves are rolled up to his elbows again tonight, and the collar of his shirt is open wide enough to bare a triangle of bronze skin and offer a teasing glimpse at the dark hairs on his chest. I'm positive he didn't have it unbuttoned quite so low yesterday; I'd have noticed. I tear my eyes away, but they snag on all the other perfect parts of him: the soft pink of his lips, which look oh so kissable, the swoop of his dark hair, which shines in the lamplight and lies over his forehead just so, like he's a movie star with a whole team to style it in the most attractive, swoon-worthy way possible. I don't linger on his lovely glittering brown eyes that remind me of an autumn bonfire in case he catches me staring, and I focus instead on his toned arms, callused hands and long fingers.

"How about one big jug of mocktail?" Luna suggests. "Any kind. We'll share."

Gabriel gives her a little salute and turns to make us something nonalcoholic and sweet. There are a few more people at the bar tonight, and I think about how that means he won't be getting his phone out, and that Rory and Luna won't be able to ask him if they can borrow it just to drive themselves back into that nervous spiral again.

Honestly, I'm relieved.

I'm also actually relieved that Rory is in crisis mode right now after all that talk about being my wingwoman to help me flirt with Gabriel. The way it's going so far, it'll be a miracle if I can get a full sentence out in front of him.

I've dated very little in the last few years, and aside from the occasional kiss with some random guy on a night out or that very, *very* brief fling with the friend of a friend with the tweed and elbow patches I asked to tutor me, I don't really go out and *flirt* with guys. At school, I was used to being the "plain" one. Ordinary enough that, for the most part, boys didn't look twice, and I didn't mind that. Or . . . I got used to it. At uni, I've been so focused on getting through my degree that things like romance and flirting are the least of my concerns.

Either way, I have *definitely* never flirted with a guy as good-looking as Gabriel.

While he's got his back turned for a second, I say to Luna, "Should we grab a table?"

"And miss out on the chance to watch you drool over Gabriel again? I think not. Besides, he seems nice. Good company, you know?"

I glance back at Gabriel and push my glasses up my nose. There's a pucker between his thick eyebrows as he concentrates on mixing juices for our mocktail, his lips parted slightly.

And hard as I try not to notice it: his arse in those shorts . . .

"Yeah," I reply to Luna. "Very nice."

Oh my God, what am I doing?

I'm pathetic. Like, properly, completely pathetic. Gawking at this relative stranger like I'm back in Year Ten or something, and he's a new guy at school, and I'm just *praying* for him to notice me, to find myself worthy of that attention.

I don't think I've had an actual crush on a guy in years. And even when I did, I never got all . . .

Well, like *this*.

Silly. Speechless.

So instead of thinking about that, I lean back on my stool to look at Rory, who's still sprawled over the bar with her head on her arms. She groans again.

"Is she okay? Are you okay?"

"No," she howls, the word muffled by her arms.

Luna stifles a giggle, and then we're pulled away from Rory by the clink of glass as Gabriel sets down three giant glasses of something bright yellow with fruit skewers in them.

"Is she sure she doesn't need something a little . . ." He waves a hand while he searches for the word, but in the end, he just says, "Tea? I know you Brits like that."

Rory lifts her head up off the counter at that to whisper, "Yes, please," before slumping down again.

I reach for my glass of yellow mocktail and take a sip from the straw.

"Oh my God," I groan. "This is amazing."

I can taste pineapple, and maybe orange. Whatever it is, it's *delightful*.

"Rory, seriously, I know you're going through something right now, but you have got to try some of this," I tell her. "Gabriel's a goddamn genius."

"Gracias, chica," he says in that smooth-as-honey voice. I feel my cheeks turn warm and hope it doesn't look like I'm blushing. I *really* hope I'm not blushing.

"She's right," Luna says after tasting it. "Rory, you've got to try it."

Gabriel leans on the bar, close enough that I can smell his after-shave, which is so intoxicating it makes me feel a little dizzy. (Is there anything about this guy that isn't completely perfect?)

"What's wrong with your friend? She was so different yesterday. Loud, ¿sabes?" he asks me. *Me*. Luna's right there too, obviously, but it's me he's focused on. My heart skitters at the attention, but I never get to answer.

"I got us kicked out of the hotel and Esteban moved us into a shack," Rory wails, sitting up enough to drink some of her mock-tail. "Damn, that *is* good."

"Ah, I heard some tonto del culo caused the power cut and flooded the hotel." He grins widely, looking between us three. "That was you?"

"Okay, we did not cause the *entire* flood," I burst out, suddenly rediscovering my ability to form a coherent sentence, and jab a finger at Gabriel. "That was a burst pipe. And Rory only left the bath on by accident because the water stopped running. And we could totally claim compensation. It ruined some of my shoes."

"Your shoes? Qué lástima," he drawls, but it doesn't sound like he thinks it's a shame. The smile is more of a smirk now, which makes it even sexier. It does something funny to my stomach, a rush of heat that seems to consume all of me.

Stupid Gabriel and his stupid perfect face.

Words fail me again and my lips move soundlessly, at which point Luna knocks her knee into mine and takes over.

"Is everyone saying it's our fault?"

"They're saying it's someone's fault," Gabriel says. His dark eyes crease with laughter. "I should have guessed it was you three alborotadores."

Rory scowls. "Us three what now?"

"Whatever it is, I'm insulted," Luna decides.

"I miss Google Translate," I say.

"Alborotadores," he repeats. "You three, up to mischief. I heard you tried to steal your phones back. Now you trash the hotel. I'm not sure I want you in my bar. You might destroy it, too."

I snort with laughter and even Rory manages a chuckle.

Gabriel looks directly at me, one eyebrow raised slightly. "Are you going to cause me trouble, chica?"

Boy, I hope so.

My heart somersaults again, and I wet my lips before I speak. Gabriel's eyes flicker down to my mouth, and it wasn't intentional, but . . . I don't hate it. I sit up a little straighter, fidgeting with the straw in my drink. "Guess you'll have to wait and see."

He gives a quiet chuckle and shakes his head. A burst of laughter from a group sitting nearby startles him back to attention, and he leans away from the bar slightly, clearing his throat. "So Esteban has put you all in a shack?"

"The beach villas," Luna explains. "The ones they're doing up that are meant to be for couples retreats or something. Except they haven't done ours up. We had to get GI Jodie here to sweep the place for wildlife. Get rid of all the spiders and lizards and stuff."

Rory fakes retching and drinks some more mocktail. "Please don't bring it back up. If I think too much about Aragog and his gang in that place, I won't be able to sleep tonight."

"I don't get the issue," I say, while Luna shudders. "They're just bugs. Same as moths or bumblebees or—"

"They're creepy. All those legs . . . Ugh!"

"You're not scared of spiders?" Gabriel asks, raising his eyebrows at me.

"Should I be?"

"You've got bigger cojones than me, chica," he says, laughing. "I despise them."

"And here I thought you had such a decent pair of melones," Luna mumbles, waggling her eyebrows at me. I snort again and shove her lightly. Gabriel laughs, too, but quickly turns it into clearing his throat.

I blush again. And hope nobody notices. Least of all Gabriel—although he suddenly seems to be *very* preoccupied with wiping nonexistent dust off the other side of the bar.

Rory pouts, scowling melodramatically between us. "I don't get it. I don't get the joke—what's the joke?"

"Just complimenting Jodie on her boobs."

"Amen to that. Me and my flat-as-an-ironing-board chest are full of boob envy," Rory says, and the two of them laugh with the sort of casualness as if they've been friends for years, ignoring how mortified I am.

To Gabriel, Rory says, "It's all my fault. The shack. I plugged in a hair dryer and tripped the power. That one was *definitely* my fault. And, you know, I *did* leave the bath running, however accidentally, in a place with some very dodgy plumbing."

"Were you behind the phone stealing, too?"

"No, that was all Luna's idea," she says, and then suddenly sits up straighter and points at me. She whispers, loud enough that we can all hear, "Jodie was a total boss, though, telling Esteban off even after we got caught. She's kind of a badass."

Then someone calls, "Hey, uh, excuse me, mate? Can I get some more Peronis and another glass of red, please?"

Gabriel excuses himself quietly and goes over to the other side of the bar to serve the guy. I turn to Rory.

"What was that? *I* was the one *you* had to persuade! I'm not sure how 'badass' that—"

"I was doing you a favor, sweetie, believe me." Rory reaches over and grabs my arm, fingers biting in as she shakes me, eyes wide. Gravely, she says, "Plus, he was definitely checking out your melons."

"Shut up. He was not. And what about the comment he made about me being more man than him about spiders? Last time I checked, that definitely wasn't flirting."

"Oh please," Luna says. "Any guy worth your time isn't going to be emasculated over something like that. If anything, he should be grateful you'd be there to deal with spiders for him. God knows I loved it about Liam. I swear, I was almost ready to beg him to come back the first time I found a spider in my room after we broke up. It was traumatizing. Anyway. Yes, he was totally flirting. Asking if you were *trouble*!"

"But he's . . . It's not . . . I'm not flirting," I hiss. "I don't know how to, remember?"

"If we had our phones, we could find all kinds of *Cosmo* articles on how to flirt," Rory grumbles. "Even when they're bonkers, they're brilliant."

"Compliment him," Luna suggests. "He seemed to like it when you called him a genius."

"For his ability to make a mocktail? He's a *barman*. It's *literally* his job."

"So . . . find something else!" Rory tells me, as though it's so obvious. "God knows there's enough about that man to compliment," she says with a sigh, looking over at him. "Pick a part, girl. Any part. Can't go wrong."

"Although that could be creepy," Luna pitches in. "Maybe don't, like, compliment him on his toes. Unless you have a foot fetish. Not trying to kink-shame here."

"I think I liked you better when you were being melodramatic and moping," I snap at Rory, and shake Luna off my arm because Gabriel's coming back.

"Say something," Luna hisses at me.

So I tell him, "You have lovely earlobes."

16 *Luna*

Jodie groans for the billionth time, snatching her pillow from under her head and pressing it over her face to scream. She tucks the pillow back under her head and sighs.

"Why? Why did you make me say something? Why?"

"It wasn't that bad," I tell her, even though it really was. It was *terrible.*

Gabriel had been speechless after the earlobe compliment, looking around at us all with a confused, self-conscious chuckle. Jodie, meanwhile, had been busy downing her drink as if the fruity mocktail might numb the sting of embarrassment, and ended up dumping almost the entire thing down her front instead. She'd bolted so quickly when Gabriel tried to get her some napkins that she'd knocked her stool to the floor, babbling some excuse about "just remembering something she had to do" before running away. I'd grabbed Rory and gone after her with barely so much as a good-bye to our friendly bartender and fellow rule breaker.

She's only just stopped hyperventilating.

The whole scene makes me dread thinking about getting back

into the dating game. Liam and I had always just seemed to . . . *fit*. It had been so easy. Or it used to be. Sometime since going off to uni, things had slid out of place so gradually that I hadn't even noticed it happening.

Maybe I was too hard on him. It isn't Liam's fault that he's such a social butterfly or that I'm not the spontaneous type like he seemed to want me to be. I hadn't exactly been clearheaded, either, snapping after that awful exam I was so sure I'd failed.

Would I have broken up with him if the exam had gone better?

Would I have only broken up with him later down the line, or would he have changed—calmed down, maybe, after the excitement of the first year of uni and turned back into the boy I'd fallen in love with? Does he want to, knowing he's lost me—or was I such a nag that he's glad to be rid of me?

It makes my head and heart ache just thinking about it.

It's just as well I don't have my phone. I can't call him for answers.

Seeing Jodie turn into a blithering, clumsy wreck in front of a guy, though, I am more than happy to forgo any and all boy drama for a while.

Like . . . a *long* while.

Rory comes out of the bathroom, rubbing pale-pink moisturizer into her face with careful circular motions, her eyebrows raised and lips puckered. "What're we talking about?"

"The fact that I can never show my face at our one little escape haunt ever again. Sign me up for improv night for the rest of the week. It can't be any more humiliating."

I give Jodie a sympathetic smile, but she's got her face screwed up and eyes closed, so I look at Rory instead and shrug. She shrugs right back and plops between us on the bed.

Even with her hair scraped back in two French braids and no makeup on, Rory somehow manages to look effortlessly glamorous. Watching her put moisturizer on, I can just imagine opening YouTube and finding her on the home page with some unboxing video or beauty vlog. I feel a pang of envy looking at her in her navy silk nightie and fluffy white slippers. (Although they're slightly less fluffy and white after being drenched in her room, at least they're dry now, from sitting out on the deck of the villa through the night.)

She puts me to shame in my Primark cotton shorts and an oversized T-shirt from freshers' week, the motif of which has long ago peeled off in the wash. I bet Jodie, in her faded Winnie-the-Pooh nightie, feels the same.

I hope she does, anyway.

"You just need to . . ." Rory sighs, eyes roaming the ceiling while she finds the right word. "Rethink. *Rebrand!* Be the badass Jodie we know and love who stole our phones back last night. Not the earlobe-adoring goofball we saw spill her drink over herself and flee the bar tonight."

Jodie groans again like she doesn't need the reminder.

Rethink and rebrand. I could do with a little of that, too. Become someone less of a party pooper, less of a homebody. More spontaneous. More . . .

More. Just—more.

Someone Liam might have stayed in love with.

Someone our friends might have cared to stay in touch with.

"Here's what we do. We just write off today. *Bloop!*" Rory sweeps a hand through the air, fingers snapping. "Act like it didn't happen. And tomorrow we fix up your hair, you put on your favorite dress and we try again."

"What's wrong with my hair?"

"I'm just saying, a little back-combing for volume wouldn't kill you."

"Here, look. Pretend I'm Gabriel," I say, a little worried Jodie will get offended if Rory carries on like this, and that they'll argue. I sit up and turn to face her. "Practice what you'd say. Flirt with me, chica."

"I'm not doing this," she mumbles, but sits up anyway. Rory crosses her legs under her, settling in more. "Fine. Uh, you look very nice tonight, Gabriel."

I do my best impression of a Spanish accent and a guy's deep voice (both of which add up to something pretty terrible) and say, "Thank you. You look lovely tonight, too, Jodie. Especially your earlobes."

Rory shrieks with glee, her crisis of earlier apparently all forgotten. Even though it's taken Jodie being humiliated to snap her out of it, I'm glad; I've never seen anybody look so hopeless and helpless as she did when she was ranting about her art and social media. Now there's light back in her eyes, and she falls backward between us just as Jodie throws her pillow at my face.

"They are some badass earlobes," I go on, in my terrible impression. "Oh no, I've found a spider behind the bar. Maybe you could help me get rid of it. You and your lovely melones."

"I hate you both," Jodie tells us, snatching her pillow back and throwing it at my face again when I break into peals of laughter. Rory smacks my arm, face creased as she gasps for breath between giggles.

Even Jodie has started laughing, though, despite the pained look on her face.

I don't remember the last time I laughed like this—especially with Liam, who has taken up so much space in my life, particularly during the past year. Ironic, when that was when he felt furthest away. Definitely not with our friends, who were—honestly—only my friends because of Liam, and not really my kind of people.

Is that why they're excluding me? Was I always just an unfortunate extra, tagged on because of who I was dating?

I'm too busy laughing with Jodie and Rory to let that realization drag me down.

"Oh, Luna, why did you start talking about his toes? You put weird body parts into my head. And you, Rory! Trying to wingwoman me, pushing me to compliment him! This is your fault, Miss Melodrama. His earlobes! I actually *complimented* his *earlobes*."

"And spilled your drink on yourself trying to down it," I remind her.

"And literally ran away when he turned around to get you napkins," Rory adds.

Jodie shoves her—and the twin beds that have been pushed together to make a double bed split apart, and Rory crashes right down between them with a yelp.

We all fall silent, and Jodie and I lean down to look at Rory in the tiny gap between the beds, the sheets cradling her like a makeshift hammock. She stares back at us in shock and says, "Ow. My *butt*. I think I broke my butt. Like this day couldn't get any worse, I'm going to have to go to hospital with a broken butt."

"Come on." Jodie offers her a hand, but Rory flails her legs uselessly, battling the sheets as she gets exactly nowhere, which sends me into another fit of laughter. I'm wheezing by the time we haul her to her feet. Jodie pushes the beds back together and we readjust the sheets.

"On that note," Rory says, rubbing her coccyx, "before I can trigger any more disasters today, I'm going to bed. By which I mean that lumpy-ass sofa. Night, ladies."

"Night," we call after her.

Jodie snaps off the lamp next to her, and the light downstairs is turned off, too. The blinds are broken, but at least we're far enough from the lights of the hotel that it doesn't matter.

I bet it'll matter when the sun comes up, though.

Maybe we'll even be up in time for a yoga class, I think wryly. There's no alarm clock in this place—just one clock on the kitchenette wall downstairs (which I checked against my watch earlier and found was fifty minutes behind).

"I cannot work that girl out," Jodie says quietly to me in the dark. "She's bursting with confidence, and I bet if *she* was the one flirting it up with some sexy Spanish bartender he'd be wrapped around her little finger by now. But when she was saying all that stuff about why her sisters sent her here, how she can't do anything right . . . And did you notice how she let us take charge? With Esteban? And Oscar when he tried to sign us up for stuff?"

I make a small noise of agreement, debating over what to say.

I know exactly what Jodie means, but Rory's overzealous attitude seems to flicker in and out of existence at the slightest sign of trouble. I wonder if it's because she's younger than us, or if it's more to do with having such protective big sisters, but . . . What if it's all a front? Amped up to protect her own feelings, or maybe the exact opposite—that this is all a more modest, toned-down version of Rory, one she thinks is more palatable for a family who don't quite understand her.

I start to say as much to Jodie but catch myself. I'd hate it if I thought *they* were talking about what I'm like behind my back— even as innocently as this.

So I just say, "I don't think she'd stand a chance with Gabriel. He's only got eyes for you, in case you hadn't noticed."

Jodie lets out a breath of laughter, unconvinced and probably blushing, and mumbles, "Maybe. Night, Luna," as she turns over, the sheets rustling.

I turn onto my side, too, but I'm not tired. After a few minutes, Jodie's breathing evens out, and it's obvious she's fast asleep. I wish I had my phone with me so I could scroll mindlessly until I got tired. I'd turn the lamp on and read, but I don't want to wake Jodie up.

I lie there and wonder what these girls think about me. Could I be just an unfortunate extra they got lumped with, too, like the crowd at uni?

Who do they see?

Someone quiet, probably. I hope they don't see me as nervous or boring or bland.

I'd hate for them to think that. To feel reduced, overlooked. Lesser, because I'm not loud like Rory or bolshy like Jodie.

I'm not, I think fiercely. Just because I'm quiet, because I like to think things through, because I have a tendency to worry—*I'm not small. Don't make me small.*

And I realize: Did Liam make me small this last year, or is it all in my head?

That's all it takes for my mind to be consumed by thoughts of him. His short brown hair and long face, the scar on his blunt chin from rugby a couple of years ago, and that broad, warm frame that would cradle me close when he wrapped his arms around me. I think about the way he kissed me, how he liked to press kisses to my palms, and the hand he'd trail over my hair when we were snuggled up together.

I run my hand over my hair now, mirroring the gesture in my memories, but my fingers meet empty air quickly. I cut it, the day after the breakup. I donated the long curls he told me he loved, craving some physical change abrupt and blunt enough to reflect how badly my world had turned upside down.

How *I'd* turned it upside down.

My entire life for the last four years has been Liam; my entire life going forward was supposed to be Liam.

I miss you, he'd said, but does he really?

How is he adjusting to this new life without me?

I remember, all too suddenly, the girl from his Instagram. What if she *was* wearing a Casa Dorada polo shirt in that picture I saw? What if she's spending her summer out here as a rep or something?

What if he comes out here with her?

I feel like that's too crazy, but the way this week is going . . .

He's allowed to move on. I don't have any right to want him to miss me when *I* broke up with *him*.

But there's a part of me that is terrified he's moved on so easily, because it proves I meant so little to him. That the guy who told me he loved me, who said he understood when I was exhausted by parties and nights out and meeting new people, who spent quiet afternoons snuggled up with me and a laptop to watch a film on Netflix together, who'd tuck my hair out of the way and kiss my neck and tell me he *loved* me . . .

Had he still loved me?

If he hadn't, when had he stopped?

When had I stopped loving him the way I used to?

When had that warm, rosy feeling and the butterflies in my stomach given way to familiarity and routine, and eventually been overtaken completely by a constant irritation gnawing at me, the stress that I wasn't doing enough, the exasperation when he moped around, hungover or bored?

And I realize it's not even *really* him that I miss. If anything, it's a relief not to have to steel myself for a night out I don't care for, be around a bunch of people I don't really like all that much and struggle to keep up with. I'm not sorry to have left that messy room of his behind, with its overflowing bin of smelly takeaway containers and laundry he'd leave until it annoyed me so much that *I* did it for him.

What I miss more is the idea of the relationship we had. It was having someone who knew me, who I felt comfortable with.

Realizing that makes me feel like a horrible, horrible person. The darkness of the room seems to swallow me up, and the shadows wriggling on the ceiling press in close, muffling the sound of

Jodie's breathing, Rory's snoring, the sea outside the window, and I disappear into that guilt and worry.

But . . . would I really have done that?

Stayed with Liam, just . . . just because?

I didn't *just* stay with him because I was scared of being alone. I am *not* afraid to be alone, I try to tell myself, but it doesn't seem to stick.

Who do I have without Liam? I mean, really?

The crowd I've hung out with for the last year apparently couldn't care less about me; they've clearly taken Liam's side. Like some pet in a divorce he gained custody of. I haven't really seen the gang from school this past year, and when we do talk it doesn't feel like it used to. It doesn't feel like it *should*.

I know that. I've known that for a while. But it never mattered because I had Liam, and we always had plans to do things together or with a group of people, and it was fine. I was fine.

I'm totally fine.

And I'm not afraid to be alone.

I repeat it in my head, scowling at the wall, until it feels like I can believe it. I do have some of my own friends at uni. Not a *ton* of them, not like Liam does, but a couple of friends from my course that I can lean on and laugh with, and that's more than enough for me. I've got my big brother, my parents. And I suppose there's always a chance I'm overreacting about my friends because I can't talk to them right now. If I had my phone to go into our group chat, maybe I'd convince myself I'm just being silly.

That's all this is: it's me spiraling because I don't have my phone and because this whole trip has turned into some kind of disaster, rather than the week of luxury I was expecting. If I had my phone, I'd be thinking differently.

(And I definitely *wouldn't* be wasting my time Instagram-stalking some girl my ex went to the pub with.)

I'm fine. Everything is fine.

I am not afraid to be alone.

And I am not imagining all the ways I should've replied to his text.

> I miss you too

Me too. I'm sorry. Can we talk when I get back, please?

Was that a drunk text? Have you already moved on? Is she just a rebound?

I never should've broken up with you, especially like that. Can you forgive me? Can we work this out?

Please stop calling me and texting. We're done. We've been done for a long time

> When did you stop loving me? Was it something I did?

Liam, I love you. I screwed up. I'm sorry

Eventually, somewhere between drafting texts to Liam in my head, thinking about the fact I haven't really connected with most of my at-home friends in way too long, and worrying over the wild possibility of Liam and his maybe-new girlfriend showing up here of all places, I manage to fall asleep.

17 Rory

~The Vacation Bucket List~

1. Write pros and cons list of actually doing the law degree you got an UNCONDITIONAL OFFER FOR
2. Write pros and cons list of doing literally anything but that
3. Consider other degrees to apply to through clearing?
4. Write pros and cons list of a gap year, just in case
5. ~~HAVE FUN! BE RESTFUL! PRACTICE MINDFULNESS!~~
6. ~~Talk to strangers (make friends??)~~
7. Try something new!
8. Figure out how to tell Mum and Dad and Nic and Hannah I don't want to do the law degree, never wanted to do the law degree, never will want to do the law degree, and might cry if someone mentions the law degree one more time
9.
10.

All right, I think, looking over my notebook. (Which is thankfully not as ruined as I expected it to be now that it's dried out. The pages are crinkled and some of the writing is a bit warped, but it could be a lot worse.)

It's not so ruined it won't still look cute in pictures.

Okay, this isn't so bad, see?

I tick off number six with a flourish and a grin. Talk to strangers and make friends—absolutely, check. After our phone jailbreak episode and sharing this shack, I reckon Jodie and Luna definitely count as friends at this point.

And I kind of hope they'll stay that way once this week is over. I think some of my friends back home would like them a lot. Sammy from art club would *love* Luna: she's an old-soul type, too. And the girls from netball would find Jodie an absolute riot. I cannot wait to tell them about the earlobes episode; they'll get a total kick out of it.

As for being restful and mindful—screw that. This vacation is a goddamn shambles. *Let's not pretend otherwise,* I think, and scribble it off the list. And as for trying something new . . . Hmm. Does aqua aerobics count? I don't know exactly what I had in mind, but something a bit more exciting and . . . fulfilling than that.

Definitely something more worthwhile and uplifting than "blow up the hotel's fuses and cause a cataclysmic flood that took out your entire room."

I'll leave number seven unchecked for now.

Which only leaves me with almost the entire rest of my Vacation Bucket List to try to do in the next few days.

I run my finger down the page, pausing at each item as I debate it.

Maybe I'll just stick with one of them for now.

Right, pros and cons of a gap year. That's no big deal. It's just a list, I'm not *committing* to doing anything. And it's just . . . *postponing* the law degree, which feels way less intimidating than not doing it at all.

I hear the girls start coming downstairs and snap my notebook shut. They're chattering about a movie, I think, and are changed, ready for the day. Luna has her massive bag slung over her shoulder, the bright strap of her bikini poking out from beneath her cover-up.

"Took you long enough," I say, shoving my notebook out of sight, beneath the book I've borrowed from the Traveling Library of Luna. I get up and drop both into her bag. I didn't even *think* to bring a beach bag with me, but hers is plenty big enough for all three of us.

"I couldn't find my caftan," Luna tells me. "And this one couldn't find her lipstick. Then decided to take it off anyway after she *did* find it."

I squint at Jodie. Her lips look distinctly pink and full. She's wearing mascara, too, and her skin has a dewy look that makes me think she's slathered on sun cream rather than concealer, like I would have if I were her. I ask, "Aren't you wearing lipstick?"

"She put it back on." Luna rolls her eyes.

"Oh. Well, anyway. Remember the plan?"

"It's a horrible plan," Jodie tells me, biting her lower lip. I resist the urge to tell her not to because she'll spoil her lipstick. "Ugh, I feel sick. No, I'm not doing it. I'm out. I'm so out."

"*Nooo!*" Luna says, putting an arm around Jodie to usher her forward and toward the door. I loop an arm through Jodie's to join in the frog-marching. "Come on. You can do this! Just don't bring up last night."

"What do I do if *he* does?"

"You laugh it off."

"Tell him you were drunk," I suggest. "Usually works for me when I do something embarrassing."

The nerves are rolling off Jodie in waves. She fidgets with her clothes like she wants to bury herself inside them. "This is a really bad idea. You—you guys should come with me. I think you should come with me. Make sure I don't make a complete fool of myself."

"I think you already managed that," I point out. "It can't get any worse, right?"

She pulls a face at me while Luna locks the villa door behind us. She comes back with a big, beaming smile all for Jodie, who only looks more nervous for it.

"Come on, you'll be great! We have a plan, right? It'll be fine— trust us."

"What if he says no? What if he's not even there?"

"Then you can stop panicking about it and come hang out with us by the pool. And if he says no, you know he's not really interested, so you don't waste the rest of the week swooning over him. It's win-win," I say.

"Hmm."

I squeeze her arm. "Glad you're onboard. Now go. Flirt your melones off."

Jodie gives us an uneasy look, but takes a breath to steel herself and nods, determined—the girl who was ready to snap Esteban's head off the other night, not the one who spilled an entire drink down herself in front of a cute guy. I reach out to readjust her baggy camisole so it flatters her cleavage instead of hiding it, but she's so in her head she doesn't even notice.

"Okay. Okay, I've got this. I can *do* this. Right, I'll . . . see you guys later."

She leaves us and heads down the beach toward the bar instead of the hotel pool with us. She let me plait her hair this morning and the fishtail braid hanging over her shoulder really suits her, and the shorts with crochet detail that Luna convinced her to wear look adorable. She thinks *I* have long legs, but hers look great in those shorts.

Gabriel will have to be a fool not to go along with our plan.

Well, Luna's plan. Luna's pretty great with plans, it turns out. It was her idea for Jodie to ask Gabriel for a little one-on-one lesson on how to make cocktails, which we plotted out while getting ready for breakfast this morning. It's totally genius.

And foolproof, we hope, given how she went off the rails last night.

I have to bite the insides of my cheeks so I don't laugh again, thinking about the way she sent her stool clattering to the floor when she leapt off it and ran out of the bar and the bewildered look on Gabriel's face before Luna dragged me after Jodie.

I *so* wish I'd had my phone to immortalize the moment in video.

"She'll be great," Luna says, but it sounds like she's trying to convince herself more than me. And she kinda sounds like a mum who's just dropped her kid off for their first day of school. "She'll be fine."

"Hey, at least if it fails miserably, she should have a funny story to tell us."

We've barely been by the pool for an hour when someone moves into my sun, and stays there.

"Ah, Miss Rory, there you are. I missed you at breakfast."

Esteban. I suppress a sigh. Of *course* it's Esteban.

I turn my book over before I put it down to keep my page (Luna's books are in pristine condition, and I don't think she'd thank me for dog-earing it) and then I roll over so I can see him. I don't care enough right now to even pretend to smile at him. And after a bad night's sleep on that shitty sofa, I don't even feel too sorry about accidentally cutting the power yesterday.

"Oh, uh, yeah. I slept in."

Luna, bless her, had brought me croissants back from the buffet after I passed out on their bed partway through getting dressed to go to breakfast.

"I have been looking for you."

I glance at Luna, who tilts her head to peer at me over her sunglasses, ignoring her book to listen in on our conversation.

This can't be good.

"Oh?"

"After your little . . . *incident* yesterday, with the hotel electricity, we are still trying to restore power to several rooms. It is most inconvenient, as I am sure you can imagine. And it appears to have damaged one of our freezers, which has cost us several hundred euros' worth of food we have had to dispose of."

"Uh, that's . . ." I clear my throat, shuffling on my sun lounger and sitting up straighter. Where's he going with this, exactly? "That's annoying."

"And, of course, you left the bath running in your room, which caused damage to the renovated rooms below yours, including personal items belonging to our guests."

Fuck.

"Um," I say, then try to joke, "just as well there weren't any electronic devices there, then?"

Esteban smiles thinly. "Perhaps you're not aware, but part of the Casa Dorada policy covers intentional damage to hotel property by guests and the payment for such damages. Cost of reparations. It was all detailed in our booking terms and conditions. There is approximately five hundred euros of damage to other guests' property, and in the range of eight hundred in supplies and labor to repair the ceilings and paint . . . This will be offset against the fact we are not charging you for the accommodation for the remainder of the week, of course, but we shall have to bill you for the difference."

"Payment?" I repeat, my mouth turning dry. "Reparations?"

Crap. Crap, crap, crap.

He can't be serious.

I would switch places with Jodie's "lovely earlobes" moment in a heartbeat.

I am so screwed. So unbelievably screwed.

I swallow the lump in my throat, but it doesn't go anywhere.

I probably can't even afford to pay for *dinner* right now, never mind all *that*.

And I cannot ask my sisters or my parents to send me God only knows how much money to fix the mess I made here. They thought this week was going to be good for me. It was supposed to *help*. It was supposed to . . . fix me.

I ruin *everything*.

Then Luna bursts out with, "What?" before I can come up with a proper reply to Esteban. "No, I'm sorry, but that wasn't *intentional* damage. It was a complete accident. You were there! You saw. You can't possibly call that intentional damage and expect her to pay for it. It would never have happened if you weren't messing around with the plumbing for your renovations!"

Esteban turns to regard Luna for a long moment, one eyebrow arched, distinctly unimpressed. She falters quickly and ducks her head.

I wish Jodie were here. Jodie would really put him in his place.

Then he looks back at me and says with that awful, smarmy smile of his, "You will be able to find further details on this in—"

"The information pack?" I mutter, stomach churning.

His smile stretches wider, one side of his twirly mustache twitching. It makes him look like a knockoff cartoon villain. "Precisely, Miss Rory. I will be adding the cost of these damages to your final bill."

He turns sharply on his heel, hands clasped lightly behind his back as he begins to walk away, and all I can think is, *Hannah and Nic can never find out about this.*

I have to fix this. I have to—to—to do *something,* anything, to make those charges disappear from my final bill. Is this the sort of thing you can claim on travel insurance? I wouldn't even know where to start with that, and what if it doesn't cover the cost of the damages anyway? Maybe whatever policy they've got wouldn't stand up if I tried to fight it, but that'd probably require a lawyer, and it would *definitely* lead to my family finding out.

I can't. I can't bear that.

I cannot go home from this week, which is supposed to do me so much good, and look them all in the eye and say that I broke the hotel and now need someone to bail me out to the tune of hundreds of euros, and, hey, guess what? I am *still a complete loser,* who even fails at going on vacation for a week.

Bolting up from the sun lounger, I cry, "Wait! Esteban, what if . . . what if there's some kind of compromise we can come to here?"

He turns back, blinking at me patiently. "A compromise, Miss Rory?"

"Yeah. S-something . . . I don't know, something I—I can do to . . . um, so you won't . . . charge me for the damages," I stammer, floundering. "Like, I could . . . help out at reception? I'm good with computers. Or I could, er, wash . . . dishes?"

I'm aware of how batshit crazy I sound even as I'm saying it all, and Esteban looks mildly amused by my desperation, but I can't just let him walk away and slap some huge fine onto my bill. If I were more like Jodie maybe I'd stand here having a go at him until he backed down—but I'm not, and she's not here to do it for me.

And besides, I think, it's probably about time I started owning my shit and cleaning up my own messes, not relying on everyone else to do it for me.

I fully expect Esteban to laugh at me and tell me that's not how it works.

My heart is thundering so hard I think it might erupt right out of my chest. It's all I can feel; the rest of my body has turned completely numb. As soon as I notice it, I become way too aware of how difficult it is to breathe right now, and it all makes me feel so *stupid* that as I drag in an uneven breath through my nose, trying to focus on that, my vision goes blurry.

Oh my God, I *cannot* pass out right now.

I blink and my vision clears, but there's something wet on my cheeks.

Brilliant. Even better. I'm *crying*.

"Please," I beg, actually *beg,* because I can pretend to my family this week was totally great even if I spend the next few days mopping up the flooded rooms if I have to, but I might actually have a breakdown if I have to see the disappointment on their faces when they find out the truth.

"Or what about—hey, you've got that Kids' Club, right? I have experience working with kids. I helped out at a nursery for work experience last year, so I have like, a bunch of background checks and things, you know? If you give me my phone, I can show you. Maybe I could help out with that?"

Maybe Esteban finally takes pity on me and my tears, or maybe he can sense I'm about to have a full-on meltdown, because he says, "Actually, Miss Rory, I think that would be perfect. One of my staff did not show up this morning due to a family emergency, and I don't believe he will be back for the rest of the week. It will be nothing too difficult. We only need someone to be Larry the Lobster for a few days, until Stephen returns. A few hours a day, no more."

"I . . . er . . ."

What the hell is Larry the Lobster?

But this is what I was asking for, *begging* him for, and it's my way out. Larry the Lobster is my light at the end of the tunnel, my golden ticket.

So I nod as enthusiastically as I can manage, wiping the tears off my face, and say, "Yes! Yes, of course! I'd be happy to!"

"Excellent!" Esteban claps his hands and smiles more widely at me, showing his pearly whites. "I will give you a moment to finish your drink," he says, gesturing at the half-full cup of lemonade next to my sun lounger, "and then you can meet me in reception, where I will introduce you to your colleague for the rest of the week."

After he breezes away, hands clasped lightly behind his back once more, stopping every so often to have irritatingly cheery conversations with people, I sink back onto the sun lounger and bury my head in my hands.

"Oh God. I can't do *anything* right. I can't believe this."

"Just refuse to do it," Luna tells me, scowling behind her sunglasses. "He can't make you. Tell him you're not doing it."

"He's not making me," I point out. "You heard me. Offering to spend my vacation washing dishes instead of paying that bill."

"Well, he can't make you pay for that! He's a chancer. Like bad landlords who try to scam uni students out of their deposits for a busted toilet seat. He won't have a leg to stand on. I bet you could take him to court. You *are* about to do a law degree; you might not even have to get a proper lawyer—"

Just what I need. A sterling reminder of the life I absolutely do not want.

"No! No, I can't . . . I mean . . . Look, this is *fine*. I promise you. It's easier. And I don't mind, really. A couple of hours a day. It might even be fun."

"But—"

"This is *my* problem, Luna—not yours. I don't need you butting your way in, okay? I've—I've got this."

I have not, in fact, got this. But I have to try. It's easy for Luna to sit there and say I shouldn't stand for it, but she's not the one facing a massive fine and family disappointment. She's not the one who's poured her heart and soul into what she *really* wants for the last two years only for it to fizzle out into total failure.

I *have* to fix this.

So, if that involves being Larry the Lobster—whatever the hell that means—for a couple of days, then I need to suck it up.

Time to take some responsibility, Rory.

"It'll be fine," I tell Luna again, but it's more to try to convince myself than her. She looks a bit taken aback, her shoulders hunched. She doesn't quite meet my eye, which makes me bristle a bit. *All right, so I screwed up, I get it, I don't need you judging me, too.*

I finish my lemonade in a few gulps and hand Luna the book I borrowed from her. I leave my hotel towel on the sun lounger and put on my cover-up.

Larry the Lobster, here I come.

18 *Jodie*

The idea of even seeing Gabriel again after last night makes me wish the ground would just open up and swallow me whole. The entire walk to the beach hut, I'm hoping to stumble into a patch of quicksand. I would love to just disappear and not deal with this.

I mean, I *know* I could turn around. I don't have to humiliate myself like this.

But . . . I'm starting to feel like I have something to prove. Not just to the girls, or to Gabriel, but to myself. How long has it been since I really put myself out there? With someone I really, *really* liked?

How long has it been since I *liked* a guy, full stop?

And Gabriel . . . Apart from being maybe the most attractive guy I have ever seen in my life, I feel drawn to him in a way I've never experienced before. I can't stop thinking about the butterflies in my stomach when he looked at me, or the tingle that ran through my whole body when his hand brushed mine the other night. Don't I owe it to myself to see what that means? To find out if it was all in my head, or if he felt it, too?

Besides, what have I really got to lose if he rejects me?

So what if he does? I think. I can handle that. I'm a badass, like Rory joked yesterday. I'm *totally* capable of handling a little rejection.

I complimented his earlobes, spilled my drink all over myself, knocked over a stool and ran away—I cannot, in any conceivable manner, humiliate myself more than that.

I cringe again, replaying it in my head.

Rory was too convincing this morning for me to argue. She talked me into this about eight times over, like it was her new life's mission to make Gabriel fall in love with me. And then Luna had jumped on the bandwagon, coming up with the cocktail class plan, and I'd had the two of them finding me a perfect outfit and doing my hair and even picking out my jewelry for me.

I could've told them no, point-blank refused, and they'd have probably listened (okay, they definitely would've listened), but they'd looked at me like . . . like I could *do* this, like they really, honestly believed I could turn it all around. I didn't have the heart to disappoint them. Or myself, for that matter.

Because I *like* the version of me that they seem to see. This badass who can tell off hotel managers, rid the bathroom of creepy-crawlies . . . flirt with attractive bartenders like they're not way out of her league.

Mum and Gran would definitely be on their side, I think. They'd be pushing me to do this, and Gran would probably be cracking jokes and saying, "If I were fifty years younger . . ." They'll get a real kick out of the earlobes story, too.

For the first time all week, I actually, genuinely wish I had my phone—so I could call them, tell them everything, and we could all laugh about it. I want to tell them what a perfect specimen Gabriel is—yes, even his earlobes—and how I seem to forget how to be a functioning human around him, which is just so not like me. I want to call them so I can hear how excited they'll be for me.

I miss them.

My heart feels heavy with it, and it's more than just not talking to them for a couple of days. It's two years of rare visits home and being preoccupied with uni work most of the time I am back home. I probably won't get to see much of them next year either, and once I graduate . . .

I shudder, thinking of that future. Buttoned-up and corporate and impressive enough to make the girls from school jealous, always attached to my emails and probably with some horrible boss who expects me to work weekends and . . . *Ugh*.

But it's the dream, isn't it? That's the life I'm supposed to want.

Grimacing, I bury that thought as far down as I can. If this week is all about switching off, what better distraction than hoping for a date with one of the most drop-dead gorgeous men I've ever seen in real life?

Instead of some bleak, nightmarish future, I swap it out for a much sweeter, more enticing daydream—I start imagining flirting with Gabriel, that wonderful smile of his, working up the courage to kiss him . . .

Assuming I can work up the courage to ask him on a date first, of course.

I'm not far from the beach hut now, and my steps become slower, more reluctant.

It'll be a miracle if I can get a coherent sentence out.

It'll also be a miracle if he even gives me the time of day after last night.

According to Esteban's bible (aka the information pack), the beach bar serves drinks and light snacks after breakfast in the hotel ends. There's a small crowd there already. The beach isn't exactly quiet, either, with one exercise class (tai chi, maybe?) in progress, a handful of people sitting on towels and some swimmers already in the sea. A few hotel reps—Oscar included, I notice—are setting up a volleyball net.

An audience for my humiliation. Wonderful.

I come to a stop just in front of the bar, heart thundering in my ears and palms sweating. I can't do this. Can I? Am I really going to walk up and ask this total stranger to teach me how to make cocktails so we can have some privacy for me to flirt with him? He probably doesn't even fancy me. He was just being nice, and it's all in my head, and—

And, after all that, he's not here.

The man behind the bar is someone I don't recognize. He's old, with a weathered face covered in deep lines, thick gray hair, a full beard and a friendly smile as he talks to a guest while pouring their drinks.

My heart sinks, despite my reluctance. My nerves.

Of course he's not here, I think. *He must work night shifts. Why would he be here now?*

Then the old man turns to call over his shoulder, "Gabriel!" followed by a string of Spanish so quick I'm surprised even a native speaker can follow it.

"Sí, sí, vale," responds a silky-smooth baritone voice.

And . . . there he is.

Gabriel steps out from the back and sets down a broom, then goes behind the bar to do . . . something, I guess, for the old man. He moves around for a few minutes and I stand rooted to the spot.

God, he's fit. How *dare* anybody look that fit? His skin glows like bronze in the sun, and with his perfect hair and long eyelashes and toned arms on show once more, and the low, lovely sound of his voice—nobody should be allowed to be that attractive.

I suddenly feel so silly. Like the fishtail plait I let Rory do or the lipstick I put on is going to make *any* difference. My shoulders hunch and I readjust my camisole, not sure when it slid down so low. I'm plain and ordinary and have permanent bags under my eyes from being on the verge of burnout for the last two years straight. Why would he even bother to look twice? My hand goes to fidget with my glasses before I remember I put contact lenses in.

He hasn't seen me yet . . . I could just leave. I could walk away, find the girls at the pool and say he wasn't here. Pretend that he didn't just appear in all his swoopy-haired, dimpled glory.

I give myself a mental slap.

Come on, Jodie, you're better than this. You're getting yourself through uni when it's way beyond you, and you can do this. If you like this guy so much, go for it.

My attitude has always been "fake it till you make it." Throw myself in headfirst and hope for the best, not let anybody know that I can barely stay afloat, and figure it out as I go.

I'm not sure that's something I can apply to this situation.

Flirting is all about confidence. I'm scared that he'll see right through me and realize I don't have a whole lot of it.

Sure you do. You're a badass, remember? You'll only regret it if you go home and always have to wonder "what if."

I'm still mentally wrestling with myself when Gabriel reappears carrying a plate of nachos loaded with cheese and dips and jalapeño peppers. As he steps out from behind the bar with them, he catches sight of me standing there, scowling and lips pursed, fidgeting with my ring as I give myself a pep talk.

He doesn't smile or wave, just glides right on by to the table of a guy who was at the bar when I arrived and places the nachos down with a warm smile, saying, "Enjoy."

It feels like a slap in the face that he ignored me.

I mean, I know I made an absolute fool of myself last night, but still.

Ouch.

I'm about to spin around and storm back to the hotel to join Luna and Rory at the pool and hate myself a little more (and begin to hate him a whole lot) when Gabriel walks down from the cabana, his eyes fixed on me. The corners of his lips are quirked up and his dark eyes gleam, crinkled at the corners like he's trying not to smile.

"Buenos días, señorita," he says, acting all professional, although his face twitches. He's trying not to *laugh,* I realize quickly. I find myself relaxing a bit. "Can I get you a drink?"

I hesitate, tongue-tied.

He steps a bit closer—and it's not as though he's *that* close, but if I put my hand up, I could definitely touch him. My heart skitters unevenly. His grin splits wider now; he can't help himself. "Or have you only come here for my lovely earlobes?"

I'm torn between hurling myself face down in the sand and hoping for the tide to wash me away, and cracking up.

Luckily for me, my body reacts before my brain has a chance to think about it, and I'm laughing. *Giggling.* I'm even tucking a piece of hair behind my ear. "I'm so sorry about that. I'm not usually . . ."

"Faced with someone so charming and handsome as myself?"

I blush, biting my lower lip. (Since when do I bite my lip when a guy is flirting with me? Since when has that become a thing I do?) "Something like that."

Gabriel's smile turns soft, but his eyes stay fixed on mine, and sweet baby Jesus, those *eyes.* His brown irises catch the sunlight and glitter gold and copper.

Never mind throwing myself headfirst into things and figuring out how to tread water later: I could drown in those eyes and be happy about it. The way he's looking at me, maybe the girls were right—maybe my hopeless crush on him isn't quite so hopeless after all. I feel anything but plain and ordinary all of a sudden. I stand a little straighter, the tension in my shoulders unfurling.

"Where are your friends today?" he asks.

"Busy." I'm not trying to be all Mysterious Woman, but somehow it comes off like that, and I don't entirely hate it.

With renewed confidence, I take a breath and say exactly what Luna told me to: "Actually, I was hoping you could teach me how to mix cocktails. You know, kind of like a . . . private class. Just the two of us."

I don't cringe, which is a relief. I just wait for his answer.

Gabriel's mouth curves up on one side, bringing out his dimples and sending a new flurry of butterflies erupting in my stomach. "It would be my pleasure."

"What on earth are you doing here?"

Luna strides toward me, pool water dripping off her. I've barely sat down after getting back from speaking to Gabriel and she's already caught sight of me and gotten straight out of the pool midswim. She grabs her towel and pats her face off, then wraps it around her shoulders.

She looks behind me, eyes following someone, kind of like she's seen a ghost. Before I can look behind me, or to ask what she's looking at, her eyes snap back to mine.

"What happened?" Her face screws up into the most adorable pout. She looks downright heartbroken on my behalf already. "Did it go badly? Did he say no? Did you bail? Did you do something else weird?"

I laugh and tell her to shut up, waiting for her to sit down before I carry on. "He just told me to come back after the bar closes for siesta, when it'll be quiet and he doesn't have to work."

Luna squeals and stamps her feet, clapping excitedly. A few people look over, but I don't even care. I'm laughing and grinning, and I feel a thrill run through me.

I have a *date*. With *Gabriel*. A private mixology class on the beach with the sexiest bartender in the world.

Who am I? I hardly recognize this girl, but I love her.

Maybe she's—*I've*—got some self-confidence after all.

"Ohmigosh," Luna gasps. "I'm so excited for you! This is amazing. Did he say anything about last night?"

This time I do cringe, but relay the whole conversation to Luna as best I can remember it. It all feels like a blur. The only thing I can recall with any real clarity is that smile on his face, the way his eyes sparkled at me.

"Hang on," I say afterward, cutting off Luna's enthusiastic babbling. "Where's Rory?" I don't spot her in the pool, but some of her things are here.

Luna rolls her eyes, her expression twisting into something that borders on being pissed off.

Uh-oh. What drama did I just walk into?

"So Esteban waltzes over, right, like he does, and starts spouting all this rubbish about hotel policy, and terms and conditions, and how she'll have to pay damages for yesterday—"

"*What?*"

"I know, right? And then she panics and volunteers to work the debt off, and he agrees for her to step in as children's rep for the rest of the week. It's absolutely *ridiculous* if you ask me."

"That *is* ridiculous! Why didn't she just, like . . . I don't know, but I'm sure if she took it to an insurance company or a lawyer or something she'd never have to pay for damages. He can't do that."

Luna snorts, brow furrowing. "Try convincing her of that. I'm telling you now, Jodie: this place is *not* getting a good write-up from me online."

"Hmm," I say, trying to lighten the mood, not entirely sure if she's mad at Rory or at Esteban and not really willing to open up that can of worms. "I don't know. The beach bar more than makes up for it if you ask me. Twelve out of ten."

She cracks a smile, and I launch into chattering about what my private mixology class might be like and how I bet Gabriel is the best kisser on the planet, not caring how shallow I might sound or if I'm getting carried away, until a shadow falls over us.

A giant orange lobster stands there. Rory's voice, muffled by the suit, says, "If you don't kiss him, I will. Nobody can resist the raw sensuality that is *Larry the Lobster*."

19 *Luna*

By the time Rory leaves, I'm collapsed on the sun lounger with a stitch in my side, breathless, tears streaming down my cheeks, laughing harder than I can remember laughing for *months*.

She only stopped by to show off the costume and ask me to take her things back to the shack (I mean, our luxury private villa), because she doesn't know how long she'll be tied up with Kids' Club, and she'll just see us for dinner.

At least she doesn't seem mad at me anymore for trying to defend her. I didn't *mean* to interfere with her problems, but . . . I thought we were friends. Isn't that what friends do for each other? And for all her confidence and bluster, she doesn't strike me as especially independent . . . I was only trying to help.

Maybe she was just upset and didn't really mean to snap at me. But, even though it stung, the ridiculous sight of her in that lobster suit more than makes up for it.

The costume looks kind of cheap and a lot tacky, and Rory lumbers about in it when she makes her way back to the kids' pool, which is far enough away that we don't hear them shrieking and having fun or crying when they scrape a knee. She walks into an umbrella, barely catching it in her claws and arms before it can hit the ground.

"I wish I had my phone," Jodie laments.

"Why? To get a picture of her?" I snort. "She always looks so flawless—imagine if we'd uploaded a photo of her in that suit and tagged her in it or something. Made a joke about her sunburn getting out of hand—like a before and after!"

"That too," Jodie says, "but I meant so I could do some research. I've got like an hour till I go back to meet Gabriel. I could've been looking up things about cocktails so I actually have some idea when he's talking to me about them. Seem a bit less clueless."

"What? But you *asked* for a lesson. He's hardly expecting you to be an expert. What would be the point in him teaching you if you already know stuff?"

"Well, yeah, but—"

"And you don't want to do that thing where you pretend to be dumb just to make him feel smart so you guys can bond and he can feel good about himself. He seems like he'd see right through that. And somehow I can't imagine you pulling that off anyway."

"I know, but . . ." Jodie sighs, looking annoyed with herself.

Admittedly, maybe I don't know her half as well as I think I do after our three days of intense bonding, but I *do* know that she strikes me as the kind of person who doesn't like to be on the back foot or kept in the dark about something.

I can see she's getting worked up, so I take a different tack and reach across to squeeze her hand.

"You don't have to be the best at everything, you know. It's all right to not know what you're doing."

Something I say must hit home because Jodie goes quiet for a while.

When she does speak again, her hands are flapping and she's still frowning as she says, "Tell me to shut up and stop obsessing over a boy any time it gets old, please. I promise I'm never usually like this, and I mean *never*. I'm not this person."

"I hate to break it to you, Jodie, but I think you are exactly that person, obsessing over a guy you've just met and losing your *shit* over him and his earlobes."

And I'm so glad she is, because I get the feeling I'm going to be *exactly* like this when I start dating again.

(There's a chance I might already be losing my shit a little bit, though. I could've sworn I saw Liam walking by earlier.)

Jodie groans and presses her knuckles to her eyes.

I reach across to slap her hands away. "I saw you spend fifteen minutes on that eyeliner. Don't go messing it up now."

She drops her hands and looks at me with what I can only assume is complete and utter despair, her blue eyes big and sad, her lips twisted.

"It's okay," I tell her. "I like this Jodie."

She blows me a kiss.

Jodie and I grab some lunch in the hotel restaurant before she heads back to the beach for her date with Gabriel. I'm a genius, if I do say so myself, a matchmaker extraordinaire: Rory and I were sure he wouldn't be able to resist spending some time with her, and a beginner's class in making cocktails is the perfect excuse. I'm so glad she didn't chicken out.

I hope it goes well for her.

If only because it might give me a little more confidence about getting back in the dating game; if Jodie can make a comeback after last night's epic fail, I can make a comeback after breaking up with the guy who was meant to be The One.

And I hope Rory's afternoon as a giant foam lobster doesn't go too badly either, even though she did sort of get herself into that mess. Esteban never would've been able to claim reparations or damages from her, and I think she's backed herself into a bit of a corner by trying to make amends. It's as good as an admission of guilt, and I bet he *still* tries to slam her with a huge bill at the end of the week.

She's been gone for a few hours now, and I *still* haven't been able to work out why she went along with it all and offered to be a giant lobster at Kids' Club. I hate the nagging idea that it might just be so she doesn't have to spend so much time with me, that maybe she doesn't like the idea of hanging out with me without Jodie around. That maybe they *do* think they've been lumped with me, like everyone back at uni.

I can't be so bad that she'd pick Larry the Lobster over lying on a sun lounger next to me, can I?

I know it's not my problem to get so wound up over, but with Jodie on her fabulous date and Rory having ditched me to help run Kids' Club—it's just me and my heartbreak. All alone.

Although, I remind myself sternly, I AM TOTALLY OKAY WITH BEING ALONE.

It's not that. Obviously. Absolutely not.

It's just . . .

All right, maybe I *was* getting a little too used to them being around all the time, and to the feeling of having friends after weeks of loneliness in the wake of my breakup with Liam. I latched onto them when my phone and all connection to the outside world was snatched away from me. That's normal, isn't it?

Jodie was a bit short with me this morning, though. I thought she was just stressed out about her potential date, but maybe it wasn't only that. And Rory snapped at me, too.

Maybe it *is* my fault. They just want to enjoy themselves, and here I am, forcing my company on them and being a total pain just because I can't cope with being by myself.

Back at the pool with a fresh glass of Diet Coke, I put the umbrella up for some shade. A few people from this morning have disappeared somewhere out of the sun, and a few new groups have appeared. An aqua aerobics class starts running, led by Oscar. He tries to drag me into it, but I tell him I just ate, I couldn't possibly, I wouldn't want to make myself sick. He gives up pretty quickly.

Jodie had pointed out that they probably thought they could walk all over us because we're young solo travelers, but at least now it looks like we've lived up to their expectations of unruly youngsters spoiling the hotel's peace and charm. Blowing up the electrics, being patient zero for flooding . . .

I wouldn't want me involved in aqua aerobics, either. Who knows what havoc I might wreak next?

I settle onto my sun lounger, open my book and find my eyes flitting around the group of people by the pool. There are twenty-three of them. Twenty-five, if you count me and Oscar.

And I feel like every single one of them is looking at me. Wondering why I'm here by myself. Are they wondering if my friends have left me and what I must have done to get them to leave? What kind of person even goes on vacation on their own? I feel like they can all see it on me: her boyfriend didn't bother spending quality time with her anymore; their friends picked him over her; she's sad and boring and that's why she's all alone.

A rep walks past carrying a pile of towels, and I squint at her from behind my sunglasses, wondering for a moment if she does look like the girl off Liam's Instagram—until I realize she's probably about forty years old.

God, I *really* need to get a grip.

It makes me feel enough of an idiot that I finally manage to get stuck into the book I'm still holding open on my lap.

I finish the book before long; I hadn't expected to get through it so quickly, but I hadn't expected Rory to be gone all day, either. Instead of gathering everything up to go back to the shack and pick a new book, I reach for my beach bag and rummage through it for the book Rory was reading; if she's busy being Larry, she won't need it.

My hand closes on something papery and I pull it out.

But it's not one of my books. It's a notebook. Turquoise, with swirly gold writing on the front that says *boss babe*, and I can't decide if that's supposed to be ironic or not—knowing Rory, it could go either way. The pages are slightly warped from the leak in her room yesterday, I assume.

Despite everything in me that says this is someone else's private property and to *put it back where you found it, Luna,* I flick through the pages, curious.

It's not a diary—that much is obvious. It's lots of rough notes, a few sketches. The sketches are cartoonish—mostly of people, and they're good. Actually, no, they're *amazing*. There's even one of Esteban: she's got his twirly mustache and villainous, smarmy smile down pat. I knew Rory said she did art, but *this* isn't what I expected at all. There are some Post-its taped down on odd pages in the notebook so they don't fall out. A few cluttered pages that look like they used to be plans or schedules of some kind are scribbled over in thick blue felt-tip.

The notebook falls open near the middle when I let it, like they're pages Rory has spent a lot of time on.

~The Vacation Bucket List~

1. Write pros and cons list of actually doing the law degree you got an UNCONDITIONAL OFFER FOR
2. Write pros and cons list of doing literally anything but that
3. Consider other degrees to apply to through clearing?
4. Write pros and cons list of a gap year, just in case
5. ~~HAVE FUN! BE RESTFUL! PRACTICE MINDFULNESS!~~

6. ~~Talk to strangers (make friends??)~~
7. Try something new!
8. Figure out how to tell Mum and Dad and Nic and Hannah I don't want to do the law degree, never wanted to do the law degree, never will want to do the law degree, and might cry if someone mentions the law degree one more time
9.
10.

A vacation bucket list.

I stare at it for a long while. Rory's outburst last night makes a little more sense now; I remember what she said over dinner our first night here, about her family being worried for her mental health, and how she'd been struggling over what to do with her future. She and Jodie were stunned when I mentioned that I had a five-year plan, but it looks like I'm not the only person who wants some structure and organization in their life.

Reading the list, a pang of sympathy twists my stomach. I try to picture Rory doing something serious and studious, imagine her standing up in a courtroom in one of those wigs—and it's impossible. "Artist," though, that fits the person I know perfectly.

Can her family really not see that? Do they not want to, or does she not let them? She did mention all the art she'd shared on social media that she hadn't told them about . . .

For someone who seems so happy to be wholly herself, this list drives home just how much she must have to put a damper on that.

My heart aches for her; and just as I think I can't imagine pretending to be someone I'm not for other people's sake, I realize—that's exactly what I was doing with Liam and our friends. *His* friends.

Like last night, it's a realization about my so-called friends that cuts deep and makes me wonder if it wasn't a mistake to break up with Liam after all.

Turning back to the notebook, I realize how focused Rory's list is on things to appease her family rather than pursue her own goals, and I can see why she was so keen to fix things with Esteban to avoid having to pay damages.

I look at the items she's crossed off the list, too, and snort at "BE RESTFUL!"—not exactly how I'd describe this week so far . . . But she's also crossed out "make friends??" Because she has already? Or is that as much of a wasted idea as this week being "restful"?

I hope it's the former, but doubt starts to snake in, dark and venomous, digging its claws in as I look at the empty sun loungers on either side of me. Maybe Larry the Lobster *was* as much an excuse not to have to hang out with me as it was to make amends with Esteban.

Someone walks past my sun lounger and I jump, snapping the notebook closed.

My overtly guilty reaction reminds me I really shouldn't be invading Rory's privacy like this. It's none of my business, not unless she wants to bring it up and talk to us about it.

We all came here to run away from our problems. Who am I to dredge it all back up? I wanted to leave behind my heartbreak over Liam, Jodie needed a breather from pushing herself so hard, and Rory—she's faced with a future she can't see for herself.

I can relate to that.

So I put her notebook back where I found it, swapping it out for the book I lent her, and escape into the comfort of a fictional romance to try and numb the sting of how completely and utterly alone I feel right now.

20 *Rory*

The kids get picked up for lunch at one o'clock by their parents.

There aren't exactly many of them: only seven, between the ages of four and nine. I have a coworker with far more experience than me. Both of these things should go a long way to making this situation better.

And I guess they do, but it's still pretty damn awful.

When I've wagged my claw in a goodbye wave at the last kid (and possibly the only truly cute one of the bunch, with his missing front teeth and extremely polite manners and little round glasses), I finally, at long last, get to remove this godforsaken lobster head for a while.

The suit smells . . . not entirely *bad* or anything, but it's definitely got something distinctly *funky* about it.

And it's disgustingly hot.

My hair is plastered to my face and neck, and my face must be red and blotchy. I could probably still pass for Larry even without wearing his head. I have never felt so desperate to take a shower in my life. Whatever kind of snarky, self-deprecating captions I could come up with right now, there is no *way* any of this would be making it onto my social media.

The *actual* children's rep for Casa Dorada, Zoe, helps me out of the suit. She's way more practiced at it than I am and doesn't even wait for me to ask this time.

(I'd tried to go to the bathroom earlier before admitting defeat and waddling back, waving my giant claws helplessly, to ask her to help me out of the damn thing.)

Zoe, for her part, is lovely, and exactly how I'd picture a vacation resort children's rep. She's a couple of years older than me, curvy, with sandy-colored hair pulled into a high ponytail and an unfaltering, wide smile. She even manages to pull off the polo shirt, khaki shorts and white sneakers combo pretty well.

When Esteban introduced us this morning, Kids' Club was already underway, and she looked so grateful to have me there I felt slightly less resentful about this whole thing.

"Oh thank gosh," she'd gushed. "The twins have already cried because Larry isn't here, and I've had a tantrum from Danny about it."

The guy I'm replacing, Stephen, is nineteen years old and on a gap year, and has apparently bunked off to meet some friends in Barcelona for a few days. Zoe told me all this quietly, after Esteban had gone and out of earshot of the kids, while she helped me into the Larry the Lobster costume.

"I thought he had a family emergency or something? That's what Esteban said."

"Did he hell," she said, rolling her eyes, but there was something fond about it. Like an indulgent big sister. "He's already on a warning for showing up hungover once too often, so he came up with this whole scheme, rang in last minute this morning. Texted me to explain and apologize. Didn't think about leaving me in the lurch in the middle of the week with these kids, did he? And I couldn't get anyone at such short notice to fill in for him—it's a bit all hands on deck right now, trying to fix the flood damage and everything . . ."

I winced, and still couldn't help but ask, "Couldn't *you* have been Larry?"

(I may have volunteered for this, but I kind of thought I'd be playing ball games or doing finger painting. Larry the Lobster is looking less like my ticket out of this mess and more like my own personal nightmare.)

"Believe me, if I could be Larry, I would. It took me half an hour to calm the twins down. They're only five," she added, "and Stephen just made all the kids fall in love with Larry. I'm too short for the costume. I tried before, but the head fell off. Which, trust me, was its own kind of disaster. I had parents file complaints about the nightmares a giant headless lobster gave their kids. Besides, it'll be easier this way. I'll deal with the kids, you just have to . . . be Larry."

"What does that even mean? What do I do?"

"You'll see."

Being Larry, as I've now discovered, mainly means making slow, exaggerated gestures with my limbs and letting the kids clamber all over me and saying whatever Zoe prompts me to say.

"Isn't that right, Larry?" she'd ask.

"That's right, Zoe," I'd say, putting on my most exaggerated cartoon voice, my own personal parody of SpongeBob.

"And we never push someone, do we, Larry?"

"No, Zoe, we never push someone."

"We all know how to wait in a nice line for a drink, right, kids? Even Larry knows how to wait in a line."

"That I do, Zoe. Line up behind me, kids."

It should have been easy.

It was, I guess, but it was also hellish.

(And did I mention the suit smelled funky?)

I'm in no position to complain, on balance. This way, my family remain oblivious to the fact that I broke the hotel and incurred several hundred euros' worth (at least) of damage; I'm not responsible for *paying* that money back, or fighting Esteban over it; and everything will be hunky-dory.

Correction: *funky*-dory.

As the morning wore on, I kept expecting Esteban to burst back in and say, "Ah, Miss Rory, I am so sorry, but I made a mistake. This will not work out after all. You'll need to pay the money, señorita."

I kept hearing a phantom phone ring and Hannah demanding to know why she'd just received a massive bill, or my dad asking how I could be stupid enough to try to plug a hair dryer into a flooded room, and I could *hear* Mum's eye roll over my doing something as basic and incompetent as leaving the bath running.

As shitty as being Larry the Lobster is, it's not quite enough to distract me from the crushing anxiety of this entire situation.

Now that it's our lunch break, I give Larry's suit a wary look.

"Do I have to put that thing back on again?"

"Only for a bit at the end of the day," Zoe reassures me. "The kids like to say goodbye to him before they go."

That's a relief at least. Esteban had given me my own Casa Dorada polo shirt and a pair of shorts that is just a bit too small: the button cuts into my belly when I sit down and they're giving me a permanent wedgie.

Still better than wearing the lobster outfit, though.

(Even if they are currently all sweaty from me having worn them inside the costume for a few hours.)

Zoe has glitter smudged on her cheeks, arms and the front of her shirt from the arts-and-crafts session we ran earlier. There's a chocolaty handprint on her shorts, and her hair is forming a frizzy halo around her face.

She doesn't seem in the least bit bothered by it.

I run my fingers through my hair, trying to tidy it up, but I keep snagging on knots, so I quickly give up and pull it up into a bun instead, hating that I must look a gross, sweaty mess.

I've never been so glad this place doesn't allow phones. I think I'd die if someone caught me on camera right now.

With Larry the Lobster set carefully in his place in a back room of the Kids' Club area, Zoe leads me through the hotel to a staff room near the restaurant where there's a small kitchen and some tables.

"I brought lunch with me, but the restaurant will still be open for you to get something from there. You can just bring your plate back here; nobody will mind. Or, if you want to head out and find your friends, go for it."

I tell her I'll be back soon, and go and load up a plate with chicken Caesar salad and some of the freshly made, still-warm baguette that's so to die for I could eat a dozen sticks of it. *If there's one thing I've done right this week,* I think, *it's giving into my craving for carbs.* I get in and out of the restaurant quickly, not even pausing to look around for Luna or Jodie. I *really* don't want people seeing me in this state if I can help it.

Back in the staff room, Zoe is flicking through a magazine and eating pasta from a Tupperware container. She throws me a smile when I come in and sit down.

"So, Esteban said you were the one who tripped the electrics yesterday and caused our little blackout—*and* that you're responsible for the Niagara Falls coming down through the first floor."

I groan. "That so wasn't—"

"You don't have to convince me." She interrupts my outrage with a laugh. "I know what he's like, and the plumbing's already been a bit on the fritz. I'm not surprised he roped you into this. I bet he threatened to make you pay or something, right?"

"Exactly right," I mumble, and stab my fork into a chunk of lettuce.

Zoe nods, her round face all sympathy.

I can see she's about to ask more questions and I don't think I can deal with them right now, so I jump on the offensive, smiling as I ask, "How did you get roped into this, then?"

"It started out as something to earn extra money while I was studying, but I really love this kind of work, so I've come back every summer. I graduate this year, but I'm thinking of staying on beyond that. It's a nice place and the money's good. Esteban can be a bit . . . Well, you know. But everyone's so great. We're like a little family. I always thought I'd get a job in a secondary school or something, but working with little kids just feels like my calling."

"Makes one of us," I mutter.

I've quickly remembered why I decided against applying to be a primary school teacher after that stint doing work experience in a nursery last year. Kids are not my forte.

"Oh, they're not that bad! They're just energetic."

I look at Zoe like she's lost her mind—as if I am in *any* place to judge.

"You wait, they'll be sleepy this afternoon. We'll pop them down in front of a movie and some of them will doze right off. Piece of cake."

I hope so, I think, but stuff some bread into my mouth instead of saying it out loud. Zoe has such a great energy, and I feel bad for being such a buzzkill, but these next few days are looking like they'll be exhausting.

Still better than the alternative, I know, but it doesn't mean I don't get to feel bitter.

I am *nothing* if not a self-indulgent, dramatic bitch, after all.

Lunch done, we head back to Kids' Club to set the room up for the afternoon. Zoe chats away happily, seeming to not notice (or at least not mind) that I'm being a real mardy arse.

When the kids get back from lunch with their parents, they don't seem to notice my bad mood, either. The craft table is still set up, and one of the little girls sits there, scribbling away with Crayola, while the rest of them settle in front of the large projector screen for a movie. I sit at the craft table, too, slumped forward over my knees and half-asleep, my mouth hanging open and eyes drooping.

The girl tugs my arm.

"Psst," she whispers, not very quietly. "I made this for Larry when he comes back later."

"Uh, what . . ." I squint at the paper she's holding up and catch myself before I ask, *What is it?* The orange scribble on the page has four limbs with balls on the end of what I think are the arms. "Is that Larry?"

She beams, thrilled it's so instantly recognizable. There is dried tomato sauce smeared around her mouth. Ew. "Yeah! Do you think he'll like it?"

"He's gonna love it," I tell her, trying to sound enthusiastic. "How about you give it to Zoe to look after and go watch the film?"

The girl shakes her head. "No. I think I'll do another one. I didn't get his eyes quite right."

I try not to laugh out loud at that, but don't discourage her. Hey, my drawing skills used to be pretty bad, too. I find myself picking up a piece of paper for myself and a couple of crayons from the pot. Most of the drawing I've done in the last year or two has been for a specific purpose: because it's the kind of thing that's popular and when I post a video of it, it does well and makes me feel like I'm not wasting my time with it, and if it can just do well *enough,* then just maybe I can prove something to my parents, my sisters . . .

For a second I wonder when it stopped being so fun.

Nope, don't open that door, Rory. That is a shit show you do not want to deal with today.

My mouth contorts in a self-deprecating smirk. I know full well that I stopped enjoying it long before my followers and views and likes started their steady decline—the whole endeavor was something I kept pushing, kept trying, because I couldn't admit to myself that it had failed before it even started.

That's a door I don't need to open, because I know exactly what's behind it.

"Wow," the girl whispers, leaning over my arm after a while. She peers up at me with wide eyes. "What is it?"

"What do you mean, what is it? It's Larry."

She wrinkles her nose and squints at my page again. "But it's blue."

"You were using the red and the orange."

"Hmm. Well, it's *okay*," she says grudgingly, and then smiles proudly at her second scrawled drawing of Larry the Lobster. I grin at her, then look at the cartoon lobster on my page. So what if he's blue? I don't think it's too shabby.

I spend the rest of the movie drawing any animal the little girl tells me to, and teach her how to draw a basic cat, which blows her mind and keeps her quiet for a full twenty minutes as she draws a bunch of them in different colors.

And I'll never admit it to Esteban, but . . . I'm kind of having *fun*. I'm willing to concede that maybe I overreacted thinking how awful this was all going to be. But then the movie is over and the kids are going wild, and Zoe helps me back into the suit once more.

21 Jodie

It turns out I really do know nothing about cocktails. Sure, I already knew that, but I thought I had a *vague* idea from having at least drunk them before.

Not the case.

Gabriel and I stand close, not quite touching, removed from the rest of the hotel—the rest of the world—in that little cabana on the beach. Gabriel's near enough that I can feel the heat of his body, and every so often his elbow brushes against my arm and sends a little zing of electricity through me.

And I'm *sure* that he goes out of his way to touch me.

"Excuse me," he murmured at one point, one hand braced against my bare arm while he leaned around me, his chest brushing my back as he reached to grab a liquor. I'm sure he lingered, just a bit.

I can't say I minded in the slightest.

"So what got you into bartending?" I ask when we've exhausted the initial small talk and he has paused between instructions and explanations.

He shrugs, and it's a small, contained gesture that looks almost shy. "I needed a job, and the rest is history."

Oh. Not the answer I was expecting. Not that I'm really sure *what* I was expecting, but it's closed off, a total contrast to his otherwise easygoing manner, which makes me all the more curious.

"Did you go to uni? Or, um, do you?" I'm not totally sure how old he is.

Gabriel shakes his head, preoccupied with cleaning a cocktail shaker. A faint smile tugs at his mouth, his eyes far away. "I wasn't exactly the, ah . . . type. More of a free spirit when I finished school a couple of years ago." He glances at me with a twinkle in his eye. "I was quite a troublemaker, too."

"You're not anymore?"

He shrugs. "A while ago, I signed up for online classes. I am training to qualify as an accountant."

"Oh wow. That's—" Bland. Boring. Very, very normal.

It must show on my face because Gabriel laughs. "I know. It's not what I saw myself doing, either. My old teachers wouldn't believe it if you told them. But I'm interested in how businesses operate, and I'm good with numbers. The classes fit around this job well, and Esteban has been good about moving my shifts to accommodate exams. He's open to offering me a role here dealing with the hotel's finances, too."

I almost snort. That's the first I've heard about Esteban being good at *anything*.

But I say, "Wow. That's amazing. So is that your plan, then? To stay here?"

I cringe as soon as the words leave my mouth, but if Gabriel thinks I sound like I'm putting him through a formal interview, he doesn't acknowledge it.

"Sí, quizás. I grew up here, and I never imagined myself staying. But who knows? By the time I've qualified, things might be different. I always liked the idea of living in England after my cousin moved there and enjoyed it so much, so perhaps I will look for a job there like she did. Or maybe I will like it here too much with a new job to leave."

"You don't like this job?"

"I love this job," he says, and I can tell he means it. "But that doesn't mean it is my only passion. There are other things out there. I would like to try everything. Isn't that what it's all about?"

He flashes me that dashing, devastating smile of his, and my heart gives a little squeeze, making it suddenly hard for me to breathe.

But—isn't that *exactly* the point of a summer romance like this? After all, I didn't ask him for this date with the idea that if it went well, he'd chase me to the airport to propose at the security gate.

"Totally," I say as breezily as I can manage. "Like, I've been working super hard at uni, and I feel like now I deserve to have some fun. Let loose a little. Just enjoy myself for a few days."

Gabriel picks up a couple of bottles, then grabs a lime out of a bowl and sets it on the counter. And then he says, "I understand. So, think you are ready to try making your first drink?"

As he guides me through a couple of measurements and talks about the ingredients and method, I ask him what sort of troublemaker he used to be at school, and he tells me stories about harmless pranks pulled on teachers, an endless string of detentions for being too talkative and disruptive, the after-hours party in the school gym he helped organize, and how, when the caretaker almost caught them, he and a few others ran out to cause a commotion to let everybody else get away before they were caught, too.

"I bet you had the girls falling all over you," I say.

"I broke my share of hearts. But I was young and reckless then."

I raise an eyebrow. "And you're, what, old and wizened now?"

He blushes a bit. "I'm twenty-one. Not quite."

Before I can ask if he's still breaking his share of hearts, he tells me about the tattoo he got in secret when he was seventeen, but when I ask where, he just winks, leaving me to wonder.

I'm a little more forward, emboldened by his flirtatiousness, and I pull down one strap of my camisole and let it slip low enough to show off my tattoo.

Gabriel laughs at it, his callused fingertip tracing lightly along the edge. His touch sends a shiver down my spine. "A flower?"

"What's so funny about it?"

He laughs again, then drops his hand and leans back to look me in the eye. The sunlight catches his face, making his skin glow and his eyes sparkle. "You seem so . . . so tough, ¿sabes? I would not have expected you to have a tattoo of something so delicate."

I blush, oddly flattered, and explain, "It's honeysuckle. My grandma's favorite. Traditionally, it means gratitude and love."

"You're close to your grandmother?"

I nod, smiling. "It's always just been the three of us, you know? Me, Mum and Gran. Mum worked a lot when I was growing up, so Gran was always there to help look after me. She lived with us till I was about thirteen—she moved out because she said we were, and I quote, 'cramping her style.' But she only moved down the road, so she was still there if we needed her. And, I mean, Mum still works a lot now. Not that that was ever a bad thing. She was always around when I needed her, same as Gran was. Always showed up to hockey matches and things; she just wanted to give me the best life she could."

Gabriel smiles, looking a little amused—and I realize how snappy and defensive my voice turns as I tell him about my family, when there's no need to be. I bite my lower lip.

"Sorry. Um, yeah. The short answer is, yeah, we're close."

I feel like an idiot; he didn't ask for my life story, after all. So I tell him his English is really good, hoping to change the subject.

It works, or maybe he just senses I'm done talking about my family for now.

"I watched a lot of British television to improve it. I'm a big fan of *Doctor Who*." He sings a few bars of the theme song, eyes lighting up. "I think you would call me a, ah, ¿cómo se dice? A Whovian. I have seen all of the classic episodes. But, ah, Ten and Rose . . . Forget any of this Nicholas Sparks, chica; now, *that* was a romance."

He teaches me how to make a Harvey Wallbanger because it reminds him of the episode "The Unicorn and the Wasp," with the Doctor and Donna.

I can't help but laugh when he tells me this, even if I have no idea what he's talking about. "Oh my God, you're *such* a nerd. You're a *proper* nerd. You know the episode names and everything."

Gabriel blushes, but his smile doesn't vanish—he knows I don't mean it in a bad way. I'm not ripping into him for it.

I just . . . didn't expect it. At all. The MCU, maybe. Star Wars, sure. But *Doctor Who*? I watched a few episodes with Gran on a

Saturday when I was little, or the Christmas specials, and when I tell Gabriel, he launches into an impassioned speech about just how great the show is. He tells me he will recommend episodes for me to watch so I can let him know what I think of them.

It's my turn to blush, then. He says it like he's going to get my number and text me after I leave.

He asks what I do, and I say I'm about to start my final year of a biology degree and need to start applying for jobs soon.

"What do you want to do?" he asks.

And, quite honestly, I tell him, "D'you know, I have no idea."

I feel like that should terrify me. It's the first time I've admitted it out loud.

But . . . it doesn't.

Gabriel's handsome brow furrows. "Don't you enjoy it?"

"Yeah, I guess. I mean, I'm . . . It's what I was supposed to do. Mum and Gran worked so hard, and I was meant to be the first one in my family to go to uni, and I liked biology. I like some of my classes. The data stuff, mostly. Computational methods, that kind of thing."

"And you called *me* a nerd," he says, his tone affronted, but there's a gleam in his eye and he nudges me playfully with one shoulder. He doesn't quite move away after but leaves his arm pressed against mine, and for a moment it's all I can think about. I'm pinned by the weight of his gaze, breath catching in my throat.

I tear my eyes away from his, fumbling to recover the thread of what I was saying. "Anyway, I guess I only went because I was supposed to, and I've worked myself to the bone trying to do well enough to make it all worth it, but now I'm faced with the reality that it's almost over, and I have to apply for jobs . . . I guess it just . . ."

The words taste like iron, and I can't quite manage them.

But Gabriel says quietly, "You wonder if it is all worth it?"

"Yeah," I whisper. "And I'm not sure what to do about that. It's kind of why I agreed to come here. My family thought I deserved a break, and . . . I wanted to not have to deal with reality for a little while. A little fun and escapism, like I said, you know?"

He nods and shifts away slightly, as if to punctuate the end of that conversation, acknowledging the space I wanted from that particular problem.

And, of course, we chat about cocktails.

Gabriel talks about the entire process, the difference little things make, the various flavor combinations and presentation styles. He speaks almost with reverence for what is, ultimately, just booze and fruit juice.

But honestly he could be saying just about anything and I'd still be hooked on his every word. He could be telling me about the tread on car tires or Victorian architecture for all I care; it's just nice listening to him speak. I let myself get carried by the low cadence of his voice, like a tide pulling me out.

But I am glad he's not talking about the tread on car tires or Victorian architecture.

It also turns out I don't know how to cut a lime—or at least don't know how to cut it the right way, because when I start carving out a wedge, Gabriel chuckles and says, "No, querida, así."

And then he steps behind me, leaning unashamedly over my shoulder and placing his arms around me and his rough hands over mine, guiding the knife.

I don't think I would have noticed if I'd sliced my own hand open, I'm so pathetically wrapped up in the fact that *Gabriel has his arms around me and is pressed up against me and nobody has ever smelled this good and oh—my—God.*

I'm acutely aware of how his hips slot behind mine, the firm, lean muscles of his legs and the brush of fabric against the back of my bare thighs. His breath is hot and tickles the sensitive skin of my neck, and it takes all my willpower not to drop my head back onto his shoulder.

Heat pools low in my stomach, and I hope he can't see how flushed I am.

When Gabriel steps back beside me, smiling and saying, "You see?" I get a little more control of myself. Enough to look at the lime wedge he's cut that, considering it's *just a piece of lime,* looks much better than the one I'd done.

"Oh! Right, yes," I say.

He puts his right hand on the bar and leans against it, but his left hand is on my back and my heart is hammering like I can't remember it ever doing before. It wasn't beating this hard when I had my first kiss, I don't think, or even when I was frantically refreshing the UCAS website on A-level results day to see if I'd got into uni. I don't remember ever feeling this delirious. I'm completely swept up in everything *Gabriel* in a way that feels so new I kind of hate myself for giving in to it so quickly.

It's been a while since I've been seriously interested in a guy, but it feels second nature when I turn and lean more toward Gabriel. His hand shifts slightly on my back. His smile is small and his eyes are fixed on mine.

He looks at me in a way that makes me feel I'm the only thing in the world worth seeing.

It makes me feel anything but plain or ordinary.

I put the lime slices into the caipirinhas we made. I hold one of the glasses out to him, and his fingers brush against mine as he takes it.

"Cheers," I say. My voice sounds softer and quieter than I'm used to. Sultry, almost.

"Salud." His own voice is a murmur that feels like a caress.

Our glasses clink against each other, and we both take a sip. It's colder than I expected and it's got one hell of a kick to it. I have to work hard not to sputter—that would definitely ruin the mood.

(And, unless I'm very much mistaken, there is a *mood*.)

Gabriel doesn't take his eyes off me as he takes his own sip of caipirinha and makes a small appreciative hum. "Not bad. For a beginner."

I laugh, nudging him. "It's all down to the teacher."

"Well, in that case, I am an excellent teacher."

I poke the straw around the crushed ice in my drink absently before saying, "Thanks for this. I've had a really fun afternoon."

"Me too. I'm glad we spent this time together. I've enjoyed getting to know you, Jodie."

His accent is a little more pronounced when he says my name, but it doesn't grate on me the way it does when Esteban calls me "Ho-dee." I feel my cheeks flush and hope he'll think it's just from the alcohol.

Gabriel seems to shift closer. There's hardly any space between us now. He sets his glass down and takes mine from me and puts it down, too. It feels like it's all happening in slow motion, and I can only watch and try to remember to breathe.

(Am I breathing too loudly?)

Thinking about that only makes me more conscious of how I'm breathing, and I can *hear* myself catch my breath when Gabriel lifts a hand to cup my cheek. His fingers are cold from holding the drink. He tilts my face up toward his and the rest of my body follows suit. I lean up toward him, my hands coming to rest on his shoulders for balance. His left hand is still on my back, warm through my shirt, anchoring like a magnet behind that heat pooling in my stomach. I bite my lower lip lightly, only for half a second, and Gabriel's eyes flit down to my mouth.

Instead of waiting for him to kiss me, I close my eyes and lean the rest of the way in, and it—is—*heavenly.*

The hand on my back tugs me closer so I'm flush against him, his other hand splaying back into my hair, which sends a shiver down my spine and makes me arch into him. I feel the low moan in the back of his throat, and it's not like the pull of the tide—it's a whirlpool, one that makes me lose all sense of everything as I get pulled under by it. I cling to his shoulders as his mouth moves over mine, and my tongue is in his mouth. He tastes like lime and cachaça.

It's been a little while since I kissed a guy, but I'm pretty sure that I've never felt so weak in the knees before.

When we do break the kiss, it feels like it takes an age for us to peel away from each other. Gabriel's nose bumps against mine until I drop down from my tiptoes, and then he lifts his head. My hands slip down from where they hooked around his neck and rest lightly on his chest instead. I can feel his heart thundering, an echo of my own. The fingers of his right hand trail from my hair to my cheek to my elbow and the arm around me slackens a little.

"We will be opening soon," he says quietly. He looks over at the clock, giving me a view of his profile. His full, pouting lips, swollen from kissing, and his slightly upturned nose and—in all fairness, he does have nice earlobes, I suppose, as far as earlobes go. Then he looks back at me. "In ten minutes. I will need to clear this away."

"Then we've still got plenty of time," I tell him, and lean in for another kiss.

22 Luna

Jodie returns to our shabby little villa totally giddy, which is kind of weird to see. She doesn't strike me as someone who would be head over heels for a guy she barely knows, but . . . well, I guess she is. And she looks a million times more relaxed than the girl from the beginning of the week with bags under her eyes and such tense shoulders. I toss her a smile and finish wrapping my wet hair in one towel, then hold the other firmly around me as I bend over my suitcase for some clean underwear.

"Date went well, then?" I ask.

Instead of telling me it wasn't a date, she beams and collapses onto the bed with a wistful sigh. "I never want to leave. This place is paradise."

I cast a disparaging look around the room we're sharing. The more I look, I swear the more things I notice wrong with it. Right now, it's a crack in the ceiling running from the overhead light to the window. "Well, they say love is blind . . ."

She just laughs.

While I get ready, Jodie gushes about how well the date went and how perfect Gabriel is and how good-looking and funny he is and how sexy his voice is and how she has never met a guy who smelled half as good as him—*and* how she's never heard anybody sing the *Doctor Who* theme tune so well before.

"You what?"

"He's a big ole nerd," she tells me with that same wistful tone in her voice. "Anyway . . ."

She's only been talking a few minutes (and a mile a minute) when Rory gets back. We hear the door slam downstairs, some muttering and then feet stomping up the staircase. Jodie falls silent and sits up and both of us turn to see Rory standing in the bedroom doorway with her hands on her hips and her pretty face twisted into a scowl.

She's in a Casa Dorada polo shirt and a pair of shorts like the rest of the staff wear. Her hair is a complete mess: frizzy and sweaty, half fallen out of the bobble. There are sweat stains and a wet orange mark on her polo shirt.

"You are aware," Jodie tells her slowly, "that those shorts are giving you a camel toe."

"Please," she mutters, "that's not even the worst of it. This wedgie is going to haunt me for years, I know it."

This is worse than the lobster outfit she showed up in earlier. Instead of laughing, I just feel sorry for her. (Which, okay, may or may not have something to do with the stuff I read in her notebook earlier.) "Rough day?"

"Don't even."

This time, at least, I'm pretty sure her curt tone has nothing to do with me.

Rory storms past me close enough for my nose to wrinkle. She smells like she's done an intense cardio session at the gym. She slams the bathroom door behind her.

And then she opens it a second later. "Are you gossiping about the date?"

"We are."

She hesitates, looking torn, before saying, "Nope, sorry, I need to shower. You'll have to hang fire on the gossiping. I can't deal with the stickiness."

Jodie and I sit in silence until we hear the shower running. I hold my hands up. "I tried telling her. I told her she didn't have to do this. I hate to say it, but she got herself into this mess."

"I don't blame her," Jodie mumbles. "I bet Esteban would've found some loophole and made her pay up, even if she *did* get a lawyer to fight it."

"Hmm," I say, although I know that if *I* were the one being confronted by Esteban, I wouldn't be half as outspoken as I am with Jodie or in my head. I tried earlier, and I didn't exactly hold my ground very well.

Jodie fidgets, pottering about and rearranging her clothes while we wait for Rory to finish up in the bathroom. I'm using the hair dryer so that she can't really talk to me, and it's obvious not being able to is eating her up inside. She's *desperate* to gossip more about her afternoon with Gabriel.

I try to remember the last time I felt like that about Liam. I draw a blank—but then again, they don't call it a honeymoon period for nothing. Isn't that just how relationships *get* when you've been in them a while? Who needs sparks and excitement when you can have stability and comfort?

Not that our relationship had been very comfortable by the end, I have to admit to myself. Not when it was peppered with resentment over the tiniest things, terse sighs and constant bitter compromises.

I keep blasting my hair with the hair dryer, if only to stall Jodie while I try to get Liam out of my mind. It definitely doesn't help that I thought I saw him and the girl in the photo around the pool earlier, even though I was mistaken both times. How typical when this is the first time all week I've actively *wanted* to put our relationship behind me rather than cling to it.

Eventually, Rory comes out of the bathroom, looking more like herself. Even with her hair wet and scraped back and a green face mask smeared on, she looks infuriatingly pretty. I'm quite sure I've looked worse *after* putting makeup on.

I almost wish we'd been able to take a photo of her when she got in. That'd be the kind of photo you set as the group chat icon, just to constantly remind everyone of a funny memory you shared.

I'm hit with a weird sense of something that feels like nostalgia as I wonder if the three of us will stay in touch after this week is over.

I wonder again, fleetingly, if this is just a bond borne out of convenience—something to tick off a vacation bucket list. I shove the thought down, though, and refuse to dwell on it.

With a while until dinner, we sit on the bed to chat.

Jodie, obviously trying to be polite and show some restraint, says, "Did you get up to much today, Luna?"

"Not really," I say. "Did some reading. Swam a bit. Took a nap. Exactly what a vacation should be."

Which it was, but . . .

Actually, it was kind of boring and miserable compared to the other days we've had here so far. I missed having the girls around, far more than I expected to for people who'd been complete strangers to me only a few days ago.

But that sounds clingy and weirdly intense, so I don't say it for fear of making myself come across like some desperate loner.

"Tell us about the date," I prompt Jodie, and she doesn't hesitate. Her whole face lights up and, cheeks flushed, she tells us all about it. She has Rory and me cooing and squealing and laughing as she recounts as much of her and Gabriel's conversation as she can remember and then launches into an epic tale of their steamy kiss.

"I mean, I just totally get it. All those moments in the movies where the camera spins around and the music swells and it's this electric moment. I *get it*. It was just . . ." She trails off with a stupid smile still plastered on her face.

"Well, let me tell you," Rory cuts in, after Jodie doesn't carry on, "my day was every bit as magical. And by magical, I mean cursed by some vengeful hag. I had to let the kids climb all over me in that god-awful costume and act like a complete prat and, ugh, it's so sweaty in that thing. And the *smell* . . . Larry is haunted by the stench of a thousand sweats. Actually disgusting."

She explains that by the time she joined everyone they had just finished a game of volleyball in the kiddie pool and started crafts and story time. She gets up to prance around the room, gesturing wildly as she mimics all the ridiculous things she had to do wearing the lobster costume.

"And then we put them down in front of a movie—"

"You got to watch a movie?" I burst out in shock, and then put a hand over my mouth. "Sorry. It just feels like forever since I've seen a screen. It's a bit weird."

"Don't get too excited. It was only *Paddington*."

"Great film," says Jodie.

"Anyway. They would not. Sit. *Still*. Or shut up. Zoe said they're normally not like that, but I bet they are. I honestly don't know how she does it. She actually *enjoys* it, too. Which either makes her crazy or me a terrible person."

Jodie laughs. "Obviously, you're a terrible person. Right, Luna?"

"Right. The worst. Utterly heinous."

"Call up the subreddit: Am I the Asshole? The verdict is in. The internet says, 'Rory, you are, in fact, the asshole.'"

She pulls a face that I've never seen anyone achieve without a TikTok filter, a weird Grinch-like smile that gives her about five chins and shows all her gums. "Why, thank you, I do try. But seriously—it was hell. I mean, you know. It wasn't *all* bad, I guess. I did have a little bit of fun. But I don't know how Zoe does it day in, day out like that. All it did was make me remember why I decided not to go into teaching. I don't have the patience to be dealing with little kids like that all the time . . ."

"Didn't you say your sisters have kids?"

"Nicola's got a baby. Who is adorable and who I love very much and don't mind babysitting, but he's family. That's different."

"And just think," Jodie says brightly, patting Rory's knee, "you get to do it all over again tomorrow!"

Tipping her head back, she groans, the noise going on for a good long while.

When she finally quiets down, I say, "You know, you don't *have* to go back tomorrow. Just tell Esteban it's not happening. This is *your* vacation. He can't force you to help run Kids' Club, and you shouldn't put up with it. Plus, I mean, you volunteered. You can just . . . *un*volunteer, I'm sure. He can't stop you."

Rory's face twists like she's got half a dozen responses to that and can't decide which one's best. In the end she just shrugs and looks at her lap, saying, "I mean, for all my complaining, it's not so bad really. It's okay. Doing drawing with the kids was fun."

I stare at her, unable to help the way I'm gawping. Am I the only one who thinks this is nuts? I can't be.

And apparently I'm not, because Jodie pipes up, "But this is your *vacation.* You're meant to be spending the next few days enjoying yourself, not—not being miserable and putting up with all that crap."

"It's fine. I don't mind. Not really."

It's clear she does mind, very much, but it's also clear that we're fighting a losing battle; Rory doesn't want our help. Jodie throws her hands up in defeat, and I think about Rory's notebook, about her ongoing crisis and what seems like a deep-rooted need to people-please. I want to say she's not messing things up if she tells Esteban where to stick it and that she doesn't need to seek *his* approval for anything, but I bite my lip to stop myself, knowing it's absolutely not my place. She's made that quite clear.

Suddenly Rory perks up, clapping her hands, her face transformed by a huge grin. "Oh! Oh man, I totally forgot! We were talking about a girls' night. Tomorrow."

My stomach gives a funny twist, that nasty, creeping doubt from my afternoon alone at the pool starting to rear its head again.

"We?" I ask.

"Zoe and me! I was saying how we've been going to the beach bar and—"

"You didn't mention about me, did you?" Jodie blurts, paling. "Please say you didn't tell her what an idiot I've been about Gabriel. I made enough of a fool of myself without that getting back to him."

Rory grins. "Course I didn't. But Zoe said there's this great club in town, not too far."

My face scrunches up. "Are we even allowed?"

"*Technically* there's no rule saying we can't leave the resort." She waggles her eyebrows. "So? What do you guys think? We'll get out of this place for a bit. Have some proper fun! Think we deserve it after all the chaos, don't you?"

"Sounds like a great idea to me. I didn't bring my littlest black dress for nothing." Jodie scrambles off the bed and rummages in the wardrobe, swinging out a black tube dress with thick straps crisscrossing in the front. It's so tiny I don't think it'd go over one of my legs, and it'd probably fit Rory's willowy frame like a tube top.

Rory squeals, wriggling with glee. "I love it! Ooh, it's going to be so fun. First round's on me!"

They both look at me, which is when I realize I haven't so much as nodded yet.

I paste on a smile. "Sounds great!"

My idea of "fun" has never really involved a night out. I've enjoyed myself well enough when I've gone along with my flat-mates or friends from my course this year at uni, but mostly my experience of it has been tainted by Liam getting blackout drunk and acting like a tool, showing himself up in front of his friends and then being completely miserable when hungover.

The idea of a night out in some random Spanish club doesn't exactly fill me with excitement—not the way it clearly does Rory and Jodie.

And I hate that I feel weird about Zoe being invited along. I'm too busy trying to shove the feeling down to work out *why* I feel this way in the first place. Some petulant, childish part of me wants to argue that we don't even know her, and why can't we hang out just the three of us?

But I know that's selfish and silly of me, especially when Zoe sounds perfectly lovely from everything Rory's said so far.

"You sure?" Jodie crosses her arms, the hanger still in her hand, one eyebrow raised. She smirks at me. "You don't look very enthu-siastic."

Boring, boring, you're so boring, you're never fun or spontaneous, and that's why things didn't work out with Liam and all your friends picked him and—

"Well, we don't have to go. I just thought it'd be fun. A bit dif-ferent," Rory says quickly.

I refuse to be a sourpuss.

"No! No, it—it does sound lovely. Really. I . . . It's only that I don't have anything to wear."

Rory snorts. "Don't you worry about that. We'll find you something."

The two of them haul my suitcase onto the bed before I can stop them and then they're grabbing clothes and pulling things from the wardrobe. My immediate reaction is to be horrified and resent all the refolding I'll need to do later, but it's not long before I get swept up in it. It's nice to be so actively included and not just brushed off. They put together outfit after outfit for me, and for each other, the three of us giggling over the awful clothes we used to wear when we first started going to parties at school and the ridiculously big heels we thought looked so cool. I start thinking that maybe a night out on the town might be just what we need.

23 Rory

At breakfast Luna tries to talk me out of being Larry the Lobster again, which I don't totally appreciate. We're all up early today—me because I have to be at Kids' Club for half nine, Luna because she decided to go to the yoga class at six and Jodie because she couldn't sleep through the two of us pottering around and getting ready.

(Not that I'm entirely sure why I bothered to put makeup on or do French plaits when I'm only going to be stuck in that lobster suit and sweating buckets all day.)

"I don't understand why you don't just sack it off," Luna says, looking at me crossly while I dig into my pancakes. "He's not *actually* going to make you pay up."

Jodie snorts. "Bet he will."

Luna rolls her eyes, cutting Jodie a look as if to say she's not helping. Which she's absolutely not. I immediately imagine Esteban with a cartoon villain grin under his mustache as he slaps some hideously expensive reparations bill on the desk when I check out.

"I don't want to chance it," I tell them. "It's fine. This is my shit to deal with, okay? Besides, Zoe will be there with me. Maybe it won't be that bad."

It will be, but I'm determined to get through it. That's all I have to do—get through it. Then it can just be a funny story we all laugh about, and maybe I'll even eventually tell Hannah and Nic about it and we'll scream with laughter as I paint them a picture of how silly I was "back when."

Luna huffs, stabbing a hash brown with her fork. I don't know what *she's* got to be so worked up about. *She's* not the one who has to put up with screaming kids all day dressed as Larry the Lobster. *She's* not the one who'll get it in the neck if Esteban decides to send home an invoice. Luna looks like she's got a lot more to say about it, but I'm grateful that she doesn't.

I'm not like her or Jodie, with a five-year plan or a fierce work ethic. I'm not put-together, independent or decisive, and I've never been good at standing up for myself. Up until this whole debacle with the law degree, which is one thousand percent my own damn fault, I haven't *needed* to. I've always had my parents and sisters to lean on.

I've also never been good at taking responsibility. And this feels like the kind of thing I should take responsibility for—even if it is ridiculous as all hell.

Not that any of that is easy to explain, so I just roll my eyes, stay quiet and let Luna, who clearly thinks I'm being a prize fool, avoid my gaze and let Jodie sigh because she thinks exactly the same.

Of course, a short while later when I've changed into the ill-fitting Casa Dorada uniform and am stepping into the lobster costume, I wish I had listened to them and just said *fuck it* and not gone along with this and damn the consequences.

"I asked Luna and Jodie about a girls' night out," I tell Zoe in an effort to distract myself. "They're up for it."

"Brilliant! That's great news. Oh, I've been dying for a girls' night out lately. I'll book the taxi for ten."

"Ten? Didn't you say the club's half an hour away?"

Zoe laughs. "It probably won't start getting busy till one! You might want a little siesta before we head out."

My impulse is to text the girls and forewarn them, which I obviously can't do. I'll just have to remember to find them at lunch and let them know.

Zoe is chattering away about how great the place is—the cheap drinks, the cheesy music, the fit bouncer she tries to chat up every time she goes there . . .

I haven't had a proper good night out in a long time—all my friends have been so *boring* with knuckling down to revise for exam season—and I'm already feeling buzzed just thinking about it. Zoe seems to be endlessly chirpy, and judging by our previous nights here at the resort, I know Jodie and Luna will be great company too. I'm actually feeling pretty cheerful by the time I'm about to pull the lobster head on.

And then Zoe says, "Oh, er, and just to let you know, we're taking the kids to the big pool today. It's the coastal walk this morning. Lots of the guests signed up to go."

"Huh, I thought breakfast was quiet."

"Yeah. Well, it'll be quieter at the grown-up pool today, so we're taking the kids there for an hour or so. Give them some floats, you know. Play some games with them. We'll do a mini aqua aerobics–type thing with them, put some music on."

"Sounds great." I say it with as much enthusiasm as I can muster—which is less than none.

Zoe laughs and hefts a big, sturdy bright-blue speaker off the table. "Come on, Larry. It's twenty-five past. Better get out there."

We're halfway out the door when Zoe says, "Oh sugar—I forgot the CD player."

"I'll get it," I volunteer. Any excuse to keep Larry's stinky head off for a couple more minutes. I tuck the offending piece of the costume tighter under my foam-wrapped arm and make my way back to the staff room for the old-school boom box. I thought Zoe might've got special dispensation or something to have a phone because of the kids, but any hope of persuading her to let me use it to check on my profiles was dashed when she showed off the snazzy little walkie-talkie device clipped to the waistband of her shorts.

The staff room is past reception and down a corridor. Voices float out from the cracked door, and the sound of a few guys laughing about something. One says something in Spanish that sounds teasing, and another says in a posh, put-on British accent, "No, we must speak English for him, like his new *friend*. Eh, ¿cabrón?"

I hear a little scuffle, like the guys are shoving each other, and roll my eyes. *Boys.*

But then there's a very sexy, very familiar voice saying, "Cállate, Eduardo. She doesn't mean anything."

"Let's hope she's worth it in bed, then. I hear Luis wasn't too happy about your little *private class*," says another guy, and there's more laughter.

My stomach twists, my heart in my throat as I pause just before I reach the open door. *Private class.* There's no way they're *not* talking about Jodie. And Gabriel just said she didn't *mean* anything.

And then Gabriel adds, "Oh, she will be. *You* know what these girls are like. The lonely ones just looking for some fun? You're only jealous you didn't get there first."

There's more laughing and jeering, and in spite of how stifling Larry's suit is, I feel cold all over. God, how did I even have the most momentary little crush on this absolute *douchebag*? Does Jodie know he only sees her as a fling? That she's one of many? I mean, maybe that's all *she's* expecting from this, but . . .

Crap. Do I have to tell her? I should, I should definitely tell her, but—would I want to know if I were in her shoes? It's not like it was ever really going to go beyond this week anyway . . .

I'm all for drama, and I love being at the center of it, but not like this.

Unable to stomach hearing any more—and also dreading overhearing something awful that I absolutely *do* have to tell Jodie about—I make as much noise as I can walking the last few steps to the door and barging through it, Larry-head first.

"Oh hey! What's up, guys?" I say.

The three guys are sitting around a table with coffees. The other two don't look much older than me; I've seen one of them doing maintenance and stuff around the pool. He's the one who mutters something in quiet, quick Spanish that makes the other guy laugh. Presumably at my expense. Gabriel's eyes widen when he sees me, but I play it cool, and he says, "Hola, Rory."

"Not Rory today, my friend." I gesture at the costume and

collect the boom box as best I can with the unwieldy claws. "Adios, dudes."

And before our scandalous, womanizing bartender can look guilty enough that it guilts *me* into telling Jodie about this whole thing, I get the hell out of there.

With Zoe leading the kiddie aqua aerobics to some teeny-bopper version of Lil Nas X's "Montero" (which, I swear to God, is a thing that *actually* exists, and I crack up inside the suit at how unrecognizable the song is), this should be easy. I wobble side to side in the costume, trying to mimic some of Zoe's movements, which are a seriously pared-down version of any kind of aerobics I've ever seen.

The kids seem to be enjoying it, which I guess is the main thing.

I'm sweating and miserable, and the waistband of my shorts is cutting into me, and I could really do with a drink. I think I could guzzle down an entire liter of water in one go right now. I know Luna and Jodie are lying on sun loungers somewhere nearby, but I can barely see out of this damn costume. That feels like a good thing right now, though. If I can't see them, I can try to pretend they aren't there and aren't laughing at me.

We take a short break for the kids to get a drink and use the loo.

A couple of them tug at me and ask if I'm going in the pool.

"I can't swim."

"But you're a lobster. Don't you live in the sea?"

Smart-arse.

"I moved when I was a baby lobster and didn't learn to swim," I say.

"Well, you could learn. Zoe can teach you!"

"You know what they say: can't teach an old dog new tricks."

"But you're not a dog."

I am never, ever working with kids again.

"Are you afraid?" one of them asks, and then suddenly I'm being swarmed by grabby little hands and upturned faces with wide eyes, and all the children are asking me if I'm scared of the water and is that why I can't swim and it's all right, they'll help me, and I can use the floats.

It's sweet, but also, I am not here for it.

So, with as much patience as I can manage, I thank them all and say maybe next time and ask if they're excited to play in the big pool. This seems to satisfy them. Zoe does a quick head count and plants her hands on her hips.

"Great! Everyone's here. Thank you, guys. Now, are you all ready to get back in the pool and have some fun?"

The kids start bouncing and whooping. Zoe tells them to line back up by the steps to get in the pool, which for the most part they do quickly and quietly.

Except for one little *demon* who peels away from the group and shouts, "Larry first!" and runs at me.

"No running by the pool!" Zoe shouts, but it doesn't do any good.

Everything happens in slow motion.

Zoe cries out, and the little boy laughs, and everyone shrieks with a mixture of horror and delight as he shoves me.

I shuffle in the giant lobster feet, stumbling and losing my balance. Larry's head flies off as I topple backward.

I hit the water hard.

And I sink fast.

The suit is heavy, and I sputter into the water. I flail for a few seconds before my head breaks through the surface. It's a good job we were near the shallow end. It feels like something grabs my foot as I try to kick it up and then I'm underwater again.

I think: *I'm going to drown dressed up as Larry the Lobster in this shithole of a hotel.*

And then I think: *Oh, God, if I die like this, Mum and Dad and Hannah and Nic are going to find out about the damages bill and how I broke the hotel.*

And finally: *Well, that's one way to get out of having to do that law degree.*

Somehow, some way, I wrangle myself out of the lobster suit far enough to get my head above water again. Coughing and blinking the water from my eyes, I kick the costume the rest of the way off and get to the ladder at the side of the pool, where I start to drag myself out.

The second I put a leg up to step out of the pool, I hear a rip.

I don't even need to look to know, but I do anyway.

My shorts have ripped along the entire crotch. They're basically two halves held together only by the waistband.

I have never—*never*—been so glad to be in a phone-free zone.

Most of the kids are laughing.

A couple of younger ones are definitely crying.

Zoe is scolding the boy who pushed me.

Jodie and Luna are right in front of me, hugging me, asking if I'm okay. They wrap a towel around me, which is nice, but I'm dripping water everywhere, and I think everyone can still see my knickers. I cough up some pool water. Jodie is saying, "Sod the charges, I bet *you* could sue Esteban."

"Come on, sweetie, let's get you back to the room to dry off."

"Oh shit," I say. My brain is whirling and rattling around inside my head. I pull away from them. "Larry. He's gonna kill me."

"Larry's going to kill you?"

"No," I tell her. "*Esteban*. He's gonna kill me for this. I bet Larry is ruined."

I lower myself back down to step into the pool, which only comes up to my waist. Larry is a big, indistinguishable orange blob under the turquoise water. Well, two blobs. His head is a little farther away. I remember Zoe saying that parents had complained when their kids had nightmares after Larry's head fell off last time she wore the costume.

My heart beats a tattoo of *fuckup, fuckup, fuckup*.

"No, no, sweetie, Larry's not going anywhere." Between them, they drag me back up. "Come on, let's get you dry, okay?"

"Zoe. Zoe." I step away from them again and walk over to Zoe. "I'm so sorry."

A little girl tugs at my shirt. "Are you okay?"

I think I smile at her, but I'm too busy grasping at Zoe's elbow to know for sure. "I'm so sorry."

"It's okay," Zoe says with a pitiful frown and an earnestness that makes me think it *is* actually okay. "You go sort yourself out. I'll deal with it. I'll see you later, though. Night out."

"Night out," I confirm, even though that feels like worlds away.

Luna draws me away gently, and I let her and Jodie lead me from the pool and back toward our shack on the beach. The sun is hot, and my shoulders feel rubbed raw from the sunburn I got earlier this week and from wrestling my way out of that damned costume. My legs move along numbly; my lungs burn from swallowing half the pool.

"Do you think she's in shock?" Luna asks from my right.

"Should we slap her?" Jodie asks from my left.

"You fucking dare," I tell her.

"You okay?"

"*No,* I'm not *okay*. I got pushed into the pool in that lobster outfit by a malicious monster of a seven-year-old and ripped my shorts and flashed everyone. This is literally, genuinely the worst day of my life. I nearly *drowned*."

Jodie laughs, but she smothers it quickly and turns it into a cough. Not quickly enough, though, because I shoot her a glare.

"It's not that deep," Luna points out, and I know that objectively the water wasn't, but—

"Are you not listening to me? I nearly drowned. I could have died as Larry the Lobster."

"We wouldn't have let you drown," she murmurs, and shrinks back a little before rubbing my back. "Come on. Nice hot shower and a cup of tea, that's what you need."

"Esteban is gonna be so pissed off . . ."

How can I try to make amends for flooding the hotel only to make things *worse* and break even more things? I'm a one-woman disaster zone. I'm usually a bit reckless and impulsive, and sometimes I get in a little trouble, but never anything like *this*. This is a total horror show, and I don't even have the good grades or anything to back me up this time.

Maybe this is the universe's way of driving home the point that I'm a total failure and should just give up and go along with what everyone else thinks is best, the way I have the entire rest of my life.

"Screw Esteban. And besides, you have *witnesses*," Jodie tells me.

"All right, calm down, Elle Woods," I mutter, managing a half-hearted smile. "Did it look as bad as it felt?"

"Honestly?" Jodie sounds apprehensive.

"Honestly."

"Then honestly, and I say this with love and affection, it was *hilarious*."

24 Jodie

I slip away during siesta to the beach bar, leaving Rory shaken, speechless and horizontal across some towels with a giant sun hat covering her face. Luna is beside her, reading a book in the shade of an umbrella and occasionally patting Rory's arm in sympathy.

They won't miss me. Not for a couple of hours.

When I find Gabriel leaning against the bar with a book, the cabana otherwise totally empty, my heart does a somersault. Not that we'd made any plans, but . . .

He looks up at the sound of the sand on the decking crunching under my feet, and I'm floored by that smile. I'm beaming back at him before I know it and practically skip the last few steps, planting my elbows on the bar and leaning toward him.

"Hi."

Instead of "hello," Gabriel hooks a knuckle under my chin and tilts my head up as he bends down and presses his lips gently to mine. I melt into the kiss, the countertop digging into my stomach as I lean in closer. When we draw apart, he gestures for me to come around the bar, where there are two stools waiting. Was he hoping I'd show up?

"I wasn't sure if I'd see you," he says, and I wonder if he noticed me staring at the stools. "I heard your friend, the loud one, got into some trouble at the pool."

I snort. "That's putting it mildly."

"She really fell in wearing the Larry suit?" He raises an eyebrow, like it's so ludicrous he can't quite believe it.

"Some kid pushed her," I say in Rory's defense, and Gabriel lets out a hoot of laughter. He shakes his head and strands of hair fall across his forehead, enticing me to reach up and brush them back.

"That's even better," he says. "I wish I could have seen that. Is she all right, though?"

"Bruised pride, mostly." I scoot my stool over until my knees slot between Gabriel's. One of his legs curls around mine, and I feel the shift in the air as his eyes focus on mine. "But I don't want to talk about her."

"Oh?" His voice lilts, teasing. "Then what do you want to talk about?"

I lean the rest of the way in and kiss him again.

But later, when I'm back in our room after a delirious couple of hours in Gabriel's company, alternating between kissing and getting to know each other better, I have to admit, "I think we should be worried about Rory."

Luna's face twists. If she's trying to express sympathy, it looks more like pity. "I can see why her sisters packed her off on vacation. I feel like I've been worried about her since before we met her."

I smirk. "Seriously. D'you think she's okay?"

"She seems okay," Luna says with a shrug. "You know, considering she fell into the pool dressed as a giant lobster and showed off her wedgie to the whole hotel."

I have to press a hand over my mouth to keep from laughing; it feels so mean. Apart from her bright-red shoulders, Rory has acquired a nice tan over the last couple of days—but the sight of her pasty white arse flashing the world *was* kind of hysterical. Objectively speaking.

The sound of Rory coming back upstairs makes us stop talking.

"So," she announces, "I found some wineglasses in a cupboard, but we have no wine. I don't think we can predrink and do the classic getting ready for a big night out without the wine. I did, however, find one minibar-sized bottle of Malibu. I'm sorry to say I was selfish and drank it."

"Better to ask forgiveness than permission, right?"

I point at Luna before climbing off the bed to get my shoes. "Lady's got a point. I've got this. You guys wait here. I won't be long."

Although, thinking about it . . .

I correct myself. "I will *try* not to be too long."

"Where are you going?" Rory asks.

"To visit a very sexy bartender and get us some vino, obviously."

Rory calls after me, a bit too casually, "So, you and Gabriel have been getting pretty cozy. Is that . . . I mean, considering it's just a vacation fling."

I pause, turning around to face them both.

"I suppose so," I say, but it doesn't *feel* that way when Gabriel and I are talking. He's flirty, of course, though he seems genuinely interested in finding out more about me, asking about my family, my interests, his eyes lighting up when he makes me laugh, like he's so pleased with himself for putting that look on my face . . . I think the butterflies in my stomach are because this is more than some fling.

"Maybe, but I don't know. He did say he might want to move to the UK at some point, so . . ." I trail off. "And he's said a couple of things that make me think he'll ask for my number and stay in touch when I leave."

Luna beams like this is the most adorable thing she's ever heard.

Rory, however, turns a queasy shade of green. She swallows hard, face and shoulders screwing up like she's bracing herself, but before I can ask what that's all about, she blurts: "I heard him talking about you to some guys earlier. He said he's basically just looking to get laid by some lonely girl up for some fun."

Her words are a punch in the stomach, winding me.

"What? What're you talking about?" Luna asks, and Rory needs no more prompting to spill the entire thing, relaying a conversation between Gabriel and two other guys that I can only assume must be word for word, given that she butchers the Spanish that's sprinkled in her recollection of the whole thing.

Then the echo of Gabriel's voice flashes in my mind, telling me only yesterday: *There are other things out there. I would like to try everything. Isn't that what it's all about?* And: *I broke my share of hearts.*

Rory's face creases again and she jumps forward to snatch my hands, squeezing them tightly. "I'm so sorry. After all the Larry carnage it totally slipped my mind, but, like, I just thought you should know? I think—I think I'd want to know. So, shit, I don't know, I just . . . Was this the right thing? I'm sorry."

I shake my head, numbness prickling across my skin. Was that why he asked me about Rory earlier—not actually because of her fall, but because he wanted to suss out if she'd told me about the conversation? And he'd kissed me before we started talking, so maybe it *is* more of a physical connection where he's concerned . . .

Maybe it's not much of a connection at all, and it really was all in my head that he was flirting with me. Maybe I just showed up, throwing myself at him, and he figured he might as well have some fun since I was so obviously up for it. I even *told* him that I was looking for fun. To "let loose."

Has he been laughing at me all this time?

Yeah. I bet that must've been hilarious. Plain, regular old Jodie, acting like I was so damn special, like *of course* I'd be the one he was interested in.

"I'm . . ."

I need some air. It's impossible to breathe. The lingering clouds of perfume in the room are choking me, the weight of the girls' sympathy too much to bear.

"Sweetie, I'm so sorry," Luna says, stepping forward, eyes wide and sad and—*no, I can't bear that, either.* "Even if it is just a fling, he shouldn't be saying those things. What an *arsehole*."

"Well, you'd know," I blurt, still reeling.

"What?"

"Liam was no peach, was he? God. Um . . . right. Okay. I'm— I'm gonna go . . . go get us some drinks. I'll be back in a few minutes, okay? This *really* won't take long."

Neither of them try to stop me this time as I stride out of the room, choking back the tears.

Gabriel is nowhere to be seen. I don't know if that's a good thing or not.

It's only eight o'clock, so lots of people are likely still at dinner. But I guess there's no planned entertainment in the hotel lounge tonight because the beach bar is *packed*. I have to queue for a while and eventually get close enough to the bar to plant my elbows on the counter and lean in.

A woman with a neat ponytail is serving, and she hands me two bottles of white wine. When I say no, I don't need any glasses, she raises her eyebrows, unimpressed and looking ready to ask me if I would like a straw to go with it instead. I mutter, "Gracias," and clutch the sweaty, cold necks of the bottles, ducking to leave.

It's best Gabriel isn't here. I wouldn't have wanted to cry in front of everybody, and I'm not even sure what I'd say anyway. I've never liked anyone enough to string things along to the point of having to end it. I should've asked Luna's advice on how to have that conversation before I left, but at least now I don't need it. Maybe I can just avoid Gabriel for the rest of the trip and then bury my embarrassment over it for the rest of my life?

I weave back through the people packed around the bar. The music is louder tonight, and people are standing around, swaying to it and chattering noisily and laughing and having a great time.

Look at them, I think irritably. Not a care in the whole damn world. They're not worried about being just another lonely girl along the trail of hearts broken by a gorgeous, lovely, charming guy because they got too caught up in trying to be someone they're not, too busy trying to have fun to be *smart*.

"Jodie!"

No. No, I won't even think about him. He doesn't deserve it. Instead, I'll think about how I hope our night out is everything we want it to be, that the club is as good as Zoe, the Kids' Club rep, has made out to Rory it is, that Luna enjoys it since she seemed so reluctant when Rory suggested going out yesterday and that Rory doesn't get too in her head about what happened earlier.

The four of us will have a brilliant time, totally free of awful ex-boyfriends and degrees we don't want to do and everything we came here to get away from in the first place. We'll have some drinks and dance and laugh, and maybe there'll be another guy just as cute as Gabriel I can kiss to take my mind off him, and we'll all have such a great night that it won't even matter anyway.

I can't remember the last time I went *out* out. Definitely not since before exams. I am desperate for this in a way I hadn't expected. Gran's always telling me I should be going out and enjoying myself more, and Mum has tried more than once to drag me to a pub quiz when I go home for the weekend—something that always felt even sadder than not going out at all.

"Jodie!"

I can't ignore it anymore. I turn, and I swear my heart actually skips a beat when I spot Gabriel just behind me, skirting around the tortolitos, who actually look like they *are* lovebirds tonight. They're dancing. And Linda is *smiling* for once. This digital detox is doing someone some good, at least.

My heart plummets, landing like a stone in the pit of my stomach.

Who was I kidding? This isn't some epic whirlwind romance that might lead somewhere.

Gabriel pushes his hair back from his face. There's a cloth slung over his shoulder. His sleeves are rolled up to just above his elbows, and I decide he must do it on purpose—must *know* how good that looks on him. His eyes dart from my face to the bottles of wine in my hand. "You're . . . staying in tonight?"

Not that I owe him an explanation, but there's a tiny part of me that's vindicated by how let down he looks. *Good, that makes two of us.* I stick my chin out and announce, "They're predrinks. We're going out. To a club."

"Ah," he says, eyebrows rising and lips quirking up. "This must be the ladies' night Zoe mentioned? You're going to Alto, ¿sí? I think you'll like it there. It's always popular with the turistas."

My chest clenches, and I can't help but wonder—

"Oh really? Is that where you go to pick up other sad, lonely girls looking for some fun?"

Shit. Shit, I did *not* mean to say that out loud. Not at all.

Gabriel recoils, those brown eyes I thought were so lovely turning wide and guilty, and I don't even try to take it back. It's a look that tells me Rory's vivid recollection of everything she overheard is bang on the money.

"I know I said I was looking for some fun," I tell him, "but that doesn't mean I want somebody to treat me like shit. It doesn't mean *you* get to swagger around and make it so fucking obvious I'm just another notch on your bedpost."

248

"Jodie . . ."

But that's it. That's all he says. There's no, "Sorry, querida, I don't know what you're talking about," or, "No, you misunderstood, I wasn't talking about you and me at all." He just trails off, defenseless, speechless.

Swallowing down the lump in the back of my throat, I haul together the scraps of my dignity and tell him, "For the record, *you* didn't mean anything to *me,* either. Maybe I'll find another guy tonight who can see if I'm *worth* it."

Gabriel cringes and says again, "Jodie, querida . . ."

But the endearment only makes me balk, skin crawling. I can't believe I fell for this—especially when he *told* me, outright, he had a history of breaking hearts . . .

God, I was such an *idiot.*

He reaches for me and I snatch my arms away, avoiding that touch I'd started to crave so badly. I give him the most disdainful look I can muster—which is not exactly difficult when I'm so disappointed in myself right now—and walk away without another word.

We're on our last glasses of wine, pleasantly tipsy and dressed, ready to go. After a quick debrief with the girls, I'm ready to shove Gabriel to the very back of my mind and focus solely on having *fun.*

My black dress is shorter and tighter than I remember, but I find I don't really care.

Rory, of course, looks effortlessly glamorous, with her beachy blond waves loose down her back, a strappy white camisole and high-waisted black shorts with four bright gold buttons. Her outfit would look casual but for the chunky wooden bangle, the long pendant around her neck and some dangerously high heels. She towers over us. Luna looks positively *minuscule* beside her.

Luna took longest to get ready, critical of every outfit even after her first glass of wine. We finally convinced her to settle on a buttercup-yellow ditsy floral sundress she brought with her, and Rory helps her accessorize by picking jewelry for her and pinning some of her ink-black hair back in cute twists to frame her face.

Rory tries to improve my ponytail by fluffing it out and softening it around the front, but I bat her away, feeling too much like a twelve-year-old playing dress-up. I'm not confident about my body as it is, but I *am* confident in my dress; I don't need to feel more insecure by worrying over my hair or makeup.

The only thing that could make our evening better is some music. A cheesy Spotify playlist or even a *NOW* CD, like my mum keeps in her car. But on the other hand, who needs our phones and Spotify for some music? We've basically turned into Donna and the Dynamos from *Mamma Mia!* all on our own.

Luna, now three glasses of wine into the night, is jumping between the kitchen and the lounge area, arms above her head and her head thrashing as she screams the lyrics to a Dua Lipa song. I can't guess which one it is—Luna sings tunelessly and improvises half the lyrics when she can't remember the right words, but her enthusiasm more than makes up for it.

Rory forgets she's holding a glass as she throws her arms up and starts to wiggle her hips, sending a splash of wine across the floorboards.

"Oh bugger!" Luna says, bursting into giggles. "Good job it's only white wine or I bet Esteban would be sending you a cleaning bill!"

"Please, don't even," Rory whines, shaking her head and holding her hands near her ears like she can block out even thinking about it. "No Esteban, no Larry the Lobster, no flooded rooms, none of that stuff. Tonight, we're gonna let loose! You know why?"

And she launches into an off-key, screechy rendition of Kelly Clarkson's "Stronger."

As perfect as Rory looks, she can't sing for toffee.

Not that it matters, but I'm easily the most tuneful out of all of us.

When it's time to go, our mood is high and we're giggling and grinning in a way that has more to do with the new friendship we've forged than how much we've had to drink. We gather our bags, put our shoes back on and teeter toward the front of the hotel arm in arm.

Rory stumbles almost immediately out of the door. She nearly takes me down with her like a set of dominoes, and I shriek.

Even a bit drunk, Luna is in full mother hen mode when she asks Rory, "Are you sure you can walk in those?"

"It's the sand," she whines, and slips her shoes off, slinging them over a finger to carry until we're on even ground.

As we make our way through reception, I feel Luna tense up next to me.

"Here we go," she mutters through her teeth, the words strained like she's bracing herself to get whacked in the face with a frying pan.

I follow her gaze to realize she might as well be—our dear friend, the one and only Esteban Alejandro Álvarez, is hopping out from behind the desk to block us off, his twirly mustache twitching.

"Ah, ladies, buenas tardes. Miss Rory, I wonder if I might have a word . . ."

Rory freezes beside me, but there's no *way* I'm letting Esteban ruin tonight. I need this too badly.

"Not now, Esteban," I sing, tightening my hold on the girls' arms and sticking my chin out. "Places to go, people to see! Have a muy bueno evening!"

He calls after us, but I tug the two others along. Rory is only too eager to get away from him before she's slammed with blame for scuffing up his reception floor with her heels or something equally ridiculous, but I can feel Luna hesitating.

The girl from Kids' Club at the pool earlier, obviously Zoe, is waiting for us by a taxi out on the drive where the shuttle bus first dropped us off. She's wearing a pair of denim dungarees, a white T-shirt and well-worn sneakers, looking more casual than any of us. She bounces on the balls of her feet and waves us over, a beaming smile on her round face.

"You guys ready?"

"So ready," Rory says.

We climb into the taxi. Zoe sits in the front and I end up in the middle of the back seat. The seat belts are broken. Rory's window is down and when she tries to roll it back up, it sticks. The cab smells of smoke—and not the kind from regular cigarettes.

Luna must notice because her face scrunches up. I decide not to say anything.

As the taxi lurches off, Zoe twists around, and Rory leans forward and waves a hand at us. "This is Jodie and that's Luna. Guys, this is Zoe."

"Yeah, we sort of met at the pool earlier," Luna says. She sounds funny.

Maybe she's not feeling very well. Maybe she drank too much. Or maybe it was the shrimp she ate at dinner. Maybe it's the smell of weed. Maybe it's just that we blew off Esteban, and she's such a stickler for the rules.

Whatever it is, I make a mental note to get her some water when we reach the club.

Zoe is chatting away to Rory already. "Are you okay? After what happened at the pool? Did you hurt yourself?"

"Not a scratch on me," Rory says, blasé in a way she definitely wasn't earlier. I smirk to myself, but don't call her out on it. "I'm fine. I mean, completely humiliated, but fine."

Zoe gives a hum of sympathy and then says to me, "And you're the one who fancies Gabe, right?"

I feel a prickle somewhere in my gut because she called him *Gabe,* which is so silly, and I wonder if he told her all about the drab, awkward girl throwing herself at him. However nice Rory made Zoe sound, I don't really want to rehash the whole thing with her right now, so I try to keep my voice light and casual when

I reply, "Sounds like Rory's been gossiping about me, which she totally swore she didn't do. But sure, I guess that's me."

Zoe's smile falters a bit, but then she starts talking animatedly, mostly to Rory, about the rest of the morning with the kids and how she'd told Esteban all about it. She says he was so sorry to hear what happened, and that some of the kids were *so* upset about the whole thing . . .

By the time we get to the club, the buzz of our predrinks is wearing off a bit and I'm pretty sure Luna is sulking. But when I nudge her and mouth, *You okay?* she just whispers, "What do you think Esteban wanted to talk to her about?"

"Don't know, don't care," I whisper back, not wanting Rory to overhear and spiral into a panic; she's kind of a messy drunk as it is. I do care, but whatever it is we can deal with it tomorrow. Hopefully he just wants to apologize to Rory, not terrorize her further, the poor thing. Luna pouts, but doesn't push it.

Tonight is meant to be *fun*. And I'm determined to make sure it is.

25 *Luna*

I'm either high from the stench of weed in the taxi or else I'm actually losing it, because I'm sure Zoe looks *exactly* like the girl in Liam's Instagram photo that I caught a glimpse of on Gabriel's phone the other night (and whose old Instagram photo I accidentally liked). It's not like the woman I saw by the pool earlier or that guy who had the same build and same hair color as Liam. From what I can recall of that photo, the resemblance is *uncanny*.

I know Liam has a type: short and curvy. Like me. Like Zoe.

And he came to Majorca on a boys' getaway last year. I don't remember the name of the hotel, but I think it was near here. I remember seeing some girls who worked at the hotel in their vacation photos. I'm racking my brain, trying to remember if Zoe looks like one of those girls.

She's chattering away to Jodie about Gabriel, unaware of the mess she's wading into, but Jodie tells her that she was only after a bit of fun when she asked him on a date. She acts like she's above it all, totally unbothered. I wonder if she is and if it was more the shock of hearing the things Gabriel had said that made her look so hurt earlier.

Zoe winks at her. "Can't say I blame you. Nothing like a little vacation romance, is there? Although long distance can be *so* cute. There's someone back home I've just started a bit of a thing with, but I don't know. It's early days! We'll see how it goes. He's barely out of a long-term relationship, but it sounds like they were really over *ages* ago."

The words feel like a slap in the face. I'm dying to grill her about this guy and his ex, to see if it really *could* be Liam, but maybe it's better to tread carefully. If she *is* the girl from the photo, if her "someone back home" is him . . . I don't want her thinking of me as a jealous maniac of an ex and that getting back to Liam.

"So how long have you been working as a vacation rep?" I ask Zoe as we walk to the club from the strip where the taxi dropped us off.

"The last couple of summers," she says.

"Did you work somewhere else here before Casa Dorada?"

She laughs. "How do you think I got into this?"

"Where are you from?"

I sound like I'm interrogating her, but I can't make myself stop. It's as if I've lost the ability to hold an actual conversation—and, apparently, the ability to *pretend* to have one. If Zoe thinks I sound like I've lost the plot, she just writes it off as how I am when I'm drunk.

"Manchester. I go to uni there, too."

"I'm from Manchester."

"Are you?" She perks up and starts chattering away about the city, leaving me struggling to keep up with the conversation while still busy trying to think of a way to ask her about Liam. (If only I could remember the name of the hotel he stayed in on his boys' getaway . . .)

But even quite drunk, I know there is no way in hell to ask that without sounding like some stalker who's obsessed with her ex and jealous of his potential new girlfriend.

Which I'm absolutely *not*, I tell myself, but the thought doesn't stick like I need it to.

Oh, who am I kidding? I *am* jealous—but not of Zoe. Or who-ever the girl is Liam had his arm around in the photo. I'm jealous of *him* for moving on so quickly.

I'm jealous because it feels like his life is still together some-how and I'm clinging on to what's left of mine, and the more I think about it, the less it feels like there's anything to hold on to, and I just want back what I had. Because if I've lost Liam—lost that future together I thought we *both* dreamed about—I've lost so much more than just my boyfriend. I've lost the friends we shared and an entire year at uni trying to please other people who didn't even want me around, and more than a little bit of dignity.

I just have to hope tonight's not a repeat of that.

Before long we come to a stop by an old neon sign that says *ALTO*. Loud music spills out of a set of dark doors. Our conversa-tion halts while we dig through our purses for some euros to pay the entry fee, and I fall to the back of the group as Zoe leads the way to the bar.

Rory buys us a round of shots. They're bright green.

"Salud, bitches!" she shouts above the music, and we down the shots.

It's not exactly packed, but it is busy. Alto is long and narrow with a DJ booth at the far end and an upper floor that's more glorified balcony than anything else, lined with booths overlooking the ground floor.

At least it's not a completely desperate scene; I'd had visions of us arriving at some empty dive, like something out of *The Inbetweeners Movie*. My brother loves that film.

Zoe promises us it'll get better later. I don't mind the quieter atmosphere so much—it's more my speed for a night out.

Jodie said that Gabriel mentioned this place was popular with tourists, and it looks like he was right. There's a hen do in a booth in a corner that has spilled out onto the dance floor, feather boas and cheap pink beaded necklaces flying around. There are groups of school-leavers in matching T-shirts who look positively tame compared to the hen do, and half a dozen guys in suits who are chugging pint after pint and egging each other on. I guess there are some locals here too, but they must be completely outnumbered by the tourist types.

I'm drinking my vodka lemonade way too quickly, sipping constantly through the straw while the others chat animatedly. I'm waiting for Zoe to say something that either completely confirms or denies my suspicions, or for me to come up with a good question.

I mean, she can't be the girl from the photo. She can't be. And if she *is* . . .

I finish my drink first, but Rory isn't far behind.

"Another?" I ask her.

She nods, and we cast a look at the other two. They're barely halfway through theirs and wave us away. Jodie is talking loudly and brusquely about how she's out on the pull tonight and doesn't Zoe think that guy over there in the khaki-colored shorts is cute?

"What about Gabriel? I thought you guys were . . ." Zoe says.

"So did I. So should I go and talk to him, d'you think?"

We leave them to it. Jodie shut me down when I tried earlier tonight to talk to her about the whole thing with Gabriel, and Rory looks eager to get away from the conversation, probably still feeling guilty for her part in it.

Not that it's her fault Gabriel said those things. And if Zoe *is* the girl from Liam's photo, that's not Rory's fault, either.

"You all right?" Rory asks me at the bar. She has to shout over the music.

I should tell her that of course I'm fine.

But everything is a little out of focus and a little too bright and it's very noisy, and I'm too hot from the buzz of it all, so I yell back, "I think Zoe is seeing Liam!"

Rory scrunches her face up. "What?"

I repeat myself.

"Your Liam? The ex? From back home? The one with the sneakers and the puka shell necklace?"

"Well, I don't mean Liam Hemsworth, do I?"

Rory frowns at me, baffled. She sways on her feet, one elbow on the sticky bar. "Are you sure?"

"She looks like the girl in the photo we saw on Gabriel's phone. The one Liam had his arm around. And he vacationed around here last year. I think Zoe worked in his hotel. And she's from

Manchester, too—if she was there when he went home from uni, maybe . . ."

Instead of telling me I've gone properly bonkers, Rory looks over at Zoe with a thoughtful frown for a while before saying, "Nah, the girl in that photo was skinnier, wasn't she? And Zoe has a tattoo on her wrist. I've seen it. We'd have remembered a tattoo, wouldn't we? Especially a Japanese one like she's got. We'd have probably said something bitchy about how we bet it means 'butter-nut squash' instead of 'harmony' or something."

"Oh."

Did the girl in the photo have a tattoo?

I don't think she did.

"Besides, I'm pretty sure Zoe has been here all week, working with the kids. I feel like she'd have mentioned if she'd been in some pub back home getting chatted up a few days ago."

"Oh, because you're *such* good friends," I say.

"What's that supposed to mean?"

I don't know. I don't know why it sounded so nasty, either.

I look at Zoe, who's totally relaxed and having a great time out with us. With total strangers. Life and soul of the party. Spontane-ous. *Fun.* All the things I'm—I'm *not.*

And it doesn't matter if Zoe *is* the girl Liam was with. The fact that she's more his type than I have been for the past year is enough.

So I ignore Rory and lean over the bar, waving to the bartender. "Can we get some vodka lemonades, please? Doubles!"

"Are you sure you're all right?" Rory asks.

Instead of saying yes, what comes out of my mouth is: "Why did you invite her, anyway?"

Rory blinks at me, her brown eyes annoyingly wide, her lips in a pout and slightly parted. The picture of innocence. I bet that's the exact kind of look that got her sisters to pack her off on vacation, the look that always gets her out of trouble. "She suggested this place when I said maybe getting out of that hellhole wouldn't be a bad idea. I was hardly going to *not* invite her, was I? She's really nice. I thought you guys would like her, too."

Once more, I think about that list I found in her notebook and the few times over the last day or so that she or Jodie have been a bit short with me, the fear that I've latched on and am only weighing them down. And I think about the group chats that have winnowed away bit by bit over the last few weeks since the breakup—over the last *year* since we all moved away from home and on to the next phase of our lives.

Boring, you're so boring, nobody wants you around. Liam wasn't sorry to see you gone, was he, not if he's moved on so quickly? And your "friends" must have thought good riddance, too.

"Guess I should be grateful you bothered to invite *me* along, then," I say.

"Miss Lola," Rory snaps at me while I pay the bartender for our drinks, "you're being really weird, d'you know that? What've I done to make you so pissed off?"

"*Nothing.* I'm *not.*"

"You sure sound it."

"I'm not!" I yell at her, bristling. "Just drop it, will you?"

"No! You're shouting at me and being mean over nothing. Because—what, because I said Zoe wasn't the girl in the photo? Do you not like her or something?"

Picking sides, she's picking sides. She doesn't want to choose you, either. Nobody does.

"Oh, shut up, Rory. You know, you wouldn't even have met her if you hadn't let Esteban push you around like that and if you hadn't been so stupid, so irresponsible—"

"What?"

"What's going on, guys?" Jodie asks, coming over.

"Luna's being a bitch, that's what," Rory says, glowering at me.

Her big brown eyes have turned narrow and icy, the sharp flick of her eyeliner only adding to the sternness of her look. She taps her long fingers on her crossed arms, hips tilting as she shifts her weight to one foot. I hate how tall she is, especially in those heels. Combined with that expression, she makes me feel all of two inches tall. She looks haughty and pissed off, and her cheeks are rosy from all the booze.

Jodie glances between us, baffled, and I can't say I blame her.

I have no idea what's happening either, but I can't stop myself. All that heartache from everything that happened with Liam, all the weirdness about the distance with my old friends and the stresses of this week suddenly come spilling out of all the dark, faraway corners I've been pushing them into, not wanting to have to confront them in case it hurts even more. They rip through me like a tornado, swallowing every rational thought, every smile the girls and I have shared this week. I cross my arms too, but I doubt I look half as intimidating as Rory does.

Jodie puts a hand on my shoulder. "Luna? What's going on?"

I shake her off. Her niceness feels as fake as her blasé attitude to the implosion of her summer romance with Gabriel earlier. She *said* in the car she didn't care why Esteban wanted to talk to Rory. Maybe she really doesn't, and we're just distractions like Gabriel was.

"Is this all about Liam?" Rory says, and rolls her eyes. To Jodie, she adds, "She reckons *Zoe* is the girl in his photo. Can you even? For God's sake, Luna, get a *grip.* You were the one who ended things! And from what you've said, he's a total prat!"

"You don't know the whole story," I say.

Jodie says, "Let me guess—he was *so* perfect, and *so* great, and you were *so* in love. Yeah, you told us. And you told us he cheated on you, which, honestly, I'm not surprised about."

I flinch.

Something flickers across Jodie's face at my reaction, but I bite back at her. "What would you know? You were so *lonely* and desperate for any kind of romance you flung yourself at the first guy who looked twice! You think *I've* been going on about Liam? Of course I have—we spent four years together! But you've only known Gabriel for a few days, and I feel like that's all we've talked about this week, you and that bartender! You wouldn't even pass the Bechdel Test the way you carry on."

"Uh, you seemed to join in with those conversations, too. You *encouraged me,* if I remember rightly," Jodie snaps, and she squares her shoulders as she straightens up, scowling at me. "And that's rich coming from you. You're acting like the fricking poster girl for lonely and desperate!"

Because you latched onto them, and they don't want you around, and they know you're terrified of being on your own.

Before I can say anything else, Rory barges her way in front of Jodie, interrupting my argument and sending me racing back down this path of self-destruction I've laid with Rory instead.

"You're *wrong*, you know. About me. I'm not stupid," she tells me. "And I didn't let Esteban push me around. Don't tell me I'm irresponsible when I was *trying* to take some responsibility."

"Was that on your bucket list as well?" I snap, too far along the path to think about what I'm saying. Rory startles, mouth dropping open and arms falling slack at her sides. She seems to shrink, but I don't feel any taller.

"What did you say?"

"Is that the only reason you even bothered talking to us? So you could—I don't know—write a blog post about it? Put it on your TikTok? Use us as a funny story in your hashtag influencer lifestyle? Trying to make yourself *look* like a better person doesn't *make* you a better person, you know. And acting like we're friends just so you could tick it off your bucket list doesn't mean we're *actually* friends."

"What bucket list?" Jodie asks, but we both ignore her.

"You read my notebook," Rory says, and she's seething, shaking, pale beneath the blotchy flush of alcohol and her makeup.

I feel possessed. Overtaken by something—someone—I don't recognize. Someone not small or quiet or boring . . . Someone horrible and nasty.

Someone who glowers at Rory and snaps, "What were we, some little pet project? An ego boost? Your own personal fan club now you haven't got all your online followers making you feel important? So you didn't have to feel like you'd *failed* at this, too, and you could go home and prove to your family what a disappointment you *aren't?*"

There's a short pause before she swallows hard. "I can see why Liam and you didn't work out," she snarls.

The words hit their mark a bit too well, and I lash out again before I can stop myself.

"At least I'm not a people pleaser too busy pretending online to actually deal with my problems in the real world!" I shout.

"You're such a controlling, condescending little—" And then Rory falls back half a step. "You know what? Fuck you, Luna."

I glance at Jodie, but she's busy scoffing and shaking her head and sipping angrily on her drink. She's turned away from me, I guess already back to scanning the dance floor for the guy she wants to pull tonight. I spot Zoe not too far off—close enough to hear but not close enough that she has to get involved. She looks away when I catch her eye.

I down the rest of my drink and slam the glass onto the bar before storming out.

Good riddance to them.

The second I've walked far enough down the strip to find a taxi to take me back to the hotel, that hurricane inside me vanishes, leaving me hollowed out and breathless, and I break down in tears.

26 Rory

The worst part is Luna was *right*. Not about treating the girls like a pet project for likes and views, but . . . I *am* a people pleaser. Isn't that why I'm here, to stop my family worrying about me? Isn't that why I went along with the law degree even when I had zero interest in it, and hid how hard I was trying with my art from them when they thought it would only ever be a "hobby"? Hell, it's definitely why I was quick to volunteer for Kids' Club to get Esteban off my back.

It's a sharp, sobering realization that makes my heart squeeze.

Still. It doesn't get Luna off the hook for snooping *or* for being so horrible to us.

Although, you know, in some ways she probably has a right to be so mad at me, because I'm responsible for ruining her and Jodie's vacation. If it weren't for me, we wouldn't have been cast out of the hotel and into that dilapidated ruin on the beach.

But I have no idea why Luna's suddenly lashing out like this. I *tried* asking what was up and if she was okay, but she bit my head off. If she wants to be a bitch, well, fine. *She's made her bed,* I think bitterly. *She can lie in it now.*

As she storms out of the club, the fight leaves me, and I look at Jodie, feeling a stone settle in the pit of my stomach. Something like concern starts to creep into her expression, clouding the anger that was there a moment ago, and her eyes follow Luna out the door.

I've left plenty of parties by myself before or wandered off during a night out. Someone's always come after me, even if I've been a total mess and it means they have to sort me out before they can go back to enjoying their own night. I've never understood why they bothered until now: it doesn't feel right to let Luna, drunk, upset and riled up as she is, go off into the night alone in this strange place. Especially without a phone.

"We shouldn't let her go back on her own," I say.

Jodie nods, already setting her drink down. She mutters, "What the hell was all that about? She's not serious about thinking Zoe's got a thing with her ex, is she? And what was all that about a bucket—"

But she stops when someone grabs my arm and whirls me around. It's some bony thirtysomething with a garish feather boa so bright it's almost fluorescent wrapped around her neck. Before I can ask her what the hell she thinks she's doing, she shrieks with delight.

"Oh my God! Kells, you were right! It is her!"

"What?" I say.

For a mad second, I think, *Maybe she follows me online.*

And then the hen-do lady laughs and pulls out her phone, posing next to me with a duck-face pout and saying, "Don't suppose you've got the lobster head with you, babe?"

A shiver of dread runs down my spine, and I go cold all over.

I can't even get excited about seeing a phone.

"The what?"

"It is you, isn't it? The lobster girl? From Hashtag *LobsterFail*?" She lowers her phone to make the hashtag sign with her fingers and looks crestfallen for a moment. "I could've sworn it was you."

"Lobster fail?" Jodie says, because all I can do is gawp in horror at this woman. A few of her friends have come over, and Zoe has drifted nearer. I noticed that she'd kept her distance when I was fighting with Luna, and I *so* can't blame her.

"Oh my God," the woman gushes, grabbing at Jodie's shoulder with her thin fingers. "You haven't seen it? *Everyone's* seen it. It was on BuzzFeed. It's trending on Twitter and TikTok. Even me *mam* has seen it."

Before Jodie or I can answer, and before I can pinch myself to see if this is maybe just some horrible nightmare, the woman's friend is shoving her phone toward us with a TikTok video playing on the screen.

The last few days have dragged by without a phone, but this is not how I wanted to get my hands on one.

The four ladies from the hen party are bickering between themselves (it must be me, they're sure, but no, maybe the girl in the video was more strawberry blond? She could have been a bit ginger. If it was me, I wouldn't dare show my face in public, so it can't be me, I'm too pretty to be Lobster Girl anyway . . .)

Jodie takes the phone, and we lean over it together.

She presses Play, and we watch the horror unfold.

It looks worse on-screen, I decide. The way I flail when the kid pushes me is cartoonish. The pool isn't even that deep, so you can see me floundering wildly in the costume while everyone looks on, laughing. As I drag myself out of the pool, the camera gets a clear shot of my shorts ripping apart before it swings to my face and zooms in. I look like a drowned cat. You can sort of see Jodie and Luna trying to talk to me and look after me, but then I make a bid to go back in the pool and they have to haul me away.

Finally, the camera turns back to the pool, focusing on Larry's head sinking under the water for a few seconds before the screen goes black and the video ends.

I can feel Jodie looking at me, so I keep staring at the phone.

I snatch it from her to get a better look.

#LobsterFail at Casa Dorada Resort—kid pushes lobster girl in pool (repost from YouTube) is at over two hundred thousand views. There are hundreds of comments. Tens of thousands of likes. "It *is* her! I told you it was—look!"

A different phone is thrust in my face. Without thinking, I take it and look at the screen, with Jodie peering over my shoulder.

It's my Instagram feed.

Except instead of 8,392 followers like I had when I last checked, I now have 17,000.

All I can do is grip the phone so tightly my fingers hurt with the effort and stare at the women, the blood draining from my face. "How did you find that?"

"Eh?"

"How did you find my Instagram?" I bark.

And it's not even the fake personal one that my family and friends follow. It's *mine,* the one I curated with such devotion, the one that points to my TikTok in the hope of growing my followers further.

Jodie puts a hand on my arm, but I jerk away.

Two of the ladies look at each other. One of them, taking the phone back from Jodie, says to me with a shrug, "It's just on Instagram, in't it? Whoever uploaded it there tagged you."

"They tagged me?"

"It is you, though?" the first lady says, squinting at me. "I knew it was! Kelly *said*. She said she was sure it was you. Didn't you, Kells? Can we get a picture, babes? Me mam'll love that. I'll tag you in it if you like. Group selfie!"

I gawp at her, only ducking away when she lifts the camera. I don't think I've avoided a camera in my whole *life*, but right now . . . Nope.

I bump straight into Zoe.

And she looks so apologetic that I jump straight down her throat.

"Did you know?"

"No! Honestly, I swear I didn't. I'd have told you if I'd seen it."

The women behind me are clucking and cooing. "Didn't you know they got it all on video, hon?" one of them asks.

"It's supposed to be a device-free resort," Jodie says.

And suddenly, I'm furious. "She's right. Device-free. Esteban and his fucking *policies*. First, I'm pushed into the pool, and now this. I should *sue* him. I should. Device-free! Who posted it?"

I'm still clutching one of the ladies' phones and dithering over the open Instagram app. I look up at them. "Who posted it?"

"Dunno. Some meme account reposted it, didn't they? Everyone's been reposting and sharing it. It's all over the internet. Sorry, chick."

Either some guest smuggled a phone into the resort—and got away with brazenly filming the whole incident at the pool—or one of the staff did it. And either possibility feeds my outrage and panic in turn.

"Are you all right, babes? Do you want a drink? Ooh, girls, let's get some shots! Tequila for Lobster Girl! Go viral, too, we will. Hashtag *lit*."

I look at the phone again.

My Instagram feed is full of carefully curated photographs of some scenery or a coffee shop. The occasional selfie, an immaculate *#outfitoftheday #ootd* and precise arrangements of jewelry or makeup. The occasional Reel reposted from my TikTok account showing the entire GRWM process.

It's a feed I'm proud of and have worked hard on. It's a personal brand I've put so much effort into building and a social media presence I was trying so desperately to grow.

And now I have seventeen thousand followers.

Eighteen.

It's gone up already.

Eighteen thousand followers who only have this fleeting interest in me because I flashed my knickers and almost drowned in a cheap lobster costume and have become the latest internet joke. I don't dare look to see if my TikTok following has had a similar trajectory.

I feel the lump in the back of my throat and the prickle in my eyes, and a split second later tears are running down my cheeks.

"Oh, Rory." Jodie sighs, putting an arm around me. "It's not that bad. It's all right."

"Not that bad?" I cry, looking at her and the pity in her face. "Not that bad? If someone googles me if they want to work with me, this is the first thing they'll find! Luna was—she was— Oh God, Jodie, I'm a joke! I'm *never* going to come back from this. Nobody's ever going to take me seriously again. And—*shit*, my family is going to find my accounts, and they'll—they'll see . . ."

They'll see all the effort I've been putting into social media, into my art, after nodding along when they said it wasn't a viable career, and they'll see all the videos that flopped and that will prove them right, and . . .

Her mouth twists. "I think you're overreacting . . ."

But she doesn't sound so sure, and there are more than two hundred thousand people who've seen that TikTok, and that's not even counting the ones who have seen reposts across different platforms . . .

Some guy—my age, maybe seventeen or eighteen—barges his way into the gaggle around me.

"Are you Lobster Fail Girl?"

My life is over.

I shove the phone blindly at the hen-do women, who scramble to take it and are asking me if I'm okay, the group selfie they wanted to take forgotten, but I shove past them, running for the glowing sign that says WC to seek sanctuary.

27 *Jodie*

Zoe and I spend a solid half hour in the toilets, trying to coax Rory out of a stall. At least it sounds like she's stopped crying now; all we can hear are soft, intermittent sniffles. I'd rushed outside to look for Luna when Zoe went after Rory in the wake of the *#LobsterFail* reveal, but she'd already gone.

As pissed off as I am at Luna for dragging me into the firing line when I've done nothing wrong, I hope she got back to the hotel okay. I don't know why she had to take out how wound up she is about her heartbreak on *me*.

It's not as if my own love life is so good at the minute.

The "lonely and desperate" dig was too far, and so at odds with how nice she's been all week. The quiet, gentle voice of reason, looking out for Rory and helping coax me out of my lifelong confidence crisis . . . What the hell happened to trigger whatever *that* was?

I knead my forehead with my knuckles, head still fuzzy from all the predrinks and the shots we did when we got here. Zoe ducks out to grab us some waters, and I knock on the stall door again.

"Rory, open the door, please."

"No. No, I can't face it. Please, just . . . You and Zoe go have fun. Go find that cute guy in the khaki shorts. I'll come and join you in a bit."

I don't point out that we both know that's a lie, and she'll either still be locked in this stall tomorrow or will make a run for it and jump in a taxi back to the hotel without telling us. I feel like I know Rory well enough that I'm convinced she won't be persuaded to come out and enjoy the rest of the night or laugh about the whole thing. Especially given the way she reacted to finding out.

Not that I can blame her, I guess. I'd be mortified if it were me.

(I'm glad it's not me. I'm so, so glad it's not me. I'd never live it down. And she's got a point—prospective employers google you. They'd find that video. I can do without something like that. Much as Mum and Gran might think it absolutely hilarious, my friends would lord it over me forever.)

"Look, why don't you just come out and we'll head back to the hotel, yeah?"

She doesn't reply.

"Rory?"

A sniff.

I sigh and lean against the tile wall. This is *not* the fun, carefree distraction I'd envisaged for tonight. Not that it's Rory's fault the video's gone viral and threatened to uproot her whole life, but it *is* kind of Luna's for picking a fight with us . . .

Although if she were here right now, and not in a mood, I bet *she'd* be able to talk Rory out of that toilet stall. She'd have some rational, reasonable plan to help fix this, and *she* wouldn't be too busy thinking about how relieved she is that it wasn't her or feeling bitter about the night being spoiled.

Or maybe she *would* be every bit as useless as I currently feel. Maybe we don't know her as well as we thought we did.

Zoe comes back at last.

I take a cup of water off her. "Finally! You were gone ages. Has it started to get busy out there at last, then?"

She wavers. "Um, kind of. Some of the guys from work have showed up, actually. I got caught talking to them. I guess after I mentioned we were all coming out here tonight . . ."

Her tone is casual enough, but she looks uneasy, not quite meeting my eye.

And then it clicks. Even though we've only just met tonight, something about that look makes me realize suddenly, deep in my bones, what she's not saying.

Mouth dry, I ask, "Is *he* out there, too?"

Zoe's cringe is answer enough.

There's a little bit of movement from inside Rory's toilet stall and her voice floats out. "Is that guy Eduardo there?"

"Yeah." Zoe rolls her eyes at me. "Ugh, honestly, they're fine to work with, but that crowd—they're so immature. Real 'poo-poo heads,' as my kids would say. But you didn't hear that from *me*," she adds with a laugh and a wink. There's a wobbly giggle from Rory.

No surprise Gabriel's out with those guys, I guess.

Did he encourage them to come here, or had they already decided? Was he disappointed that he didn't see me out there? Do I even care if he was?

Then Zoe pulls a more sympathetic face and asks, "What happened? Rory said you guys had really hit it off! And Gabe seemed super into you! Honestly, that little cocktail class you guys did—it was the *worst*-kept secret. Like, he shouldn't have been doing it, but he was dead excited about it, and it was so adorable."

"What makes you think something happened?"

"I—well, um . . . It's just . . ."

I'd been so careful to keep my answers short and sweet earlier when she was talking to me about "Gabe," but I'd tried to make it clear to her that I wasn't interested in him anymore. It was bad enough that I was already a subject of ridicule and gossip, I didn't need to add fuel to the fire, and Zoe didn't owe me any kind of loyalty over Gabriel if I'd explained the whole thing to her anyway.

And if he said it didn't mean anything, well, she was hardly going to judge me if I hooked up with a different guy tonight, was she?

"You know what, Rory? I'm gonna go back out there for a little bit, after all. Find that guy, like you said."

The lock on the stall door slides open. "Jode, maybe that's not—"

The bathroom door opens again and half of the hen do spill in. They recognize me and Zoe and one of them crows, "All right, gals! Where's your friend, Lobster Girl?"

The lock bolts shut again. As Zoe makes up an excuse about Rory not feeling well and the women start to coo in sympathy and crowd around Rory's stall, I slip out. I pat down my hair, brushing some of the frizzier strands off my face, and then steel myself as I emerge from the bathroom corridor and out into the club.

It's busier now, but still not exactly packed to the rafters. The dance floor is half-full with bodies surging and writhing in time to the too-loud music pouring from the DJ booth, and there's a queue at the bar.

I immediately spot Gabriel, nursing a bottle of beer, among some guys around my age. I think I vaguely recognize a couple from the hotel in the half-dark. They're chattering away, laughing and jeering, drinking fast, their eyes roving over the other people in the club.

Gabriel's easily the best-looking of the group, and even though he's not the tallest, the way he holds himself upright against the bar, looking a little bit bored, makes him stand out from the others. My heart gives a traitorous flip-flop in my chest.

One of the guys points at me suddenly. I can't make out what he shouts, but Gabriel's gaze snaps toward me, pinning me to the spot, and I fight the urge to fidget with my dress or hair. His expression is closed off, unreadable, and as someone digs a playful—or maybe mocking—elbow in his ribs, I whirl around and make for the dance floor, launching myself into the fray.

I push through to the middle, hoping to lose myself in the joyful delirium of everyone else. The school-leaver boys are nearby, and I spot the bride with her tacky veil and a few of her friends. I could probably do with a little more liquid courage if I plan to dance, but there's no way I'm going up to the bar to face Gabriel and his friends right now, so I throw my arms in the air and dip my hips to the music with a confidence I definitely don't possess.

Fake it till you make it, I tell myself.

At least this far into the crowd, nobody can see me very well if I'm making a total fool of myself. I always preferred hanging out in the kitchen at house parties or holding down a table at a club whenever I went out with people at uni. It's not something I've had a lot of practice at.

I must do something right, though, because before long a guy sidles up to me. He might be my age, or maybe the beard adds a year or two. He's blond and has a streak of sunburn across his nose and cheeks that mark him as a tourist. He's broad-shouldered, muscular in a way that makes me think he must spend all his free time at the gym. He's not much taller than me. He's cute, but he's no Gabriel.

Which makes him perfect.

I smile back at him when he ogles me in a way I think is supposed to be an attempt at a flirty smolder, and when he steps in close and puts his hands on my waist, I keep dancing, my arms up in the air as we sway out of time with each other to a club remix of an Ed Sheeran song blaring from the speakers.

The bass thrums through me so fiercely it overtakes my pounding heartbeat, and I close my eyes, trying my best to lose myself in the music. To be part of the current, to let it carry me along this wave with everybody else and wash away the sting of being pursued because I was lonely and desperate, the humiliation that I ever believed a guy like Gabriel might have genuinely been interested in me . . .

I just want to forget about him. Salvage what's left of my trip—as difficult as that might be with my plush hotel room exchanged for a shack, Luna unreasonably pissed off with me and Rory hiding in the toilets.

Turning, the blond guy pulls me in closer to him, hands

snaking around to hold my front while he presses his lips to my shoulder. I squirm a little, the sensation of his lips on me pulling me too close back to reality. His breath is warm and damp against my neck, and I give up, forced to admit to myself that for all my posturing earlier, this is *not* the distraction I'm looking for.

When I open my eyes, I find Gabriel standing right in front of me. Something burns in the depths of his lovely brown eyes, and his mouth is pressed into a grim line. A furrow has set in deep between his eyebrows.

I stand still and meet his gaze.

"Oi, shove off, mate!" the boy behind me shouts to him.

I extricate myself from his arms and step up to Gabriel. The guy mutters, annoyed, but goes back to dancing and enjoying himself without me quickly enough.

For a moment, Gabriel and I stand there, people twisting and swaying around us, bodies bumping into us as we stay completely still, the eye of the storm.

"Well, muchas gracias for scaring him off," I tell Gabriel, as though I didn't push the guy away all on my own. "Did you come here just to spoil my night? Just because we kissed, it doesn't mean—"

"It does," he interrupts, shifting closer. Close enough that I can feel the heat of his body, that I can't help but glance at his lips and notice the sadness etched into his frown. In spite of how loud the music is, his voice is low and makes me shiver when he says, "Significas mucho para mí."

But I shake my head, refusing to be drawn in by that sultry voice and his good looks.

"I don't mean anything to you. You *said* so yourself. This is just you playing games with me. Trying to convince me to get into bed with you to make it all *worth it*." I give him a mirthless smirk, hoping if I sound sharp enough it'll push him away and he'll give up. Maybe his friends egged him on, or this is to appease a guilty conscience because he got caught.

Gabriel swallows hard, Adam's apple bobbing. My eyes catch on the movement and drop down to the planes of his chest beneath his plain white T-shirt, his arms . . .

I snap my gaze away.

One of his friends appears out of nowhere, grabbing his shoulder and shouting something in his ear with a laugh. My Spanish isn't good enough to follow it, but it doesn't sound especially kind, whatever it is. Gabriel pushes him off with a scowl and shouts something back that I don't understand either, but I recognize his tone well enough to understand it probably means "piss off."

The music shifts, and it's Abba. The crowd goes nuts, jumping into the air with arms flailing as everyone yells along to "Voulez-Vous."

I'm about to join them, to turn my back on Gabriel and let him know just how little I think of him, how little he means to me, too, but, as if sensing what I'm about to do, he catches my wrist, his fingers warm and light on my skin, and steps close enough that his body brushes against my side.

"Please, Jodie." His head dips low, probably so I can hear him better, but it makes me shiver and want to lean into him. "Let me explain. Please."

I don't owe him anything. Not even the chance to talk his way out of this.

But he sounds so earnest, so regretful . . . And, just like the girls pointed out that I'd regret not putting myself out there and always wondering "what if" when I went back home, I know I'd regret not hearing him out now.

So I nod, and Gabriel gives a sigh of relief. I let my hand slip into his and follow him away from the commotion of the club so we can talk, just the two of us.

28 *Luna*

The taxi fare is extortionate. The hotel reception is quiet as I trudge through it. There are lights on around the pool, and the water casts an ethereal glow, turquoise shadows dancing on the umbrellas that are still up.

By contrast, the beach bar is lively. I slow down as I get closer and can hear it: music and chatter and people having a great time, enjoying themselves and their vacation. I keep walking.

When the path turns toward the luxury villas under renovation—to the sorry shack we're staying in—I don't follow it. I walk straight on, into the sand. My heels sink quickly and I stumble, throwing my arms out to brace myself.

I give up and flop down, reaching for my feet to wrestle off my shoes. These awful, awful shoes I didn't even really want to wear. I'm so bloated from all the drinking earlier, and from my period being due, that the waistband of my dress feels like it'll cut me in half now that I've sat down. I undo the zip down the side, not caring what it looks like or who might see, but I don't seem to be able to breathe any easier for it. I hook the straps of my shoes over a finger and push myself off the sand.

I struggle to get up, but once I'm up I keep going.

The sand is warm and soft on my bare feet, and I make my way toward the sea, where the sand is packed tight and cooler. I drift closer until the waves wash over my feet, and continue walking along the shore, my shoes and bag swinging from my hand, dress gaping loose at my side.

It's dark, but out here the stars seem so bright.

After a while, I get to a patch of rocks. I climb onto them, knowing that Sane Luna, Normal Luna, would never do something like this. Climbing onto a big pile of rocks next to the sea in the dark after getting drunk is a terrible, terrible idea, a recipe for the sort of cautionary article I'd send my friends with a headline like "Young woman drowns at luxury beachside resort!"

I throw down my shoes and bag and press my hands over my face.

I am such a fool.

I can't believe I went off like that. It's not the adrenaline-fueled blur that breaking up with Liam was. No, this time I can remember every word I said, every glimmer of emotion on the girls' faces, and my whole chest seems to cave in on itself. I can't believe I was so nasty to Rory and that I made those remarks to Jodie about Gabriel, and . . . I was so horrible to them.

And why? Because I can't deal with the fact that my closest friends might be two girls who I've known for all of five days? Because I was jealous that they're both so much more outgoing than I am, with their vacation fling and new friend Zoe, and I feel like I've lost my boyfriend, my future and my old friends in one fell swoop?

I like to be in control of my life. I'm a problem solver. I like to have things in order and to think about consequences, and I like to be prepared. Those are all things I'm *good* at.

And what's it got me?

A vacation from hell. An ex-boyfriend I'm starting to think I probably should have dumped a long time ago and friends who are really just people whose Instagram stories I watch and react to.

I'm aware that I might have latched on to Rory and Jodie a bit much, what with the three of us being more or less the same age and thrown together without any of the outside world on our phones to distract us. But—but you don't just *click* with people like that unless you've got a real friendship, right?

Maybe I'm deluding myself.

Jodie said it wasn't a surprise Liam had cheated. Rory told me I needed to get a grip. Have they been sick of me and my heartache all week but too polite to tell me to shut up about it before tonight? They must have been. Maybe that's why they've been a bit short with me.

Did they complain about me behind my back? Whisper to each other about what a loser I am, like when Jodie wanted to talk to me about Rory on our first night in the villa? They must be by now—they've probably stayed at the club to bitch about what a pathetic, sad person I am and laugh at me. They'll be relieved I've gone, like all of my—all of *Liam's*—friends.

I feel terrible for all those things I said to them—things I don't mean at all, not really. I wish I hadn't been so rash storming off like that, if only to stay and apologize to them and explain it wasn't about them at all.

I've made my world so small, so centered around my relationship with Liam . . . Is it any wonder I'm so focused on me, me, me? Even at the expense of people I'd come to consider friends?

I accused Jodie of using Gabriel to feel better about herself, that she was lonely and desperate. I called Rory a people pleaser. I said she was a *failure*.

But I'm the one who's alone. I'm the one who's failed.

"You're a mess, Luna Guinness," I tell myself, pushing off from the rocks and picking my way back down to the sand. *"A mess."*

29 Rory

I've got no idea how long I've been shut up in this toilet cubicle, but I know it's getting late. The place is noisier now, the music louder and the bathroom busier. I can see Zoe's shoes on the other side of the door. The well-meaning, giggly women from the hen do are long gone.

Jodie never came back. I wonder if she had some epic showdown with Gabriel in front of Eduardo and the other arseholes and put him in his place. I would've loved to have seen that, but tempting as it had been, it didn't quite outweigh the crushing humiliation of my fifteen minutes of fame.

Because now not only am I a people pleaser who refuses to live in the real world, I'm also the worst kind of viral sensation and currently the world's biggest joke.

Which is just great. Totally awesome.

A real fricking *blessing*.

Ugh. I bury my face in my hands, but it doesn't block out the memory of that video: me flailing wildly in the water to get out of that costume, the clean rip of my shorts as I lunged out of the pool . . . It looked every bit as bad as it felt at the time.

All the times this week I had longed for my phone, and now I'm wishing I could have lived in the internet-free bubble of Casa Dorada in blissful ignorance just a little while longer.

I wonder if Nic and Hannah have seen the video. But who am I kidding? *Of course* they have. People will be retweeting it, DMing it to their friends, posting the link in group chats. There's probably someone out there who's dug through my old posts to find every-thing and anything remotely embarrassing or overtly opinionated to drag out of context and add to the impression that I'm a joke and a loser. Maybe I've even been *canceled*.

Maybe people from the university have seen it. Maybe they'll rescind their offer because they don't want some absolute *joke* asso-ciated with them.

I wonder how disappointed my parents are going to be, because they totally will be because this is the kind of thing that sticks to you in the worst way, and, oh *God* no, they'll want to know *why* I was dressed up as a lobster helping out at Kids' Club while I was on vacation, and I'll have to tell them *everything* and fuck, fuck, fuck.

I'm *never* going to be able to show my face anywhere again.

My life is over.

Eventually, I realize I'm being horrifically selfish. Luna has bailed, Jodie never came back and poor Zoe has not moved from her post outside my cubicle. I've got no idea how long it's been because I don't have a phone to check the time, but I know it's been way too long.

Zoe doesn't want to be spending her night standing in a grimy bathroom, waiting for a relative stranger to get a grip. She wanted a fun, girlie night out and I've ruined all that.

Feeling terrible, I haul myself back up, legs aching and arse sore from sitting on the toilet seat for so long, and unlock the door.

Zoe is slouched against the wall, looking bored out of her mind, on her phone. She startles when I step out from the cubicle, and her face creases with so much concern I want to shut myself back inside.

"You all right?"

We both know I'm not. But you don't *say* that, so all I do is shrug and say, "Yeah. Course."

"Do you wanna head off?"

As though I want to stay here and go back to the fun we were supposed to be having.

Zoe looks tired and bored and ten thousand percent done with tonight. Whoops. I owe her big-time. Maybe there's something in the hotel gift shop I can get her as an "I'm sorry I'm such a hot mess and made you endure a terrible night out" present.

Nothing screams "Thanks, hon, you're a saint!" like a plastic palm tree magnet, right?

"Can do," I say. "I don't mind."

She nods. "Come on, then. There's always loads of taxis outside."

She's right; we don't have to wait for very long.

"What was all that drama with your other friend earlier, by the way? Luna? She looked really upset about something. Was she okay?" Zoe asks.

"Oh. You're gonna laugh, but she thought you were shagging her ex."

Rather than dwell on the too-true accusations of my own irresponsible, people-pleasing nature or my bucket list that Luna found and snooped at, I tell Zoe about the photograph on Liam's Instagram and all the wild, far-fetched coincidences like Liam maybe having been at the same hotel as her last summer, Zoe also being from Manchester, and—

"Oh God," I say, suddenly realizing, "and then in the taxi you were talking about some guy you had a thing with back home who'd *just* got out of a long-term relationship . . . No wonder she was so freaked out about it."

Zoe looks at me with her mouth hanging open for a long moment and then hoots with laughter. "Jeez. Okay. I mean—that makes *so* much sense. I thought she was being kind of frosty, but, you know, I didn't want to say anything and make things awkward. That would drive anybody to distraction, wouldn't it? Gosh. Poor Luna, she must be really hung up on this guy."

"Yeah," I say, not mentioning that I can't see *why* because Liam doesn't sound like a very good boyfriend at all. Instead, I double-check: "You're *not* dating a guy called Liam, are you?"

"Most definitely not," Zoe says, laughing again and then leading me to the next free taxi.

As soon as the car pulls off, I ask her, "Can I borrow your phone?"

"Do you think that's a good idea?"

"You sound like my mum," I tell her, laughing. It sounds loud and fake. I cringe.

Zoe tries to smile, and although it looks more like she's just baring her teeth at me, she unlocks her phone and passes it to me anyway.

I search "lobster fail" on TikTok—the one I saw earlier is up to eight hundred thousand views already, and the number makes me feel so queasy, I click off it quickly. I type "lobster fail" into Google, where one of the first results is the BuzzFeed article the hen party mentioned. The writer found out who I am through the Instagram video that tagged me—they're nice about my photos, even mentioning my "career as an artist" (which is laughable only for its nonexistence), and are ruthless in the way they dissect the "best" (worst) moments of the video. But BuzzFeed has at least been kind enough to link my Etsy store. Maybe I'll get a pity sale or two out of it.

I look for Instagram, but the familiar tile is nowhere to be seen, and Zoe's apps are sprawled with no apparent order across the pages rather than filed neatly. It takes me a couple of good looks before I ask her, "Where's Instagram?"

"Oh!" She blinks at me. "I don't have it."

"You don't have Instagram?"

"Nah. I just never got into it. If I like a photo so much I want to share it with my friends, I'll just send it to my friends. I don't get the whole culture of it. I only have TikTok because my friends basically bullied me into it. I don't use it unless they send me something on there, though."

As she's talking, I look at her phone again. Now she mentions it, Instagram, Messenger, even Snapchat or Twitter—I don't see any of them.

"You don't use *any* social media?"

"What's the point of it?"

"Well—to—because—it's . . ." I trail off. I can't even form a sentence because I can't get my head around it. The uneasiness of *#LobsterFail* is totally gone from my mind now, because all I can think about is how this girl doesn't have social media.

Who doesn't have social media?

It's, like . . . like . . . well, it's just *weird.* Everyone has it.

And what does she mean, what's the point?

"Isn't it in the name? It's social media; it's to be social. To connect with people," I say.

"Sure, but the people I want to connect with, I talk to. I don't get the point of sharing selfies with total strangers or posting a hundred and forty characters about some joke you'll forget about in an hour anyway."

"Its two hundred and eighty now."

"Is it? Since when?"

"I don't know. Ages."

"Hmm. Well. Yeah, I just . . . don't get it. Like, why do I want to share that stuff with strangers? What do you get out of it? If you need that much validation from people who know nothing about you . . ." She bites her lip, cutting herself off. "I mean . . ."

"But they *do* know you," I say. "They get to know your personality, the *essence* of who you are. And sure, they don't know where you went to school or if you got good grades or if you have brussels sprouts at your Christmas dinner, but you form a real bond with some of these people. You feel like you know each other in a way that really connects you, you know?"

"So you're telling me that if you post a joke on Twitter, you don't want it to go viral?" she asks.

"Everyone wants to go viral," I say, snorting.

And then I remember the phone in my hand and the fact that, according to the BuzzFeed article, I am now a trending topic on Twitter.

"For the right reasons," I add. "For making a funny joke or an insightful comment or taking a good photograph or creating something people enjoy."

"Not for being pushed into a swimming pool by a little kid and ripping your shorts."

I pass the phone back, groaning and smacking my head against the headrest. "Not for that, no."

"It'll die down, though. People forget these things."

"Not all of them. People remember Grumpy Cat, Kombucha Girl, Blinking White Guy, Salt Bae, the Corn Kid, 'Chrissy, Wake Up' . . . Some of them stick around."

Zoe gives me a sympathetic smile. "Well, hey, look, it's not all bad. If you wanted to sue, you've got great evidence now. I mean, sure, I bet Esteban will say it was photoshopped, but . . ."

She catches my eye, her expression so deadpan that, despite the knots in my stomach over the whole thing, I start giggling, and we both dissolve into fits of laughter, doing our best and most exaggerated impressions of Esteban the rest of the ride to the resort.

30 Jodie

Gabriel and I walk to the end of the strip, away from the stream of taxis zipping by and the throngs of people moving from one restaurant, bar or club to another. Away from the rush of the crowd and the pressure of his friends, my confidence in getting through this with my heart in one piece falters.

"Listen," I say, holding both hands up, palms out, in front of me, "whatever you've got to say for yourself, save it. Rory overheard everything you said to those guys in the staff room, and it's—"

It's not "fine." It hurts too much to be *fine*.

"It is what it is," I settle for saying. "I mean, we both knew this wasn't going to go anywhere. That it couldn't. I won't hold it against you. Let's just—forget all this ever happened, okay? I think . . . I think that's best."

"No," he says.

I blink, pulling away to look at him better. I don't know what I was expecting him to say, but it wasn't *that*.

He holds my gaze steadily, his expression serious. "No. I don't want to forget this—*you*—happened," Gabriel tells me, and some of my waning resistance turns warm and gooey, because it sounds like something straight out of a movie.

"Those things I said—"

"What, you weren't talking about me? You didn't mean it?" I retort, relieved that there's a bite to my voice. *Stand your ground, Jodie, come on.*

He bows his head slightly, shoulders slumping. "No, no. I said them, but . . ."

"But what? I'm supposed to believe that you realize the error of your ways and you're a changed man in all of, what, less than a day? Do you just wait around for lonely, pathetic girls like me to throw themselves at you so you can laugh about it with your friends?"

"That's not what it is."

I scoff, feeling like an idiot. "You're just sorry you got caught and want to clear your conscience."

Even if he *does* have a good excuse lined up, or suddenly declares what a fool he was because he's fallen madly in love with me, what am I going to do, exactly? Swoon into his waiting arms and kiss him and tell him all is forgiven so we can ride off into the sunset for our happily ever after? A few days ago, this was something exciting and tempting and fun, but now it's been tainted by the things he said—whether he meant them or not.

The confidence and dizzying desire that drove me even until earlier this afternoon is a distant memory. I don't think I could claw it back even if I wanted to. Now I feel every inch the lonely, desperate girl he and Luna accused me of being.

"Jodie, please. Escúchame. The people I said those things

to . . . It isn't an excuse, but they were goading me. Egging me on, I think you say."

"That's supposed to make it better?"

Gabriel lets out an agitated sigh, but it seems directed more at himself than at me. He scrubs a hand over his face, and I try hard not to think about how endearing he looks right now.

"It doesn't. And I know that an apology won't make up for the fact you are upset with me. I am not trying to explain myself so you will sleep with me or anything else, but I don't like to think that I have hurt you. Those guys—they bring out a side of me I don't like. More the person that I used to be. I want to think I have grown up a bit from that cábron I was in school. It's not someone I want to be anymore, but"—a faint, wry smile tugs at his perfect mouth, a look so *vulnerable* that it makes my heart give a little jolt—"I said those things, yes, but more out of a . . . sort of self-preservation. I did not believe them. Does that make sense?"

"Self-preservation?" I ask.

"Because I like you."

I frown, searching his face. He looks so completely sincere, and I believe him, but— "What's that got to do with it?"

He lets out a brief bark of laughter and runs his hands raggedly through his hair. "Everything! Because I believed that you were the kind of girl who could mean something to me, I felt that spark, and *you* were not looking for anything more than un ligue. A hookup, ¿sabes?"

"I was—I—what on *earth* gave you that idea?"

"You said that was what *you* wanted," he exclaims, his brow creasing. Some of his hair falls over his forehead, but he doesn't brush it away. "You were the one who told me first that you only wanted to enjoy yourself while you were here."

"I didn't—"

I did say that. *I deserve to have some fun. Let loose.* But I'd been so drawn to Gabriel, even beyond his good looks and that smile, enraptured by every story he told me and each piece of himself he revealed, giddy with how easy it had been to open up to him in return . . .

"Well, I only said that because *you* made it sound like you were only after something short term! You were talking about passions and wanting to try everything, and—"

"I was talking about my job!" he says, a laugh in his voice. His frown creases into disbelief, eyebrows twisted upward and mouth wide as he shakes his head toward the heavens. "Food! Travel! Not *women.*"

"How was I supposed to know that?"

"How was I supposed to know you didn't mean what you said?" Gabriel retorts. "You were quite clear that *you* only wanted something short-term, and I thought I would rather know you a little while than not at all, even if you were not looking for something more."

"I didn't know I *was* looking for something more," I confess, the words tumbling out of me, quiet and soft and scared, and it's only after I say them out loud that I dare to look at him again, heart thundering in my chest.

I didn't know I was so scared of losing that chance at something more until Rory told me what she'd overheard. Gabriel isn't just the first guy I've let myself show interest in for a long time—he's the first guy I've *wanted* to make an effort with or open up to. And he's right: I felt that spark, too.

"And now?" he asks softly.

I take a small step nearer. "I think I'd like to find out."

Gabriel's handsome face softens, his eyes searching mine, and something warm and hopeful blooms in my chest as we move toward each other. Gabriel wraps me in his arms as mine slide around his back, my face pressing into his shoulder. A breath shudders out of me, taking with it a lifetime of tension from feeling overlooked and ordinary. He brushes a kiss on my cheek and murmurs something softly, sweetly in Spanish to me.

I don't know what it means, but it feels like a promise.

We share a cab back to the resort, and Gabriel leads me around the hotel and down to the beach, in the opposite direction of the beach bar and the villas. Even if we haven't exactly talked about what is going on between us, it feels like something has slotted into place. Something gentle and delicate, wrapping around us like cotton wool.

That's okay. For once, I don't let myself worry about the future, about what's next. There's only enjoying where I am now.

Where we are.

Walking hand in hand along the beach, I tell Gabriel about the veritable shitstorm of our night out and all the drama. We laugh about the *#LobsterFail* video, which he saw earlier, and it really is quite funny; I'm sure even Rory will realize that eventually. I intend to gloss over the details of the fight with Luna, but surprise myself at how emotional I get relaying it all.

"I think it just hit a nerve," I find myself admitting—not just to Gabriel but to myself. "I haven't let myself have space in my life for romance, or any real, solid friendships, or even my family for ages now. Not since I went off to uni. I think I've been trying so hard to live up to this life I told myself I should want, it's . . . kind of hard to step back and admit I don't actually want any of that at all."

"What do you want?" he asks. It's a loaded question, but there's something about the earnestness of his open expression, like nothing I say could be the wrong answer, that makes it feel safe, and not like the grenade I've been skirting around for so long.

"Not that," I say, and it comes out with a watery chuckle, a couple of tears splashing down my cheeks out of nowhere. I brush them away. "I *want* romance. I want relationships. A boyfriend. Friends I actually care about and want to hear from, not ones I resent because it feels like their lives are so much better than mine and it's all one big competition, you know? And I don't want to be at uni. I hate it there. I like having something to apply myself to, and there's bits of my course I like—but the whole thing, it's just . . . It's not me."

So much for not worrying about the future, I think, as a few more tears fall.

I wipe them away with the back of my wrist, sniffling, and realize the only thing I *actually* feel for saying all that out loud is *relief.*

Gabriel's hand squeezes mine. "Then why don't you let yourself have all those things, querida?"

Like it's that easy.

But there's a weight off my chest, a clarity around the idea instead of nervousness and disappointment, and I squeeze his hand back. "I think I'd like to."

We walk a little while longer, down to the shore and then back up, swapping quiet, lighthearted stories about our families, our interests and what we want to do with our lives, the places we want to go, the things we'd like to try out there in the big, wide world.

Gabriel and I come to a stop near some neat rows of plush loungers swallowed up by the darkness and starlight. The sea washes noisily on the shore, lines of white foam illuminated in the night. He takes a seat on the end of one of the loungers and tugs me toward the spot beside him.

I don't take it.

Instead, I stand between his legs, my hands settling on his shoulders. When I bend to kiss him slowly, his tongue drags along my lower lip like a question, and I come alive. There's only the two of us, the solitude of the warm night air carrying a salty tang, the heat of his skin against mine, the burning need that makes my heart cry out for more, more, and I let him pull me down to sit on his lap. My thigh brushes against his erection, and he grips me a little closer as I deepen the kiss, my hand skating over the bulge in his shorts at the same time as his fingers squeeze my breast.

"Gabriel," I breathe, because it's all I can say, all I can find to voice the need searing through my veins and the way he makes me feel so *seen*.

As if reading my mind, he pauses to meet my gaze. "You are so beautiful, Jodie," he tells me, lowering his head to kiss a trail down my throat. His voice is even lower than usual, husky, and a thrill runs through me that it's all because of *me*. "You are . . . spectacular."

I shiver against him, his voice, his words, his touch, and just as I start to shift to straddle him, Gabriel's arm slides around me and he lowers me down beneath him, his eyes dark and fixed on mine so intently that it makes my breath hitch in my throat.

His hands rest on my waist and my fingers toy with the hem of his T-shirt.

When he kisses me, I'm floating. His lips are soft on mine and his teeth tug my lower lip. My hand presses flat against his chest, the coarse hairs there tickling my palm, and I can feel how hard his heart is beating. His belt clanks softly as I draw him closer, and I arch into the kisses he places beneath my ear, in the space between my neck and shoulder. Just the two of us, under this blanket of the night sky.

I don't think I've ever seen so many stars.

31 *Luna*

When I wake up, I have a raging headache, and I feel absolutely awful.

I'm quite sure it has less to do with the hangover lurking at my temples and the sawdust-like taste in my mouth, and a lot more to do with how horrible I was to the girls last night and how I cried myself to sleep about everything. About the new friendships I might have ruined, the ones I thought I had back home and at uni that don't exist anymore, and the ex-boyfriend who still has a piece of my heart.

Fresh tears spring to my eyes and I blink them frantically away, focusing hard on my breathing instead. In and out, in and out . . .

I match it to the sound of Jodie's deep, even breathing on the other side of the bed, where she's fast asleep.

She got in late. I'd slept so badly that the sound of the door opening downstairs jolted me awake easily. Jodie arrived back quite a long while after Rory; I wonder if she did end up hooking up with that guy in the khaki shorts after all.

Sunshine bleeds into the room through the broken blinds on the window, illuminating the dust floating around in the air.

I watch it for a while, my thoughts swirling inside my pounding head, punishing myself by rehashing all the terrible things I said last night and their exasperation with Liam, with *me,* that pushed me to it.

I hate the idea that a boy who's no longer even in my life has somehow cost me their friendship. Or, worse, that I've done that all by myself. I didn't even mean the things I said to them; I only said it to hurt them, for them to feel as I did. The shame of it is nauseating.

Feeling a bit restless now that I'm awake, and a bit worried that if Jodie wakes up I might have to deal with a cold shoulder I more than deserve, I do my best to sneak out of bed. Holding my breath, I push the covers back slowly. They scratch against each other, too loud in the absolute silence of the room. The mattress creaks as I sit up, and when I stand, slotting my feet into my flip-flops, the headboard knocks against the wall.

I stay completely still for a moment, cringing and half crouching, like I'm playing Quasimodo in a game of charades.

But Jodie snores once, which I guess means she's still out for the count. I breathe a sigh of relief and glance over my shoulder at her. Her mouth gapes open, and she has one arm flung to the side and the other hooked over her head. Her legs splay out awkwardly around the sheets she's kicked off. Her hair, which was done so carefully last night, looks matted and frizzy, one big, knotted cloud obscuring her face. There's a trail of drool across her cheek.

Part of me wants to laugh, wishing I could take a photo to giggle with her and Rory about later.

I'd have liked to be her friend.

I get changed quickly, not even using the toilet for fear of the flush making too much noise, grab my beach bag, which is still packed from yesterday, and tiptoe downstairs to make a quick and silent escape.

I know that avoiding the girls makes me a coward, but . . . isn't that part of the reason I booked this trip in the first place? To run away from the problems I'd created, the consequences of an emotional meltdown? I just can't bring myself to face how much they must hate me after last night, not yet.

Rory is curled up in a ball on the sofa in last night's clothes. Her eyes are shut, but I'm not sure she's asleep.

I don't stick around to find out.

Breakfast is busy when I get there after a quick freshening up in one of the hotel toilets. The giant clock on the wall says it's five past eight—prime in-between-activities time. Most people are wearing athleisure. It must be a busy day because there are hardly any free tables when I arrive. Oscar and his clipboard and the intensely structured itinerary seem so far away now.

I find a free table to dump my bag in a chair and set about getting myself some tea, then skip my usual muesli and fruit for the comfort of a full English.

By the time I've brought a heaped plate back to the table, someone else is there.

Skinny, hunched shoulders and long blond hair piled up into a messy ponytail, and still in last night's clothes. Rory is wearing green tassel earrings today.

When I sit down, she's bent over a cup of coffee, remnants of last night's eyeliner smeared underneath her eyes, accentuating the shadows there. I wonder if she had a sleepless night, too, and instantly feel awful in case that was to do with something I'd said.

She doesn't say anything, doesn't even bother to look at me.

I'm sorry. I'm so sorry for what I said last night. It was mean, uncalled for, and I shouldn't have said it.

She won't forgive me and has no reason to, but it doesn't mean I shouldn't apologize.

And yet . . .

I don't. The words stick in my throat, choked with tears. I don't want to cry; *I'm* not the one who has any right to be upset.

I think I'm waiting for her to yell at me—to let me know just how much she hates me, and no apology can change that, so don't waste my breath. I sit there, bracing myself for her to say her piece, because God knows I said plenty last night.

Rory's chair scrapes on the floor, cutting through the chatter and bustle of the restaurant and making me wince.

I watch her go over to the buffet, and my stomach knots with guilt.

She's back a few minutes later with a plate of toast and a handful of mini packets of jam. Rory reaches across the table for one of my half-used packets of butter, pinching things off someone else's plate like she's been doing all week, but her hand hesitates near my plate, and I look up.

"Can I have one of these?"

"I'm sorry," I blurt. "I'm really sorry, Rory. All those things I said—they weren't . . . I shouldn't have . . . I'm *so* sorry."

"Sure," she mumbles, taking the butter and concentrating on her toast. She opens her mouth a couple of times, drawing a sharp breath each time, but doesn't say anything.

And then my mouth is running off again, as if I've hit self-destruct. "Why did you sit here if you weren't going to talk to me?"

Rory puts her knife down with a clatter. "Well, *excuse me*, I didn't realize you had a monopoly on tables. In case you hadn't noticed, it's pretty busy in here."

She's not wrong. Looking around, I can't see any other free tables.

I bite hard on my tongue for a minute, hating myself.

I can't believe I'm doing it again.

"Rory, I'm—"

"Save it. Okay? Let's just . . . eat breakfast."

I can feel the tension crackling between us. I find myself wishing Jodie would show up, because even though she's probably on Rory's side, it might at least change the dynamics a little bit. I'd rather them both shout at me and shun me than this awful, shameful limbo.

As if I needed to go home with my heart even more in tatters than when I left.

32 Rory

I'm running on, like, three hours' sleep right now and probably stink of a night out I didn't actually have. I pretended to be
asleep when Luna snuck out this morning, and then I hadn't
wanted to wake Jodie by showering and changing when my stomach rumbled too much for me to ignore anymore. I figure the very
least I owe her after she spent half of last night huddled in a grimy
bathroom with me is a lie-in.

Luna doesn't look too worse for wear, considering. Actually, she
appears as bright-eyed and bushy-tailed as ever—if kind of down in
the dumps and puffy-eyed like she's been crying.

Which, you know. Makes two of us. But it does make me wonder if there was more to her big blowout last night than just having
a go at me and Jodie.

She did *try* to apologize. Sort of.

I was sort of expecting her to, but as soon as she started I didn't
want to hear it.

Because if she apologizes, I'll feel compelled to tell her that it
only *bothered* me so much because she was right, and that was all

306

the kind of stuff I'd come here to run away from. And, you know, I'd like to stay in this bubble where I don't actually deal with my shit for a little while longer, thank you very much.

Luna takes a while to decide she's done with her massive plate of breakfast while I mostly just nibble some toast and nurse a luke-warm coffee. Considering I stopped drinking pretty early in the night, I shouldn't have a hangover, but I feel like I do.

The coffee doesn't help.

I don't even *like* black coffee.

I don't know who I'm trying to impress with it.

It just leaves a bitter taste in my mouth and makes me feel even more gross and run-down.

"Done?" I ask when Luna has poked her fork at the same bit of sausage about eight times and is slumped with her elbow on the edge of the table and fist pressing into her cheek.

"Mm," she says.

We get up, Luna slinging her bag over her shoulder, and then the two of us trudge out to the pool.

I can't bring myself to ask if she's still got my bottle of sun cream in her bag, or a hairbrush rattling around in it somewhere.

She looks in such a sulk I start to think maybe I'm wrong, and last night *was* about me.

We don't talk as we pick out sun loungers. (By which I mean I hang back a little as Luna walks along the row of loungers a couple of times before deciding which one she likes best. She's chosen all week, and each time manages to nab the best of what's available, rather than tossing her stuff on whichever is nearest like I would've done.) There are hotel towels already folded on the bottom of them. Someone immediately shows up to provide us with chilled bottles of water.

I busy myself wrestling with the giant umbrella so that I won't burn. I figure I'll head back to the villa in a little while and take a shower, freshen up, put my bikini on.

It's the last day of the vacation.

It doesn't feel like it.

Whenever I went away with my family, the last day of a vacation meant we were all annoyed at having a little bit too much of a lie-in before rushing to the pool, fighting over who would have to go back up to the room for whatever we'd forgotten to bring along. (It was always Dad who'd trudge back up, except the year Hannah was in sixth form and decided the chlorine was bad for her fake tan and dyed hair, so she was sent up instead. We pushed her in the pool in the end, though, and she tried to be annoyed for all of about two minutes before Nic tried to dunk her, and then we all burst out laughing.)

And Mum would always manage to miss putting sun cream on some part of herself and end up with a bright-red patch on an otherwise perfect tan. Kind of like my peeling shoulders right now, which are still pink compared to my bronzed arms and legs.

I tuck my legs up into the shade of the umbrella and smile thinking about those vacations.

"Ah! Miss Rory! I have been looking for you, señorita."

Aaaand my momentary good mood is gone.

Shit. I forgot all about almost getting cornered by Esteban on our way out last night.

I suck in a long breath through my nose before looking up, my smile taut.

"Esteban, my good buddy. What can I do for you?"

His smarmy smile is a bit less confident than usual, and his thick eyebrows are drawn together, with a single, deep line cutting across his forehead.

If I didn't know better, I'd say Esteban Alejandro Álvarez was nervous.

I sit up a little straighter and notice Luna lowering her book. She's wearing sunglasses, but I'm more than certain she's looking at me and Esteban. We might not exactly be on speaking terms right now, but she wants in on all the drama.

Can't say I blame her, really.

"Esteban?" I prompt, sugary sweet.

Is that a bead of sweat on his upper lip, or am I delusional?

No, I think it is.

"Ah, sí, Miss Rory, I heard about what happened yesterday. Zoe informed me of the incident. Such an unfortunate accident."

"Unfortunate?"

"Most unfortunate. But I, ah, would like to remind you of the agreement you signed the other day, when you agreed . . . *volunteered* . . . to work at our Kids' Club. Casa Dorada cannot be held liable for any minor injury in the course of—"

"Yeah, I remember."

I'm not exactly about to sue the resort because some kid pushed me in the pool or because my shorts were too small—if only because I don't think I could actually get away with it—but it's *so* good to see him sweat.

"Yes, yes, well . . ." He clears his throat.

Despite everything, I can't stop myself glancing at Luna. Her eyes are still hidden by her sunglasses, but her lips twist upward. She's trying hard not to grin or laugh, enjoying this every bit as much as I am. I bite the inside of my cheek, fighting to keep a neutral expression as I face Esteban again.

"Well," he repeats, standing up a little straighter, "I have found someone else to help with the children today. And, of course, we shall not be charging you for the damages the blackout caused, under these, ah, new circumstances. I hope there are . . . no hard feelings, hmm, Miss Rory?"

No hard feelings?

I'm not sure if I want to laugh, scream or shove *him* into the pool and watch him flail around as he tries to work out what just happened. No hard feelings, my arse. Literally. My arse that is plastered all over the internet, no thanks to him.

And besides . . . did he honestly think I'd be showing up at Kids' Club to help out today? Zoe told me yesterday she'd already asked someone else to muck in and help her out, and that she'd deal with Esteban. I guess he didn't need much convincing, seeing as he's come over to check that I'm not going to slap Casa Dorada with a lawsuit the second I get home.

"Mm-hmm," I say.

I might let him off the hook, but he still hasn't actually apologized.

Esteban dithers for a moment. His hands are clasped behind his back, and he rocks back and forth on the balls of his feet. He clicks his tongue.

"Well. Yes. Good."

Just as he's about to leave, I pipe up, wanting to get the last word in—and make him squirm a little more.

"You know someone here has a phone, right?"

"¿Perdón?"

"Someone here has a phone. I don't know if it's a guest or staff, but you punished *us* for our little stint the other night, and someone else here is taking videos and sharing them online. Just, like, so you know. Clearly, your whole policy thing is *totally* working out."

Esteban's ears turn pink. "I see. Gracias, Miss Rory, for the information."

He still doesn't apologize, but turns sharply on his heel and stalks away, bristling and irked, and that feels more rewarding than any half-baked apology.

Luna leans over. "That jackass. Good for you, putting him in his place like that."

"Mm," I say, wondering if I should have done that days ago and stood up for myself rather than try to do everything I could to avoid the fines he'd threatened. I guess he can't have been *that* serious after all, if he let them go so easily.

A hotel rep calls out that the game of pool volleyball will be starting in five minutes, which sends around a murmur of excitement.

I tell Luna, "I think I'm gonna head back to the villa, take a shower and put my bikini on. I should probably wake Jodie up, too. She'll be mad if she misses breakfast."

"Oh," Luna says quietly. "Sure. Okay."

I stand up and put my shoes back on.

"I *really* am sorry about last night," Luna exclaims suddenly, throwing off her sunglasses to give me a plaintive look, lower lip pinched between her teeth. "I don't know what came over me. I wasn't . . . Rory, I'm so sorry. You didn't deserve any of those things I said."

As Luna starts pouring out more apologies, I hold a hand up to stop her.

"Come on. You totally meant it, and I deserved it. I've been a pain in the arse all week—getting you guys roped into living in that shack after I flooded my room, wrecking your luxury week away . . . And I was quick enough to go along with the phone jail-break that got us in trouble in the first place, wasn't I?"

But Luna shakes her head vehemently. "No. *No*, you haven't been a pain in the arse at all! How can you even think that? I'm the one who's been dragging you two around all week! To dinner that first night, and then—"

"What are you *talking* about?"

Luna's lower lip wobbles, but she takes a deep breath and says, "I'm sorry. I am. And I don't expect you to forgive me because what I said was unforgivable, but—"

I have to laugh, because seriously? Can she hear herself right now?

And I thought *I* was the dramatic one.

"Girl, come on," I say. "Shit happens. Friends fight. That's how it goes. And while, yes, you definitely, totally owe me an apology for going through my stuff and bitching me out like that—come on. It's hardly *unforgivable*, is it? It's not like most of what you said wasn't *true*."

"But—"

I cut her off. "Luna, listen, I appreciate that you want to clear the air, I do, but I'm telling you: *I need a shower.* So that's what I'm gonna go do, okay? And then when I don't smell like an armpit, we can talk."

A huge sigh rushes out of her, and she bites her lip again before nodding. I swear she has to swallow down another "sorry," too.

I add, "You know, I don't think I can stomach the sight of the pool after the Larry incident yesterday. Why don't you find us a spot down on the beach? We can come find you in a bit."

Luna nods eagerly, grabbing up her stuff. We walk quietly away from the pool, but I'm glad to notice some of the tension from breakfast has disappeared.

I know I don't need to hear her out; after tomorrow, I never have to see her again. But I can't imagine going from our tight-knit little trio this week to *nothing,* and . . . it feels like the grown-up thing to do. So maybe I don't owe it to Luna, but I owe it to myself.

The thought buoys me, a little glimmer of pride sparking in my chest, just like when I stood up for myself with Esteban. If this is what a little independence and responsibility looks like—I think I like it after all.

33 *Jodie*

"Fair warning," Rory announces, barging up the stairs as I scramble to finish pulling my knickers on and snatch my towel back up to cover myself. "Luna is in a super apologetic mood this morning, so brace yourself for major puppy-dog eyes and groveling. Which, like, she totally owes us, I know, but it's kind of a lot to be on the receiving end of. So brace yourself or whatever."

She swans into the bedroom looking disheveled and with a stale smell wafting off her. Which is unsurprising given she doesn't look like she's even brushed her hair since last night.

"Good to know," I tell her.

I hadn't been very sorry to find Luna gone when I woke up; having it out about the fight first thing this morning was a sure-fire way to kill the good mood I woke up in after such a wonderful end to the night. At least she wants to fix things, though. I don't think I could have coped with us ignoring each other all day, especially when we're still sharing accommodations until tomorrow.

Rory starts peeling off her top and shorts and jewelry, throwing them on the bed. "I left her down on the beach, if you want to come find us after you grab some breakfast." She cuts me a deadpan look. "Which I came *back* to wake you up for, FYI. You can get kind of hangry, you know?"

"Us?" I say instead of "thanks." "Did you two make up, then?"

"Ish. I think so?" She sniffs her pits and gags. "I need a shower before I tackle that whole thing, honestly. But it'll be fine. I think something else was going on with her—maybe all the drama around Liam or something? Not that there *is* any drama, but . . ."

"But she's still madly in love with him," I finish for her, agreeing. "God knows why. I mean, I'm sure there's a whole other side to the story we haven't heard, but it's not like she came here furious with him, is it?"

"I reckon she wants to fix things with him. Which, no. She was out of line last night, but letting her get back with that *arsehole* is way beyond any kind of punishment."

I laugh. It's kind of a relief to know that Rory's not holding a grudge, that there must be more to the story than Luna just secretly being a bitch and suddenly showing her true colors. But Rory's right: breakfast first.

"I'll see you guys on the beach," I tell Rory as she makes her way into the bathroom.

"Good. I still need to hear all about where you vanished to last night! You owe me a story after ditching me!"

With a full belly and a clean beach towel tucked under my arm, I make my way out onto the sand. I spot Luna lounging well out of the way of the ongoing tai chi class and am relieved when I see Rory settling in next to her. At least if this all goes badly, Rory might act as a bit of a buffer . . .

I don't *actually* know if Luna wants to apologize to *me*, after all. I could very well be jumping to conclusions.

"Hey," I say, announcing my arrival.

I spread my towel out and drop down to sit with them, legs stretched out in front of me to soak up the last sunshine of the trip. In spite of the tension crackling in the air and the despondent look on Luna's face, the combination of sand in my toes and the sound of the waves and the distant music from the cabana feels like absolute bliss.

Well. Close second, after last night.

It's about three seconds before Luna starts blurting apologies, telling me that she knows she was out of line and didn't mean any of those awful things she said about me and Gabriel, and that she doesn't expect me to forgive her . . .

"It wasn't about you guys," she says, head snapping between me and Rory, eyes wide and pleading. "I promise. I was upset about— about some other stuff, and at myself. I think I got all in my head thinking that you didn't like me, and I know I shouldn't have taken any of that out on you, but—"

"Hang on." I lean forward, and she catches herself mid-sentence. "Why the hell would you think we didn't *like* you?"

Once Luna starts speaking again, she talks a mile a minute about how none of her friends from uni have bothered to even do the bare minimum and get in touch with her since her breakup, and how she's realizing that they were never really her friends in the first place, which she says isn't surprising when she was always so boring and serious compared to Liam, so it's no wonder *he* preferred spending time with everybody else rather than her . . .

"And I guess, coupled with the fact my friends from home barely speak in the group chat anymore and you guys were short with me a couple of times, I got really paranoid that *you* were just putting up with me, too. Especially when you said that you weren't surprised Liam had cheated on me," she adds in a small voice, to me.

"What?" I rack my brain before remembering what I said last night at the bar. "No. I meant it wasn't surprising because he sounds like a really shitty boyfriend! Not because of *you*."

Rory nods sagely. "Such a shitty boyfriend."

Luna gawps at me, and I can practically hear the gears whirring as she adjusts to this new information. "R-really?"

"Yes! Is that honestly why you went off at me yesterday, about throwing myself at Gabriel?"

Her eyes dart between us, tears shining in them, shame coloring her cheeks.

As much as her words last night had upset me, all I feel now is sorry for Luna—and frustrated that things got so out of hand. I shuffle up to sit on her towel so I can put an arm around her.

"You poor thing," I tell her, just like Gran says to me. "As if we would have hung out with you all week—*and* shared a room with you—if we didn't like you!"

She lets out a watery laugh. Rory nudges her thigh with a foot and asks, "This is why you were all upset I invited Zoe? Not just because you thought she was seeing your ex? Which, for the record, was *bonkers* to even think, but I did check, and she isn't. So, there's that."

Relief shudders out of Luna in a big sigh, tears running down her cheeks as she talks about how silly she was being. She tells us how she regrets breaking up with Liam even though she's starting to see that there are so many reasons why she should have done exactly that, and she can't tell if she misses him or is just scared of not being in a relationship.

"Because it's not just him I've lost—it's having someone to share everything with. It's all our friends, and . . . the worst part is, I didn't even *notice* they weren't my friends! Because Liam was always there inviting me along, and it's— Don't laugh, okay?"

"We would never," Rory says with such deadly seriousness that it sounds more like she's promising to absolutely laugh.

"You guys feel more like my best friends than anyone back home I'd actually think of as a best friend. Which I know makes me sound crazy and like some weird, clingy stalker—"

"And thinking Zoe from Kids' Club was dating your ex *didn't*?" I blurt.

"I hate to break it to you, sweetie," Rory says, leaning across to put a hand on Luna's shoulder, "but you're stuck with us. If you think I'm letting you two losers go after we leave this place, you are sadly mistaken. And if you think *you* sound sad, I have a bunch of friends but nobody I'd call a *best* friend. Nobody I feel I can be real with, like you guys."

Luna sniffles, teary-eyed.

They both look at me.

"Friendless dork right here, too. I'm *so* glad it's not just me. The only times I ever message anyone from school is on LinkedIn. I probably won't end up staying in touch with most of my uni friends after I leave, either."

Which . . . might be sooner than I was expecting.

"Seriously," Rory carries on, "if you guys think I'm not sending you follow and friend requests on every damn platform the second we're on that bus and have our phones back, you've got another thing coming."

"This is where I admit I only really have LinkedIn, isn't it?" I deadpan.

"Excuse me?" Rory chokes, eyes bulging. She throws her arms in the air and her head back. "What is it with people not having social media? Zoe barely has anything! Please tell me you at least have Instagram, Jodie?"

"Er . . ." I feel myself flush, not really sure why. It's never bothered me before. But then, I guess, maybe I haven't had people in my life that I wanted to be on social media for. It was just another way for them to rub their lives in my face, to make me feel inadequate.

I say as much to Rory's and Luna's gobsmacked faces, then add, "Plus, I was trying to make a point to my friends that I was better than them because I didn't need it, but . . . I don't think they ever cared, let's face it. It just meant I could say, 'Ooh, I'm not on social media,' like people tell you they're vegan, or that they go to Oxbridge. But for you guys," I say in the grandest voice I can, hoping that overdramatizing will hide the genuine emotion behind my statement, "I can make an exception."

"Thanks, you two," Luna mumbles, her voice wobbling. She squeezes Rory's hand and tips sideways to lean her head on my shoulder for a second before sitting back up. "I'm really sorry I yelled at you both like that and ruined the night."

"Believe me," Rory snorts, "that didn't even come close."

34 Luna

I'm dizzy with relief that the girls have forgiven me—even if I'm still mortified over my behavior and the paranoia that led me to lash out at them. I've never been so happy to be so wrong about something.

Without further ado, Rory takes over and seizes the spotlight, launching into a vividly detailed description of everything that happened from the second I stormed out, telling me all about her viral success and *#LobsterFail,* even giving scarily good northern accents to the women from the hen do as they appear in her storytelling.

"Like, I don't think I'd even care so much if nobody knew it was me," she says.

I sneak a glance at Jodie, who smirks. *Who's she kidding?*

"But someone knew it was me and they tagged me and now *everyone* knows. The *whole world* knows that Rory Belmont is Lobster Girl. It's going to follow me everywhere. People will google me, and the first thing they see will be that video and my pasty arse."

"Maybe you can just say it's not you and they made a mistake? I bet you can't even make out your face that clearly in it."

Jodie pulls a face at me.

Oh. Well. Never mind.

"Doesn't help that you can hear me shouting her name when she falls in," Jodie adds. "You can see us running over to help."

I suck my lips in, chewing on them for a moment.

"Right. Er. That's not . . . ideal, I suppose."

"And," Rory goes on, her eyes wide, "they tagged my *public* Instagram. Well. Okay, so bear with me, but I don't tell people I *know* about that account because I've been trying to build an online presence and promote myself as an artist to try and prove that I *can* do it, and like if I can get enough of a platform, my parents would have to admit I didn't need the law degree. So now *everyone's* gonna find out I've got this other Instagram, they'll find my TikTok and Etsy store and see just how much I've been failing being an artist, which my family are going to think is *so* sad, and—"

"Ooh!" I blurt. "Do you post all your drawings on there, like the doodles in your notebook? Sorry, I know I shouldn't have looked, but you're a good artist."

"Wait," Jodie says, looking totally baffled. "That's what that Instagram account was for? I thought that was just . . . you know, *yours.*"

Rory's lips draw into a pout, giving me the impression she's offended, but I can't work out why. "What do you mean?"

"Don't get me wrong, it was cute," Jodie replies, backpedaling. "But I would never have guessed that was what you were trying to promote. Like, your art stuff, I mean. I thought it just looked pretty and . . . influencer-y."

"What?"

Jodie shrugs. "I dunno, I guess I would've thought I'd see . . . more of your work? I mean, if you'd said it was all the brand you'd built to try and launch yourself as an *influencer,* I totally would've bought that. But hey, I pretend that not having social media gives me some bullshit moral high ground. What do I know?"

Rory laughs, but it's borderline hysterical. She slumps back down to lie in the sand, dragging her hands over her face a few times.

"Oh my God. Oh my *God.* I can't . . . You're *right.* I never promote my own damn work on there anymore. I've been trying so hard to do what typically does well on *other* accounts that I stopped posting the kind of content that *I* wanted to share. Which was doing well when I *did* post it! No wonder I was losing followers and not getting so many likes or views anymore! No wonder nobody was visiting my Etsy store. God. It's so obvious now you've said it!"

She lets out a loud, mournful sigh. "Face it, guys. Whatever I thought I could do, I can't. Even if people did take me seriously as an artist, nobody's going to care when they only want to see Hashtag *LobsterFail.*"

"So own it," I say, shrugging, remembering her "Rethink! Rebrand!" pep talk to Jodie the other day, after the earlobe incident. "Start putting 'Lobster Girl' in your bio and stuff. If people are going to find out anyway, you might as well be up front. Buy yourself an orange dress and post a picture of a Lobster Girl glow-up. Brands do ad campaigns with people from memes now, right? Maybe it'll even *help.*"

Rory's braids swish across the sand as she whips her head around to look at me.

"Sorry," I mutter, backing down as her brown eyes pierce right through me. "I was . . . just trying to be positive about it. Find a silver lining."

"No," she snaps, and breaks out into a grin that goes from ear to ear. "That is *perfect*. Oh my God. Why didn't I think of that? You're so right. How are you guys so good at this? I thought *I* was a social media guru, but I can't even promote my own work or think of a good way to spin the whole Lobster Fail fiasco. I need to—ugh, what's the phrase?—take control of the narrative! I need to make it my story. You are *so right,* Miss Lola."

"I am?"

"She is?"

"Yes! I can't believe I was too busy throwing myself a pity party to even think of capitalizing on it. Oh my God. I mean, I have a viral hashtag now! Granted, I bet it'll die down soon, but hey, I can make it mine, keep it going. I can totally use it. I totally love the glow-up idea, it's genius. I'm absolutely stealing that."

"You're welcome to it."

I'm too startled by her complete one-eighty in attitude to say anything else, quite honestly. Rory has gone from moping and sullen, her pout hardly shifting since I saw her at breakfast, to, well, this. Her eyes are wide and shining, her smile is so big that if she smiled any harder I think it might break her face, and she's all but vibrating with energy.

She looks a little manic, but in a good way.

It's the most energetic I've seen her all week.

"Are we sure she didn't smack her head yesterday?" Jodie stage-whispers to me, making Rory laugh and shove her.

"Shut up, I'm fine. I'm just . . . Ugh, it's such a great idea! I wanted all those followers, and now I've got them! I need to use them. And to *think* I was actually considering after yesterday if I'd be better off shutting down all my social media completely. Luna, you've saved my life."

"Ahem!" Jodie cries, clutching a hand to her chest. "I believe I also helped drag you from the pool yesterday."

Rory gives her a sardonic look. "And, my sweet knight, I shall be forever in your debt. I shall have a feast arranged in your honor. Oh man, you realize what this means, don't you?"

"What?"

"I can never do a law degree now. Nobody would take their lawyer seriously if they'd been a *viral joke.* That's it—that's my gateway into telling my parents I'm not doing it and that I should apply for something else I actually *would* suit through clearing instead. Or take a gap year! Say I'll wait for it to blow over, while I capitalize on it instead!"

Jodie rolls her eyes, but says sincerely, "Good for you, honey, good for you. We're glad the pity party is over."

Rory flips onto her stomach and scrambles up, spraying sand everywhere. She lunges for my bag and scrabbles through it. "You've still got my notebook, haven't you? Where's . . . aha! And pen, pen . . . Where's . . . Got it."

My stomach clenches a little at the mention—and sight—of her notebook.

"I'm sorry I read your journal," I say, "or whatever it is. I didn't . . ." No, that's a lie, I *did* mean to. "I shouldn't have done it."

"It's fine," she says, waving her hand and pen at me as she

balances the notebook on her knees, then tears the cap from the pen with her teeth and starts scribbling away on a fresh page. It's a different attitude from her reaction last night—but I guess it probably hadn't helped that I'd been yelling at her.

Jodie snaps her fingers and sits up a bit straighter. "Oh yeah! I forgot about that. What was this bucket list thing you were on about?"

Rory doesn't answer for a minute, too busy scribbling away, grunting and jerking her head at me as if to signal I should take over. So I explain to Jodie about the list I found in Rory's notebook—admitting in a mumble that her goal of making friends and talking to people had just made me feel even more insecure.

I feel so pathetic, so foolish.

But Jodie doesn't laugh at me, just nods with a sympathetic twist of her mouth like she gets it.

How could I have ever thought they weren't really my friends?

I say as much out loud, and Rory spits the pen cap into the sand to say, "There are some things you go through that forge a friendship. For the Party and El, it was the Upside Down and the Demogorgon. For us, it was a digital detox resort, too much sangria and a crumbling shack on the beach."

"I think next time I'll take the mountain troll," Jodie responds.

We sit quietly for a while, letting Rory scribble away. The page looks like a mess of scrawled, frantic notes. It's covered in arrows, things are starred, and some are in haphazardly drawn circles. Finally, she huffs and snaps the notebook shut. She glances at us, blushing and cringing visibly.

"Sorry. I just—had a lot of ideas."

"It's okay."

"From now on, Luna, you have permission to shout at me as much as you want, if this is what happens after. I am going to turn this thing *around*. You wait. I'll be hitting a million followers in no time. Let those Etsy orders roll in!"

But she says it with a self-deprecating wink so that we know she hasn't got her head completely in the clouds, and we smile back at her.

Rory knocks Jodie's leg with her foot. "What about you, then? You vanished last night. Did you go after that guy in the khaki shorts? OMG, and what happened with Gabriel and his cronies showing up?"

"Hang on—*Gabriel* was out last night?" I blurt, eyes wide. I look at Jodie with ready sympathy, remembering how hurt she was yesterday before our night out. "Are you okay?"

"Actually . . ."

I'm stunned when a wide smile splits her face and lights up her eyes.

Rory levels a finger at her, peering over the top of her giant sunglasses. "Girl, that is *not* the look of a lady who got her heart torn to shreds after having it out with lover boy last night. Spill!"

And giddy, girlish Jodie is back with a vengeance, perching up on her knees and gesturing widely as she tells us about wanting to prove to Gabriel she didn't care, dancing with another guy, and their tense little showdown on the dance floor. She explains how they'd completely misunderstood each other, how sweet and genuine he'd been . . .

I can't help but feel a flicker of jealousy, wishing Liam had shown that kind of self-awareness about his own immaturity at some point. But it vanishes quickly, replaced by something a lot closer to feeling like I dodged a bullet by breaking up with him when I did.

Moony-eyed, Jodie flops back onto her elbows to tell us about their nighttime stroll. "We spent . . . God, must've been hours . . . just walking along the beach, talking."

"And kissing," I guess.

"Quite a lot of it, actually," she says, sounding rather pleased with herself.

"And shagging?" Rory waggles her eyebrows, and Jodie's blush is answer enough, even if she's tight-lipped on details, which makes us all giggle.

"It wasn't just that, though. I really felt like I could open up to him. Things just . . . make *sense* with him somehow, you know? Like, I've decided I'm going to quit uni."

"What!" Rory and I both cry.

I know Jodie had mentioned that first night how unhappy she was there, and that thinking about her final year and her career afterward was what she'd come here to run away from, but she suddenly sounds so sure of her decision and so at peace with it. *Happy* about it.

"It's what I've wanted for a while," she says, nodding to herself, "and it's time I started going after what I want a bit more."

"Teach me your ways," Rory declares with a self-deprecating snort, but stretches a leg to nudge Jodie with her foot in a way that seems to say, *Proud of you, girl!*

I ask, "Did you and Gabriel talk about—about you . . ."

The way Rory looks at me makes me stop talking. Bad idea, I guess.

But Jodie seems to know I was about to ask if there was any future for the two of them, and shrugs. "Not really. I told him I'd see him today, but we didn't discuss anything about *after* that. It's his day off, so I figured . . . I dunno. Maybe I'll say bye later. It was just such a perfect night, and if that's all it can be . . ."

She sighs wistfully.

"Well, excuse me, Miss Ho-dee," I say, doing my best impression of Esteban, "just what do you think you're doing here with us?"

"What?"

"You have one day left to enjoy this piece of paradise." I sweep a hand out at the view we've got right now.

The white sand, the bright-blue sea, the beach bar . . . The hotel itself looks like something out of a magazine, glowing in the sunshine and surrounded by palm trees and flowering bushes. Even the volleyball game that's started up a way down the beach looks inviting.

"So *what* are you doing sitting here with us when your man has a day off work and you could be spending it wrapped up with him?"

Jodie blushes, mumbling incoherently, but there's a smile tugging at the corners of her mouth.

"Go on," Rory encourages. "Go find him! We'll be hanging around here if you want to come back or change your mind or whatever. But for now go and kiss his face off."

"Are you guys sure? I mean, it's . . . it's our last day. And—"

"And we'll be stuck together for most of tomorrow on a bus to the airport and on the plane home," I point out. Jodie's face lights up, but she ducks her head to try and hide it. I can't help but smile at that. "If you don't go, one of us will. And I'm newly single. Don't tempt me."

Jodie laughs and climbs to her feet, dusting sand off herself. "Okay, okay, I'm going. I'll see you guys for dinner, though?"

"The last supper," Rory says.

"A final hurrah to the vacation from hell," I add.

Jodie picks up her shoes, gives us a little wave and heads off, and Rory and I both shout after her, whooping and cheering for her. Jodie stops to throw her hands in the air and give a little wiggle before jogging up the beach.

"That girl," Rory declares, "is living her best life."

She twists to lie on her stomach, opening her notebook again. I get a book out of my bag, but after a minute or so I realize I'm not really reading any of the words.

I close the book again, hugging my knees to me and watching the sea wash up onto the shore and back out. My eyes slide shut, and I enjoy the warmth of the sun on my skin, the quiet of it all.

Jodie is, as Rory put it, out there living her best life. Off to get her guy, and determined to make changes in her life and rethink her priorities. Rory is writing furiously with a newfound zest for all her ambitions.

Which just leaves me.

And maybe I don't have many good friends to go back home to, or a boyfriend anymore. Maybe I don't have a five-year plan that's remotely on track or even *any* kind of plan right now.

And I'm . . . okay.

No, that's not right. I'm better than okay.

I am *brilliant*.

35 Rory

"You should put more sun cream on," Luna tells me.

"Please! What kind of pasty-arse Brit would I be if I put sun cream on, on my last day on vacation?"

"A burnt one, risking skin cancer and wrinkles."

I wave a hand at her. "I put some on this morning, and I haven't even been swimming. I'm fine, Miss Lola. But," I say, softening, "I appreciate your concern, babe."

Luna rolls her eyes, and I have to smile. Hannah and Nic would love her. She is every inch the responsible young adult they are trying to train me to be.

We sit out on the beach for a while after Jodie leaves. I'm wrapped up in my notebook and plans, scribbling video ideas and Instagram captions and my new bios. I find myself thinking about the drawing of Larry the Lobster I did at Kids' Club with the little girl, and sketch it out again as best I can remember. I redraw him a few more times until I think he looks perfect.

I could do something with that. I'm not sure *what* yet, but something will come to me. Today my brain is on fire, and I am determined to fan every ember and keep it going.

I can't believe I didn't think of this sooner—and I can't *believe* I needed Jodie to point out the obvious to me: all my efforts to "build a brand" were ultimately not focusing on the product I wanted to sell. The passion I actually wanted to *share*.

I flick back a few pages to my bucket list. I bite the inside of my cheek as I cross a few things out:

~The Vacation Bucket List~

1. Write pros and cons list of actually doing the law degree you got an UNCONDITIONAL OFFER FOR
2. Write pros and cons list of doing literally anything but that
3. ~~Consider other degrees to apply to through clearing?~~
4. ~~Write pros and cons list of a gap year, just in case~~
5. ~~HAVE FUN! BE RESTFUL! PRACTICE MINDFULNESS!~~
6. ~~Talk to strangers (make friends??)~~
7. ~~Try something new!~~
8. ~~Figure out how to tell Mom and Dad and Nic and Hannah I don't want to do the law degree, never wanted to do the law degree, never will want to do the law degree, and might cry if someone mentions the law degree one more time~~
9.
10.

I think my stint as Larry counts as "try something new," and as for all my worry and indecisiveness about the law degree . . .

My family will all have seen *#LobsterFail*, I have *zero* doubt. I'm also willing to bet that means they've found my TikTok, Instagram and Etsy store. They'll *know*.

And for once, that . . . doesn't horrify me the way it used to. The way it did mere *days* ago. So what if my views were declining and I was losing followers? Look at all that effort I've put into something I *love*, I'll say! It's easily way more effort than I ever put into my studies, and just because I've coasted through school so far doesn't mean uni will be a breeze. Jodie's proof enough of that.

I'd like to go to uni, though. Whenever Jodie and Luna have talked about it, it's made me look forward to it. Just, like, not the "law degree" part.

My family will have to suck it up, that's all.

And then help me figure out how clearing works, because I don't actually know.

I look up when Luna says, "I might get a drink, if you'd like one? Or I think lunch should be open by now . . ."

Hint taken. "I could eat."

"Are you sure? If you're busy, I don't wanna disrupt the flow."

I shake my head, closing my notebook. She holds her bag open for me to drop my things into—I make sure to dust the sand off first—and we head back toward the hotel.

"So," she says, dragging the word out and looking at me uncertainly, "your bucket list. Any, um . . . any progress? All that frantic note-making?"

I mock gasp, clutching my chest. "You fiend, Luna, reminding me of your snooping. I am heartbroken by your betrayal."

She looks a little awkward, even though she rolls her eyes and nudges me with her elbow. "Oh, shut up."

I tell her about the pros and cons lists I've just been working on, which are remarkably short given how stressed out I was about the mere idea of them and how decisive I feel now. I say I'm going to be a big girl, act like a goddamn grown-up for once and just tell my family I want to study something else.

If I can stand up to Esteban, then Mum and Dad will be a *breeze*.

"Good for you, Rory. That's—it's great, really."

Luna beams at me, and something warm blooms in my chest. Kind of like pride. It's a nice contrast to the sinking dread I felt when I got that letter with my unconditional offer, by a mile.

"What about you? Are we totally over that drag of an ex with his cheating and his awful sneakers?"

Luna gives a small, uncertain laugh, and as she rolls her eyes again, I find myself barreling on.

"He didn't deserve you, you know. I realize that probably sounds weird coming from me because we only met a few days ago, but I mean . . . We're friends. And you deserve better than a guy who was more bothered about going out and having a good time than respecting what he had with you. You were together for *ages* and it's a lot to get over, I understand that, but it sounded like things hadn't been good for a while, and like you'd bitten your tongue a whole bunch of times rather than tell him he was pissing you off before you finally broke up with him. You're stunning, you're sweet—you're the whole deal. If he couldn't see that, then it's *his* problem, not yours."

Luna stares at me, stunned, listening intently. Maybe I sound like a total weirdo or maybe (I hope) it's the kind of stuff she's been wondering herself and needs to hear out loud. But she's been so kind and supportive—up until last night, anyway—trying to build me and Jodie up and lend a sympathetic ear. And I doubt her awful ex-boyfriend—or any of the shitty friends who've been ghosting her—gave *her* that kind of courtesy.

"And," I press, "if your friends would rather pick him than you, then that says a lot about *them*. They're probably not your kind of people anyway. You'll be better off without them, too. You said you've got other friends on your course, though, right?"

"Yeah," Luna says quietly, eyes focused on the ground as she nods, taking my words in. "I do."

"You're not boring, either. For the record, I think you're pretty fucking cool."

Luna flushes, but says in a soft voice, "Thanks, Rory. I appreciate that."

When we get to reception, along with a stream of people heading toward lunch, I spot Zoe across the room and tap Luna's arm.

"Hey, uh, you go on ahead, okay? I'll meet you there in a minute."

"Sure," she says. I think she's only half listening, but she makes her way toward the restaurant anyway, and I head over to Zoe. She's leaning against the reception desk, filling in a form. I linger for a second, but she doesn't seem to notice me.

God, why do I suddenly feel so awkward? We were getting along great. We didn't click the way I did with Luna and Jodie, but she was nice, and we were never stuck for something to say. So why do I feel so weird now?

Oh right—because I got her to come out to a club with us, unwittingly went viral, lost my shit, shut myself in a toilet cubicle and made her wait around in the loo for me all night.

I clear my throat. "Hey."

Zoe jumps, startled, and looks up with wide eyes before setting down her pen and smiling widely at me. "Rory! Hey! How're you doing? Are you, um, feeling better?"

"Loads," I say, and I really mean it. "I just wanted to say I'm *so* sorry about last night. I promised you this awesome, fun girlie night, and I totally ruined it."

"Would you believe I've had worse?" she jokes.

I'm so relieved she doesn't seem mad. I know I would have been, in her shoes.

"I'm glad you're doing better today. That video stuff—it'll all blow over."

I don't explain that I'm kind of hoping it doesn't. "Well, yeah, anyway, I just . . . wanted to apologize. And say thank you. I really appreciate you sticking around like that all night, and it was kind of fun working with you at Kids' Club."

"Hey, you know, the day is young . . ."

I give her a deadpan look. "Not *that* young."

Zoe laughs loudly. "It was fun having you around for a while. Thanks for being Larry."

"I'd say *anytime,* but what I really mean is *never again.*"

"You should know I'll be telling people about you for years," Zoe says.

"I would despair if you didn't. If you're ever back on social media, look me up, huh?"

"Will do, Lobster Girl."

36 *Jodie*

Gabriel is nowhere to be found. After maybe half an hour of meandering around the hotel, hoping to spot him, I start to give up hope. He'd said he'd see me today, but he never said *when,* and it's not like I can just text him . . . And it's also not like I can just barge into the staff room to see if he's there. Not least because I don't want to run into Eduardo or any of the other guys Gabriel was hanging out with last night.

"Hola, señorita," a friendly voice calls to me when I'm walking back through reception for maybe the eighth time. "¿Cómo estás?"

I look around to see Rafael, the driver from our first day, smiling at me. I smile back and say, "Estoy bien, ¿y tú?"

"Your Spanish is very good, Miss Jodie. I see you wandering around the hotel. Have you lost something?"

"Oh! Um, no, I just . . ."

"Have you forgotten which activity you are supposed to be at, perhaps?"

He says it with such an air of sarcasm that I can't help but laugh. "Not exactly. I was just . . ." I take a gamble, bracing myself to ask, "Have you seen Gabriel anywhere?"

"Ah," Rafael says, smiling again, "do not tell me, there are more tortolitos about. Sí, I heard he was quite taken with one of our guests!"

All I can do is give a sheepish laugh and an even more sheepish smile.

Rafael takes pity on me, though, and beckons me to an office behind reception. He flicks through a book and finds a phone number. Saying nothing to me, he calls from the office landline and greets the person on the other end enthusiastically when they answer.

After exchanging some pleasantries, he says in English with a sidelong glance at me and a smirk, "I am calling because I have a lovely young lady here who is looking for you. Mm-hmm. Sí, sí . . ."

He says goodbye and hangs up. "Gabriel is on his way. He won't be long."

"Thanks," I say, pleasantly surprised by the lack of interrogation and how damn *helpful* he's been. (After the way Esteban has been and how we got press-ganged into activities at the start of the week, I kind of forgot the staff could be *nice*.) "I appreciate the help."

"I believe he likes you," Rafael tells me with a certain tone of conspiracy, reminding me of the time when I was little and Gran told me where Mum had hidden my Christmas presents. "He is quite lonely sometimes, I think. I haven't seen him excited about a young lady in a while."

"Er," is all I can manage.

In my head, I'm punching the air and doing a pathetic happy

dance because *hell yeah,* Gabriel doesn't come on to every girl in this hotel who shows an interest in him and compliments his earlobes!

Not that I really *thought* he did, given the things he said last night, but . . . it's still nice to hear that he doesn't from someone else.

Rafael hangs out talking with me for a while. He finds it hilarious that we got shunted to one of the ramshackle villas on the beach ("Not even fit for the cockroaches," he says), and has seen the video of *#LobsterFail*. He's a little more sympathetic about that one, even if he does crack up laughing just thinking about it.

When a shadow falls across the room and someone stands in the doorway, Rafael and I stop snickering over the tortolitos, who he saw bickering over eggs at the breakfast buffet this morning. It's Gabriel, standing there smiling at me, his eyes sparkling, and my mouth goes dry.

"Hola."

"Hi," I rasp.

"I will leave you tortolitos alone, hmm?" Rafael says, winking at me. He claps Gabriel on the shoulder on his way out, and Gabriel stays leaning against the open door and smiling at me for a moment longer.

He's wearing an old, faded pair of jeans and a black V-neck T-shirt that shows off his strong arms and clings to his broad chest. I thought he looked pretty dishy in his uniform, but this is . . . Wow.

I want to run my fingers through his dark hair and—

Like I'm possessed by someone more confident and flirty, I'm already getting up to do just that. His soft hair slides between my fingers, and I pull his head down to kiss him. A shiver passes through me as his hands settle on my waist and his tongue drags over my lower lip.

I break the kiss first; Gabriel leans forward as I pull back, groaning melodramatically as his lips finally part from mine. I feel him smile, and don't mind that his hands tighten around my waist to stop me from going anywhere.

"Okay, that was all," I tell him, patting his chest. "You can go back home now."

He chuckles. It's such a loud, hearty sound, and it wraps around me like a hug.

"I'm sorry I dragged you in on your day off. I didn't realize, um . . ."

He doesn't even shrug, just keeps smiling at me. "I was glad Rafael called. I thought you would be with your friends today."

"I did promise I'd meet up with them for dinner."

He tugs me back closer to him with a wink. "If I can spare you."

My heart skitters, and all I can think is: *I'm done for.*

Gabriel sweet-talks the kitchen into packing us a picnic. They make us chicken salad sandwiches with baguettes that are still warm and soft and some fruit salad, and they even throw in a bottle of cava, glasses and everything. The bottle is still sweating when Gabriel pops it open on the beach.

He brought me in the opposite direction of last night, beyond the villas and far out of the way of any wandering guests. The palm trees are thicker here, and there's a cluster of rocks near the shore. We sit on the sand and munch our way through the picnic and sip our cava, the sun beating down on us. It's quiet all the way out here—private, almost. You can only just see the beach bar—if you squint. The people are dots in the distance.

"You're not going to ask if me and Rory made up with Luna after last night?" I ask Gabriel eventually.

He scoffs, leaning back on one elbow and reaching for a piece of mango from the fruit salad. "Por favor, querida, you were always going to make up. The three of you, it's like . . ." He considers it for a moment. "Like the Doctor, Rory and Amy."

"I guess Rory is Rory in that analogy."

He laughs, only hearing it once I point it out.

"I think that's a compliment," I go on. "I'm going to take it as a compliment."

"Claro que sí. You three have a bond, ¿sabes? If you hadn't told me, I would have thought you had all been friends for years. One fight is nothing. But I am glad to hear you made up."

I tell him that Luna apologized and seems to be in crisis about how she doesn't have any friends back home and about breaking up with her boyfriend, and how Rory has decided to make the most of the #LobsterFail thing. Gabriel is in stitches just thinking about the video—laughing so hard that he wheezes and even snorts.

It's maybe the most unattractive laugh I have ever heard—and it is utterly infectious.

I get a warm, fuzzy feeling thinking how much more I like him now that I've found something *not* flawless about him.

Oh God, why do I like him so much?

Gabriel takes a sip of his cava, but when I say, "And the fact she tried to go *back into the pool* to get the costume . . ." he chokes on it and cava shoots out his nose, which sends me into hysterics.

I fall onto my back and roll on my side, turning away from him as he wipes his face and tries to stop coughing and I try to calm down. I genuinely think I might wet myself laughing—and it would *still* be less unattractive than Gabriel is right now.

By the time we both get a grip and he's tidied himself up, I've got a stitch and my cheeks ache. My eyes slide closed behind my sunglasses.

"You're lucky you've got such lovely earlobes," I tell him, "or I'd be long gone."

He throws a grape at me. It bounces off my nose.

"Don't," I whine. "I haven't got the energy left to laugh again."

"How about for this?"

He is *smooth.* Cava shooting out the nose and all.

Gabriel has shifted so he's leaning over me, his hands planted beside my shoulders, and he leans down *so slowly* to kiss me. His soft lips skim lightly along my jaw, under my ear, bite gently at my skin, suck at the base of my throat. And I *swoon,* making soft little humming noises as my hands grip his shoulders and arms, then rake through his hair and eventually move under his shirt . . .

His skin is hot and smooth, and his hips press against mine as my hands slide up his chest and pull his T-shirt off. His lips leave my skin for the split second it takes for him to duck out of his shirt, and I ogle him shamelessly, making up for the darkness of last night. He chuckles when he catches me looking, but then he's busy returning the favor, undressing me bit by bit, kissing and caressing my body as he goes. He lingers over each of my breasts, tender in a way that feels reverent, my self-consciousness melting away under his mouth and hands.

I arch into Gabriel's touch, heat pooling in my stomach as his hands travel lower; he murmurs sweet nothings in a mixture of English and Spanish against my skin, compliments that make me every bit as dizzy and delirious as the curl of his fingers and caress of his tongue. My fingers fist in his hair, my hips canting toward him as I moan his name before dragging his head back up to kiss him. I fumble to undo his trousers, and a low groan stutters out of him when I wrap one hand around him with long, slow strokes, and the sound makes my heart flutter, scattering the last scraps of my self-consciousness. I draw him in close, my legs wrapping around his hips, and cup his face in my hands, the sand on my thumbs brushing off as I trace the lines of his face.

He presses his forehead to mine, our breath mingling, and I have that same feeling as last night: that whatever happens next, this is worth it, and it *means something.*

I'm not the kind of girl who goes totally giddy over a guy she fancies, and I didn't think I was the kind of girl to have sex on the beach—twice—with a guy she's only known for a few days.

But it turns out I am exactly that girl. And I've never been so happy about it.

I am also, it turns out, the kind of girl who goes skinny-dipping with a guy she's known for five days and just had sex with on a beach.

Droplets of seawater glisten on Gabriel's olive skin. With his wet hair slicked back off his face, he has kind of a big forehead. I'm weirdly thrilled to find something else that's a little less than perfect about him.

We float near the rocks. The water is calm, waves rocking gently against us. I can just about stand on tiptoe here, but Gabriel's arms are holding me up and my feet don't touch the bottom. I'd make a joke about him sweeping me off my feet, but it would be a little too accurate.

"I wanted to kiss you the day I met you," he tells me. "When you asked me for that cocktail class, I almost said no."

"You did?"

He nods, looking grave, but a small smile tugs at his lips. "I knew I would like you. Y me dio miedo. It scared me, ¿sabes? But it is like I said—I thought a short while with you would be better than wondering 'what if.' I haven't met anybody before who makes me want to be . . . so much myself."

Oh, man. Just when I thought he couldn't be any sweeter. He looks so *vulnerable* right now, too, with that pucker between his thick eyebrows and the way his lips pout. I can't resist pressing a kiss to them.

"It's hard for me to open up to people, too," I say. "Luna and Rory—and you—are the first people I've been honest with in . . . God, *years*. I didn't even tell my mum and my gran exactly *how much* I've been struggling being away at uni. I didn't want them to think I was . . . being soft. Giving up."

"Are you going to tell them?"

"Yeah. Yes," I say, more definitely. "My friends—so-called friends—make everything feel like a competition, and all that does is drag me down. The people who matter, like my mum, my gran . . . even Rory and Luna—they won't see it as a wasted opportunity or think I'm letting anyone down."

"What are you going to do next?" he asks.

I've always known what's next. Not in the way Luna did, with her five-year plan and her whole life so carefully thought out, but in terms of *school, exams, uni, graduate scheme, job.* It's a path that's been trod by the thousands of students who've gone before me, and I've been following it blindly.

My arms hook a little tighter around Gabriel's neck, both of us bobbing through the water on a fresh wave. A giggle slips out of my mouth as I smile and kiss him and say, "I don't know. Isn't that exciting?"

And then, stealing a bit of this newfound courage about my future, I ask him why he wanted to kiss me on the first night we met.

"I liked the look on your face."

"You mean when I was gawping at how fit you are?" I blurt.

He laughs, though looks flattered. "You seemed like you were the kind of person who"—he takes a minute to find the words—"doesn't take shit off anybody. Like you know who you are, what you want, and nobody can take that from you."

Well, now *I'm* flattered.

I think that's the nicest thing anyone's ever said to me.

"Gracias."

His eyes are hooded, and he tugs me closer, fingers dancing up my sides. "I like when you speak Spanish, querida."

"I like when you call me querida."

I sense the shift in the conversation before he speaks again, the seriousness that we've allowed to sneak in around the edges of our flirting and gentle confessions. "Are you . . ." Gabriel stops, glancing down, a frown slipping onto his beautiful face. I feel his spine stiffen and shoulders tense. "You leave tomorrow."

"Yeah," I murmur. I get what he's angling at, and I can feel my heart racing. But somehow I gulp down the lump in my throat and say, "We could stay in touch, maybe. If—if you wanted. I mean, I'd . . . I'd like . . . that."

His forehead is pressed to mine once more, and his lips ghost over my skin. He draws me closer and I wrap my legs around him. "I would like that, too, querida."

I kiss him again, and I have never been happier to be *that* kind of girl.

37 *Luna*

"You done?"

"I think so."

I've borrowed some pages at the back of Rory's notebook, at her insistence, to make a list of pros and cons of my relationship with Liam. After her little pep talk before lunch, I admitted that I hoped that this week would somehow magically cure my heartbreak, but I'm a bit scared that when I get home, I'll see a text from him or run into him somewhere and cave and beg for him back.

To which Rory declared, "*No.* You know what you need? A good old-fashioned pros and cons list."

I took a *lot* of convincing to do this.

Partly because I was afraid of what I'd find out. (What if there were so many pros that I realized I'd made the world's biggest mistake, and Liam wouldn't take me back, like I'd been worried about all week? And what if there *weren't* as many pros as I thought, proving how much time I'd wasted on him and been a fool to stay with him?)

But honestly, it just made me feel like a terrible person. I like planning. I like lists. But reducing *Liam,* and our four-year relationship, and all the plans I had to marry him and have kids with him, and the way I'd pictured our lives together . . . Reducing all that to a *list* just felt wrong.

It took me ages to get about three things on the list, but once I found my groove it became frighteningly easy to add to it, an outpouring of months of feeling like I didn't know who he was anymore, feeling left behind and lesser, not fitting into his new life at uni. Rory was right when she said I had probably bitten my tongue around Liam plenty of times, rather than be honest with him about something he'd done that upset or annoyed me.

Most of the list consists of fleeting moments that it feels petty to hold a grudge over, but they all add up to something larger—something that made me have a complete meltdown and end things, unable to take it anymore.

I skim through the three pages of "cons" while Rory watches me.

"It kind of turned from a list into one long rambling rant," I confess in a mumble, a little ashamed now that I'm sitting back and reviewing the pages. I cringe, groaning and pushing the notebook to the edge of my towel. "I don't need Reddit to pass judgment. Oh gosh. Why did you make me do this? No, don't *read* it!"

Too late—she's already grabbed the notebook and is flicking through it. She arches her eyebrows at me and says, "Hey, if you can snoop, I can snoop."

I bury my face in my hands, pull my knees up to my forehead and groan again.

Rory scoffs after a moment. "You are *definitely* not the one in the wrong here. The cheating was totally out of line, obviously, but are you kidding me? He could find the money to go out with his friends and buy video games, but not to get you a *Christmas present*? Are you shitting me? What a *douchebag*. God. I'm sorry, Miss Lola, but why did you put up with this guy for four years? He sounds awful. Ugh. You are *much* better off without him."

I expect to cringe again, and I'm about to defend Liam, but the words die on my tongue when I realize I'm *not* embarrassed.

I'm . . . relieved?

I'm relieved.

I'm *glad* Rory thinks that about him. I'm glad she's looked at my list of pros and cons, read all the sweet, lovely things about him that I miss, and still believes I'm better off without him.

She thinks he's a douchebag. And awful. And that I *put up with him*.

"You know what?" I say suddenly, sitting up a bit straighter. "You're right. I *am* better off without him. He was never going to change. Not for me, not with me. He just made me *tired,* and what kind of relationship is that? What kind of person would I be if I stayed with him?"

"You'd be settling," Rory says. "That's what! And you'd be miserable and resentful and you'd get divorced after your third kid when he forgot to buy 'the big present' for the first kid's tenth birthday, and by then all the stress would've given you wrinkles and gray hair and saggy boobs."

I gasp and clutch my boobs. "Don't say such blasphemous things." I crack a smile, though, and say more softly, "Maybe I should've broken up with him a long time ago."

"Nah. Nuh-uh. Don't go worrying about stuff like that. Look, you guys had a great run, but it ran its course, and now you realize what a goddamn catch you are and get over him. Which, honestly, you *really* need to do. I mean, you thought Zoe was Liam's rebound. *Zoe.* The *kids' rep.*"

I laugh, but it quickly turns into a pitiful moan of humiliation. I feel my cheeks flame. "Please don't remind me."

Rory's face scrunches up, her brown eyes glittering. "Mm, you did go a bit bananas. But it's okay." She pats my leg. "All the best ones do."

I get a similar pep talk from Jodie when she meets us for dinner. Her hair is matted with salt water and sand, her clothes are rumpled, and she looks so completely happy that we immediately know how well her afternoon with Gabriel went.

So instead of sharing all the sordid details, she and Rory quiz me on my relationship with Liam until I feel like they know everything about our four years together.

And *they're right.*

I deserve better.

Liam made me happy, for a while, but not toward the end. Not really, and not enough. And that's not his fault. (Well, it *is*, but . . . not completely.) What I mean is, I'm sure he will make someone else very happy one day, maybe. But that someone is not me, and that's okay.

"I'm not saying I need someone better than Liam," I declare, placing my hands flat on the table. Rory's shoveling profiteroles into her mouth and tries to say something, but then shakes her head and waves it off while she chews. "I'm just saying I need someone *different*. I am a grown-ass woman," I tell them. Jodie nods and Rory slaps the table in support. "And I did the right thing. I deserve someone who *fits* with me and doesn't wear me out."

"Oh, babe, you need someone who wears you out," Rory tells me. "Just, you know, in the *right* way."

Jodie hoots.

"You're right! And I *can* be on my own," I go on. "I don't need Liam around to make me happy, because he didn't anymore. I'm *better off without him*."

And for once I don't feel like it's something that if I say it enough, if I pretend hard enough, I might be able to convince myself.

I say it because it's *true*.

38 Rory

Gabriel, God bless him, helps us with our luggage. He walked Jodie back this morning (from . . . wherever they spent the night) and stuck around to give us a hand with our things.

For that alone, he is the new standard by which I will hold all romantic interests in my life.

(After Jodie hung out with us for a while at dinner, positively glowing and with a huge smile plastered on her face and a dreamy look in her eyes, she went back to find Gabriel. And I can only guess, judging by the fact she's still smiling and humming away to herself while she packs and gets ready, that it was a *really* good night.)

And when I say Gabriel is helping us with our things, I mean mostly mine.

I have to admit defeat and get the girls to help me repack my suitcase. I have no idea how Hannah got everything in there. Luna does her best to help me roll my clothes up as tiny as possible, but I still end up with a handful of bras and a pair of wedges in my carry-on bag. In the end, Jodie has to sit on top of my suitcase, with Gabriel wrestling the zips to make it shut.

I also don't remember my suitcase being *nearly* this heavy when I got here.

"Must be all the memories you're taking back with you," Luna jokes.

"I swear to God, if this is the cheesy crap you come out with, I will stop being your friend the *second* that plane lands."

She only laughs, though.

At reception, I take my case from Gabriel. He and Jodie hang back. Her hands are gripping his T-shirt like she physically can't bear to let go, pulling him into her. Their heads tip close together as they talk softly. Gabriel's lovely, lovely arms are wrapped around her, his thumbs stroking her back.

I can't decide if it's sickly sweet or the most romantic thing I've ever seen.

Kinda makes me wish I had someone like that to cozy up with.

When it looks like they're going in for a kiss, I turn around to give them their privacy and follow Luna, joining the queue at reception to check out. It's a slow process—people are collecting their things and signing something to say they've received all their devices. They're all asked about their stay and the receptionists discuss with each guest the activities they participated in.

I guess it's a nice touch, but I just huff at Luna and roll my eyes.

"Miss Rory."

Oh, wonderful.

Just what I wanted. One last chance for Esteban to fleece me for ruining his hotel.

He smiles at me, looking much calmer than he did yesterday. "And, Miss Lola. Bueno. I trust you both had a pleasant stay?"

Luna just gives him a look that would terrify anybody. And, to my utter shock and awe, with all the self-assurance she had last night when she was talking about being single, she tells him in a haughty voice that would make my *sisters* quake in their boots, "I'm not sure 'pleasant' is the word, Esteban, given that we stayed in a hut that looked like it would fall apart any moment, had our rooms flooded and were *banned* from certain activities."

She's channeling her inner Ice Queen and, honestly, I'm living for it.

Esteban's face tightens. "As we discussed during the week, your Hidropark visit was—"

"Save it," she says, lifting a hand, palm out. She even does a dramatic turn of her head, eyes closing for a moment. I have no idea where this has come from, but it is dramatic as all hell and I *love it.* "I have heard *quite* enough of your hotel policy for one week. It was all made perfectly clear in the fine print."

He purses his lips.

"Other than that," she goes on, with a sudden brightness, "it was a lovely stay."

"I am pleased to hear it, Miss Luna," he replies rigidly.

I gawp. Did he—he didn't, did he?

That smarmy git.

Luna just gives another Ice Queen smile and turns around, leaving every impression that she will be writing a damning, scathing review on Tripadvisor when she gets home.

Esteban clears his throat to say something to me, but I get in first. I'm so done with his attitude—especially after he failed to apologize for the whole pool incident, and after Luna put him in his place so well.

"I was thinking," I tell him. "After the . . . problems . . . the other day with Larry the Lobster, do you think you could send me his head?"

Esteban gives a small scoff of disbelief, unable to hide his astonishment. "I'm sorry?"

"His head. The head from the costume. I'll leave my address at reception. Could you post it to me? Call it . . . a gesture of goodwill."

"I'm not sure—"

"We'll have to remember to book tetanus shots," Luna tells me loudly. "I'm not convinced that villa was safe at all. And the splinters . . . Gosh, and the rash from the bedsheets . . ."

There is no rash from the bedsheets. Or splinters. And we definitely don't need tetanus shots. But before I can look at her like she's gone mad, Esteban is saying, "Sí, claro que sí, Miss Rory. I will make sure that is arranged for you, after we have had the costume cleaned."

"Muchas gracias, Esteban. So kind of you."

I fix a toothy smile on my face, looking at him until he caves.

"Well, señoritas, I am delighted to hear you have enjoyed your stay here at Casa Dorada. We hope to see you return soon," he says.

He moves away to talk to a couple near the doors, and Luna scoffs. "Not likely."

"I don't know what you're talking about," I tell her. "I'm dragging you two back next year. We'll smuggle in phones next time. It'll make a brilliant TikTok series."

I put the cap on my felt-tip and nod once, satisfied I've got it now.

"Okay. What do you guys think?"

I hold the notebook up to show them. Jodie and Luna are across the table from me in one of the airport cafés with paper mugs of not-too-great tea and subpar pastries, leaning over Luna's phone. She's just made the mortifying discovery that, when booking this trip completely drunk, she somehow *mistyped her own name,* and that's why they called her Lola. Jodie can't stop laughing.

Getting my phone back was weirdly blissful, but my mind has been going a mile a minute. I did a quick rundown of *#LobsterFail* and my social media accounts. I'm now at 24.7 thousand Instagram followers and my TikTok following has increased by half, which I'm totally thrilled about. I've also updated my bio to declare that, yes, I am indeed Lobster Girl. There are more than 3.5 million views on the TikTok video.

I've got what feels like hundreds of messages from my friends about it, and a shedload of DMs, but I'm less concerned with those right now.

I haven't even checked any of the comments on my profiles.

Luna had a great idea about owning this. I can't wait to upload a photo of me (looking good this time) with Larry the Lobster's head when it arrives. Maybe doing some dance trends while wearing it. I need to make the most of this, and that's exactly what I'm doing.

So I show the girls the cartoon I think I've finally nailed, based on the drawing I did at Kids' Club. It's a caricature of me, drenched and clutching my torn shorts, with a giant bright-orange lobster drowning in the pool I'm standing by.

"I didn't realize you could *actually* draw!" Jodie cries, snatching the notebook from me to get a better look. "I figured you just meant you could do a bit of Photoshop! This is amazing!"

"You think?" I ask.

"She looks *so* like you," Luna says.

"That is the point."

"This is *so* good," she tells me reverently, wide-eyed and grinning.

"What's the plan, then?" Jodie asks.

"I'm turning our Larry the Lobster into my own personal brand while it's still going viral. I'm thinking I'll post a couple of pics of this cartoon of him, bump up the likes, get those followers, and turn him into a bit of a comic to try to promote some of my other art."

I set the notebook down, swapping it for my phone and opening up my emails—my last port of call, and probably overloaded with junk, but . . .

Holy shit. Holy. Shit.

I let out such a shriek that Luna and Jodie jump and several people look over. I clutch one hand to my mouth and flap the other at the girls.

"Guys. Guys. Oh my God, look at this. Look!" I shove my phone under their noses, but before they can look I'm already squealing, "I'm sold out! My Etsy store! Look at all these restock requests! *People are buying my art.*"

This isn't happening. This isn't happening.

It's happening. It's so happening and I'm—I can't—it's—

I let out a long rush of air, trying to steady myself and not get swept up. This is crazy. But a good kind of crazy.

This is all happening. And I know it's my fifteen minutes, but that doesn't mean I can't make something of it after that. This was just a nudge in the right direction.

Not the greatest nudge, granted, and not one I'd have chosen, but hey, I can work with it.

And I will.

My family have all seen the video—and my artwork on social media. In our family group chat, Mum said that maybe I should be pursuing a more creative degree after all, *and* said how proud they are of me for "all the initiative and hard work you've been putting in when we thought you were just endlessly scrolling!"

So I guess that's a good start for the whole big "Mum, Dad, I'm sorry, but I don't want to do a law degree, it's *your* dream, not mine!" speech I was thinking I'd have to give.

Hannah and Nic found some of the comments from people on my Instagram asking when items in my store will be restocked and if I do commissions and texted me screenshots of them. Hannah's offered to sit down and work through the finances with me to make sure I'm charging "enough." Nic has mostly just sent me some of her favorite tweets about the *#LobsterFail* video and told me how amazing it all is.

And it is.

It's so amazing.

"Oh my gosh," Luna whispers. She smacks Jodie's arm hard

and flicks her fingers in my face, eyes widening as she looks down at her phone. "You guys. You guys!"

"What?"

"Well, I looked at the account that uploaded the original Lobster Fail video to YouTube. You will *never* guess who posted it."

She looks at us, phone cradled to her chest, a manic gleam in her eyes. Whatever it is, it's gotta be good. Maybe it's some celebrity we didn't know was staying at the hotel and didn't recognize.

And then she says, *"Esteban."*

I shriek (again), turning several heads (again), and we scrabble for her phone. And yep—there it is, clear as day: an account belonging to one Esteban Álvarez, with a familiar smarmy smile and twirly mustache in the profile photo.

"This cannot be real," Jodie breathes, wheezing with laughter and almost bent double. "Oh my God, stop—take it away. I'm going to wet myself!"

That slimy git.

But I can't help the grin on my face as I laugh right along with Jodie and Luna, and I think, I'm so glad I got to share all this with them.

39 Jodie

"Right," Luna says, all serious and in planning mode, her favorite place to be. We've just stepped through the arrivals gate. I'm still feeling a bit wobbly from the flight; we hit some turbulence, which was not fun at all, but the girls were really sympathetic about it, not even teasing me. Rory held my hand, and I'd been so grateful for Luna's request when we checked in that we be seated together. "Now. You've both got me on Facebook."

"And Instagram," I say, having created accounts on the bus ride from the hotel.

"And TikTok," Rory says.

Luna taps her phone. "And . . . that's a group WhatsApp set up. And we've all got each other's numbers."

"Roger that."

She lowers her phone, nodding and beaming at us. "Oh! I can't believe this week is already over! I can't believe I've only known you two for a week!"

"If you start crying . . . ," Rory threatens.

Luna's head wobbles. I think she actually is on the verge of tears. "Shut up. I'm going to miss you both so much!"

"I will literally be messaging you as soon as I'm on the train," I say. "You'll be sick of me before you even get a chance to miss me."

The three of us hug goodbye for what must be the eighth or ninth time.

I'm with Luna on this, though. It doesn't feel like I've only known them a few days, or that this time last week we were total strangers.

Something tells me that all this talk about messaging and visiting each other, hanging out and having group chats isn't just an empty promise that will quickly dissolve into bland "Happy Birthday" messages once a year and liking a post on social media from time to time.

They feel like friends for life.

And I've not had friends like this for a long time.

Admittedly, I felt an initial pang of jealousy at Rory's sudden internet fame and newfound success as an artist, but it disappeared quickly. Mostly, I just feel excited for her because things seem to be working out the way she wants them to.

Which, for me, is a new feeling.

I'm so used to competing with my friends.

This is a nice change.

"Rory!" a voice yells. "Rory! Oi! Lobster Girl!"

We all look around. A blond woman with a round face, a nose like Rory's, and dressed in an expensive coat and high-heeled shoes is waving at her.

"That's Hannah," Rory says. "Looks like my lift's here!"

"Lobster Girl, who're your friends? Who are you wearing? Watch out for the paparazzi!"

"Oh my God," Rory mutters. Her cheeks are red and she gives an awkward smile when she realizes people are looking at us. "Better go before she starts making a scene."

She hugs us again before giving her suitcase a kick and dragging it after her as she strides over to her sister. They hug and kiss on the cheek, and Rory tries to give her sister her case. Hannah flicks Rory's hat, laughs and starts walking off.

Rory turns around with a flourish, holding her sun hat to her head.

"Love you losers! Goodbye, Miss Ho-dee, Miss Lola!" she yells, and blows us a kiss before following her sister out of the airport.

Luna's phone buzzes and she looks around, letting out an excited, "Oh!" when she sees someone. "My ride's here, too."

I follow her gaze and spot a short, stocky guy wearing round brown-framed glasses, waving to Luna with a slightly bored, put-upon look that can only mean he must be her big brother.

"Looks like your cue to head home," I tell her. "I'll see you soon?"

"Yes! Definitely!"

We hug again—what's that now, the tenth time?—and Luna takes a breath as if to steel herself.

"You sure you don't want a lift to the train station? My brother won't mind."

"Yeah, it's fine. I've already got my bus ticket. And it's out of your way anyway."

"If you're sure. Well . . . see you."

I let her get halfway to the doors before firing off a text: *Miss you already xoxo*

She stops to check her phone. She turns around, laughing, and then waves over her shoulder as she leaves.

My turn now, I guess.

It's weirdly bittersweet to have watched them go. It was the same with my goodbye to Gabriel. We promised again we'd stay in touch.

"I really like you," he'd told me before I checked out. "I could fall for you, Jodie."

"Don't say things like that."

"Why not? It's true."

"I know. But it makes me not want to leave."

But I had left, and there's a text from him waiting for a reply, asking how the flight was and hoping I got home safe. (With four kisses.) (Not that I'm counting. But I am.)

I can't see me losing Rory or Luna anytime soon—and honestly, I don't want to lose Gabriel, either. I feel so silly admitting it, given that I've hardly known him any time at all, but . . . there was something so *real* about the spark between us. Maybe I'm a gullible fool, or he's uncovered the hopeless romantic within me, but . . .

I'd like to think there *is* something there, with us.

And he seems to feel the same way.

This past week feels like it's gone on for years.

And I don't know why, but I just feel . . . different.

Like a new Jodie.

I guess Gran was right: a vacation was exactly what I needed.

The arrivals gate is starting to empty out and I realize it really is time to go. I pocket my phone with plans to reply to Gabriel once

I'm on the train, hoist my bag higher onto my shoulder and make my way toward the bus station, suitcase dragging behind me.

"Excuse me," says an all-too-familiar voice, making me stop in my tracks. "And where do you think you're going?"

Mum steps in front of me, her arms crossed, car keys dangling from one finger, looking at me expectantly.

All I can do is stare at her.

"What the hell are you doing here?"

"Fine way to greet your mother! What about, 'Hey, Mum, good to see you, thanks for coming to collect me and save me from a bus and a train ride'? Didn't even wave back at me, too busy talking to your new friends. Not even a hug?"

I laugh, still not believing it, and give her a hug. We're not exactly a surprises kind of family, so this has thrown me completely.

"Thought I'd come and pick you up! Hmm? Nice surprise, isn't it! We can head over to Gran's so you can see her. Thought you'd probably want to go straight there for a cuppa and a natter—and even if you don't, *we're* dying to hear all about your week away, so tough!"

"Thanks, Mum. And that sounds brilliant, you're right."

"When am I not? Here you are." She takes my case from me, and we walk out. "So? How was it? You're looking very tanned. Very *relaxed*, for once."

"It was . . ."

I think for a minute. This past week was a lot of things, and such a roller coaster I don't even know where to start.

"You know what, Mum? It was perfect."

Luna Guinness

Aaaand one group WhatsApp sorted!

PS here's the link to that resort in Portugal we were looking at for our next vacation! They've got quite a good deal on at the minute, if we book soon

Jodie Davenport

Perfect! Thanks, Luna. Let's book it!

Rory Belmont

Ditto

Don't even have to beg my parents for a handout now I'm flush from selling out my store lol

All sixteen items xo

Jodie Davenport

Sixteen more than yesterday!!!

367

Luna Guinness

I want dibs on your restocks of that Tenby landscape btw! My grandad's bday is coming up and he'll love it

Rory Belmont changed the name of the group chat to "Casa Dorad-nah"

Rory Belmont set Luna Guinness's nickname as "Her Name Was Lola"

Rory Belmont set Rory Belmont's nickname as "Lobster Girl"

Rory Belmont set Jodie Davenport's nickname as "Sangria Slut"

Sangria Slut

Why am I Sangria Slut????

Lobster Girl

Uh, you did have wild, fantastic sex with a Spanish bartender on a beach

But also I have never seen anyone embody the heart-eye emoji so much as you whenever you saw a jug of sangria, so

Her Name Was Lola

Casa Dorad-nah, LOL

Love it

Luna Guinness set Jodie Davenport's nickname as "Steve Irwin"

Jodie Davenport set Jodie Davenport's nickname as "Sangria Slut"

Sangria Slut
Nah, I kinda like this version of me

Anyway, guess who has a FaceTime date with Gabriel tomorrow night!?

Acknowledgments

In all honesty, I don't think I'd cope for a week without my phone half so well as Luna, Rory and Jodie do—but if I had to, I know the friends who'd make me forget all about the internet and who deserve a thanks for always being there for me. Lauren and Jen, I miss your faces and am forever grateful to have you in my life. The Gobble (née Cactus) Gals, where would we be without the life updates that go completely unmentioned for weeks and giggly brunches and board nights? (Hannah and Ellie—it wasn't Casa Dorada, but I'm glad we got lumped together for *that whole thing* and then went out into the world as besties.) Aimee, the lifelong friend I love to bits. The Cluster/Squad Ghouls—love you nerds. What's a few thousand miles and a couple of time zones when you have the group chat!

A special shout-out and hug to the Physics gang. Two of the main characters in this book are struggling with the big life changes that university brings and the impact it has on their friendships, and I genuinely cannot imagine that time of my life without you lot. Seriously—who would I have held up drunk on the way to a club, or cried with in the library, or had in-depth discussions with about the Doom of Valyria instead of making sure I'd nailed Planck's law of blackbody radiation ahead of an exam? Who would I still be laughing with over silly memes and games of charades all these years later? Katie, thanks for always being on the other end of the phone and making me smile; I know I can trust you to share my standards when it comes to an overnight stay—especially one involving an air bed. And, Amy, aren't you so glad we bonded over academic diaries after being put into the same tutor group in freshers' week, now that you have me in your life to annoy you constantly and send you all the goblincore TikToks I find? Aren't you??? Love you all tons, my wonderful Physics gang xo.

As ever: big, big thanks to my family. To Mum and Dad, to Gransha (who can truly find fans of my books anywhere!), to my auntie and uncle, and my sister, Kat—lots of love to all of you, and thanks for always being supportive of my books. Also, to Katie and Harriet—on the one hand, I'm sorry our girls' trips don't involve life-changing epiphanies and sexy bartenders, but . . . c'mon, who doesn't love aqua aerobics?! *Cue the jazzy arms*

And of course, no book is complete without a MASSIVE thank-you to the team behind the scenes. Clare, you're a true rock star, and I couldn't do any of this without you. To Naomi and Sara, thanks for believing in my book and helping bring the girls to life with me, and to the rest of the team at PRH UK—thank you for bringing this to bookshelves!

And a big thank you to the brilliant team in the States—Noreen, Megan, Colleen, Trisha (who designed such a stunning cover!) and my editor, Kelsey. Thanks for bringing my stories across the pond!